The Best
of
Sydney J. Harris

Also by Sydney J. Harris

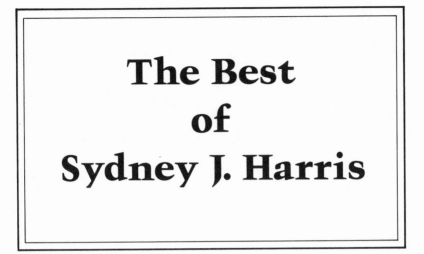

The Best
of
Sydney J. Harris

Houghton Mifflin Company Boston

1976

Library of Congress Cataloging in Publication Data

Harris, Sydney J
  The best of Sydney J. Harris.

  I. Title.
AC8.H36678 1975   081   75-28012
ISBN 0-395-21980-9 ISBN 0-395-24973-2 pbk.

Printed in the United States of America

W 10 9 8 7 6 5

For John S. Knight

whose encouragement
made it all possible

Contents

I.
Of the Life
of the Spirit

World Lacks Lovers—of the Truth

A YOUNG MAN at a college where I recently lectured was trying to bait me during the question period. He seemed cynical and defensive and disbelieving—but he didn't fool me for a moment. I knew he was a lover, and this is how lovers behave when they are young. He was a lover of truth and goodness, and the one thing he hated above all else was "phoniness."

And he was engaged in a typical lover's quest with me. He had a deep and desperate desire to believe what I said, to believe that I was sincere and honest.

But, at the same time, he felt compelled to attack me, to probe for soft spots in my nature, to expose me if he could as a pompous fraud and a windbag.

It is easy to dislike or disdain rude young men of this sort, until you realize that they are lovers. Somewhere along the line they have been hurt and disillusioned; they feel betrayed by the world's falsity; and they will not rest until they either prove that everything in the world is phony—or until they find a truth they can cling to.

Much of what is called "rebellion" in bright young people—I am not here speaking of the obviously disturbed youngsters—is really a search for faith.

Their scorn and their immature cynicism reflect their secret desire for goodness and their unwillingness to compromise with the shoddy standards of older people who have, weakly and sadly, come to terms with the Devil.

And these rebels, if understood and treated intelligently, can become the most creative and effective of citizens. I much prefer them to the sheep who are docile because they are dumb, who accept what they have been taught without question, who are tractable because they lack imagination, and who never do anything bad because they have no passion for either good or evil.

There are not enough lovers in the world. There are too few people who care deeply enough about such sublime abstractions as Truth. Time itself is corrupting: as we get older, we become flabby in the mind and the spirit as well as in the body.

These boys see it happening to us, and they resent it. Their cynicism is just the reverse side of their idealism, put on to conceal their hurt. It should be our task to heal them and to guide them, not to become like us, but to become what we once wanted to be.

But Can You Sympathize with Joy?

IN GERMAN, the word "sympathy" takes two forms—one form means sympathizing with another person's sorrow; the second form means sympathizing with another person's joy.

To sympathize is to be in harmony with someone else's feelings. But in English, we always use it to mean "feeling sorry for," and the opposite sense of the word is wholly lost.

Yet it is much easier to sympathize with sorrow than to sympathize with joy. We always have a slight feeling of superiority when someone else suffers a tragedy, and it makes us feel good to feel bad about it.

But when someone we know is rejoicing, is radiant, is successful, how much sympathy do we then feel? Are we able to harmonize our emotions with his, or do we rather feel a pang of bitterness and envy?

I know a good many unpleasant people who are eager to sympathize with disaster; in fact, some of them spend a lifetime in looking for disaster to sympathize with.

When, however, a friend of theirs is riding the crest of good fortune, these unpleasant characters are totally unable to sympathize. Instead, they sneer, they pick flaws, and make dire predictions.

It takes no great moral or spiritual qualities to feel sorry for a person who has fallen from a tremendous height, or has suffered an irreplaceable loss. We can easily put ourselves in his place, and feel sorrow for ourselves, in a vicarious fashion.

A genuinely sympathetic person is a rare and wonderful creature. He not only mourns when we mourn, he rejoices when we rejoice, he is able to identify with us in happiness as well as misfortune.

Many people delude themselves that they are warm and sympathetic because they cry easily over the death of small children or animals or miners trapped in a slide. Julius Streicher, one of the most bestial of the Nazi leaders, used to weep copiously when one of his 20 pet canaries died.

The true test of a sympathetic nature, however, comes when a friend or a neighbor or a colleague has risen in eminence and is sitting on top of the world.

Then we are not quite so sympathetic; then we look for the world to turn, for reverses to set in, even for a tragedy to strike—so that we can again sympathize with him. On our own terms.

This may be worth reflecting about the next time we pride ourselves on our compassion.

"If Only the Reds Would Disappear"

IF EVERY COMMUNIST government were wiped off the face of the earth in a single stroke—the remaining capitalist governments would sooner or later come to blows among themselves.

If every white person were wiped off the face of the earth in a single stroke—the remaining black people and their nations would sooner or later come to blows among themselves.

If the state of Israel were wiped off the face of the earth in a single stroke—the Arab countries would sooner or later come to blows among themselves.

If any living, breathing "enemy" were to disappear tomorrow morning, a new enemy would make its appearance the day after, or the week after, or the year after.

It is hard for contending groups to see this, but it must be seen. Otherwise, by destroying the enemy, we only create within ourselves the precondition for a new enemy.

The living, breathing enemy can only be absorbed, not conquered or destroyed. Taken in, not struck down. Changed, as we ourselves change. Otherwise, the vicious circle of history will be unending—or will end when we all perish in the ultimate confrontation.

A few years ago, in a Baptist church in Atlanta, the late Peter Howard said to the Negroes what must be said to all contending groups everywhere in the world:

"Be passionate for something bigger than color. Be passionate for an answer big enough to include everybody, powerful enough to change everybody, fundamental enough to satisfy the longings for bread, work and the hope of a new world that lie in the heart of the teeming millions of the earth.''

Most of all, we must begin to learn the ancient lesson that the only true enemy is within, not without. *The enemy is that part within us which makes our differences seem more important than our similarities.* This is the human trap almost all of us fall into—the trap that makes us act so inhumanly.

If we can mature as a species, and learn to avoid this trap, then we can unite against our real and common enemies—injustice and inequality, disease and decay, flood and famine and pestilence and all the ills that flesh is heir to.

We expend our passion on objects too small, on enemies too temporary, on goals too trivial. We must learn—as our children are beginning to recognize—to become passionate for something bigger than color or creed or geography or ideology or any other partial loyalty that has always seduced man away from largeness of soul. If we can diminish the enemy within us, the enemy outside us will begin to look more like a friend, a neighbor, a brother.

The Great Failure of Capitalism

IN ALL THE SCATHING CRITICISMS that the communists make against capitalist society, they have never put their finger on the one just accusation that can be leveled against us.

For the big failure of capitalist society is neither economic nor political, as the communists wrongly insist. It is social, cultural and educational. We have failed to raise the *quality* of life nearly as much as we have increased the mere *quantity* of goods and opportunities.

The general quality of life in our society is low and brutish. The violence we are lately so concerned about is merely an extension of our incivility, our bad manners, our coarseness of values and crudeness of sensibility.

The original idea of the American Revolution was to raise the level of all citizens, to educate them, civilize them, make them responsive to the grand ideas and broad sentiments expressed by Jefferson and his colleagues. Americans were to become a different breed of people.

But something went wrong. In the process of exercising our economic and political freedom, we somehow forgot that these are just *means*, not ends. The ends must include a citizenry ruled by *reason* and *compassion*.

We have failed dreadfully, thus far, in this crucial area. Just walk along a crowded downtown street in any American city and you will see what I mean. Or visit a beach on a hot day. Or drive along a congested expressway at rush hour. The spirit is sour and cheap, the very quality of life is disputatious, uncivil, mean and petty.

Our massive educational system has not educated. Our imposing religious establishment has not Christianized the tribalism of our people. And our affluence has merely convinced us that *possession*, rather than decency or merit, should be our prime and ultimate goal.

We do not understand the meaning of law, the workings of democracy, the relevance of religion, the roots of civilization—we do not even comprehend the virtues and limitations of capitalism in a way that will permit us to benefit from the former while escaping the dangerous consequences of the latter.

Most Marxist criticism of us is a mad mixture of malice and ignorance, half-truths and utter distortions. The kind of "capitalism" they fulminate against disappeared a long time ago. But if our enemies are too dumb to disclose our true defects, we should be smart enough to see them and to take prompt steps to rectify them. For if the quality of American life keeps degenerating, there will be no need for a revolution. We will disintegrate from within, as our own worst enemies.

We Need Heart and Mind

SINCE THERE ARE MORE people in the world with good characters than with good minds, the world makes a lopsided judgment of its leaders. We are perfectly aware of the danger in a man with a spacious mind and a small character; but we are not aware of equal, if different, dangers in a man with a lofty character and a small mind.

The brilliance of an Iago or a Richard III cannot conceal their lamentable deficiencies of character; but if we study history, instead of literature, we shall find that more troubles have been visited upon humanity by the well-meaning, upright man with a deplorable deficiency of mind. For every war that has been started by an unscrupulous genius, a dozen have been started by honorable men whose narrow and rigid mentality made it impossible for them to see beyond the ends of their noses.

The tragic mistakes of the British Empire in the 18th and 19th centuries were not the result of intellectual cunning, but the stupidity of men who were not broad enough to forsee the evil consequences of colonialism and imperialism. And, in Germany, the men who paved the way for Hitler were honorable, patriotic dullards like Hindenburg, whose moral rectitude covered an abyss of ignorance and befuddlement.

We appreciate good character because we know that it means well toward us; and we suspect brilliance of mind because we know that, unless checked by a high ethical sense, it can be fatally used against us. We feel more comfortable with amiable simplicity than we do with the complex personality of a first-rate mind. This is only natural, but it would be prudent for us to be as aware of the perils on the one side as on the other. The ideal answer, of course, is a man who has both character and brains; but a Lincoln or a Lee arises with pathetic rareness in the history of mankind.

According to the Buddhists, there are only three sins: ill-will, sensuality and stupidity. We may not look upon stupidity as a sin, for it is not a voluntary act—but the consequences of a limited mind can be as damaging as the consequences of ill-will or unbridled appetites.

But as long as the world lives in fear, we shall respond to people emotionally, not rationally. The man of character soothes our fears and gives us the faith that somehow we shall muddle through together.

In the highly organized, not to say explosive, society of the 20th century, this is scarcely a sensible or farsighted attitude to have.

Knowledge without character is wicked, and character without knowledge is wasteful. We tell the man of mind, "It is not enough"; we should tell the man of character the same.

If you want to know what a man's character is really like, don't ask him to tell you his creed or his code (for everyone has a prettified public version of these), but ask him to tell you the living person he most admires—for hero worship is the truest index of a man's private nature.

*

If you cannot endure to be thought in the wrong, you will begin to do terrible things to make the wrong appear right.

Giving Must Be Based on Need Alone

ON MY WAY to the office this morning, I was approached by a shabby and shuffling old man who stretched out his hand and whined, "Will you give a member of the 83rd Division a dime for a cuppa cawfee?"

Now, I happen to be a soft touch for panhandlers; not out of any deep sense of generosity, I suppose, but perhaps merely to propitiate the gods for having been so good to me. This, after all, is much of the source of charity.

But my hand stiffened on its way to my pocket as I heard his words, and I passed him by with a curt shake of the head. He had insulted me.

Whether or not he had ever been a member of the 83rd Division I do not know; it seemed highly improbable, but this was not the point. It was that he had felt it necessary to make a sales pitch to win my help.

The whole virtue in giving, it seems to me, lies in the evident fact that the recipient needs it. Not that he is worthy, not that he is a veteran, or the father of six, but simply that he is a human being in distress.

No appeal can be greater than that; anything added to it just lessens the essential humanity of giving. If we offer charity because it is "merited," then we should abolish charity and instead hold competitive examinations to determine the moral qualifications of the distressed.

This is why so many of those high pressured charity drives make me resentful even while I am giving. They try to appeal to our self-interest, to our prudence, to our fear, our sense of guilt—but rarely to our basic humanity.

If I give to a medical campaign because I or my family might some day fall victim to the same dread disease, I am merely taking out a kind of insurance. If I give to a home for crippled children because their pitiful condition moves me to tears, I am responding to the condition and not to the child. I am indulging in sentiment, not expressing the "loving kindness" that we have poorly translated into "charity."

If the scriptural phrase "It is more blessed to give than to receive" means anything, it means that we are doing ourselves a spiritual favor when we give, and that we ought to be grateful for the chance to make better men and women of ourselves. By placing the emphasis on the good we are doing for others, we run the risk of becoming smug and self-righteous, and corrupting our virtues until they begin to look like vices.

The Way to Persuade Someone

WHAT I WISH I HAD KNOWN AT EIGHTEEN:

— That the weakness in ourself we recognize as a weakness can be made either endearing or compensated for; but the weakness in ourself that we regard as a *strength* is what will ultimately betray and defeat us.

— That we do not grow up *uniformly,* but in spots and streaks; so that we may be mentally mature but *still* emotionally underdeveloped, or have a good practical grasp but *still* lack spiritual depth; and we must not make the mistake of confusing our categories of grown-upness.

— That candor in order to cure is very different from candor in order to hurt, and putting someone *right* is quite a different thing from putting someone *down.*

— That the way to persuade someone is not to beckon him to come and look at things from where *you* stand, but to move over to where *he* stands and then try to walk hand in hand to where you would like both of you to stand.

— That the best (and, ultimately, the only) way to make a "good impression" is by *becoming who you are,* not by trying to conform to anyone else's standard of what you ought to be.

— That wanting to be liked and admired by persons whose opinions or characters you do not really respect is the most common, and pernicious, form of emotional prostitution in the world.

— That if you do not find pleasure in solitude, you will not develop enough resources within yourself to find genuine pleasure in company; and, conversely, if you do not find pleasure in company, your solitude will be barren and involuted rather than creative and expansive.

—That while it is true in the world of arithmetic that two and two make four, it is not true in the world of real things that two apples and two lamps make four of anything; and thus, we cannot add up disparities and expect to come out with a neat sum, but must accept the fact that the real world is composed of "irrational numbers."

— That, in the deepest Platonic sense of the word, you do not truly "know" something until you act upon it; and that "know thyself" is a meaningless injunction unless and until such knowledge compels you to put it into action, in immediate and practical terms.

— That the world of experience is divided, roughly, into those things which are matters of *taste* and those which are matters of *judg-*

ment; and the rigid relativist who turns matters of judgment into mere matters of taste is as foolish as the rigid absolutist who turns matters of taste into matters of judgment.

Virtue Needs to Be Cultivated

AN OLD FRIEND of the family, named Aristotle, once told me that "virtue is a habit." I was too young to understand what he meant at the time, but as I get older I see his point.

Last week, we bought a couple of goldfish in a tiny bowl—to give someone as a joke on his birthday. He was called out of town, however, and the goldfish remained on our fireplace mantel all week.

Now, I have always disliked goldfish swimming around in a bowl. They seem to be supremely uninteresting creatures, and I could never see any reason for humans feeding and housing them.

Somehow, we didn't get around to giving them away, and we reluctantly began feeding them and changing their water. After a couple of days, against our will, we started to look upon them in a different light.

The goldfish suddenly acquired personality. Dumb as they are, they ceased being "objects" and became "creatures." I would not go so far as to say we quickly grew to care for them, but we assumed the responsibility for continuing their existence.

We may not have cared *for* them, but we began to care *about* them.

This "caringness" is a natural instinct in man, but it must be cultivated. It is a virtue because it finds values where none seemed to exist before—and the more values we find in life, the more full and satisfying our life becomes.

We can easily see how selfishness is a habit, but it is harder to see how virtue is the same. We commonly think of virtue as being a "quality" deep in the soul, which one either has or hasn't. I am convinced that everyone has it, but not everyone cultivates the habit.

Our old friend of the family also told me that virtue must be "active"—which is another thing we generally forget. It is impossible to be passively good—to wish the goldfish well, but let them starve to death or die in dirty water.

Millions of people think they are good simply because they are actively doing no harm. But this smug and self-righteous attitude is more responsible for the consequences of tragedy than the evils these people comfortably deplore from their easy chairs.

When we take care of a goldfish, it is less for the sake of the goldfish than for our own sake—for the caringness makes us more of what human beings ought to be. When we realize that taking care of our fellows is more of a blessing to ourselves than to them, we shall understand why the habit of virtue is the first rule of human conduct.

How Would You Label This Man?

THE CENSUS TAKER from Rome was sent to Galilee around A. D. 28. As he entered the region, he came across a man sitting on a donkey. The man had long hair and a flowing beard; he wore an old tattered cloak, sandals and beads.

"Pardon me," the census taker said, "but I'm taking the census. Do you mind answering a few questions?"

"Not at all," said the man on the donkey. "I believe in rendering unto Caesar the things that are Caesar's."

"What is your job?" asked the census taker.

"I have no job," replied the man. "Consider the lilies of the field—they toil not, neither do they spin."

"What is your family?"

"I have no family," the man answered. "I have left my parents and my brothers and sisters, and I live alone."

"What is your address?"

The man sighed. "The foxes have holes, and the birds of the air have nests; but I have not anywhere to lay my head."

"Humph," muttered the census taker to himself. "No job and no fixed abode. Now, do you belong to any clubs or social affiliations?"

"None," said the man. "For no man can serve two masters."

"Do you go to school?"

"Nay," replied the man, "for which of us by taking thought can add one cubit to his stature?"

"Do you have any money or visible means of support?"

The man shook his head. "Lay not up for yourselves treasures upon earth, where moth and rust doth corrupt," he chanted.

"Have you registered for military service?"

"I resist not evil, but return good for evil," replied the man. "And whosoever shall smite me on the right cheek, I shall turn to him the other also."

"Who are your friends?"

"I go among publicans and sinners."

"What political party do you belong to?"

The man shrugged. "Only this—a new commandment I give unto you: That ye love one another."

The census taker scribbled on his sheet: "Hippie character, school dropout, no permanent address, no job, probable draftdodger and pacifist, alienated from family, no wife or children, no church attendance, dubious associates among lowest elements in town."

"One more thing," he asked. "What is your name?"

The bearded one smiled sadly. "Some call me the Son of Man."

How to Be a Selfish Druid

AFTER A COLUMN of mine about Jesus appeared in the paper around Christmas, a woman called and asked me what religion I professed. I told her I was a Reform Evangelical Druid. She didn't seem to know what that was.

We Druids—small in number, but ardent in faith—have a most peculiar theology, but it seems to work for us. Most of the time.

We don't think it's important if you "believe" in God—as long as God believes in you. And there is only one way to make Him believe in you—to be as selfish as possible at all times. This means to want whatever is best for you, and you alone, in every situation.

If you are truly, deeply, unremittingly and wholly selfish, you are saved. We don't know what you are saved *for*, but that is none of our business. That is God's business, and we don't interfere in it.

Now, the art of being selfish seems to most people to be the easiest thing in the world, but that delusion is just a trap of Satan. Pure unadulterated selfishness is about the hardest thing in the world to accomplish, and it often takes a lifetime of unceasing effort.

In order to be genuinely selfish, you have to *want* what is best for the self, and to *do* what is best for the self. This implies *knowing* what is best for the self—and this is what makes Druidism so hard.

To be a Druid in good standing (even a non-Reform un-Evangelical one), you first of all have to understand the nature of man. You have to know that he was designed for something, just as an acorn is designed to be an oak tree.

If you properly understand the nature of man, even in part, then you know that the basic need, and the basic aim, of your true self is *to become as human* as it is possible to be. The only way your self can ever be satisfied is by turning its *potentiality* for humanhood into *act*.

Next, you have to understand what it means to become as human as possible: how the reason and the will and the appetites work together, how man can *live* and *control* his humanhood without falling into the error of angelism on the one hand or bestiality on the other.

When you have mastered this knowledge—which involves retraining the emotions as much as the mind—then you are ready to become the most selfish person in the world, doing only those things which are of benefit to your true self. This is why we are such a small sect.

Charity Doesn't Start at Home

NOT LONG AGO in the column I mentioned the Biblical phrase, "an eye for an eye, and a tooth for a tooth," observing that it is invariably misunderstood by people who use it as an excuse for retaliation, when it originated as a plea for justice.

There is another common phrase that is damaged even more in popular usage, and that is, "charity begins at home." Whenever this saying is trotted out, it is to justify taking care of one's own before concerning one's self with the needs of others.

Yet this is not at all what the phrase originally meant. As first published, in 1642, in Sir Thomas Browne's *Religio Medici*, it meant "charity" in the Pauline sense of "loving-kindness," not almsgiving or philanthropy.

And it did not mean that we should first "take care" of our own, but that if we do not display loving-kindness to our family and our friends, then whatever alms or philanthropy we engage in is done out of pride or vanity or ostentation, not out of deep human compassion.

I have known more than a few celebrated philanthropists who gave away huge sums to worthy causes of all sorts, but whose personal relationships were devoid of loving-kindness, and who used public magnanimity as a cloak for private skullduggery.

This common subterfuge, of course, is the reason for another widely misunderstood saying—Jesus' injunction that your left hand should not know what your right hand is doing.

If anyone troubled to read the whole verse, he would learn that Jesus is addressing himself to the philanthropists of his time, who would stand up in public and make known their large donations to charity. He is telling them to give so quietly and anonymously with one hand that not even the other hand is aware of it, much less the community.

Charity, of course, does *not* begin at home; it must begin where it is *most needed*, whether this be at home or in some remote Indian village. What must begin at home are love and respect and tender treatment of those closest to us—for unless we radiate such feelings in our daily, intimate relationships, the money we give away to others is simply a bribe, allowing us to maintain our self-esteem while we continue to injure the fabric of social life.

The poor know it and resent it when they are the objects of help without the commensurate feelings of respect; when they are aided to make the giver feel better, not because they are worthy of aid. In a psychological sense, the philanthropist needs the poor more than they need him—charity brings him honors, but leaves them only scraps.

How Does One Judge "Obscenity"?

IT'S INTERESTING how people are "relativist" about things it suits them to be relativist about, and "absolutist" about other things it suits them to be absolutist about.

A man called me on the phone this morning to ask about a play I recently reviewed. He wanted to know if it is "morally offensive." All I could reply was that it didn't offend me, but I couldn't speak for him or his friends.

Now, this man would never call me up to ask whether a certain piece of music is "beautiful." He no doubt believes that beauty is in the eye (and the ear) of the beholder. If I recommended a certain poem he didn't like, he would shrug it off with a phrase about "a matter of taste."

People tend to be relativistic about their aesthetic standards, but absolutist about matters of "sex" and "decency" and "obscenity." They want the right to judge for themselves whether a painting or a piece of music is beautiful and appealing, but ask for an objective judgment on whether a play or a novel is "immoral" or "offensive."

But if "beauty" is in the eye of the beholder, so is "obscenity." I personally happen to find the collected works of Mickey Spillane "obscene" in their crude combining of indiscriminate violence and mindless sex—but the public bought such books in the millions, while at the same time regarding D. H. Lawrence as "obscene."

In my own view, aesthetic judgments are much more absolutist than sexual ones. There is not a trained musician in the Western world who would not agree that Beethoven wrote greater music than Grieg, or that Schnabel was a finer pianist than Liberace—no matter what the uninstructed in such matters might believe.

But the very people who would bellow with outrage if we tried to impose such aesthetic standards upon them ("I may not know music, but I know what I like") are the same ones who demand absolute conformity in sexual matters, and who think that "dirtiness" can be defined by counting noses and accepting the majority opinion.

There *are* certain absolutes for the human race—in that the nature of our being cannot be violated with impunity—but sexual customs and practices and attitudes are not among them. It's odd that the people who worry whether certain plays are "morally offensive" so rarely worry about the moral offensiveness of war, poverty and bigotry.

We Want a Messiah, Not a Leader

PEOPLE KEEP SAYING, "We need a leader" or "We need better leadership," but that is not what they really mean. What most of them are looking for is not a leader, but a Messiah.

They want someone who will give them the Word. And the Word would be one that is agreeable to them, that appeals to their preferences and prejudices, so that they can follow it wholeheartedly.

But this is not what a true leader does—a leader tells people hard truths, gives them a difficult path to follow, calls upon their highest qualities, not their basest instincts. A true leader does not tell us what we *want* to hear, but what we *ought* to hear.

Indeed, this is the difference between a false Messiah and a true one. A false Messiah—such as a Hitler, in our time—caters to and inflames the fears, hates, angers and resentments of his people, and drives them to destruction rather than to salvation or self-realization.

A true Messiah—such as Jesus, even taken on the worldly plane—rebukes his people, shows them their errors, makes them want to be better, not stronger or richer, and asks them to make sacrifices for the common good and for the good of their own souls. He is never followed by very many, usually killed by the majority, and venerated only when he is safely dead and need not be taken seriously.

What we are looking for, I am afraid, is neither a true leader nor a true Messiah, but a false Messiah—a man who will give us oversimplified answers, who will justify our ways, who will castigate our enemies, who will vindicate our selfishness as a way of life and make us comfortable within our prejudices and preconceptions.

We are seeking for leadership that will reconcile the irreconcilable, moralize the immoral, rationalize the unreasonable and promise us a society where we can continue to be as narrow and envious and shortsighted as we would like to be without suffering the consequences. In short, we are invoking magic, we are praying for the coming of the Wizard.

But there is no Wizard. There are only false prophets—and they come equally from left, right, center and below. Wherever they come from, no matter how they differ, they can all be distinguished by the same sign: those we like make us feel better, instead of making us feel worse. We want to follow them because they "understand" us.

But all the true prophets, from the Old Testament through Jesus, made us feel worse. They knew, and said, that the trouble wasn't with our enemies, but with ourselves. They demanded that we shed our old skin and become New Men. And this is the last thing we want to do. What we are looking for is a leader who will show us how to be the same old men (or women) only more successfully—and his ancient name is Satan.

What "Love Your Enemies" Implies

MOST PEOPLE look upon the Biblical injunction "Love your enemies" as either impossibly utopian or impossibly sentimental. This is because they fail to understand the meaning of *agape,* or love, as Jesus meant it.

To love your enemies does not mean that you have to like them. It does not mean that they are no longer enemies. Nobody can command us to like what we do not like, for emotions cannot be directed by moral laws.

And enemies remain enemies if their ultimate goals conflict with ours, no matter whether we love them or not. So that "Love your enemies" does not order us to something either utopian or sentimental.

What it means, properly understood, is that no matter what we "feel" about another person, or how we oppose his beliefs, there must be an acknowledgment that what binds us together is greater than what divides us.

It is the "personhood" of the other that unites us in something that is above, and greater than, both of us; and our respect for this common ground of being must take precedence over our likes and our beliefs. This is the hardest lesson for any people (and any church) to learn.

We mistakenly imagine that if we could "love" our enemies, then we might become friends or allies; but this is not necessary, nor even possible in many cases. We would still be enemies—but we would treat our enmity as athletes do in a contest, not as soldiers in a war.

It may sound odd, but true athletes "love" their adversaries. That is, they respect them as other persons striving toward an opposite goal. And they oppose them only within rules that both obey, so that the winner wins on merit, not on fouls.

This is the kind of spirit Jesus was urging upon us, not a sticky sentimentality that tries to blink away human conflict or pretend that people can like each other better than they do. He was saying that it doesn't matter if you like someone or not, it doesn't matter if you agree or not—the only thing that matters is treating the other as fairly and cleanly as athletes do in a championship game.

This is a union that goes beyond sympathy or friendship, for there is no merit in behaving nicely toward the people we like; the only merit is acting decently toward people we don't like or disagree with—for this kind of "love" is an act of the will, not an emotion or an intellectual conviction. What a tragedy that we honor it only in our games, which we take so seriously, but not in our lives, which we play away with such perilous flippancy.

Men Can Fear and Love God

IF THERE IS SOMEONE you respect enormously, and whose good opinion you value highly, what is it that makes you act well in this person's presence? It is the fear that otherwise he might withdraw his favor from you, might lose his good opinion of you.

There is nothing wrong with such fear; it is perfectly logical and legitimate. All love relationships are controlled by an element of fear—that of acting, or becoming, unworthy of the loved one's approbation.

When modern people, however, deplore the Bible's emphasis on "fear of the Lord," they fail to understand what it properly means. Worship of the Lord, they insist, should be based on "love," not on "fear"—but there is no love unless it is accompanied by the kind of fear that helps us to live up to the loved one's conception of us.

The reason for this widespread confusion is that we equate all "fear" with fear of punishment. This, indeed, would be the worst reason for doing honor to God—that we are afraid of being eternally punished. Fire-and-brimstone religion has fallen into a deserved disrepute because it stressed such punishment, which would be unworthy of any God we would care to worship.

But not all fear is of this punitive kind, which is a childish conception of God's power. Fear of losing respect, of the loved one's withdrawal, of the severing of the bond, is what is psychologically true in our relationships. All moral authority is based on this legitimate form of fear, not on power or punishment or retaliation.

Hell is to be loveless. To be abandoned. To have forfeited one's interdependence. To live only for oneself. No fire and brimstone can equal this desolation. God has no need to "do anything" to us; we are our own punishers, we create our own Hell, we either become what we were meant to be, or go to our death without ever having known what it was to live.

All this has nothing to do, incidentally, with "believing" in God. Avowed atheists can be closer to Him than devout churchgoers. God is not "religious" in any petty human sense of the word; this is why there can be no "right" religion—only right people, many of whom profess no religion at all.

Those who respect the cosmos, who treat all men as brothers, who know there is a law higher than that of self-aggrandizement and self-preservation, "who walk humbly and act mercifully," live in constant fear of the Lord, whether they know it or not. They fear becoming unworthy of the humanhood they were created with, and for.

When a Thou Becomes an It

EVERYONE is at the center of his own universe, like a spider sitting at the heart of his web. This is the condition of man, to be self-centered, in the most literal sense of the word.

And when we engage ourselves with another person, our own existence seems necessary and absolute, while the other's existence seems contingent and relative. We are essential to our world; he is not.

Yet, while this is our deep emotional conviction, on the intellectual level, we know it is not true. The other person is as real as we are. He, too, is the center of the universe; he is necessary and absolute to himself.

Treating ourselves as absolute, and others as relative is, of course, the primal sin. It converts persons into *things* to be manipulated, used and discarded; into *means* for our own ends, not for their ends. In Buber's terms, it turns a Thou into an It.

And when a Thou becomes an It—when the createdness of the other person is not viewed as necessary as our own—then there is no reason (beyond expediency) to treat the other as a person. All injustice and cruelty come, basically, from this distorted view of reality.

Seen in this light, the great commandment "Love thy neighbor as thyself" becomes something more than a sentimental injunction or a pious wish or even a purely religious precept. It becomes an imperative for mankind—a self-protective measure to keep us from wiping out one another, as we seem about to do on a global scale today.

The great commandment means that our neighbor, however he differs from us, is just as real, just as worthy and as worthless, just as much the center of creation. It means that the only way we can like some people is by loving them—by loving not the accidents of their personality, but the essential createdness of them, the residual humanity that makes us all much more alike than we are different.

The kind of love we are commanded to have is not a *feeling*, in the ordinary sense of the word. Nobody could be "commanded" to love his neighbor as he loves his mate or parents or children or friends. It is an *act of the will*, a turning of the whole person to the other, in open recognition that what unites us is much greater and deeper than what divides us.

Man will never lose his self-centeredness. He can only mitigate it, by accepting the realness of the other, and regarding him as an absolute. In the crisis of our times, the I can save itself only by reaching out to the Thou and saying "We."

We truly possess only what we are able to renounce; otherwise, we are simply possessed by our possessions.

*

"Conscience" is a much abused word in our society, for we commonly use it to worry over personal trifles instead of training it to be troubled about big things; and this dissipates our moral energy and permits us at the same time to develop an insensitiveness to the monstrous inequities of our time.

The Way to Achieve a Good Life

AMERICA IS A public speaker's paradise. Nowhere else in the world are so many people in so many organizations so indecently eager to hear speakers on every topic from atom smashing to zinnia growing.

As I contemplate my lecture schedule for next season—with a mixture of horror and greed—it occurs to me that this passion for information is a dubious blessing. What are the audiences really getting?

Basically, they want to be told *what to do*. What can we do about Russia or China? What should we do about our schools? How can we get better plays on the stage, better films on the screen, better programs on television?

Yet, advice on what we can do is usually futile—for we will do nothing except applaud the speaker, accept those ideas of his we already agreed with, and reject those ideas that run counter to our prejudices.

What is important in our lives is to be told *what to be*, before we can learn what to do. And audiences resent being told what to be; that is preaching, it is moralizing, and it is uncomfortable to hear, except in church, when we listen as a matter of good form and promptly forget it.

I once heard a brilliant speaker at a Quaker meeting. He was talking about charity and working for philanthropic organizations. He said that there were three steps each person must take.

The first step is *giving*. That is the easiest. Writing a check makes us feel virtuous and involves little personal participation. This is the lowest rung of charity.

The second step is *doing*. That is harder: it means giving up time and expending effort on tedious and unrewarding tasks. It is a higher rung on the ladders of charity.

The third step is *being*. That is the hardest of all: it means transforming oneself into a kind and loving person, not merely in relation to a project or an organization, but in relation to everyone around us.

Achieving the good life is more a matter of being than of doing or giving. It calls for intense self-scrutiny, a relentless honesty about one's motives, and a persistent feeling that we are no better—and perhaps worse—than those we are trying to help.

This is the only lecture worth listening to, and the only one that could ultimately help us in solving the problems of Russia and China, the schools, the movies and the atom bomb. In this profound psychological sense, charity does begin at home.

The Whole World Is a Huge Legacy

THE BOY IN THE GARAGE was bickering with his father. "I don't owe the world a thing," he said, as adolescents are wont to. "I didn't ask to be born."

It is true that nobody asks to be born, but it does not follow that we don't owe the world a thing. We have a tremendous debt to the past, which we take for granted, as part of our "rightful" heritage.

The boy in the garage has never taken a good look around him. Everything he enjoys doing is a free gift from the past. His tools, his machinery, his clothes, indeed his health itself—all were invented or developed or fortified by his ancestors.

How many of us could survive at all without this tremendous inheritance we accept so thoughtlessly? Consider the brilliant men, the patient men, the dedicated men, who labored (often without reward) on projects both great and small, from the steam engine to the safety pin.

This boy would be like a beast in the forest if not for better men than he: unclad; unshod, ravaged by disease and riddled with misery.

Not one of us contributes more than one millionth of 1 per cent to the accumulated knowledge and comfort we call "civilization." The farmer inherits his tools from his wisdom of the past; the manufacturer depends upon the kind of brains that were more interested in progress than in profit; the schoolboy benefits from untold man-hours of research and devotion.

The whole world is a gigantic legacy. Imagine having to start afresh each generation: who would invent the wheel, devise the lever, construct the alphabet and the multiplication table? I could not; could you?

We owe reverence to God; but, beyond this, we owe loyalty and gratitude to the past. We were born into a world where most of the basic elements were already waiting for us; we merely combine and rearrange them for our pleasure or profit. Not more than a handful of us in any century leaves something permanent for the future to use.

Ungratefulness to the past is a barbarous trait. The boy in the garage is greedy for all the advantages that ancient minds can confer upon him, but he will not pay any homage to history. He did not ask to be born, but he is asking to die, as a sullen savage, crouched in a motorcar he did not make, behind an engine he cannot control.

Realistic Prayer for Atomic Age

GOING THROUGH the notes crammed into my desk drawers the other morning, I came across a clipping that I had stored away on the day the United States opened its nuclear detonation season.

The test began with a short prayer intoned over the intercom by the warship's chaplain, and it went as follows:

"Unto us who are privileged to draw aside the curtain into the secrets of Thy universe, teach us that our whole duty is to love Thee our God and to keep the commandments."

Presumably there is at least one commandment that a chaplain on a warship is in no position to invoke. It would seem a trifle awkward to enjoin "Thou shalt not kill" just before the detonation of a bomb with the power of several million tons of TNT, capable of killing a few hundred thousand of His children.

Instead of the pious sonorities of this prayer, I suggest a much more realistic invocation to be given by the Representatives of the Lord whenever they happen to be present on similar fraternal occasions. It would go something like this:

Unto us who have the pride and the presumption to release the most devastating forces of nature, O Lord, be merciful;

Protect us from cardiac contusion;

Preserve us from cerebral or coronary air embolism;

Guard us from the dreadful consequences of respiratory tract hemorrhage;

Allow us not to suffer from pulmonary edema;

Save us from the trauma of distended hollow viscera;

Withhold from us the horrors of hemorrhages in the central nervous system.

Visit these catastrophes upon our enemies, not upon us, and we promise to love Thee and keep the commandments—all except one, O Lord.

This, at least, would be an honest and meaningful prayer. No nonsense, no hypocrisy, no solemn theological jargon to disguise and sanctify the purpose and the power of the bomb.

The Lord, I am sure, would not grant this prayer—but it would not, at any rate, be an insult to His intelligence and an affront to His benevolence. Sometimes I think He must be more discouraged by the blindness of his shepherds than by the folly of his sheep.

You Can, Too, Argue with Success

TWO YOUNG MEN, evidently salesmen, were having lunch at the table next to mine. "I couldn't do it," one of them was saying, "but Bill gets away with it. And, after all, you can't argue with success."

I have heard this vicious phrase a thousand times, but I have never heard its justification. Why can't you argue with success? It is the only thing worth arguing with.

There is no need to argue with failure. And failure doesn't want to argue; it just wants to be let alone and lick its wounds. But success is too often brassy and argumentative, self-satisfied and superior about itself.

The man who won't argue with success has already been corrupted without knowing it. He accepts the world at face value. He thinks that things are what they seem to be. And he is, at bottom, a traitor to Western civilization and to the whole Judaic-Christian tradition.

It was the duty of decent Germans to argue with the "success" of a Hitler. It is the duty of good Russians to argue with the "success" of the Soviet dictatorship. It is the duty of good people everywhere to argue with the "success" of all violence and fraud and greed and inhumanity.

It is only by rebelling against these false conceptions of success that man has raised himself from the jungle. It is only by weighing and judging and evaluating the worth of his leaders that man has overthrown tyrants and deposed despots.

Success is the one thing in the world that *must* be questioned, that cannot be accepted without the proper credentials of morality. From the Mosaic Code to the Sermon on the Mount, the Bible insists that the mighty shall be toppled when their ways are wicked.

And good sense confirms this. It knows that man's end is not power, but peace and justice. And peace is impossible, and justice is a mockery, unless we see that power is put where it belongs—in the hands of men who cherish wisdom and righteousness.

Success, rather than being venerated, must be carefully defined. It should include the whole man, in his spiritual and social life, and not just his capacity for taking, for impressing, for commanding. The truly successful man, by these rigorous standards, is a rare and wonderful creature.

But he is the only creature worth imitating. To imitate or worship his shabby counterfeits is to sacrifice the most distinctive part of our humanity.

Well, How Would You Answer the Hindu?

I COULDN'T ANSWER the Hindu. Maybe you can. Maybe you can make a better defense of so-called Western civilization than I could.

"Since traveling in the Christian world of the West," he said at dinner, "I have been puzzled by my readings in the New Testament. How do you people interpret the words of Jesus?"

"What do you mean?" I asked, afraid of what was coming.

"I mean," he said politely, "how do you reconcile his plain doctrine of nonresistance with your guns and your planes and your wars every few decades?

"Which Christian nation has ever turned the other cheek? Who among you are willing to return good for evil? How can people who share in the good news of His message continually kill one another, while both sides are praying to Him?"

"Well," I stammered, "after all, that's a doctrine of perfection that Jesus preached. Ordinary mortal men can't always live up to it."

"That I understand," he nodded, "but it should be your goal—and I can only see that you go in the opposite direction. Gandhi was not a Christian, and yet it seems to me he practiced the New Testament more than Westerners do."

"But Gandhi was a saint," I protested. "Surely the mass of Indian people are no better, morally and spiritually, than Westerners are."

"Perhaps not," he said. "All the same, we do not claim to have a special revelation from the Son of God. We do not insist that we follow the Prince of Peace, and then follow the Prince of War."

"Not everybody agrees that Jesus was a pacifist," I objected. "Some people point to his scourging the moneychangers out of the temple."

"Ah, but there is a difference between scourging—as you might a disobedient child, out of love for him—and wantonly killing millions of innocent men and women and children, all in the name of God. You are commanded to love your neighbors—and today, in this shrunken world, everybody is a neighbor."

I had one defense left; my Sunday punch, if you'll pardon the expression. "Don't we have a right, an obligation, to fight against injustice and wickedness and tyranny?" I demanded.

"Yes," he said "you must fight against it—but in your own minds and souls, for that is where it begins, not in some foreign land.

"When you have purified yourselves, the example of your goodness will be the most effective weapon in the world—if not for now, then in the future."

Maybe you can answer the Hindu. I could not, in all honesty.

Man–the Marvel of the Universe

REREADING SOME of the brilliant and bitter works of Jonathan Swift last night, I was reminded of the old German saying that "every stick has two ends."

One's view of humanity depends on which end of the stick one chooses to grasp. If you look upon man as a spirit corrupted by flesh, it is hard not to become disgusted and revolted with human behavior.

But, if you consider man as an animal infused with a spirit, then it is a constant source of wonder and delight that this animal has attained as much as he has.

Swift took the former view. He plunged from dizzy idealism to degrading cynicism. He saw only the great gap between our pretensions to nobility and our selfish animal passions.

Gulliver's Travels is, of course, not a children's book; it is a savage attack on mankind. Swift was nauseated with our sight, our smell, our sound. That we can rise so high in our thoughts and sink so low in our conduct was, to him, a terrible indictment of our hypocrisy.

Seizing the stick from the other end, however, it becomes perfectly plain that man is the marvel of the universe. He is an animal, at one with the shellfish, the buzzard and the hyena.

If we can look this natural fact in the face, and accept our animal heritage, it seems biologically incredible that we can ever conceive of such things as honor and nobility and love and sacrifice.

We often, or usually, do not live up to our concepts. This is regrettable, but not condemnable. Physically, we are forced to live in the animal world; but the soul, or spirit, or psyche—call it what you will—gives us a set of values that goes far beyond the animal kingdom.

We need not like what people *do;* but we must admire what a part of them desires to do; and what a few individuals in every society succeed in doing. We can modify our basic pattern of behavior—something no other animal can achieve.

It is easy to be cynical about the defects in human nature; but deep in every personality is the yearning for goodness and truth and beauty.

Holding mankind by this end of the stick, we cannot but have reverence for an act of animal creation that so vastly transcends the lusts of the jungle and the laws of the swamp. Man is a greater miracle than anything else in the universe.

Time Is Past, Present and Future

THE PEOPLE WHO INSIST that one must "live for the present" are as foolish and lopsided as the people who live wistfully in the past or the people who live hopefully in the future.

Time is seamless. Past, present and future are woven into the same fabric. The present is continually disappearing into the past, before we can grasp it. And, in a real sense, the future never comes.

Time and space are part of the same continuum, Einstein taught us. We must also learn that time itself is indivisible, that every act is a blending of past experience, present situation and future expectancy.

Living for the present is a senseless philosophy. The man who most perfectly lives for the present is the criminal: he forgets the prison sentence of the past and he ignores the probable prison sentence of the future. He lives from "score" to "score."

We must not look behind too much, we must not look ahead too far, and we must not fix our gaze too steadily on the immediate. Each of these angles of vision has its own particular dangers.

What is necessary, it seems to me, is a delicate combination of the three. Those who focus on the past become apathetic; those who peer exclusively into the future become unrealistic; and those who live on a day-to-day basis become incapable of learning from the past and incapable of controlling the future.

The mind likes to break up life into categories—but these categories are illusions. For instance, we think the past is behind us, but it is not; it is very much with us, very much alive, very much a part of everything we do now.

We think the future lies ahead, but its seed is contained in the present. There is no sharp break between the two: the lie we tell today can send us sprawling a year from now; the way we treat our infant determines the way he treats us when he reaches adolescence.

Life is a flow, a stream. The current is everywhere. Like mariners, we must learn the shoals, the rocks, the rapids. No man can navigate only from wave to wave, for the waves are part of a ceaseless pattern in time.

Live for the present? It is impossible; and if it were possible, it would be fatal. To live for the present is the surest way of forfeiting the future to barbarism and bestiality.

When Knowing We Know Little Is a Virtue

IT IS TRUE that a wise man is one who knows how little he knows—but I am tired of hearing ignorant people defend their ignorance on this ground.

What most people fail to recognize is that you have to earn the right to be wrong; physicians sometimes make incorrect diagnoses, but we do not therefore take our ailments to shoemakers.

As Montaigne remarked long ago: "There is an ABC ignorance that precedes knowledge, and a doctoral ignorance that comes after it."

Newton said he felt like a little boy playing with pebbles on the seashore, and Thomas Aquinas, at the end of his life, declared that his great *Summa* was little more than rubbish.

But these geniuses at least knew what there was to know about their respective fields, and their ignorance began only where human reason ends. They pushed their minds as far as they could go, and only then did they bow before the ultimate mystery of the universe.

Lao-Tse, the Chinese sage, beautifully illustrated this in one of his sayings: "To the ignorant man, a tree is a tree, and a river is a river. To the learned man, a tree is not a tree, and a river is not a river. To the wise man, a tree is a tree, and a river is a river—but they are not the same tree or the same river that the ignorant man sees."

What he meant, of course, is that we progress from a naive realism to a scientific understanding of things; and then, if we proceed far enough, we return to realism, but with a heightened awareness of what it means.

For instance, to a child, love is love, unquestioning and unqualified. As we acquire knowledge, we learn that love may be different things, and that it is a complex and contradictory bundle of emotions. But if we become really wise, we return to the child's concept of love, only on a much higher plane. We are still ignorant of its final meaning, but our ignorance is now doctoral, and not the ABC ignorance of the child.

To know how little we know becomes a virtue only *after* we have tried to learn all we are capable of knowing.

The ignorant man is arrogant in his profession of humility; as Einstein once said of a mediocre colleague: "He has no right to be so humble—he is not great enough."

Why Evil Always Defeats Itself

IT IS A COMFORTING thought on a grim day that what keeps the world from falling wholly into crime and corruption is the psychological fact that evil is a *separatist* thing, while goodness is a *unifying* thing.

We would be utterly under the rule of evil, were it otherwise; for evil is industrious, while virtue is too often apathetic; evil is cunning, while virtue is credulous; evil is attractive and exciting, while virtue makes no similar appeal to the senses.

But the one redeeming factor, the one element that tends to cancel out all the other advantages of evil, is that by its very nature it separates itself, not merely from the good, but from other evil as well. It is not only destructive; it is ultimately self-destructive.

Samuel Johnson put it pithily two centuries ago: "Combinations of wickedness would overwhelm the world did not those who have long practised perfidy grow faithless to each other."

Thieves fall out; thieves *must* fall out, for it is the essence of their character, the mainspring of their behavior. They can have no enduring loyalty to one another, no basic trust, no disinterested activity. What is anti-social in them in the beginning turns into anti-one-another in the end.

This is worth remembering in an age when evil seems ascendent, powerful, organized and ruthless; when society assumes the dimensions of a magnified racket; when expediency becomes the mark of polity; when nations, like sophisticated gangsters, engage promiscuously in threats, bribes, blackmail and all the lower forms of intimidation.

It is no mere sentimentalism to insist that—barring some cosmic cataclysm—evil cannot survive and flourish; for it contains the seed of its own destruction. Its center does not hold, it flies apart, it cannot cope with the one thing it wants above all—success.

For success, to have any meaning, requires order, coherence, unity, proportion and equity. All these factors are alien to the spirit of evil. Most of all, success calls for co-operation at the deepest level—and co-operation is impossible for the separatist spirit.

Rival gangs kill one another off; within each gang, struggles for power disintegrate the group. Hitlers and Stalins cannot maintain "non-agression pacts" for very long. Tyrants are assassinated by their own lieutenants. The same instinct that drives a man into wickedness drives him to dominate and destroy his associates in the enterprise. Evil in its very nature is self-defeating; in dark days, this truth is sometimes all that good men have to cling to.

"Authenticity" and Teaching

DISCUSSING A COMMON school problem, a parent recently asked me: "How is it that some teachers are able to control their classes with a very light rein, and have no disciplinary troubles, while others must shout and plead and threaten and still get nowhere with the trouble-makers?"

I don't think the answer has much to do with teaching techniques or even experience, beyond a certain degree. I think it has almost every-thing to do with the "authenticity" of the teacher.

Notice I do not say "authority," but "authenticity." For genuine authority, which is more than a matter of official position and the ability to reward or punish, comes out of the depths of the personality. It has a realness, a presence, an aura, that can impress and influence even a 6-year-old.

A person is either himself or not himself; is either rooted in his existence or is a fabrication; has either found his humanhood or is still playing with masks and roles and status symbols. And nobody is more aware of this difference (although unconsciously) than a child. Only an authentic person can evoke a good response in the core of the other person; only person is resonant to person.

Knowledge is not enough. Technique is not enough. Mere experi-ence is not enough. This is the mystery at the heart of the teaching process; and the same mystery is at the heart of the healing process.

Both are an art, more than a science or a skill—and the art is at bottom the ability to "tune in to the other's wavelength."

And this ability is not possessed by those who have failed to come to terms with their own individuated person, no matter what other talents they possess. Until they have liberated themselves (not completely, but mostly) from what is artificial and unauthentic within themselves, they cannot communicate, counsel or control others.

The teachers who meant the most to me in my school life were not necessarily those who knew the most, but those who gave out of the fullness of themselves; who confronted me face to face, as it were, with a humanhood that awoke and lured my own small and trembling soul and called me to take hold of my own existence with my two hands.

Such persons, of course, are extremely rare, and they are worth more than we can ever pay them. It should be the prime task of a good society to recruit and develop these personalities for safeguarding our children's futures; and our failure to do so is our most monstrous sin of omission.

If Christ Returned on Christmas

IF THERE SHOULD BE, on Christmas night, a second coming, would there not be soon a second crucifixion?

And this time, not by the Romans or the Jews, but by those who proudly call themselves Christians?

I wonder. I wonder how we today would regard and treat this man with His strange and frightening and "impractical" doctrines of human behavior and relationships. Would we believe and follow, any more than the masses of people in His day believed and followed?

Would not the militarists among us assail Him as a cowardly pacifist because He urges us not to resist evil?

Would not the nationalists among us attack Him as a dangerous internationalist because He tells us we are all of one flesh?

Would not the wealthy among us castigate Him as a troublemaking radical because He bars the rich from entering the kingdom of heaven?

Would not the liberals among us dismiss Him as a dreamy vagabond because He advises us to take no thought for the morrow, to lay up no treasures upon earth?

Would not the ecclesiastics among us denounce Him as a ranting heretic because He cuts through the cords of ritual and commands us only to love God and our neighbors?

Would not the sentimentalists among us deride Him as a cynic because He warns us that the way to salvation is narrow and difficult?

Would not the Puritans among us despise and reject Him because He eats and drinks with publicans and sinners, preferring the company of winebibbers and harlots to that of "respectable" church members?

Would not the sensual among us scorn Him because He fasts for 40 days in the desert, neglecting the needs of the body?

Would not the proud and important among us laugh at Him when He instructs the 12 disciples that he who would be "first" should be the one to take the role of the least and serve all?

Would not the worldly-wise and educated among us be aghast to hear that we cannot be saved except we become as children, and that a little child shall lead us?

Would not each of us in his own way find some part of this man's saying and doing to be so threatening to our ways of life, so much at odds with our rooted beliefs, that we could not tolerate Him for long?

I wonder.

Such Things Youth Should Know

WHAT I WISH I had known at 18:

• That a "free offer" is usually the most expensive kind.

• That a man isn't judged by what he knows but by how he wears it.

• That it's useless to get into a spraying contest with a skunk.

• That when a man's position in life depends upon his having a certain opinion, that's the opinion he will have.

• That nobody has the power to hurt us or help us as much as we fancy, and mortal hurts are almost always self-inflicted.

• That the best person to borrow from is one who doesn't have much.

• That the cynic is goodhearted beneath his facade, whereas the sentimentalist is flint-hearted beneath his.

• That the worst sins are committed by indifference, not by vice.

• That the people who are suspicious of certain things are the very ones who are the most capable of doing that of which they are suspicious.

• That friends who break fast at the wire often fade in the stretch.

• That the atheist who believes in man and scorns God can be closer to holiness than the religionist who believes in God and scorns man.

• That the more neurotic partner in a marriage is the one who is *not* seeing a psychiatrist.

• That ends never justify means, but, quite the contrary, means tend to corrupt ends.

• That being able to do exactly as one pleases is the surest way to remain perpetually unpleased.

• That human nature doesn't need to change: it just needs to ask itself continually what is meant by "human" and to give itself an honest answer.

• That the way in which we say something is often more important than what we say.

• That the "liberal" who gets power can be violently illiberal, just as the "conservative" who gets power can be greedily unconserving.

• That it can take less courage to face death than to face life.

• That nobody can misunderstand a child as much as his own parents.

• That women who seem the most "feminine" turn into the most feline and most feral.

• That it is impossible to have a good opinion of one's self and a low opinion of others; the downgrader is projecting his self-contempt.

• That "pleasure" and "joy" are not synonyms but may be as profoundly different as Heaven and Hell.

The Real Spirit of Christmas

EVERYONE SAYS that what is wrong with Christmas is that it is "too commercial"—but that is not the trouble. What is wrong with Christmas is that it is "too spiritual"—in the wrong way.

The commercial aspect of Christmas can easily be ignored or repudiated by anyone who wants to take this holiday seriously. But the false "spiritual" aspect is harder to separate from the true message.

The three wise men and the star of Bethlehem and the babe in the manger and the mystery and the miracle—all these make it tempting and easy for us to forget what the whole story is about.

And the whole story—the whole message of the whole messiahship—can be summed up in two sentences from Jesus' own lips:

"If a man say, I love God, and hateth his brother, he is a liar." (I John 4:20).

"Inasmuch as ye have done it unto one of the least of these my brethren, ye have done it unto me." (Matthew 25:40).

This is what Christmas—the mass of Christ—must mean, if it is to mean anything. If it does not mean this to us, then what we worship is superstition and idolatry.

You cannot love God without loving every fellow creature He made; and an act of contempt or rejection or injustice or neglect toward the least—the lowest, the poorest, the weakest, the dumbest—is an act against Him.

If Christianity does not mean this, it means nothing. If this central fact is ignored or slurred or rationalized away, the whole structure of Christianity falls apart, and we are left with nothing but another primitive "magic" religion.

And it is not the impious, the pagans and unbelievers, who must be most on guard against forgetting this message. It is the believers, the "spiritual" people, who mistake form for substance, prayers for performance, worship for practice.

For Christianity is not a "spiritual" religion, like some religions of the East. It is an intensely "practical" religion, having its moral roots in the practicality of Judaism. It was not designed to change the way men *think* or *believe* as much as to change the way they *act*.

It is easy to *think* Christmas, and easy to *believe* Christmas; but it is hard—sometimes intolerably hard— to *act* Christmas. It is not our false commercialism that prevents it, but our false spirituality. Not the clang of the cash register, but the jingle of bells, calling us to sentimentality, and seducing us from the grim, patient, year-round task of brotherhood.

Western civilization has not yet learned the lesson that the energy we expend in "getting things done" is less important than the moral strength it takes to decide what is worth doing and what is right to do.

*

Why do so many people yearn for an eternal life when they don't even know what to do with themselves in this brief one?

*

Confidence, once lost or betrayed, can never be restored again to the same measure; and we learn too late in life that our acts of deception are irrevocable—they may be forgiven, but they cannot be forgotten by their victims.

Changing Human Nature

THE ONE CLICHE I cannot bear above all others is that "human nature doesn't change." I am sure that is what one cannibal said to the other cannibal, when some daring soul proposed that they stop eating people.

We use this cliche as an excuse for not making ourselves better, and the world better. But we don't really believe it. As Prof. John Platt points out in his book, "The Step to Man," all our vast educational activities would be absurd if we actually thought there was no possibility of changing human nature.

This thing called "human nature," as I conceive it, is like a musical instrument—say, an organ. Now, it cannot be changed, in the sense that the range of notes is given, and we cannot play the instrument outside that range.

But the range of possibilities is large enough so that we can play a nearly infinite number of melodies. We can play harmonies, and we can play dissonances. We can soothe or deafen. We can play war marches and love songs and lullabies and hymns. *How* we use the instrument depends largely upon social conditioning, upon the kind of culture we grow up in.

It is not necessary to "change" human nature in order to get sweeter melodies out of the organ. It is only necessary to change the social order so that more people will have an incentive to press the keys and push the pedals that make melody rather than discord.

We have within us an enormous range of possibilities for behavior, unlike all other animals, which can only behave one way in any given situation. Education is the way in which society selects the kinds of possibilities it wants to encourage in young people—but education, to be effective, cannot be limited to the schools. It must be the whole example society gives to its young people.

Human nature will always contain badness and goodness, enmity and love, destruction and production. In this sense, we cannot change, we cannot eliminate, the possibilities of evil. But we *can* place a premium on the constructive, the creative and productive impulses of man—by rewarding these impulses, and penalizing the sour notes.

It is a difficult task, and it will never be wholly successful, but we must not blame our failure so far on the fact that "human nature doesn't change." We know we can change it for the worse—as some societies have done—and so we can change it for the better. Our first step is to agree upon what kind of people we want to have; and, as in most things, the first step is half the distance.

Spurring Our Better Selves

IT AMUSES and embarrasses me that so many readers apparently think I am able to direct and control my life by my "thoughts" or my "philosophy." And they want to know how they can do likewise.

Actually, a "philosophy of life" is meaningless unless it reflects one's deepest feelings and attitudes—and then it is unnecessary. Some of the world's worst men have had the noblest philosophies, which they failed utterly to put into practice.

It is not what one consciously believes that counts; it is what one feels at the marrow of existence. Millions of people call themselves Christians, and believe every item in the Apostles' Creed, who in their daily lives are as far removed from the gospel of Jesus as if they had never heard of Him.

We cannot direct or control our lives by such inanimate things as a body of thought or philosophy, but only by following an example of a person. I have long had such a person in my life; and in times of stress, I try to imagine what he would do in similar circumstances. Most of the time, I know exactly what he would do—but I am not always good enough to do likewise.

It is no accident that the two greatest teachers of the Western world, Jesus and Socrates, wrote not a word. They taught by questioning, by parable, and most of all, by example. They were not so much concerned with how we think or what we think, as with how we behave toward one another.

Not a single thought or piece of philosophy is able to help me when I am confronted with a moral decision—for one can find all sorts of reasons to justify any sort of conduct. The crimes committed over the centuries in the name of "religion" by well-meaning men have been far greater than those committed by evil and irreligious men, as all church historians will unhappily admit.

We can draw strength and righteousness only from another person, from someone we perceive to be better than we are, to be more of what a person was meant to be. When we find such a person—and he or she can always be found if we look hard enough—we must use him as a touchstone for testing the truth of our own behavior.

just as likely to happen to us right now as to anyone we read about in Alabama, we might go through each day with a more sympathetic and humane attitude toward our fellow mortals, trapped in the same web of time.

Deathbed contrition has always seemed a little cheap to me—a form of taking out additional God-insurance just as the policy is about to lapse. Every day we live, a little bit more of us is on the deathbed. A calm acceptance of this might make us act as if each day might be our last—not hoarding our penitence until the fatal hour, but lavishing our love before the tolling of the bell we will not hear.

Nobody Sees "What Is There"

WE USED TO THINK, in our naive way, that the act of perception consisted of two independent things: the perceiver and the thing perceived. The act of perception simply meant "seeing what was there."

Perhaps the most important advance in the behavioral sciences in our time has been the growing recognition that the perceiver is not just a passive camera taking a picture, but *takes an active part* in perception. He sees what experience has conditioned him to see.

We enter a restaurant, and six persons are sitting there. What do we "see" beyond the mere fact that these are six human beings? Do we all see the same picture, either individually or collectively?

A European will note that these are six Americans, by their dress and attitudes. A woman entering the room will probably note that the six consist of two married couples, an older woman, and a single man. A Southerner will see one man who could possibly be a light-skinned Negro. A homosexual will single out one of the men as a fellow deviate. An anti-Semite will immediately label one of the couples as "Jewish." A salesman will divide the group into "prospects" and "duds." And the waiter, of course, does not see people at all, but a "station" and "food" and "drinks."

What perceiver, then, "sees what is there"? Nobody, of course. Each of us perceives what our past has prepared us to perceive: We select and distinguish, we focus on some objects and relationships, and we blur others; we distort objective reality to make it conform to our needs or hopes or fears or hates or envies or affections.

In the physical sciences we have long been aware that the very act of examining and measuring some physical phenomenon changes the phenomenon itself: What the scientist sees during his experiment is not the same object that it would be if not under scrutiny.

Now we have begun to learn that the behavioral sciences contain this same subjective element: that our eyes and brains do not merely register some objective portrait of other persons or groups, but that our very act of seeing is warped by what we have been *taught* to believe, by what we *want* to believe, by what (in a deeper sense) we *need* to believe.

And this is the main reason that communication is so difficult: We are not disagreeing about the same thing, but about different things. We are not looking at the same people in the dining room, or on the picket line, or around the conference table. How to correct this built-in warp may very well be the basic, and ultimate, problem of mankind's survival.

Science Can't Give Us Everything

THERE IS NO WAY of deciding the running argument between the people who believe in a liberal arts education and those who believe in a technical education until we ask and answer one prior question.

This question is: What kind of persons do we want our colleges to turn out? Is it enough to "train" students, or do they somehow have to be changed in outlook and attitude? If we decide it is not enough just to "train" students, then we must look to the humanities and social sciences for means of changing them.

Literature, history, sociology, philosophy, anthropology—these differ in much more than subject matter from physics, chemistry, engineering, mathematics. They differ in that the knowledge we have of them affects both the future of the subject and of ourselves.

Our knowledge of the table of atomic weights does not change the atomic system. Our knowledge of algebra or calculus does not affect those mathematical concepts. Our knowledge of metal fatigue and structural stress does not alter those physical laws.

But our knowledge of the humanities and social sciences is an essential part of those systems. In sociology, for instance, once we truly understand the nature of group pressure and the influence of prejudice, both we and the subject have been modified.

If we know what Shakespeare was getting at in *King Lear*, if we can grasp what was wrong with the Treaty of Versailles, if we see what the existentialists are trying to express—then we are able to utilize this knowledge to reshape our own views of life and to exert influence on those we live with and work with.

The humanities are not "superior" to technical studies because they are more ancient or more "cultural" or more intellectual; these would be poor, and snobbish, reasons for granting them any sort of priority.

They are superior because they expand the imagination, enlarge the personality, enable us to become something different and better than what we were before. Learning a chemical formula does not make a man different; reading Donne's sermons can change his whole life drastically.

Our great need today is not so much for better-trained technicians as it is for well-rounded persons who know how their subject fits into other subjects, and who can relate their experience to some general framework of human experience. Without this, we will breed only a generation of technical barbarians, who do brilliantly what they have been taught to do, but who are blind to the consequences of their actions. This may be an admirable quality in a soldier; it is a disastrous one in a free citizen.

We Beg to Be Despised

I HAVE BEEN browsing through the new revised edition of Walter Sullivan's book, *We Are Not Alone,* in which the science editor of the *New York Times* examines "the search for intelligent life on other worlds."

At the same time, I heard another man on a television interview discuss the "flying saucers" that have been reported around the country for many years. He, too, is writing a book to document these cases.

Most speculation and science-fiction on the subject is based on the theory that highly intelligent creatures living in distant space are either trying to communicate with us, or are actually investigating life on Earth, with a view toward attacking or conquering us.

I cannot believe this. If there are creatures intelligent enough to spy on us through vast galactic distances, then they must also be intelligent enough to let us alone after they learn what we are like.

For the human race on Earth, it seems plain to me, must rank quite low in the order of conscious intelligence. We seem to have just enough brains to make trouble for ourselves, and not enough to learn how to live together amicably. Just enough brains to create a huge technology that could turn the Earth into an Eden, and not enough to prevent us from using this technology to blow ourselves up.

Creatures from another planet, if they have observed us for any length of time, are more likely to be perplexed and disgusted with our irrational behavior than tempted to conquer us. What could they get from us but grief? They may study us, but only as we study bacteria.

Civilization after civilization has toppled in the 10,000 years of history. Wars between people have become more ferocious and fatal as the art of weaponry has developed, and the future holds grim promise of chemical and bacteriological warfare even more sinister than the threat of the hydrogen bomb.

We have made tremendous advances in living conditions—but they have been more than matched by our ominous advances in dying conditions. Prejudice and passion, hate and rivalry, are more intense today than in the pastoral environment of Biblical times. People may *be* no worse, but we have increased by a million-fold our capacity to *do* worse.

Any truly intelligent beings from another galaxy would not touch us with a 10-light-year pole. We are quite capable of attacking and destroying ourselves without their help. And not because we are ''bad'' in any grand and classic sense of the word—but because we are weak and petty and more concerned with our immediate advantages (delusive as they are) than with pledging our allegiance to the survival of the human race.

Man Finished or Finished Off?

FROM ARISTOTLE to the moderns, man has been variously defined as many kinds of animal—as a ''rational'' animal, as a ''problem solving'' animal, as a ''self-conscious'' animal, an animal with ''tools'' and ''language'' and ''history.''

But perhaps the most satisfactory definition I have ever heard is the one that calls man the ''unfinished'' animal. Alone of all the species, man seems to have been assigned the task of *completing himself.*

Every other species is complete, and has been so for countless years. The tiger, the rabbit, the dog, the eagle, the earthworm, are (so to speak) finished products. There is nothing more for them to be or do; no further possibilities, for good or evil, are open to them.

We, on the other hand, seem to have been conferred the dreadful freedom to finish shaping ourselves in whatever way we will. We can become more like Socrates, or more like the men who put him to death. We—alone of all living creatures—can elevate ourselves, or degrade ourselves, or totally destroy ourselves.

Other animals have a *nature;* we, as Ortega suggested, have a *history.* This means that we are not "given," as they are—we have an infinite number of moves and combinations on that chessboard called "human nature."

The only important question facing mankind today is "How shall we complete ourselves?" For the first time, we have the technology, the energy, the knowledge and the resources, to unify the human race, to feed everyone, to protect all from want, to lift the living level of the havenots without lowering the level of the haves.

Yet, while all this is happening on the intellectual and physical and technical fronts, precisely the opposite is happening on the political, the social and the emotional fronts. We are more divisive, more hostile, more suspicious, more chauvinistic, more irrational than at any time in the present century.

Every thinking person knows that the smallest possible unit of survival today is the human race. This has been forced upon us by atomic fission; neither philosophy nor religion, but the stark demands of science call for an ultimate decision on our part—co-operation or catastrophe.

Man is still evolving, by his own hands, with his own mind and feelings. We have the power to finish ourselves or to *finish ourselves off.* This is the frightful burden of our freedom, a burden not carried by any other creature. If we cannot rise to this responsibility, will we not perish, to be replaced with some other species more fitted for the task? For one thing is sure—we cannot continue to survive in this uncompleted state, an animal so bitterly divided against itself.

We Are All on One Space Ship

WHILE IN THE COUNTRY this summer, we watched, like most other American families, the weeklong space orbiting of our astronauts. We marveled, we applauded, we sighed in relief as they came down safely.

"I wonder what it would be like to be on a spaceship," mused my 10-year-old boy. "You're on one," I told him. "And you have been all your life."

The earth itself is a very small spaceship, by astronomical standards. It is only 8,000 miles in diameter, which makes it just a tiny speck in our galaxy. And our galaxy is only one of millions.

Yet this tiny speck has sustained billions of human passengers for more than 2,000,000 years as it has orbited around the solar system. It shows no signs of running down for millions of years more, and all it needs is radiation from the sun to keep it going and to regenerate life "on board."

If we could implant in our children, at an early age, this concept of a global spaceship, they might possibly be more prepared, in attitude and action, to treat one another as crew members should, when they grow up.

It may be too late—psychologically speaking—for most adults to adopt this approach. We see the world in narrow, sublunary terms: in terms of racial divisions and national territories, of ancient rivalries and provincial fears, of airtight compartments separating one portion of the crew from another.

But to see the world as the astronauts saw it—this fragile yet sturdy sphere revolving in the immensity of space, carrying its millions of passengers locked together for a lifetime—is the only way to make it viable in the future. When two men can circle the globe in less time than it takes us to mow a good-sized lawn, then anything less than a global viewpoint is dangerously inadequate.

Nature has provided us with a magnificently self-renewing spaceship, containing everything it needs for perpetual flight, for nourishment, for comfort—and even for beauty. If the Gemini astronauts had quarreled and fought, or sulked and sneered, even a week's flight would have been imperiled.

Everybody is an involuntary crew member on Earth I. The compartments we create are artificial and destructive. Until now, however, we only had the power to injure other members of the crew. Today we can easily blow up the whole ship and everybody on it.

The only hope is to think of ourselves as astronauts.

How Authentic Self Is Hidden

THE PERSONALITY of man is not an apple that has to be polished, but a banana that has to be peeled. And the reason we remain so far from one another, the reason we neither communicate nor interact in any real way, is that most of us spend our lives in polishing rather than peeling.

Man's lifelong task is simply one, but it is not simple: To remove the discrepancy between his outer self and his inner self, to get rid of the "persona" that divides his authentic self from the world.

This persona is like the peeling on a banana: It is something built up to protect from bruises and injury. It is not the real person, but sometimes (if the fear of injury remains too great) it becomes a lifelong substitute for the person.

The "authentic personality" knows that he is like a banana, and knows that only as he peels himself down to his individuated self can he reach out and make contact with his fellows by what Father Goldbrunner calls "the sheer maturity of his humanity." Only when he himself is detached from his defensive armorings can he then awaken a true response in his dialogue with others.

Most of us, however, think in terms of the apple, not the banana. We spend our lives in shining the surface, in making it rosy and gleaming, in perfecting the "image." But the image is not the apple, which may be wormy and rotten to the taste.

Almost everything in modern life is devoted to the polishing process, and little to the peeling process. It is the surface personality that we work on—the appearance, the clothes, the manners, the geniality. In short, the salesmanship: We are selling the package, not the product.

There is a vast disparity between our inner and outer selves; in many of us, the real person never comes to life at all, never reveals itself, never knows itself. It lives through its functions, it lives as a type, a response to an environment, and dies without ever having found its true existence. This, and not unhappiness, is the tragedy of life; this, and not "selfishness," is what causes human misery.

So long as we live behind the peeling, we can have no genuine encounter with the world. So long as we go on polishing, we sacrifice the substance for the image—until, at last, there is no substance left. What is all the good of our "individualism," if it means merely the freedom to be like everybody else, the liberty to remain secure within the peeling?

We are rarely satisfied with our portraits, for each of us carries around inside himself a self-image that is quite impervious to reality.

No Stranger Knew, None Cared

A COUPLE of weeks ago, I slipped off a ladder at home and fractured a little bone in my foot. Nothing serious, but awkward and uncomfortable. The foot was tightly taped, and I hobbled around with a cane.

What was pleasant about this otherwise painful experience was the way I was treated by everyone—strangers included. People opened doors for me, helped me into cabs and gave me plenty of room in elevators.

Their consideration almost made up for the discomfort; and it was a temptation to keep the bandage and the cane longer than I need have. My spirit blossomed under this kind public treatment.

Yet, the moment I laid aside these symbols of deficiency, people reverted to their old selfish selves: pushing and jostling and running down any object in their mad pursuit toward nowhere in particular.

And it occurred to me that everybody has some sort of broken bone somewhere, even if it cannot be seen. Not physical bones, of course, but emotional ones that are just as frail and tender (and sometimes as painful) as the visible bone that was taped and labeled.

Each man carries with him some ancient wound that has not quite healed, and that he feels he must protect from the jostling throng.

Because they cannot see this hurt, he is forced to protect it, not with tape or a cast or a cane, but with mannerisms and defensive reactions that may make him seem less likable or less approachable than he really is.

We are creatures of the visible and the palpable: If something cannot be seen or felt, we imagine it does not exist. We feel pity for the physical cripple, because we can see his twisted limbs; but we are indifferent to the psychic cripple, because his troubles are buried beneath the cranium.

There have been many days when I needed more consideration than the days I carried a cane; when my mind was troubled and my emotions churned; and no stranger knew and no stranger cared. The little broken bone was minor—but it opened a floodgate of human sympathy and warmth.

Of course, we cannot see beneath the skin: The man passing swiftly on the street may be tortured more agonizingly than the lady on crutches, who only broke a leg on a ski slide. We respond to the symbol of pain, not to the pain itself.

It could be a fruitful experience for us to take a day off once in a while and treat every person we meet as if his foot were bandaged. This might do more good than dropping alms in a crippled beggar's cup.

Even the Empty Need Solitude

SHORTLY BEFORE DINNER, one of our weekend guests went out of the house onto the terrace and sat down on the stone steps leading to the water.

He was there less than 10 minutes when a murmur ran through the entire house: Is he feeling all right? Is he angry at someone? Is he upset? Is there anything we can do for him?

Finally, one of us summoned up enough courage to walk down to where he was sitting and ask him if anything was the matter. He looked up in great surprise.

"Certainly not," he answered. "I just wanted to be alone for a little bit—to look at the water and watch the sun go down. I rarely get a chance to do this at home."

And then it occurred to us that "solitude" is an almost extinct word in modern society. Wanting to be alone with one's thoughts or dreams is considered almost antisocial.

But a certain measure of solitude is necessary for our mental and spiritual wellbeing. Man is a social animal, but he is also a thinking animal—and thinking is difficult in a crowded room.

Even without the desire to think, solitude is often a healing state, when we are bruised and fatigued from too much contact with other personalities, no matter how much we may like them most of the time.

We recognize that people who cannot be alone, who must forever have company and conversation and activity, are sick people. Yet, while few of us have this compulsive need for society, few of us seek repose in solitude. We seem almost afraid to be alone—as though it were a sign of unpopularity.

As our social order grows increasingly larger and louder and more insistent in its demands upon our time and energy, we tend to lose our sense of identity as individuals, and become as indistinguishable as ants marching up and down a hill.

Our guest who sat on the steps by himself and looked at the water was trying to recapture, perhaps, the knowledge of who he is and where he is going. And even if he was merely staring blankly at the horizon, without a thought on his mind, his desire to shut out the world for a few minutes is a more natural need than our feverish chatter over cocktails or our desperate groping for one another in the spiritual darkness of a blazing room.

We're Not at All Civilized

MAN IS STILL LIVING in the primitive world. The division we make between "barbarism" and "civilization" is compounded out of vanity and illusion.

Viewed a thousand years from now, our century will seem as much a part of the "dark ages" as the 8th Century now seems to us.

What fools us, and sustains us in our illusion, is our growth in technology. Our mechanistic world view makes us think that because of electricity, airplanes, conveyor belts and skyscrapers we are somehow superior to the Hittites, the Babylonians and the Goths.

But the true mark of "civilization" is *civility*—that is, good manners at the deepest level of behavior. And our manners are no better than they were a thousand years ago; indeed, given our awesome instruments of technology, our bad manners are now infinitely more dangerous than ever in the past.

We are now able to hate more effectively, but we do not know how to love any better. We are now able to conduct massive and mutually suicidal wars between whole continents, whereas in the past wars were limited to small city-states or duchies at the most. We are now able to poison the air everywhere, pollute all the waters and make every crop radioactive—even among people with whom we have no quarrel.

We have been able to despoil the countryside and make the city increasingly uninhabitable, so that we retain neither the consolations of rusticity nor the advantages of urbanization. Whichever environment we opt for, the discomforts are beginning to outweigh the benefits; and there is no place to live that combines the beauty of the country with the culture of the city—which is what civilization *ought* to mean.

I was born during one Great War, lived through another, and perhaps will see the third (and final) one before I die. I cannot believe this represents a significant advance in human affairs since "barbarian" times. We are able to keep many more people alive on a retail basis, through progress in science, medicine and sanitation—only to be able to kill many more on a wholesale basis, through battleships, bombs and gas chambers. The 20th Century is the most murderous era of mankind.

Let me not conclude on a bleakly pessimistic note. It need not remain this way; there is nothing inevitable about our fate. But, just as the first step to becoming better is to know you are bad, and the first step to becoming well is to know you are ill, the first step to becoming civilized is to know you are still barbarous. When we stop thinking of ourselves as "civilized," and begin to inquire what the word truly means, we may begin to cross the threshhold of humanhood.

"See Him as the Child He Was"

SEE HIM AS THE CHILD he was. These seven simple one-syllable words have taken me half a lifetime to learn. But it has been worth the long, hard-fought lesson.

For these are magic words: with them, you can rise above pettiness and spite, cruelty and arrogance and greed.

When you confront a man who shows these unattractive traits—see him as the child he was.

Remember that he began his life with laughing expectancy, with trust, with warmth, desiring to give love and to take love.

And then remember that something happened to him—something he is not aware of—to turn the trust into suspicion, the warmth into wariness, the give-and-take into all-take and no-give.

See him as the child he was.

Behind the pomp or the rudeness, beneath the crust of meanness or coldness, begin to perceive the wistful little boy (or girl) who is hurt and disappointed and determined to strike back at the world.

Or the little boy who is frightened, and tightens his jaw and clenches his fist to ward off some overwhelming fear that hovers deep in the dark past.

Or the little boy who was given too much too soon—and given *things* instead of *feelings*—and now can only clutch his power or his purse the way he used to clutch his teddy-bear, because there is nothing else he feels is really his for keeps.

See him as the child he was.

Regard the faces as they pass you on the street: adult faces on the surface, but the child is lurking not too far beneath the skin—the child who eats too much because he craves the sweetness of affection, the child who drinks too much because he cannot face a motherless world, the child who brags and lies and cheats to wrest revenge for some huge indignity that is gnawing at his heart.

And then look again, closely, and you will see what the Book means when it calls all of us "God's children"—you will see a glimmer of hope behind the hate, a glint of humor behind the harshness, a touch of tenderness that no defensive wall can wholly obliterate.

Only in this way can we guard ourselves against responding in kind, against returning pettiness to the petty and cruelty to the cruel. And only in this way can we find the path to the green plateau of adulthood, where we can look down upon God's children with a sad but loving glance.

Space Age Won't Turn Key to Peace

IT IS A HALF-TRUTH, and a dangerous half-truth, to think that the nations will become closer in spirit as they become closer in space. The world is shrinking, but our loyalties are not expanding.

Soon, by jet, it will take only a few hours to go from New York to any place on the globe. But the differences between New York and New Delhi do not thereby disappear; indeed, they may become sharpened.

The closeness of England and Ireland did not prevent the brutality and blindness of British policy in Ireland; the proximity of France and Germany did not create neighborliness; nor have the Turks been noted for their kindness toward the Armenians, who live close by.

It is worth remembering that the first act of aggression that was recorded in the Western World was the slaying of one brother by another. Cain and Abel lived less than a stone's throw from each other; and so a stone was thrown.

Rapid transportation and communication will not automatically bind the world into brotherhood. They simply make it easier to be hostile at long range.

Human beings are tied together by ideas and feelings, not by geography. The bitterest battles have been fought between brothers— between the Yorkists and Lancastrians in England's War of the Roses, between the Blues and the Grays in America's Civil War.

It is what I call "scientific sentimentality" to believe that as modern technology makes the world grow smaller, our spirits will somehow grow larger.

If we (as nations and as individuals) are motivated by fear and hate, then the closer together we are brought, the more fiercely will we bristle at one another.

This is not a plea for "isolationism," which is impossible today, even if it were desirable. But it is a caution that mere proximity is not a force for peace, and has never been.

The only force for peace lies in the heart and in the mind—that is to say, in love and in reason, not as vague Sunday sentiments, but realistically translated into the behavior of our governments.

How to accomplish this is the only significant task facing mankind; but while there are pressure groups to promote everything from highways to low taxes, there is no concerted effort by the public to comprehend and to attack the one problem whose solution will determine whether we survive or perish as a race.

What the ordinary person means by a "miracle" is some gross distortion or suspension of the laws of nature, some vulgar and melodramatic spectacle; but life itself strikes him as commonplace, when in truth a blade of grass or a neuron in the brain is a greater miracle (to the thoughtful person) than any piece of cosmic showmanship.

*

What the world most needs is a flexible fusion of the doctrine of the West—that action is paramount—and the doctrine of the East—that action is futile—so that we are neither infatuated with mere motion, nor immobilized by a sense of passivity.

*

Any creed whose basic doctrines do not include respect for the creeds of others, is simply power politics masquerading as philosophy.

*

The founder of every creed, from Jesus Christ to Karl Marx, would be appalled to return to earth and see what has been made of that creed, not by its enemies, but by its most devoted adherents.

*

Alone of all creatures on earth, man and the shark share this one dubious distinction: They are their own worst enemies, and the only creatures more threatened by their own kind than by other species.

II.
Of the Mind
and Passions

The "Love It or Leave It" Nonsense

ONE OF THE MOST IGNORANT and hateful statements that a person can make to another is "If you don't like it here, why don't you leave?"

That attitude is the main reason America was founded, in all its hope and energy and goodness. The people who came here, to make a better land than had ever been seen before by the common people, had been rebuffed and rejected by their neighbors in the Old World.

They didn't like conditions where they lived, and wanted to improve them. If they had been allowed and encouraged to, the Old World would have had a happier history, instead of the miserable tribulations that turned the eyes of the people to America as their last, best hope.

Now we find that many Americans—smug and fat and entrenched in their affluent inertia—are saying the same ugly thing to their neighbors: "If you don't like it here, why don't you leave?"

But most people who want to change conditions *do* like it here; they love it here. They love it so much they cannot stand to see it suffer from its imperfections, and want it to live up to its ideals. It is the people who placidly accept the corruptions and perversions and inequities in our society who do not love America—they love only their status and security and special privilege.

Nobody should be faced with the mean choice of accepting conditions as they are or abandoning the place he has grown up in. We not only have a right, we have a responsibility, to make our environment as just and as flourishing as our Founding Fathers declared it must be if it were to live up to its aspiration as "the standard of the world."

Those who want to leave have a right to leave, but those who want to stay and work for what they consider a better society must be protected in that right—for without it, our nation would sink into stagnation, and the process of change would harden into repression by those who benefit by keeping things just as they are.

If all the settlers who came here, with high hopes for a new and finer social order, had been compelled to "go back where they came from," we would have had no United States of America. This country was born out of dissatisfaction with the old scheme of things, and grew on the blood and dedication of men who were not afraid to speak and work for fundamental changes in the whole political and social structure.

Somebody who truly didn't like what America *stands for* ought to be invited to leave; but there is a vast difference between such a person and those who dislike *what we have allowed ourselves to become*, through greed and prejudice and provincial indifference to the great problems we now face. No community can afford to lose these good "agitators."

Just Like the General's Mule

WHEN A FAMOUS German general, long ago, heard one of his staff officers venture the sententious remark that "experience is the best teacher," the general snorted: "Nonsense—my mule has been through a dozen campaigns with me, but he knows no more now than he did before the first one!"

Experience can be a very bad teacher, indeed, or no teacher at all. It is like the silly phrase, "Practice makes perfect." In most cases, practice merely confirms us in our errors, and the longer we do something the wrong way—that is, without enlightenment and instruction—the more fixed we become in our folly.

To take a trivial example in my own case: I began playing tennis as a boy, and had many years of experience. I also practiced incessantly. But because I did not understand the basic principles of the game, the more experience I had, and the more practice I took, the more deeply I fell into the grip of bad form and losing habits.

It finally became necessary for me to take lessons if my game was to improve at all—and most of the lessons were spent in *unlearning* everything that "experience" and "practice" had taught me!

This, of course, made it twice as hard for me to become a truly proficient player. With a beginner, the coach merely instills good habits and proper form; but, with me, it was necessary first to break the deeply ingrained bad habits of years and reduce me to the rank of ignorance before I could learn to rebuild my game the right way.

Young people today are fond of believing that "experience" in and by itself is a good thing, and that we automatically learn the right after we have experienced the wrong or the dubious. But older people know—through painful examination of their own lives—that this is not usually the case.

Many people go from one bad experience to another, from one kind of mistake to a different kind—learning, perhaps, to avoid the kind they made in the past, but having no rational guideline to prevent them from making other, and more disastrous, mistakes in the future. The millions of multiple marriages in American society are tragic proof of this failure to profit from mere "experience."

Of course, we cannot learn without "living." But "living" means not only inviting new sensations and experiences; it also means studying, analyzing, generalizing, anticipating and judging from mankind's accumulated wisdom of the past. Otherwise, our experiences do us no more good than they did the general's mule.

Buying off Our Consciences

A FEW DAYS after the Clay-Terrell fight, I was having a cup of coffee with a friend, when he pointed to the front page of the paper. A lady cellist in New York had just been arrested for performing with a bare bosom during an avant-garde concert.

"I wish you'd explain to me," he said, "why this event is considered 'obscene conduct,' and the Clay-Terrell fight isn't. Why are we so repressive about sex, and so permissive about violence?

"I watched the Clay-Terrell fight," he went on, "and by my definition, it was an obscene performance. After the seventh round, Terrell was just a punching-bag. And Clay was as ugly and vicious as a man could be. Yet the public pays millions to watch such spectacles, and feels cheated when one of the fighters doesn't end in a bloody pulp on the floor."

It wasn't hard for me to agree with him that we have a perverted sense of values in Western society, insofar as sex and violence are concerned. It seems absurd that a bare bosom is considered in any way "lewd," while the brutal batterings of two anthropoids are applauded and approved as a great sporting event.

Neither a prizefight nor a cello concert cum nipples would attract me as a customer, but I fail utterly to see why one is given police protection while the other is subjected to police persecution. The lady cellist wasn't hurting anybody, or doing anything intrinsically wrong, and her bosom is certainly no more an offensive sight than Terrell's blood-streaked chest.

I am almost convinced that this curious inversion of values—where violence is condoned if not actually sanctified, while sex is still shrouded in shame—explains in large part the shifting sexual morality of young people today. A society that is so willing to send them out to be killed, that is so indifferent to human life, and yet at the same time that places so many safeguards against sexual activity, seems unworthy and hypocritical in the eyes of many youngsters.

Unnecessary *pain* of any kind is what is "obscene" in human conduct, while pleasure may be good, bad or indifferent, depending upon the other values involved in it. Surely the display of the body is not lewd by and of itself, with or without a cello; nor is there anything lewd about the mutual enjoyment of sex by two consenting adults. It may not be prudent, but that is quite another matter.

Is it possible that our strictures against sex are the way we buy off our collective conscience for our obscene addiction to violence?

What Shape's Your Mind In?

IT IS TRUE that minds are of different sizes, just as bodies are of different sizes. But it is also true that minds are of different *shapes*, just as bodies are of different shapes. And the shape can be as important as the size.

A considerable number of people feel inferior or inadequate in the mental department, when they compare themselves with mighty minds. This is mistakenly placing too much value on mere size, and not enough attention to shape.

A mighty mind can also be mighty dull, mighty ponderous and mighty closed in its frame of reference. I have known many intellectual persons, with massive brain power, who had ungainly "shapes" to their minds, and were not nearly as interesting, amusing or stimulating as persons with smaller but more shapely minds.

There is no reason to feel inferior because God has seen fit to give us a mind less vast and powerful than some others. We can do nothing about that; but we can do something about the shape of the mind, just as we can make the shape of the body more graceful and attractive.

The people I most enjoy are not necessarily those with the largest mentalities, but those who know how to use what they have with charm, humor and individuality. A four-cylinder mind, properly tuned and expertly driven, can generally run rings around an eight-cylinder mind that is cumbersome and self-satisfied.

A nicely-shaped mind, like a nicely-shaped calf, need not be large. It is the trimness and the curve that are appealing, not the bulk. And anybody who sincerely tries can improve the shapeliness of his or her mind, by getting rid of the superfluous fat of banality and conformity.

Indeed, what I personally would call an "intellectual" mind has little to do with brain-size, and even less to do with formal education. It is much more a matter of shape—of a kind of grasp, a kind of attitude, a kind of approach to the world and one's self. It involves a humorous detachment from the obvious, and a profound awareness of the personal equation in all "objective" opinions.

Many large minds are muscle-bound, just as many large bodies are. Our aim should not be to "expand" the mind, for this simply cannot be done, but to improve its contours, to enhance its charms and graces and whimsies, to trim off the ugly fat deposits of encrusted non-thinking. Given the proper exercise, our minds, like our bodies, are capable of twice as much activity—and appeal—as we ordinarily display.

Prejudice Is Never "Reasonable"

THERE IS A STORY about a man who accosted a wealthier friend and asked for a loan of a hundred dollars. "Can't do it," said the friend, "because my mother-in-law is visiting us right now."

The man was puzzled. "What has that got to do with lending me the money?" he asked. "Nothing at all," replied the friend, "but when you don't want to do something, one excuse is as good as another."

I thought of this recently when I heard someone holding forth on the reasons he doesn't care for Negroes—they are shiftless, they lack ambition, they won't accept responsibility, they commit many crimes, they don't even help one another, and they are simply unintelligent.

This same man, I happen to know, doesn't care much for Jews, either. And what do you suppose his "reasons" are? The Jews are too ambitious, they stick together and help each other too much, they are too clever and study too hard and get the best grades and run the big businesses and the most prosperous law offices and the most flourishing medical practices.

The very opposite traits that prejudice him against the Negro prejudice him against the Jews. One group reacts to discrimination in one way; another in another; and he objects to both reactions.

Many of the things that are said about Negroes and Jews are false; some of the things are true. But what is significant is that if you don't want to like and accept somebody, one excuse is as good as another. The objective facts don't matter, and the reasons are never as "reasonable" as we like to think they are.

It is interesting that, for a long time, the Americans as a group were talked about by Europeans just as we talk about our own minority groups. Even up to modern times, the educated elite among Europeans dismissed the Americans as arrogant, crude, barbarous, boastful, greedily materialistic and vulgarly ostentatious in their habits and goals.

Many of these charges were true, but the Europeans failed to recognize the historical and cultural reasons for such behavior. All they knew was that the Americans were a different breed, and their very difference was an offense to Old World standards. They both resented and envied us, and so they used the same vituperation that older and more settled communities have always used against the newcomer and the outlander. The ancient Greeks said the same things about the Romans.

If you tell a child long enough that he is unattractive and undesirable, he comes to believe it despite himself, and begins to react in an extreme manner. The real tragedy of prejudice and discrimination is that the person (or the group) turns into a caricature of himself.

Good Deeds Can Be Misused

IF YOU'RE GOING to do something nice, be nice about it, or don't do it. This is a simple and obvious thought—but it rarely seems to occur to certain types of people.

I am referring to those who will go out of their way to do something nice—a favor, a chore, an extra kindness—and then silently demand repayment in terms of gratitude or appreciation.

These are what Dr. Edmund Bergler, the late psychiatrist, called "the injustice collectors." They go around in life collecting injustices. They do nice things to prove to themselves that other people do not appreciate them as much as they should.

Then they sulk, or adopt a martyred pose, or take to their beds with some real or fancied ailment. And, in one way or another, they exact a high retribution for their "niceness." Finally, those around them begin to realize that it's not worth the price.

Many acts of generosity and self-sacrifice are not at all what they seem to be on the surface. Rather, they are techniques employed for neurotic ends; these "tyrants of goodness" would be better off—and so would their families—if they acted a little more selfishly (that is, a little more naturally) much of the time.

Self-pity is the *leitmotif* in the lives of such personalities. They enjoy demonstrating, over and over again, that others do not appreciate them, that they are victims of the world's injustice, that the bread they cast on the waters is never served up to them as toast on a tray in bed on Sunday mornings.

What they utterly fail to understand is that nice things are done for our own sake, not for the sake of others. The pleasure must reside in the performance, not in the applause. Good deeds are, in a deeper psychological way, *a favor to oneself.* If this is not grasped, then our whole sense of personal relationships becomes warped.

A kind act, a piece of generosity or self-sacrifice, must be its own reason for being, an end in itself, not part of a barter system. It must not be used later to reprove someone else with, or as a lever to pry up ancient grievances under a rock. Yet this is what the self-sacrificers tend to do.

They pile up their good deeds like misers stuffing bills in a mattress; hoard them, count them over at night, and recite their complaints. Eventually, with this hoard they try to purchase affection and admiration and gratitude—but it does not work that way. The injustice collectors only collect more injustices.

There are many people who should try to be a little better; but there are almost as many who should stop trying to be better than they can be. If their hidden feelings (hidden to themselves, if not to others) do not correspond to their generous acts, there can be nothing but bitter fruit in the end, for themselves and for those they are so "nice" to.

Ignorance can't be bliss, or many more people would be happy.

*

The only way to be meaningfully "successful" is always to compete against yourself, against your previous best, rather than against others; in this way, you win even when you lose, in gaining a knowledge of your proper limits.

Why Sammy Continues to Run

"WHY DOES HE WANT more money?" said my friend at lunch, about a third man we both know. "He's got far more than he needs, and he'll just kill himself trying to double his fortune.

This is a commonplace enough situation. And, of course, it is obvious to anyone that money itself is not what the man wants: it is the "game," the "thrill," the gratification of "winning" that makes Sammy keep running long after he has any need to.

What I think is less understood, however, is that a chase of this sort is essentially a *substitute experience*. And a substitute is always something that we can never have enough of.

The man is really looking for self-esteem, and he seeks to find it by winning the esteem of others. In our society, the fastest and surest way to do this is by amassing a great deal of money. So the money becomes a substitute, a symbol, for the esteem.

But in the deep chemistry of the psyche, things do not work out this way. Getting the esteem of others does not give us self-esteem; worthiness comes from the inside, never from the outside. This is why a substitute experience always leaves us hungry for more.

Money is only one example. Sex, of course, is another. The man who chases women (like the one who chases money) can never have enough, can never be satisfied, can never settle down to one possession. The compulsive Lothario is perpetually as insatiable as the compulsive driver in the marketplace.

For the same motives operate in this area. When sex becomes a substitute for love, it can never be gratified, but must go on from dizzying triumph to dizzying triumph (and each triumph ends in a kind of internal exhaustion and defeat, convalescence and continuation). The libertine can never find what he thinks he is looking for, any more than the acquisitive man can ever have "enough" money.

Our genuine needs are self-confidence, self-esteem, self-sacrifice. These can be achieved only by giving, not by getting. When something in the psyche blocks us from expressing and gratifying these genuine needs, we turn to substitute ones. But no liquid can quench our thirst except water itself.

Not only can the substitute not satisfy us; it also contains its own law of diminishing returns—like the dope addict who needs more and more of a "shot" in order to maintain the same level of euphoria. Finally, he needs massive doses simply to keep alive, to keep reality at arm's length. Sammy runs because if he ever stopped, he might drop dead at the mere confrontation of his real needs.

Good, Bad Traits Are Entwined

I WAS HAVING LUNCH with a magazine publisher from New York, in the course of which he mentioned a man we both knew. "Sam would make a fine editor," he said, "if only he would learn to give the other fellow a chance to speak up."

"Yes," I agreed, "but then he wouldn't be Sam any more; he would be somebody else."

One of the most frequent mistakes we make lies in assuming that a personality is a collection of traits, or that a personality is merely the sum of its parts. Personality is a *way of organizing* these parts.

Sam's "bad trait"—his unwillingness to give others a chance to speak up—is directly related to his "good" traits. They are integrated in a complex structure, like a set of molecules, and removing or changing one would affect the whole nature of the structure.

If we look at persons dynamically, and not simply as a static set of traits, we can see that certain defects are the price they pay for their virtues, just as ulcer or migraine is the price some people pay for their perfectionism or their passivity or their aggressiveness.

This is why "pointing out" a bad trait to a colleague or a subordinate—even in a kindly and well-meaning way—usually does no good, and may even do some harm. It makes him feel worse, and does not enable him to act any better.

When we single out one trait or characteristic and ask the person to change it, we are really asking him to change the *organization* of his whole personality; and this is a formidable task for which most of us are not equipped—especially when it has taken us years of effort to achieve some success and equilibrium with this particular organization of our traits.

Perhaps we can see the problem more clearly if we conceive of the personality as a closely integrated team of acrobats who stand on one another's shoulders—three men below, then two on top of them, and finally one on the top. If we change the position of any one of the men, or take one away, the whole act is different. And, indeed, it may be the man on the bottom (whom we find "undesirable") that enables the top man to maintain his precarious balance.

Of course, people change, and modify their conduct, and learn from experience if they are open to it. But it is important to know that some "bad" traits make the good ones possible, just as the pathology in the oyster produces the pearl.

"Intelligence" Has Many Facets

A COUPLE DROPPED IN while I was playing chess the other evening, and the woman made the customary remark that she wasn't "intelligent" enough to take up the game.

Yet, although I have been playing since I was 10, with duffers and experts alike, I have not seen the slightest relation between chess ability and general intelligence.

Indeed, I have seen some Masters who barely knew enough to tie their shoelaces properly away from the chessboard. They can beat me blindfold every game, but their non-chess intelligence is scarcely visible to the naked eye.

I suggest that the word "intelligence" is not a single unitary thing, but is rather a composite made up of many strands. There are different *kinds* of intelligences, and one is not necessarily better than the other.

There is social intelligence, for instance, which few intellectuals possess—the ability to understand how other people feel and to live and work with them in reasonable peace.

There is mechanical intelligence, which I don't possess an iota of—the ability to manipulate and conquer physical objects, to make, to repair, to take apart and put together.

There is mathematical intelligence, of which chess is a part—the ability to visualize abstractions in space. This is a rare gift which has sometimes been given to men who are otherwise idiots.

There is verbal intelligence, the ability to use words with force and clarity; but some of the writers who are best at this (Hemingway comes to mind) are appallingly poor thinkers and have evolved a philosophy of life that would scarcely do credit to a high-school sophomore.

And there is a deep intelligence of the blood and the bone, which is not articulate, which cannot express itself verbally, but which knows what to do in practical situations where a genius might find himself helpless or hysterical.

We must not be bluffed or intimidated by a word. "Intelligence" can cover a wide spectrum of human aptitudes; and, besides, this spectrum is so colored with our emotional lives that many people seem dumb (to themselves as well as to others) because they are merely fearful and confused.

No real gauge of intelligence has yet been devised; the I.Q. test is a makeshift device, heavily weighted in favor of those who can express themselves deftly and swiftly.

But millions of others have simply not learned to use more than a fraction of the intelligence they have.

A Good Workman Is Never Crude

THE MOST OBVIOUS TRUTHS in the world are often the hardest to grasp. The simplest facts of human relations are often the most difficult to make some people see.

Such as the equation: the more respect you give, the more respect you get back. Since everybody wants respect from others—indeed, the struggle for money and prestige is simply a means of trying to attain respect—why don't more persons try this easy, proven method?

I have had lots of men working around the house since I bought it early this summer. Two or three of them have been Old World characters, who did their jobs not only with competence, but also with dignity and courtesy.

The others have been the brash and sloppy workmen we have become so used to these days. They roll into the house as if doing the home owner a favor, are dirty in their habits, crude in their deportment, and even seem contemptuous of their own skills.

When they are treated in the manner they seem to invite—for everyone is treated in the manner he seems to invite—they build up a further supply of resentment, and the vicious circle begins anew.

The other workmen—and I am sorry to admit that they are not of native birth, but bring with them a sense of craftsmanship from Europe—are treated with the respect they earn and deserve. They carry an aura of dignity that gives them stature as human beings.

They are courteous and deferential, not because they are weak, but because they are strong and can afford the emotional luxury of politeness. When a man has genuine respect for his own person and his powers, he then has enough respect to spare for others.

Crassness is always a sign of weakness; the blusterer is full of fear; the sullen workman who is afraid of being imposed upon is secretly convinced of his own inferiority—when he has to say, or think, "I'm as good as any man," he doesn't quite believe it himself.

The good workmen never doubt their status, either as human beings or as craftsmen. They think well of themselves, and therefore are thought well of by the people they work for.

It is a curious psychological fact that the man who seems to be "egotistic" is not suffering from too much ego, but from too little.

When the ego is strong and well developed, there is no nagging need to impress others—by money, by rudeness, or by any other show of false strength.

Authority Takes More than a Title

TWO ACQUAINTANCES OF MINE work for different companies in the same line of business. Both men have the same title—an impressive title. But one is influential and the other is little more than a highly paid flunky.

This discrepancy is not so much a difference in the companies as in the characters of the men themselves. Even in this anonymous, mass-produced age of ours, the force of personality still counts for a good deal.

I know many men who are bucking for a promotion, for a new title that will presumably give them authority and prestige. But authority and prestige are not automatic—they may come with the promotion, but they do not necessarily stay with it.

Here, temperament is often more important than talent. Disgruntled sub-executives sometimes feel they have been passed over in favor of men with less talent, which may be true.

But, for an executive, knowing how to get the best out of other men is as important as knowing how to get the best out of oneself.

An honest self-evaluation of one's own personality early in one's career might save a lot of resentment and heartache. This is why I have continually stressed that the knowledge of one's limitations is fully as important as the awareness of one's capacities.

I myself would not want the responsibility of ordering other men around, nor do I like to be ordered around. I work best in splendid solitude, left to my own peculiar devices. No money on earth could persuade me to become a Mover and Shaker.

This self-knowledge has saved me a lot of grief, and in addition has permitted me to do what I do best with a minimum of friction. The peace of mind that this affords is worth, to me, far more than all the titles and perquisites and badges of authority.

For genuine authority is not something given to us with a name on the door, but a gift, like musical talent or mathematical prowess. If it comes naturally to us, then we can gracefully assume responsibility; if it does not, we merely look pathetic and ineffectual in the role, and may wind up acting the tyrant—which is always a sign of impotence rather than of strength.

Sadly enough, our society is so arranged that it offers its largest rewards to the manipulators rather than to the creators—which is why so many creative men try to fit their round heads into square jobs.

Hate Is Rarely a Personal Matter

A FRIEND OF MINE was complaining at lunch that somebody hates him, and he couldn't understand why. "He probably doesn't hate you," I tried to console him. "You may just remind him of something he hates."

And I remembered an observation that a wise doctor made to me some time ago: "One is rarely lucky enough to be hated for oneself alone."

This puzzling remark makes more sense the more you think of it. Usually, if we hate, it is the shadow of the person that we hate, rather than the substance.

We may hate a person because he reminds us of someone we feared and disliked when younger; or because we see in him some gross caricature of what we find repugnant in ourself; or because he *symbolizes* an attitude that seems to threaten us.

To be hated for oneself alone is almost a tribute; at least you feel that the person knows you and estimates you (however harshly) as an individual.

But most of what passes for hate is merely an illusion. We are hated as a type, as a symbol, as a fantasy of the past, not as a person.

The French may be straining the truth in their famous saying that "to understand all is to forgive all," but it is certainly true that the more we know of any given person, the harder it becomes to hate him. We may begin seeing him as a type, but further intimacy reveals him in the nakedness of his individual personality—and there is always more there to pity than to scorn.

Hateful people are pathetic, and no harm they do to others is so great as the harm they do to themselves.

I have known, as you have, a number of unpleasant and unattractive persons—but not more than one or two who seemed hateful in their very essence, whose souls seemed corroded at the core.

Most of us wistfully want to be better than we are; and there is a kind of redemption in this wish.

The only way to cope with hate that is directed against oneself is to realize that it is rarely (strange as this may sound) a personal matter; that the object is only a pretext for hating; that any other convenient symbol might serve the hater just as readily; and that refusing to return hate for hate is not only a great moral precept but the wisest piece of psychological advice ever handed down to man.

Best Listener Is a Good Talker

"WELL, I MAY NOT know a lot," said the man smugly, "but at least I'm a good listener."

It often seems to me that the man who prides himself on being a good listener isn't good at much else. I like men who are tuning-forks rather than sounding-boards.

A dog is a good listener. He fixes those big brown sympathetic eyes upon you and lets you pour out your woes to him, sometimes even licking your hand during the recital. But I don't know anyone who has solved his problems by having a one-way seminar with a dog. You might as well talk into a tape recorder, which is the most faithful listener and will play back to you exactly what you said, with all the gratifying intonations of pity and anger and self-justification.

An expert bartender is a superlative listener—or seems to be, even when he doesn't comprehend a word you are saying. He knows just when to put in the knowing "Ah!" and the approving "How true!" and the consoling "That's life for you!" But a man has to be pretty drunk to believe that he is achieving any real communion across the bar.

What we need are more *discriminating* listeners: and these are hard to find. We need people who know how and when to break in with "That's not so," or "You're deluding yourself," or "What do you *really* mean by that remark?" These are the people who keep us on pitch, who force us to try to harmonize our conflicting emotions, and are not mere echo chambers for our unresolved fears and our infantile wishes.

And, contrary to popular belief, it is usually the good talker who makes the best listener. A good talker (by which I do not mean the egomaniacal bore who always talks about himself) is sensitive to expression, to tone and color and inflection in human speech. Because he himself is articulate, he can help others to articulate their half-formulated feelings. His mind fills in the gaps, and he becomes, in Socrates' words, a kind of midwife for ideas that are struggling to be born.

This is why a competent psychiatrist is worth his weight in gold— and generally gets it. His listening is keyed for the half-tones and the dissonances that escape the untrained ear. For it is the mark of the truly good listener that he knows what you are saying often better than you do; and his playback is a revelation, not a recording.

Why There's Danger in Extremism

A FRIEND OF MINE, whom I have always considered a calm and stable personality, told me recently that he is regarded in some quarters as a wild-eyed radical, and in other circles as a stony conservative—when actually he is neither.

"It's an irresistible urge I have when I get together with extremists," he said. "I promptly swing over to the other extreme, just because I am so irritated with their one-sided view."

I was delighted to learn that somebody else reacts that way, too. For years I have deplored my own tendency to do this. In most cases, it gives a false impression of my views—but when I am confronting an extremist, I become a passionate defender of the opposite view.

With ice-cold reactionaries, I sound like a rabid bolshevik; with professional liberals, I take on the tone of a fascist; with the ardent culture-vultures, I pretend to read nothing but comic books and lovelorn columns; with pugnacious lowbrows, I refer haughtily to the French symbolist poets and the ontological existentialism of Kierkegaard.

This, of course, is a senseless way to behave; it is over-reacting to a situation. But, in all fairness, there is something about extremism that breeds its own opposite.

The complacency of the *bourgeoisie* makes me yearn for the Bohemian life; the sloppiness of the Bohemians brings out my primness; loud-mouth patriots prompt me to take a stand for the French way of life; and moist-eyed lovers of all things European give me the urge to hop on a chair and begin waving Old Glory.

The danger of extremism is that it forces its opponents to adopt an equally extreme view—thus hurting its own cause more than it realizes. The Reign of Terror during the French Revolution was a natural historical result of the repressive monarchy; the Satanism of Stalin sprang out of the soil of Czarist cruelty.

No single way of living is exclusively right. Combination is all. Life is the art of mixing ingredients in tolerable proportions, so that all the varied needs of man are somehow satisfied, and no important hunger is neglected. This is what all extremists forget, with their too-simple slogans for the good life.

Self-Doubt Is One Mark of Sanity

IT IS PART OF THE COMMON wisdom of the human race to recognize that "everybody is a little crazy." It is this knowledge, about ourselves as well as others, that keeps us in touch with sanity.

And it is one of the paradoxes of mental health that the person who never questions his own sanity is the one most likely to lose contact with reality.

I was speaking with a lawyer the other evening, and he remarked that he has had to deal with scores of clients who, in his opinion, were over the line. "And they all had one thing in common," he reflected. "They never doubted that they were right."

This is why I am so negative about all those believe-in-yourself books and courses and inspirational lectures. The paranoid is a person who believes in himself—and in nobody else. He has complete faith in his utter sanity, and that is the mark of his madness.

It is not only useless, it is harmful, to believe in oneself until one truly *knows* oneself. And to know oneself means to accept our moments of insanity, of eccentricity, of childishness and blindness.

In a family, for instance, when one of the mates voluntarily goes to seek psychiatric help, it often turns out that the other mate needs it more desperately.

The rigidity of the paranoid personality never questions its own sanity, but may easily drive a mate into questioning his own.

It is true that many disturbed people lack "confidence" in themselves. But confidence cannot be achieved by a magic incantation, by resolving grimly to "believe" in oneself. Self-confidence can be won only by treading the path of self-discovery—by learning all the twists and turns and dark corners of our emotional nature.

A tightrope walker gains confidence by practice, by becoming aware of his skills *and his limitations*, by a realistic acceptance of the dangers involved—not by repeating to himself, "I can, I can," and then foolishly attempting a stunt for which he is not prepared.

The man who thinks he can do anything if he *wills* it hard enough is crazy. The man who thinks he is always right is crazy. The man who believes that if only those around him would change, then everything would turn out fine—he is closer to the edge of insanity than the self-doubting creature who timidly visits a doctor to learn if he is losing his mind.

Thief Robbed of Faith in Criminals

THERE IS A STANDARD in every profession, a code in every craft. I ran into a criminal the other morning who was "shocked" at the crimes going on today.

He is an old-fashioned criminal I used to see occasionally when I was a reporter over 30 years ago. A quiet, round-faced man who was a first-class burglar and safecracker, but otherwise a quite decent sort of chap.

"I don't know what's got into young fellows these days," he shook his head mournfully as we had a cup of coffee together. "They're monsters, not human beings. I wouldn't spit on the best of them.

"In my day, a thief was a thief. He did his job and went home and tried to enjoy himself the same way other men would. "He didn't like violence, he didn't hate anybody, and he wasn't trying to prove anything.

"Now I see these punks all over the streets, and they're enough to make an honest thief's stomach turn. They don't have any brains, and they don't have any heart either. All they can do is hit and shoot and curse.

"They're not even good thieves," he reflected, as a master tailor might mourn the passing of the age of craftsmanship. "With a couple of drinks, they'll knock off a cab driver for 10 bucks in change. What do you writing fellows call them—'psychopaths'?"

"How do you account for the difference?" I asked him.

"Who knows?" he shrugged. "Something has gone out of them. They don't love anything. They don't have families or hobbies, as we used to. They don't even seem to want to be successful—just noticed—and that's the surest way to get caught."

"Then you think they want to get caught?" I suggested.

"Sure," he said. "They want to prove how tough they can be, even walking to the chair. What's the point of 'punishing' punks like that? You've got to straighten out their mental kinks when they're small, or you can't do anything with them at all.

"The old bunch I used to know are mostly dead," he sighed, "Ah, they were fine fellows, some of them, a pleasure to talk with.

"It's a funny age we're living in, when a professional thief can't bring himself to associate with the scum running around these days. That's the real reason, if you want to know, why I went straight."

Reversing the Spool of Thought

IF YOU ARE NORMALLY a right-handed person, try a little experiment for a half hour or so: Do with your left hand everything that you usually do with your right.

The most simple and obvious acts will become complicated and cumbersome. You will hardly be able to write, or cut or eat your food; and you will quickly become baffled, frustrated and exasperated.

Now imagine this lopsided process intensified a thousand-fold, and you may have some idea of how painful and difficult it is to think "with the left hand"—that is, to reverse our customary process of thought.

Why has science made such enormous strides in knowledge and development, while human affairs still remain largely as they were in the days of the Assyrian Empire? Largely because every advance in science is gained by reversing the spool of thought—by thinking in a way that is opposite of the traditional and customary ways.

Of all the habits of mankind the habits of thought are the most persistent, the most tenacious, the most enslaving. We put on an idea in the morning as we put on a shoe, left or right first, unconsciously and without ever varying the procedure by a fraction.

And our resistance against changing our habits of thought is immense and unrelenting. If we try, briefly, we find it as vexing and unrewarding as writing a letter with the left hand. What we are used to is comfortable; what is comfortable is good; and what is good is right—this is the unspoken belief of almost all people everywhere.

When a scientist, however, tackles a problem that has hitherto seemed insoluble, he abandons all his preconceptions, and all the preconceptions of the past. Only when he begins to question the basic assumptions he has always held can he make an utterly fresh start, unencumbered by the intellectual baggage of the past.

I am not suggesting that a knowledge of the past is not useful, or that history and tradition have little to offer us—but they must be used as tools, not as points of departure. Our thinking about them must involve a painful re-evaluation of our most cherished ideas and ideals.

Not one person in a thousand is willing—although many are able—to think left-handed for more than a few minutes at a time. Yet every important discovery has been made in this way, from Harvey on circulation of the blood to Freud on the role of the unconscious. And we know what derision and abuse such men were subjected to for daring to violate the right-handedness of their times.

Too Many Words and Voices

A MAN I KNOW was talking at lunch about a widely-known columnist who specializes in humor and whimsy. "Why doesn't he ever write about serious and important things?" he asked me. "Certainly he's amusing, but there are more substantial matters in the world to write about."

I disagreed with his point of view. "Each person should do what he does best." I suggested. "And this columnist is excellent as a light entertainer. He fills a need, does no harm and gives people pleasure. Why ask more of him?"

The man at lunch was a victim of what I call mock-seriousness. He wants everyone in the public prints to focus on the important issues, and he ignores the obvious fact that some writers are not equipped to comment on matters beyond their immediate perceptions.

The columnist in question is modestly aware of his limitations. He has a keen eye for foibles, a deft way with language and a puckish sense of humor. If he tried to do more, he would end up doing considerably less; like Sir Arthur Sullivan forsaking the blithe Savoyard operettas for ponderous "serious" music that is mostly unlistenable-to today.

I would make precisely the opposite criticism: that there are too many commentators who are floundering beyond their depths, who lack the background, the intellectual stature and the analytic powers to convey more than a superficial (and thus distorted) picture of what is happening and what it means.

There are many who deplore the fact that so witty and saturnine a sports writer as Westbrook Pegler, for instance, decided to cover the larger arena of world events, for which nothing in his background had prepared him. Overwhelmed by the complexity of his subject, his humor turned corrosive and his perspective became warped.

Many people, it is true, do not live up to their potential; but just as many, it seems to me, are trying to live beyond theirs. The air is filled with voices pontificating on everything from birth control to bomb-testing, and the voice of the reformed disk jockey is often louder than that of the man who has devoted a lifetime to studying such matters. Too much is said about everything, and not enough of it has any meaning.

The puckish columnist is to be commended for working within his severe, but admirable, limitations, and refusing to become an oracle. What he does is small, but craftsmanlike, and it is a real pleasure among so many pundits whose volume is equaled only by their vacuity.

The Warm and Moist vs. the Dry and Cool

THE WARM, MOIST PEOPLE always feel cheated or let down by the dry, cool people. And the dry, cool people always feel embarrassed by the warm, moist people.

I have a friend in the West who is a fine person, but warm and moist. He is full of feelings, very big on Friendship, on Letters, on Photos of the Family. He goes for "Real Human Beings."

My own temperment tends more toward the dry and cool. I write no letters, carry no photos, find any effusiveness rather sticky. This has nothing to do with my feelings, only with my way of expressing them.

This bothers the warm, moist people. They feel that their friendship is not adequately returned. They want you to be as demonstrative as they are. Their ideal of true companionship is sitting around a campfire, holding hands in a circle, and singing old songs.

It is hard to get them to understand that one can be a true friend without saying so every half-hour, without writing long, chatty letters, without celebrating the fraternal rites. Their sensitivity is so acute that every omission seems a snub, every understatement seems a rebuff. They interpret a difference of temperament as a personal affront to their own code of living relationships.

Some of them, indeed, are so excessive in their unremitting desire to prove their friendship that they remind me of what Talleyrand said about Mme. de Staël: "She is such a good friend that she would throw all her acquaintances into the water for the pleasure of fishing them out."

And, no doubt, we dry, cool personalities are just as vexing and trying to them. We must seem singularly unresponsive, changeable, uncommunicative, and frightfully offhand about the sacred bond of friendship. They must wonder if we have any "real feelings" at all.

Laissez-faire may or may not be a good economic philosophy; it is certainly the best emotional philosophy. Live and let live, each in his own way, working out his own life-style—this is the only sensible attitude to take toward those around us, close or not.

But it is devilishly hard for many people to do. Parents, especially, become infuriated if their children differ temperamentally from themselves; they look upon it almost as a rejection or repudiation—which, indeed, in some cases it may be. A warm, moist parent tends to breed a cooler and drier child, as an inevitable reaction to all that steam.

There is no right or wrong in matters of this sort; personalities are as different as fingerprints. And if we are ever going to learn to love our enemies, the best way to start is by tolerating our friends a little better, and not trying to change them.

On subjects that intensely concern us, we must not promise to be "objective" – the most we can promise is to try to be objective about our lack of objectivity.

*

When you run into someone who is disagreeable to others, you may be sure he is uncomfortable with himself; the amount of pain we inflict upon others is directly proportional to the amount we feel within us.

Are You "Round" or "Angular"?

"Do YOU KNOW so-and-so?" I am sometimes asked, and when I answer that I do, the second question is commonly, "What is he [or she] really like?"

To give a true and honest answer to this second question, I have learned that it is necessary for us to divide the people we know into "round" and "angular" characters.

The round characters are the easiest to define and describe. They are the people—which includes the majority—who present a rounded appearance to all who know them. With minor variations, they are the same viewed from any angle of vision—like a circle.

Ask a dozen different accquaintances about them, and you will receive a unanimity of opinion: Joe is a good scout, Sam is a well-meaning blowhard, Ernie is tough and slippery, Mike wouldn't hurt a fly.

Where most of us go wrong, however, is in our estimate of the angular characters, in failing to recognize their angularity. These are the people who are many-faceted—depending upon the angle of acquaintance, they assume different shapes, sizes and textures.

With an angular character, one cannot say "This is what he is really like"; all one can say is "This is how he reacts to me, and I to him."

The angular personality is viewed in one way by his wife, in another by his business colleagues, in yet another by his subordinates, and in still another by his close friends. His personality glints with different lights, refracting the atmosphere he happens to be in at the time.

Of him, one person may say "He is terribly conceited," and another that "He is really very modest"; one may call him "aloof and superior," and another describe him as "friendly and humorous." And these are no contradictions—for the angular character is all these things, depending on the stimulus he receives from his environment.

None of us can know what he is "really" like, for his essence is determined by the particular mode of existence we see him in. Work brings out one side of him, family life another; at one kind of party, he is shy and stiff, at another he is relaxed and vivacious.

When two acquaintances disagree about the nature of a third, it is hard for them to believe that both may be right—for they are discussing an angular character in terms of a round one, and are much in the position of the blind men touching different parts of the elephant.

In a deeper sense, we cannot even know what the round characters are "really" like, for they are likely to surprise us in moments of crisis; but we can at least agree on their basic elements. When it comes to the angular people, all we can say is "From where I stand . . ."

Are Stupid People Happiest?

ARE STUPID PEOPLE "happier" than intelligent ones? This seems to be the general opinion among laymen, who are fond of pointing to some stupid acquaintance and saying, "He doesn't have enough sense to let things bother him—he's just like an animal grazing in the field."

I would tend to take issue completely with this judgment. Not only do I disagree with the opinion that stupid people are "happier" than more intelligent ones; I also happen to think that much of what seems to be "stupidity" is a form of neurosis in itself.

The way some people retreat from their problems is by becoming more stupid than they really are, by dulling their senses and blunting their responses to life. This reaction itself is a symptom of unhappiness that can cope only by withdrawing in a bovine way.

We can see it beginning more clearly in a child: when a certain type of child is emotionally troubled, he will act stupid. He will shake his head at simple questions, he will seem thick and uncomprehending, and will retreat into a shell that would seem to be stupidity if we did not know him better. If persistent, this emotional upset can turn the child into a stupid-seeming adult.

It is axiomatic in the field of psychotherapy that, all things being fairly equal, the intelligent patient will recover faster and more fully than the less intelligent.

An intelligent person *seems* to be unhappier because he can articulate his discontent, and because he is more obviously sensitive to his environment; but this very sensitivity is what enables him to change, to grow, and to heal the psychic wounds.

I happen to believe firmly that most people are much more intelligent than they give evidence of being: that a great deal of what we call stupidity is really an emotional defense against pain; it is simply the way a particular kind of personality handles its problems.

In an article on Sonny Liston in a sports magazine a few weeks ago, the writer shrewdly observed, during an interview with the fighter, that Liston was smarter than the public impression he has given in the past. The writer went on to observe that "Liston is not stupid, but his insights are impeded by his neuroses. Emotionally he is a child—stubborn, obdurate, and completely lacking in flexibility."

Given his dreadful background, this is perhaps the only way the boy could have developed. And what is true of him is true of millions of others who live angrily behind the iron curtain of the mind.

Guilt Gives Rise to Double Talk

"HYPOCRISY," SAID LA ROCHEFOUCAULD a long time ago, "is the homage that vice pays to virtue." And so it is with language—for those groups which are the most ruthless in their acts are also the most devious in their speech.

Totalitarian governments do not "kill" dissenters and heretics; they "liquidate" them. Goering did not speak of "gassing" the German Jews; he spoke of "the final solution" to the Jewish problem.

The fine art of double-talk has been raised to the ultimate degree by modern communist and fascist governments; and the more vicious their policies, the more they seem to feel the need to use the soft word.

If one carefully examines a speech by a totalitarian official, it will be filled with words like "truth," "peace," "liberty," and "the will of the people." And all these words, on further examination, turn out to mean something quite different, and much uglier, than their accepted definitions.

"Truth" means the dogma of the ruling clique; "peace" means acquiescence in the party line; "liberty" means the right to stir up sedition; "the will of the people" means exactly nothing.

In a sense, such euphemisms are customary in all diplomatic and political expressions; but the unconscious sense of guilt that seems to haunt the totalitarians compels them to find the most tortuous and abstract phrasing to conceal their grim and single-minded intent.

We find this same psychological tendency among criminals: the more heinous the crime, the more reluctant they are to call it by its proper name. A thief will cheerfully admit he is a thief—a burglar, a pickpocket, a safe-cracker.

But a killer is never called a killer, by himself or by his confederates. There are a dozen euphemisms for this, the currently most popular being "hit." A man who is murdered is "hit" by a "hitter." Some nagging vestigial conscience prevents even the professional murderer from uttering the true name of his occupation.

The worse the deed, the more the need to dress it in taffeta phrases. An aggressor never goes to "war"; he "defends the boundaries of the fatherland" or he "takes preventive action." Likewise, it is the awful enemy who "brainwashes" our soldiers; what we do is "indoctrinate" theirs.

The more a person has to conceal and the more he is ashamed of—whether he is aware of his shame or not—the more pressing becomes his need to find another word for the right one, the plain one, the true one. Simplicity of speech is always the enemy of injustice.

A Strong Man Knows His Weaknesses

A YOUNG MAN I know, who is doing a study on "executive power" for his doctoral dissertation, told me at lunch the other day about some of the interesting psychological conclusions he has arrived at.

He has been studying the "strong man" and the "weak man" in executive situations, to try to find out some of their principal differences in temperament and attitudes.

"There's a real paradox at the heart of the matter," he said. "The strong man is one who knows his weaknesses consciously, accepts them, comes to terms with them and knows how to cope with them. In a funny way, this knowledge serves to give him more strength.

"The weak man," he continued, "is unconsciously aware of his weaknesses, but cannot admit them to himself or to anyone else. He has not worked out his own inner problems—the chief one being self-acceptance—and so he cannot really accept anyone else in a normal, natural way.

"As a result," he went on, "the weak executive adopts pseudo-strength. He is afraid to be kind, because it might be construed as a sort of weakness on his part; and he is afraid to be open, because it might disclose too much of his real self to others."

"What about the man who's kind and pleasant, but simply incompetent?" I asked.

"That's not the kind of 'weak personality' I'm investigating," he explained. "Men like that come and go; they're just mistakes, and they don't pose any problems. But it's the weak man who employs pseudo-strength to attain and maintain his position who creates most of the mischief in executive capacities.

"What I've learned so far," he amplified, "indicates that generosity in judgment, a certain flexibility and, most of all, a degree of tolerance toward the weaknesses in others are the marks of real strength in an executive. We can afford the emotional luxury of such tolerance only when we feel genuinely strong within ourselves.

"For instance," he added, "it is fatal for anyone to reveal a weakness to a weak man. He will either take advantage of it, or despise you for it—because the weak man unconsciously despises his own weakness and therefore cannot stand it in others. But it is safe to reveal it to a strong man—because, having come to terms with his own problems, he doesn't have to project any self-contempt toward others.

"We have some peculiar ideas in our society," he concluded, "about what constitutes strength and weakness in men. Much of what we respect is simply pseudo-strength. To that extent, we are a weak and immature people."

Friends Are to Be "Put Up" With

A COUPLE I KNOW slightly stopped seeing another couple who were their closest friends. It seems that the second couple turned up two hours late to an important dinner the first couple were giving.

"You simply don't treat good friends that way," said the hostess, who was filled with wrongeous indignation. "I won't put up with that sort of thing."

But this is exactly what good friends are for—to put up with. Friendship, of the true sort, means accepting another person, not for his good points, but in spite of his bad points.

And that is the beautiful thing about friendship: we can take liberties, we can show our frailer side, we can afford the vast luxury of giving way to our boredom when we are bored, our anger when we are angry, our peckishness when we feel downhearted.

This does not mean, of course, that friendship will stand any amount of abuse.

It must be based on genuine respect of the other personality; but once this exchange of respects has been firmly rooted, a true friendship is meant to stand a great deal of tension.

Many marriages falter, it seems to me, not because the couples are out of love, but because they have never been friends as much as lovers. They may love each other, in a vaporously romantic way, but they do not really *like* each other as individual personalities.

You can treat a good friend almost any way—short of basic disloyalty—because he understands the springs of your motivation, and knows that beneath your temporary bad behavior you are a decent sort with generous instincts and a desire to do well by your fellow men.

When a person won't "put up" with the rude or capricious antics of a friend, I suspect that such a person has never begun to have a real friendship.

After all, it is easy to like someone who is always polite and considerate and gay; the virtue in friendship consists of liking someone whose finest qualities may be hidden beneath a craggy exterior.

There are an appalling number of friendless people in the world. I have seen many among the most influential and famous of our time, and they all have one thing in common—a desperate need to be treated well at all times.

When they are disappointed in this, they break off a "friendship," never knowing that friends were made to endure mutual disappointments.

Greatest Machine of Them All

OUR VENERATION OF THE MACHINE in this computer age has led us to a subtle but definite downgrading of the human brain. We forget that in order to make a machine that seems smarter than man, man must be smarter than the machine.

The human brain contains about 10 billion neurons: each of these cells is connected with hundreds, and sometimes thousands, of others. No machine ever devised by man could approach the complexity and versatility of the human brain.

According to Arthur Samuel, consultant to IBM's research department, the chance of constructing an artificial brain that could duplicate ours is about the same "as the chance that every American will be stricken with a coronary on the same night."

In the new book, "The Computer Age," prepared by Gilbert Burck and the editors of *Fortune* magazine, the cost of duplicating the brain's cells and connections is estimated thus: even at the ludicrously low cost of only 5 cents per cell and 1 cent per connection, the cost would come to more than $1 quintillion, or $1 billion billion—more money than all the governments in the world together possess.

Samuel, by the way, is the man who taught a computer to play checkers so well that it now consistently beats him. But checkers is a relatively simple game, with a finite number of alternative moves. Chess is a different matter; no machine yet programmed can play very much better than a good novice.

The number of all possible moves in a chess game is something like 10 to the 40th power; to examine all these, even the fastest computer would take longer than the age of the universe, which is estimated at about 2 billion years.

Doubtless, the vast funds we are spending for computer research are worthwhile, for the more we can get machines to do for us, the more will our own faculties and energies be released for specifically human projects.

But at least an equal amount should be spent on developing the brains we have, the unused potential that resides in each of us, and especially in our children. My own guess is that all of us utilize no more than between 10 and 20 per cent of the intellectual capacities we have—and that adequate research could show us how to exploit the enormous mental powers that are lying unused at the mind's bottom.

It is not enough that a few brilliant men can create computers to "think" for us; for the greatest thinking machine is inside each of us.

Is It "Contrary" or "Contradictory"?

Do you know the difference between "contrary" statements and "contradictory" statements? Or do you imagine it's just playing with words, merely a semantic distinction with no practical application?

It can be shown, I think, that much of our confusion and conflict over political and social matters arises from our inability to distinguish between statements that are "contrary" and those that are "contradictory." I don't mean that better logic alone would change our opinions; but it would make us look elsewhere in support of them.

"The wall is black" and "the wall is red" are contrary statements; that is, they cannot be true together. But they can be false together— the wall might be green, neither black nor red. The falsity of one statement ("the wall is black") does not imply the truth of the other.

"The wall is black" and "the wall is not black" are contradictory statements, that is, they cannot be false together and they cannot be true together. The truth of one implies the falsity of the other, and vice versa. They are mutually exclusive terms; there is nothing in between them.

What we do, however, in much of our political and social talk, is to take contrary statements and turn them into contradictories, so that we get what the semanticists call a "two-valued orientation."

The two statements, "communism is the best system" and "capitalism is the best system," are contraries, not contradictories. It is not possible for both statements to be true together, but both may be false together. Another system, combining their elements, might be better than either communism or capitalism.

But if we take these contraries as contradictories, then we are automatically against everything the communists are for, and for everything they are against—even when they happen to be against the right things for the wrong reasons. If we adopt such a posture, then no real communication or co-operation is at all possible. It is one of the worst faults of Marxist ideology, indeed, that it does adopt such a posture.

Each side denies that there can be more than one other side—and this denial is the essence of the "two-valued orientation," which is shared by Nazis, communists and the radical right. They are all somehow incapable of seeing that the wall may be neither black nor red, and that the falsity of their opponent's position does not imply the truth of theirs.

Oversimplification is one of the most dangerous attitudes facing us. This is especially so in our complex and interrelated modern society. It is tempting to look for simple answers, but when we turn a contrary into a contradictory, we make it impossible for our answer to correspond to reality, or to find any solution in reasonable terms.

The chronic wisecracker is usually a frightened man who is scared of seriousness and uses humor as a barrier against self-knowledge; he is an emotional extremist who, if he were not laughing, would be crying.

*

The faculty that is most taken for granted by most of us is actually the rarest ability—and that is, to see what we really see.

The Deviate's Double Life

THE MOST INTERESTING aspect of that squalid Jenkins case during the Johnson election was never discussed, or even raised. It had nothing to do, of course, with politics, but with the organized idiocy of the social order.

The chief objection to Jenkins was that he posed a possible "security risk" by being a homosexual in a sensitive government position. Why did he pose a security risk? Because homosexuals are notoriously susceptible to blackmail.

Why are homosexuals notoriously susceptible to blackmail? Because the blackmailer threatens them with public exposure of their deviation, which would cost them their careers, at the very least.

Why should this threat affect them? Very simply, because our social order does not accept their deviation, and forces many of them to lead wretched double lives. In a sense, the homosexuals are "driven into crime" by the attitude of society.

Obviously, the way to remove the "security risk" that attaches to homosexuals in government service is to accept their deviation openly, as a condition as old as history, and thus to remove the pressure that makes them easy prey to blackmailers.

But this is not the rational way in which a social institution works. Instead, we must pretend to ourselves either that the problem hardly exists, or else that by ostracizing and punishing these people we are somehow solving the problem or reducing the consequences.

Quite the opposite is true. Our codified hypocrisy simply intensifies the problem in all areas. It makes the homosexuals more apprehensive and more furtive, forcing them into shameful and "illegal" activities, while, at the same time, it strengthens the hold that sinister and subversive elements can exert upon them.

Moreover, society's attitude channels them into an "underground" movement of their own, and cuts them off from the mainstream of community life. Like all persecuted minority groups, they strike back by forming cabals, by "taking over" certain spheres of activity (in the arts, for instance), and by purposely provocative behavior.

If our society were mature enough to ignore or accept their deviation, much of their unattractive social behavior would disappear, since most of it is based on an overreaction to public opprobrium. It is we who make them not only "security risks," but who give them an extra layer of neurosis on top of their own internal conflicts. The Jenkins case was more illustrative of our irrationality than of his.

Letting Others Do Dirty Work

A WOMAN IN KANSAS wants to know how it is possible that a friend of hers—"a sweet and generous woman"—can have an another close friend a woman "who is a malicious gossip of the worst sort." She is puzzled by what her friend "finds" in the gossip.

What she finds, I expect, is a deeply repressed part of her own personality. Some of us do our own dirty work; others must get someone else to do it for them. For we become friends with people not only for their virtues but also for their vices.

Her example reminds me of married couples I have known, in which the husband was mild, quiet and courteous, while his wife was loud, aggressive and contentious. People observing them in action would invariably ask, "Why does he put up with it; why does he let her get away with such behavior?"

The only answer that makes sense is that he covertly enjoys such behavior. She is acting out for him some real need to attack others—a need he is unable to express directly. A large share of her initial attraction for him, no doubt, lay in his (perhaps unconscious) realization that she would be glad to do some of his dirty work for him.

The "sweet and generous" woman who has a malicious gossip for a confidante probably resents being so sweet and generous all the time, but lacks the temperament to be otherwise. So, with the cunning with which our infantile needs take revenge upon us, she seizes gratefully upon a "friend" who allows her to enjoy malice without suffering any of its consequences.

What we consider "odd" friendships or marriages can hardly be explained on any other basis. Each of us has actualized only a part of his full personality; the unactualized parts (which are unacceptable to us) often find their expression through the friend or mate (or gang) we choose. This is the true meaning of the maxim that "opposites attract"—they attract because they are not really opposites, but complementaries. They expand our possible range of reaction to the world.

It works both ways, of course. The malicious gossip is in the grip of a compulsion she cannot understand or control; and so she buys an indulgence against her sins by making friends with someone who, in turn, expresses a buried part of the gossip's nature. For just as no one can be "all that sweet," no one can be all that malicious, without release.

Why should the German people have chosen Hitler? I look upon it as more than a political or economic choice—that Europe's most orderly, most industrious, most rational, most educated, most instinctually repressed nation should have voted in the arch-demon of irrationality.

Shyness—a Form of Arrogance

AN EXTREMELY SHY young woman managed to summon up the nerve to visit us, after repeated invitations, the other day. As she left, she stammered, "I hate to go anywhere, because I always wonder what people will say about me after I leave."

"That," I said, "is something you will never know. And that is a chance that all of us take."

It occurred to me, when she left, that shyness is really a form of arrogance—just as many traits become absorbed in their opposites. She is almost perversely proud of being shy.

The shy person really refuses to take the chance that everybody must take—the chance of being disliked, or derided, or rejected.

Who knows what others actually think of us, except for a few close friends? All we can do is offer our wares in the social market, and hope that there will be some takers.

To refuse to play this game is to take an arrogant attitude toward one's fellow men; it is to place oneself outside the ordinary judgments of mankind; it is almost, in a way, to decline the game unless you are promised that you can be a winner.

We are all of us locked tightly within our personalities. None of us is as gay or as bright or as popular as he would like to be; everybody feels left out of something or other.

The person who trades on his shyness is like the boy who won't let the others use his ball unless he is allowed to pitch. He doesn't want to be an outfielder—but everybody has to play outfield in some games.

Of course, I know there are deep psychic reasons for this attitude, going back to childhood. Yet, short of getting professional help, the victim of shyness can somewhat help himself by simply recognizing that what he thinks is "inferiority feeling" is often a kind of superior snobbishness.

It is an unwillingness to be judged for what you are, or seem to be. And this is a judgment that cannot be avoided in any society. Some people are going to like and appreciate you, and some are not—no matter what you say or do.

One cannot live one's life as a bundle of reactions to other people. For the most contemptuous remark they can make after you leave is that you are too indecently interested in winning their approval.

Opposites Attract—Up to a Point

A YOUNG LADY was waxing confidential at a party the other evening and confessed that she had fallen in love with a chap who was completely different from her in every respect.

"Is it really true that 'opposites attract'?" she asked. "I don't know whether two persons so different could really get along in a marriage."

It seems to me that there is just enough truth in the saying that "opposites attract" to make it a dangerous fallacy.

On one level, there can be little doubt that each of us is somewhat fascinated by what he does not have. We are attracted to people who have strengths where we have weaknesses, who seem to supply lacks that we feel in our own nature.

So far, so good. Yet this apparent interlocking of traits can prove treacherously deceptive—for I am just as convinced that, beneath the surface, two persons have to be basically similar to get along well.

By "basically similar" I do not mean in temperament, but in *outlook*. They must share a common view of the world, a similar sense of the things that are serious and those that are funny.

The values they place on such fundamental matters as a family, money, social activities, religion, must be at least roughly equal. They must agree on what is important and what is not to their general scheme of life.

People who are superficially opposite do attract each other; but if they are *fundamentally* opposite, I do not think the attraction can last. If one has a brutal, materialistic outlook on life and the other has a sensitive and generous viewpoint, only conflict and bitterness can be expected.

Most people, whether they know it or not, are engaged in a double quest. On the one hand, they are looking for someone who is piquantly different from themselves; on the other, they are looking for someone who squints at the world from the same angle.

If you take a close look at those genuinely happy couples who seem to be so completely different from each other, you will find that either the differences are an optical illusion—or the happiness is.

"Busy" Person May Be Running Away

"IF SHE'D KEEP HERSELF BUSY," I heard one lady say to another, in reference to a mutual friend, "she wouldn't have time to feel so sorry for herself."

There is just enough common-sense shrewdness in this remark to be dangerous. People *should* be kept busy, of course—but to be busy for its own sake is as neurotic as to be indolent and moody.

It is easy to spot the people who are listless and self-engrossed, who refuse to assume the responsibilities of adult life. We can plainly see that such personalities are running away from themselves.

What is harder to see is that the energetic, aggressive, always-busy person may be just as much in flight from reality. The compulsion to do a great deal, in fact, may be even sicker than the inclination to do little.

In both cases, it seems to me, people are trying to escape taking a close and honest look at themselves. The person who disengages himself from the affairs of the world is afraid that his participation may reveal weaknesses; and the person who is perpetually in a flurry of activity is afraid to stop and let go for a moment, for fear that he will then have to confront himself in the nakedness of his spiritual isolation.

But the human personality is a twofold fabric, as it were: the top layer is social, and the bottom layer is uniquely personal.

Just as we are composed of spirit and body, we are also composed of a part that turns outward and a part that turns inward. A personality that turns only inward is retreating from the social reality; and the personality that turns only outward is fleeing from the reality of the hidden self.

I repeat this familiar axiom only to make the point that we judge the inward-turning people much more harshly, because they contribute less to society, and society resents their lack of involvement.

Yet, the outward-turning person often does as much harm as good. Energy for its own sake sometimes explodes in unpredictable ways; and the person who is compelled to drive hard soon finds that his neglect of his own personality makes him neglect the personalities of others—in this way are big and little tyrants born.

"Keeping busy" is fruitful for oneself and for society—but only when the busyness is truly a proliferation from the inside, and not merely a brittle wall to ward off all knowledge of the private self.

You Can Be Wrong When You're Right

THE OTHER EVENING I heard a speaker attacking a subject I knew very little about. My feelings were not involved, pro or con. But there was one thing I felt as he finished: that he was a dishonest man.

He gave me this impression because he was manifestly unfair to his opposition. He attributed to them certain ideas that no rational man could hold, and certain motives that no decent person could have.

And I knew that, whatever the merits of the argument, this speaker was not getting to the crux. He was distorting his opponents, rather than refuting them.

Lord Acton, who had one of the coolest, fairest and keenest minds in history, once set down an absolute rule for disputes. I cannot quote him exactly, but this is the gist of it:

"Never try publicly to refute an opponent until you are sure, in your own mind, that you can make out a better case for him than he has made out for himself. Do not look at his weak points, but at his strong points. Then, when you have marshalled the most powerful arguments on *his* behalf, see whether you can knock them down with reason and logic."

His advice is not only morally sound; it is psychologically valuable. If an audience feels that a speaker is being scrupulously fair to his opponents, he has gone half way toward winning their respect and good will.

Most of us, unfortunately do exactly the contrary. We seize with glee upon any flaw or inconsistency in our opponents' positions; we magnify their small errors, and point with scorn to their lapses in logic. We are more interested in discrediting the speaker than in demolishing the foundation on which his beliefs rest.

Both honor and good sense demand that we first build up the strongest case for our antagonist—even to the point of finding favorable evidence he has missed. Then, if we can refute his position, we are certain to be right, for we have done a better job with his position than he himself can do.

When Darwin was working on his *Origin of Species,* he scrupulously sought for every scrap of evidence, either for or against his theory, and entered everything in his notebook. And, only when he was satisfied that the balance was on his side, did he publish his findings.

He may turn out to have been wrong, but he was more honorable than the men who are right for the wrong reasons.

Pity the Phone-Grabbers

A BUSINESSMAN has written me a heated letter about what he calls "the tyranny of the telephones." He explains: "Regardless of the importance of the subject between two people, the ringing telephone receives precedence over any matter that may be discussed, although the telephone subject may not be of prime importance.

"In fact," he continues, warming up to his prejudice, "a person on his deathbed must answer the telephone. It is allowed to interrupt almost anything in a business or a home."

Much as I sympathize with his point of view, I must enter a plea on behalf of the telephone-answerers, of which I am one.

We are a poor, weak, romantic type of character—those of us who are compelled to leap to the telephone the moment it rings.

I envy those calm, strong personalities who can continue to talk, or munch their food, or read their paper, through the insisting shrilling of a telephone.

Such people are realists: they know that the call probably is not important, or, if it is, that the party will soon call again. They are able to do one thing at a time, and will brook no interruptions of their routine.

We pathetic phone-grabbers, however, are made of flabbier stuff. In our unconscious minds, we are waiting for The Telephone Call—the one that will solve our problems, grant our wishes, transform us into something beautiful and rich.

We are the same folk who rush to the mailbox each morning, with a vision of The Perfect Letter that is waiting there for us.

Perhaps a long-forgotten cousin has died in South Africa and left us a diamond mine or two. Or it may be a cordial note from the President, inviting us to fly to Washington and unsnarl the nasty foreign situation, which has baffled the best minds in the State Department.

We are incurable visionaries. To us, a ringing telephone is potentially more fraught with significance than anything we may be doing or anyone we may be talking with. We have remained children at heart: We are perpetually waiting for "surprises" that will delight us.

So I ask the irate businessman to temper his annoyance with a little charity.

We do not mean to be rude; it is simply that our Dreams of Glory are more vivid and compelling than everyday reality. To his kind, a ringing telephone is a nuisance; to my kind, it opens limitless possibilities for a free trip to the Land of Oz.

Logic Won't Reach the Unconvincible

IT ISN'T UNTIL LATE in life—if ever—that most of us learn not to argue with the Unconvincibles. In Grandma's famous phrase, we might as well save our breath to cool our porridge.

The Unconvincibles are the people who are not amenable to reason of any sort. Their minds are not only closed, but bolted and hermetically sealed.

In most cases, their beliefs congealed at any early age; by the time they left their teens, they were encased in a rigid framework of thought and feeling, which no evidence or argument can penetrate.

"It is impossible," observed Dean Swift a long time ago, "to reason a man out of something he has not been reasoned into." A succinct and admirable statement about the Unconvincibles; for, having acquired their beliefs on an emotional level, they cannot be persuaded out of them on a rational level.

And it only makes matters worse to argue with them. They become more and more passionately partisan, more extremist, more defensive about their position. In the end, you are just exchanging invectives.

The moment I realize that I am engaged in a controversial discussion with an Unconvincible, I shift the subject to the weather, the crops, the T-formation or the relative merits of the new automobiles. It has kept my blood pressure at a happily low level these many years.

How can one detect an Unconvincible before the discussion has gone beyond the point of no return? There are several gambits they all use, which should alert us to the presence of an Immovable Object.

They are, for instance, fond of quoting texts, which they have learned by heart. They may have memorized portions of the Bible—roughly torn out of context—to bolster their position. Or they may cite historical statistics, which they have at their fingertips. Or they tell you some long, rambling personal experience they have undergone—and then generalize outrageously from this one instance.

Logic, of course, is utterly useless against them. They will not define their terms, and they commit every fallacy in the book. If pushed to the wall, they will bitterly counterattack by impugning your ancestry, your mental condition, your patriotism, your solvency, your moral character, your very motives themselves.

And the surest sign of an Unconvincible is the description he immediately uses about himself. He thinks of himself as Broad-Minded.

A Nook a Need in Modern Homes

ALTHOUGH I HAVE A HIGH OPINION of most modern architecture—indeed, I think that America's main contribution to the arts in the twentieth century has been in the field of architecture—I deplore the increasing lack of privacy that seems to mark most modern homes.

Wide expanses of glass, walls that open and combine two rooms into one, family areas with floating partitions—these all may make for spaciousness and graciousness, but they rigidly ignore the psychological needs of people. I firmly believe that doors were invented for closing, that each member of a family is entitled to be alone when he wants to, that "togetherness" should be a matter of emotional rapport and not mere physical proximity.

In this respect, the old-fashioned house is far superior to its modern counterpart. It may have been ornate and cluttered and dark, but at least it provided the inhabitants with places of refuge when the spirit of solitude descended upon them.

Children, especially, require all the privacy they want in these times of overorganized activities and the desperate race to "adjust" to others. Emerson's words of advice are still cogent: "Be not too much a parent; trespass not on the child's solitude."

The French wisely recognize these needs, and most French homes are designed to give each member of the family the maximum of privacy. In fact, the "boudoir" was invented to supply the lady of the house with a place to remove herself in a pique; *bouder* means "to pout" in French, and the *boudoir* was literally a sulking room for madame.

It appalls me to see to many new homes going up with more space devoted to the car than to the children, with a large area for a barbecue pit and no study for the father, with an all-electric kitchen for the mother to work in and no cranny for her to escape to. The great charm of old houses does not consist in the elegance of the living room or the graceful curve of the staircase, but the cool refuge of the basement, the redolent mustiness of the attic, the alcoves and turnings and just plain hiding places from the world.

People who live in glass houses can't help throwing stones at one another if they have no secret nook in which to brood or exult or daydream or simply withdraw from the mounting pressure of planned chaos.

It's the Way You Say It That Counts

WE HEAR A GREAT DEAL about "communication" these days—about our need to listen more carefully, to read more skillfully, to grasp the essence of what another person is trying to say. But it seems to me that communication, even more than charity, begins at home. The most important person to listen to is oneself, and our most important task is to develop an ear that can really hear what we are saying.

Anyone who has ever listened to a playback of a hidden tape recorder will know what I mean. It seems impossible that these are our voices—these babbling, incoherent sounds, more like monkeys than human beings. Is that raucous tone our own? How did self-pity sneak into that sentence? And listen to that phrase, unctuous with hypocrisy, or vibrating with false heartiness.

Without refraction, the voice cannot hear itself, any more than the eye can see itself. The whining wife does not know she whines, the bellowing husband is unaware of his bellow, the self-satisfied prig cannot detect the smugness dripping from his lips.

Just as we do not know what we sound like in timbre and cadence of voice, so we do not hear the unconscious attitudes that are revealed to others by our speech—the hostility thinly masquerading as humor, the fear hiding behind cool precision, the pomposity or envy or greed or any other unlovely trait we desperately try to conceal from others and from ourselves.

To communicate well and meaningfully it is not enough to make one's meaning plain to a listener. It is, first of all, to make one's meaning plain to oneself, to understand the real motives for our attitudes, to hear the half-tones and flats and sharps of our own prejudices, and to separate (however imperfectly) the voice of reason from the voice of childishness.

This is the hardest job of all, and this is where all genuine communication must begin. For people do not so much listen to what we say as to how we say it; the expression of a statement carries a stronger charge than its content; two men can make the same observation, and one will be accepted, the other met with suspicion or disbelief.

The world listens to the secret language of our emotions, and not to the bald denotations of the words themselves. And mastering that secret language calls for a true ear as much as for a true heart.

Keep Control of Your Personality

I WALKED WITH MY FRIEND, a Quaker, to the newsstand the other night, and he bought a paper, thanking the newsie politely. The newsie didn't even acknowledge it.

"A sullen fellow, isn't he?" I commented. "Oh, he's that way every night," shrugged my friend. "Then why do you continue being so polite to him?" I asked. "Why not?" inquired my friend. "Why should I let *him* decide how I'm going to act?"

As I thought about this little incident later, it occurred to me that the operating word was "act." My friend *acts* toward people; most of us *react* toward them.

He has a sense of inner balance lacking in most of us frail and uncertain creatures: he knows who he is, what he stands for, and how he should behave.

No boor is going to disturb the equilibrium of his nature; he simply refuses to return incivility with incivility, because then he would no longer be in command of his own conduct, but a mere responder to others.

When we are enjoined in the Bible to return good for evil, we look upon this as a moral injunction, which it is; but it is also a psychological prescription for our emotional health.

Nobody is unhappier than the perpetual *reactor*. His center of emotional gravity is not rooted within himself, where it belongs, but in the world outside him. His spiritual temperature is always being raised or lowered by the social climate around him, and he is a mere creature at the mercy of these elements.

Praise gives him a feeling of euphoria, which is false, because it does not last and it does not come from self-approval. Criticism depresses him more than it should, because it confirms his own secretly shaky opinion of himself. Snubs hurt him, and the merest suspicion of unpopularity in any quarter rouses him to bitterness or aggressiveness or querulousness.

Only a saint, of course, *never* reacts. But a serenity of spirit cannot be achieved until we become the masters of our own actions and attitudes, and not merely the passive reactors to other persons' feelings. To let another determine whether we shall be rude or gracious, elated or depressed, is to relinquish control over our own personalities, which is ultimately all we possess. The only true possession is self-possession.

My friend is a model of balanced conduct, and few of us can hope to attain his kind of surefootedness. But we can at least adjust our weight to lean less heavily upon the world's giddy gyrations.

A Person's Worth Doesn't Change

NO OTHER ARTICLE I have written in a year has evoked so much comment as my recent piece on "acting and reacting." Hundreds of readers wrote in to tell me how much they like it; it has been widely reprinted, and used as a text for many sermons in the last few weeks.

I mention this not by way of boasting, but to point out that the individual today is deeply concerned with his personal and social character: he knows the kind of person he wants to be, but he doesn't know how to reach this goal.

As a corollary to my previous piece, may I suggest that one of the impediments to becoming an "actor" instead of a mere "reactor" is what I call the "pulley system" of evaluating people, including oneself.

On the pulley system, we go up when someone else goes down, and we go down when someone else goes up. We have no inner stability, because our emotional position keeps shifting in relation to the outside world.

If I meet a man who writes better than I do, this does not diminish my talents. I still have exactly what I had before, no more and no less. His own gifts do not devalue mine, nor do mine devalue somebody else's.

Yet most of us judge ourselves on this false relativistic basis. If we meet someone richer, we feel poor; someone handsomer, we feel ugly; someone more fluent, we feel tongue-tied. If they are up, we are down.

Conversely, many of us cannot feel comfortable unless we are pulling others down. We rise only by their lowliness: if he is uglier, I am handsomer; if he is poorer, I am richer; if he is ineffectual with women, I am a Casanova.

Those who have a tremendous need to depreciate others are doing it not because they feel genuinely superior, but because this is the only way they can achieve any emotional parity with the world. Unless others are made to feel inferior, these people cannot feel even normal.

But human society is not a pulley system. Each person has his own value, his own place, his own distinctive gifts and limitations. A pretty woman is no less pretty because a beautiful one enters the room; I am no poorer because I am lunching with a millionaire. My own writing does not become despicable when I am reading Shakespeare.

Things remain what they were; only our opinions of them change. To act, and not merely to react, implies the acceptance of God's world, and knowing that only He is the ultimate judge of our real worth.

Advice on How to Aid Mentally Ill

HALF THE HOSPITAL BEDS in the country, as we know, are occupied by mental patients; and one out of ten persons walking the streets today will have a mental breakdown of some sort.

Given these blunt facts, it is time we were also given some blunt advice on the handling of such cases by families, relatives and friends. And the first and best piece of advice is—stop moralizing.

There is no relationship between the moral and the mental structure; the mental patient does not have free will—that is why he is in trouble.

Don't advise him or her to "use will power," which is a dangerous, arrogant and ignorant thing to say.

Don't ask him or her to "pull yourself together"—for people in serious difficulties are beyond pulling.

Don't offer such fatuous remedies as "get a hobby," or "keep your chin up," or "count your blessings." This is as infuriating (and as futile) as urging a man with two broken legs to go down a ski slide.

Don't suggest "a change of scenery"—for the mental patient takes his own scenery with him wherever he goes.

Don't urge "if you'd only try a little harder"—for this is like imploring a hunchback to straighten up a little.

Don't say "If you really loved me . . ." for the mental patient is beyond love, which is an act of the will.

Don't invoke "faith" or any religious inspiration, because religious feeling must be rooted in mental health, not in illness.

Don't imagine for a moment that a new job, or a new mate, or a new setting, will clear up the ailment—for the problems come from within the patient, not from without.

Don't preach, don't beg, don't give pep-talks, don't threaten, don't bribe, don't do anything that assumes the patient could change if he only *would*.

In a positive sense, be sympathetic but not sentimental; cool but not hard; attentive but not over-solicitous; concerned but not frightened; and, most of all, keep in mind at all times that most saving thought of all: "There but for the grace of God go I."

None of this is easy; some of it is impossibly hard. The least we can do, however, is respect the illness and not expect the patient to stand up and walk with the equivalent of two broken legs. We cannot make him better; but we should not make him feel worse.

It's Easier to Love Dogs than People

RECENTLY, IN SAN FRANCISCO, a defense attorney tried to introduce evidence that a murder defendant once refused to kill a mouse, and therefore could not have killed his wife.

The judge quite properly refused to admit the testimony, ruling it only proved that the defendant "probably liked mice." His Honor evidently has a wide acquaintance with the personalities of past murderers.

Only the sheerest sentimentalism still holds that a person who is "kind to animals" is necessarily kind to people. In actual fact, an inverse ratio often exists: Many of the people who are fondest of dogs, cats, birds and mice are most cruel, or most indifferent, to human beings.

The barbarous leaders of the Nazi regime, for instance, were great animal fanciers; Julius Streicher, after urging the gas chamber for several million humans, would go home and tenderly care for his nineteen pet canaries. Stalin is said to have loved dogs, and I have no doubt that Nero, Genghis Khan and Attila the Hun displayed a sentimental attachment to some animal or other.

Many of the world's celebrated murderers have had a passionate devotion to the lower forms of life, while brutally extinguishing the upper form. In a morbidly fascinating book called *Famous British Trials,* the curious reader can find abundant evidence of the merciful instincts of hardened killers toward defenseless animals.

It is much easier to love an animal than a person, which is why so many people transfer their affections in this manner. An animal cannot betray you, disappoint you, quarrel with you, or make excessive demands upon you. It is your creature, and enables you to play God with it —which you cannot easily do with human beings.

Please don't write in, dear readers, to charge me with saying that all, or even most, animal lovers are potential murderers, or that caring for an animal means you don't care for people. What I *am* saying, however, is that, in a striking number of cases, devotion toward a dog acts as a substitute for a more normal emotion toward our fellows.

The man who wouldn't hurt a mouse would blithely kill his wife—perhaps because she refused to be a mouse. When we treat animals like humans, it is not long before we begin treating humans like animals.

We Play Roles and Forget to Be People

A COUPLE DROPPED IN for tea last Sunday afternoon, and during the conversation the wife mentioned that they had been shopping for an apartment, but with no success.

Knowing that she owned a handsome building in a most desirable location, I asked her why she didn't take an apartment in her own property.

"It would drive me crazy," she shrugged. "As the tenant, I'd expect the owner to pay for all the repairs and decorating—but as the owner I'd insist that the tenant take better care of the apartment. My nervous system couldn't stand such a strain!"

We all laughed, of course, but her jest was rooted in serious fact. She was really saying that she prefers her functions as Landlord and as Tenant quite separate—because combining them might force her to give up a viewpoint she now finds comfortable and profitable.

The tremendous size and complexity of our society has given each of us a specialized task and role to play; and it has become dangerously easy for each of us to consider his separate function as the *whole person*.

We are the Landlord, the Tenant, the Banker, the Workman, the Stockholder and so on. These roles are usually so demanding, and so restricting, that we forget ourselves as a human entity, and become only part of a person—the part that is directly engaged in making a living and protecting our possessions.

Perhaps we can see the problem more clearly with an everyday illustration. When the average man is driving his car, he is a Motorist, and pedestrians are menaces or fools who seem to be his sworn enemies; when he is walking, however, he becomes a Pedestrian, and then the motorist is seen as the lunatic foe.

Yet, above both the Motorist and the Pedestrian is the higher concept of the Good Citizen, who wants justice and fair treatment for walkers and drivers alike, and whose attitude does not depend on whether he happens at any given moment to be walking or driving.

The lady who refused to move into her own building was denying her *unity* as a person, and preferred to think of herself only as a separate *function*. Her attitude, while understandable, is the greatest single stumbling block in the way of a decent and flexible social order—for, until we are willing to put ourselves in another person's place, to incorporate his views in ours, we selfishly obstruct any vision of a better world.

Westerns Fill a Real Purpose

WHILE I WAS HOME last weekend, coping with a late-model type of virus, a friend came calling with an armful of paperbound books for "light" reading.

There were a couple of novels, a scattering of mysteries and four Westerns. Not having read any of the latter since I was about twelve, I picked them up out of curiosity and thumbed through the casts of characters.

Not a thing had changed in three decades. The heroes were uniformly lean and bronzed, with a muscle that twitched ominously along their jawbone when they were riled. The villains still had shifty and close-set eyes, black mustaches and a greasy way with the wenches.

And it occurred to me that it is unfair to classify this sort of reading as "literature" of any sort, as mysteries might be so classified. After all, mysteries are quite different in plot from each other; the measure of their enjoyment is their unpredictability.

But in a Western there is never any doubt who is the "good guy" and who the "bad guy." It is really an old-fashioned morality play with the characters plainly labeled Virtue and Vice, and not the slightest doubt about the outcome of their conflict.

This is not to derogate the Westerns, but to suggest that they fulfill a purpose that is more therapeutic than literary. Their chief value is not even "amusement" for those who read them—it is "vindication."

The continuing popularity of the Western story, I am convinced, is attributable to the fact that they satisfy a childlike part of us that never wholly dies. I mean not the part that loves adventure, but the part that wants to see the world in black and white, with the white ultimately prevailing.

The Western permits us, for an hour or two, to return to the warm, safe, comfortable world of childhood, where we know that the police-man will always capture the robber, where Father stands guard outside the door to see that no harm befalls us.

Western stories vindicate this childhood belief in the triumph of virtue, and restore for a time a sense of values badly shaken (if not shattered) by the apparent chaos of maturity. It is a mistake to think that men read them for adventure. They read them for safety.

Motivation a Key Part of "Talent"

WHAT MOST PEOPLE—and especially parents—don't want to recognize is that motivation is an integral part of talent, and not just a kind of fuel injection that powers it.

Parents are fond of sighing, "He'd be so good at this," or "She'd make such a wonderful that"—if only he or she would *apply* himself or herself.

But the talent is incomplete without the applying. It is nothing, it is only a potentiality, and cannot be brought into existence if the motivation is lacking.

Who knows how many "mute inglorious Miltons" have lived and died without the world having been aware of their latent talents? If the drive to actualize their ability is missing, nothing outside of themselves can instill it in them. No threats, no promises, no praise.

A truly talented person is self-propelled. Not only does he not need to be encouraged (although it helps), he cannot be suppressed. He will keep on painting or writing or composing or doing whatever he does best, despite all the rejections and rebuffs in the world. And he is supremely self-confident, although despair may attack him from time to time. Despair about his future, not about his gifts.

This is true not only of the artist but of the student. The student who "could really get an A" if he wanted to, cannot really get an A because he really doesn't want to. And the wanting to is an essential part of the achieving, not a separate thing, as parents imagine, that can be injected into him like a shot of adrenalin.

All genuine and meaningful and lasting motivation comes from the inside, not from the outside. The carrot and the stick work—maybe—only as long as the carrot is in front and the stick behind. When they are withdrawn, the motivation ceases. You can get a mule to move this way, but not a person, for very long.

Parents should learn to stop nagging their children about how well they could do "if you only tried more, or cared more." Trying and caring, in specific areas, is built into people; or else it comes to them later, if they mature properly; or it never comes at all. But it is dead certain that no young person was ever motivated by a querulous, disappointed parent more concerned with his own pride than with the child's ultimate self-actualization.

If she shows "a talent for music" and doesn't want to practice, let it go—the only talent worth cultivating is that which is accompanied by patience, persistence and passion. If these are lacking, you might as well try to make a ballerina out of a "talented" paraplegic.

Bad Drivers Unsure of Virility

As I was edging out of a parking lot the other day, some Clyde in his Bonneville cut sharply ahead of me, flashed a sour smile of triumph in my direction and scooted away.

He evidently thought he had "won" something, but in my view, he had lost. He thought he was displaying strength and aggressiveness; I thought he was displaying weakness and bad manners.

What the prevailing ethos in modern American life does not seem to understand is that true strength *always* reveals itself in gentleness and courtesy; this was the whole medieval idea of knighthood and chivalry—a knight was chivalrous because he felt strong enough to afford it.

We tend to confuse rudeness with power, and aggressiveness with virility. Many, if not most, of the bad-mannered drivers on the road are slack-jawed youths who privately feel weak and insecure in their personal relations with the world; tooling a ferocious car gives them a vicarious sense of power they do not possess in person.

Genuine strength of character is always accompanied by a feeling of security that allows one to practice civility and courtesy—but, in our perverse culture, civility and courtesy are often regarded as signs of weakness or some lack of "manliness."

And it is largely this perverse evaluation of what constitutes manhood that accounts for so much of the dangerous discourtesy on our nation's highways—somehow, the education of boys here has stressed aggressiveness at the price of gentleness, so that many youths act like boors in order to be thought of as "men."

This is fairly indigenous to our culture; in other countries, a more balanced view is taken of what comprises "manliness," and one of the main criteria of an adult male is his *considerateness* for others. And the poor result of our misconception of manhood can be seen in many failing marriages, where the wives uniformly complain that their husbands are just "little boys who failed to grow up."

There is little doubt in my mind that girls here grow up to be women more easily and successfully than boys grow up to be men; or that most "immaturity" in the marriage relationship is displayed by the husbands. Women have other conjugal faults, but they tend to accept adult obligations with better grace than men do.

No one, to my knowledge, has ever made a study of the social psychology of driving; but I think that such a study would show that the males with the worst manners are the least sure of their masculinity and the most resentful toward the deeper responsibilities of manhood. For true strength always exhibits itself in generosity of spirit.

If you shout in an argument, it makes you wrong, even when you are right.

*

The way we interpret the world makes it become more that way, for us—the suspicious man makes the world more suspicious, the greedy man makes the world more greedy, the belligerent man makes the world more belligerent; for every distortion of reality becomes, in the end, a self-fulfilling prophecy.

How to Understand What's Going On

HOW TO BEGIN TO UNDERSTAND What's Happening in the World Today in Ten Not-So-Easy Lessons:

1. Start by taking a long, hard look at yourself, to determine whether you have significantly altered your views or stance in the last twenty years, or even in the last decade.

2. Ask yourself what you have done, personally and practically, to help change what needs to be changed, and to help preserve what needs to be preserved—and on what philosophical or moral basis you distinguish between the two.

3. Look around at your co-workers, friends and neighbors, and assess whether they are engaged in anything but the pursuit of affluence (and if they are enjoying it), and the pursuit of pleasure (and if they are enjoying it).

4. Recall when you last, if ever, had a serious talk with a person under twenty, with a poor person, with a Negro, with a foreigner, with a radical—with anyone whose life-position is sharply different from yours.

5. List and evaluate the kind of things you are reading now that you weren't reading twenty years ago, or a decade ago—are you aware of what's going on in the behavioral sciences, in education, in technology, in psychological research, or are you still reading the familiar and comfortable publications that tell you only what you like to hear or want to hear?

6. Are you reacting to new questions with new insights, or with answers that were beginning to be obsolete a generation ago—and are you able to differentiate between those principles and maxims that have permanent value and those that merely reflect the ''received wisdom'' of your father's time but are increasingly irrelevant today?

7. Try this imaginative process on yourself: Take a social or political position that is at the opposite pole from your own, and formulate it so that its proponents would be satisfied with the fair way you have stated it—and then, and only then, try to refute it with reason, logic and facts, not with rhetoric, emotion or name-calling.

8. Ask yourself (*a*) what are your proximate goals in life, then (*b*) what are your ultimate goals in life and then (*c*) are your proximate goals leading toward, or away from, your ultimate goals?

9. Consider Bernard Shaw's aphorism: "It is impossible for the smoker and the nonsmoker to be equally free in the same railway car," and reflect on how society can arrange optimum freedom for all.

10. Whenever some act reported in the news particularly outrages you, threatens you or appalls you, ask yourself under what possible conditions your reaction might be exactly the opposite.

How We Make Prophecies Come True

"THE WHITENESS OF A MAN'S TEETH," observes St. Thomas in the *Summa*, "primarily belongs, not to him, but to them."

If the whiteness of the teeth belongs to the teeth, and not to the man, then the blackness of the skin belongs to the skin, and not to the man. And, thus, all the accidental attributes of the body must not be ascribed to the essence of the individual personality.

This is a lesson mankind has not yet learned. We identify, and stratify, and treat persons largely on the basis of their accidental characteristics, which have no deeper meaning.

Then, because our treatment of such persons makes them sensitive and resentful and angry and out of joint with us, we turn around and blame them for being "different." This is the history of all discrimination and persecution.

Suppose we did this with a child in our family, who had some peculiar physical characteristic, one not shared by the rest of the family. By the time the child was adolescent, the weight of disapproval would have shaped (and misshaped) his whole character and personality. Our thinking him different makes him different; our dislike makes him unlikable.

We can clearly see what would happen in the case of an individual child; but we somehow cannot grasp the analogy to a whole race or section of people who are treated in the same fashion.

What social scientists have lately called "the self-fulfilling prophecy" is hard at work in such cases. Because of our prejudice or fear or ignorance, we *expect* certain groups to behave in a specific negative way; and the very thrust of our expectations tends to drive them in that same direction. Then we feel justified in condemning them, because they have predictably reacted as we thought they would.

In this truly vicious circle, all racial and religious and geographical discrimination is constantly being reinforced—because the objects of our prejudice eventually come to resemble the stereotypes we have cast them in. And our contempt becomes their self-contempt. Even their new-found "pride" is reactive, not spontaneous—black is neither "beautiful" nor "ugly," it is merely pigment.

The vast revolutions awaiting us in the latter third of the twentieth century may take political form, but they will be racial revolutions in substance, using as their tremendous lever the insane delusion of the white race that the blackness of the skin belongs to the man, and not merely to the skin.

What's Sexy About Nude Bodies?

THE WORD "OBSCENE" means "tending to cause sexual excitement or lust." I don't know why this should be considered a *bad* thing by society, but even granting that it should, what makes a naked body obscene?

Two University of Wisconsin students last fall were indicted on obscenity charges (later withdrawn when no witnesses could be found) for performing in a nude version of *Peter Pan* at two performances of the musical production.

I didn't see the performance, but I have seen naked bodies, and they are lovely or laughable or pathetic or uninteresting or droll, but none has ever impressed me as obscene, in any sense of the word.

An *act* can be obscene, an *attitude* can be obscene, but a body per se cannot be. It is only a dirty mind that can see dirt in a clean body; to the (unconsciously) impure, all things are impure.

The plain common-sense fact is that a naked body is about as unlustful and unexciting in itself as a plucked chicken. Many years ago, as a reporter, I covered (or uncovered) a nudist convention, which was about the most Puritan convention I had ever attended in my life.

Because the members of this nudist group didn't regard their bodies—at that time, in that place—as provocative or symbolic of sexuality, they were totally unself-conscious; and after an hour or so of reconditioning, I became just as unaware of their nakedness.

Everyone knows that a woman wearing diaphanous garments that tease and promise and conceal as much as they disclose is ten times more "alluring" than a stark-naked woman prancing around. It is her attitude that makes her "obscene" or not; it is not her equipment. And it is the attitude of society, not the fact of nudity itself.

Recently I saw a record album cover of two young singers, totally naked in front-face, as it were. The photograph was amusing because it was so utterly unerotic; they both looked like sad sacks, standing there smiling foolishly at the world, for no particular reason. It was enough to drive a man into a monastery.

Actually, the *more* nakedness, the *less* sexuality; the more we take the body for granted, the less we feel prompted to fumble for forbidden fruit. It is the false aura of mystery that invests the body with a meretricious glamour. Japan, where men and women freely bathe together, has fewer rape cases in a year than the United States has in one day.

Why Some Are Doers, Others Aren't

BERNARD SHAW SAID many wise and witty things, along with a good deal of nonsense. But perhaps the most mischievous comment he ever made is one that is parroted by people every day: "He who can, does; he who cannot, teaches."

This was a cheap, smart-alecky and wholly unthinking observation. *Doing* and *teaching* are two wholly different activities; and if the teacher is often not good at doing, the doer is generally much worse at teaching others how to do.

The most obvious example that comes to mind is athletics. The greatest coaches have often been mediocre players; the most astute prize-fighter trainers usually could not last a round against Tiny Tim; and some of the finest music teachers would disgrace a high school orchestra.

In the sport that interests me most, tennis, the outstanding coach for many years was Mercer Beasley, who brought an astonishing number of youngsters to court greatness. Yet Beasley himself was never more than an indifferent tennis player, as he and all his pupils cheerfully admit.

And, likewise, in the theater, some of the best dramatic coaches can barely stagger out on a stage and recite "Gunga Din" before an audience.

They know *how* a performance should go, and can superbly impart this knowledge—but there is no earthly reason why they themselves should be able to play a role professionally.

This snide attitude toward teaching comes from a mistaken view of talent. The talented person generally does not know why he does what he does, and therefore he cannot transmit his knowledge to others. The spring of his creativity resides in the unconscious mind, and when he tries to formulate it into words, he falls into incoherence.

The teacher acts as a necessary middleman between the professional and the novice. He can understand the deeper motivations of the professional and can translate these into a systematized program for the novices.

Even in academic teaching, it is unnecessary for the English teacher to be a master of prose, or for the chemistry teacher to be a marvel with the test tube. They are *interpreters* of an art, and without skilled interpreters the intuitive language of the artist could not be transmitted to future generations.

Let's revise Shaw's foolish saying to "He who can, does; he who understands, teaches."

We Read with Our Biases

IN A FEW WEEKS, I'll be beginning my twenty-fourth year of writing a daily column. When people ask me if it's "challenging," I feel like telling them that the biggest challenge belongs to them, not to me.

And that is the one challenge thrown out by every serious writer—to be understood in what he says. For most people read not with their minds, but with their emotions and prejudices. They read *into* or read *out* of a piece of writing what they want to. And when they disagree, it is usually not with what a writer says, but with what they *imagine* he said.

A nearly perfect example was a column of mine about a census taker in Galilee, which appeared some weeks ago. It was a mildly ironic piece, purporting to show that the average official or bureaucrat cannot distinguish a saint from a bum, or a prophet from a nut. The official mind is interested only in superficial and external facts.

The census taker was interviewing Jesus, and was answered by Biblical quotations attributed to the Son of Man. As far as he was concerned, these answers were either incomprehensible or evasive, and the bearded man on the donkey was merely an old-time version of the "hippie."

Those readers who approached the subject without an excess of religious bias immediately understood what I was trying to say in this oblique and narrative fashion: that we must be careful about categorizing or condemning people because of the way they look or dress or express themselves; and that the greatest figure the world has known lived and worked among the most "disreputable" elements in his society.

But many other readers wrote in bitterly to accuse me of calling Jesus a "hippie"—which would be an absurd misreading of history and theology on my part—and to attack the parable as "blasphemous," when it was exactly the opposite. Jesus himself rebuked his own countrymen, by sadly commenting that a prophet is without honor in his own country—often mistaken for a crank or a mere troublemaker.

People filter what they read through the fine strainer of their feelings and preconceptions, their prejudices and fears. If they have a stained-glass image of Jesus in their minds, for instance, it disturbs or infuriates them to hear that the living Jesus would most likely be thrown into jail in our contemporary society—and surely would not be allowed into the "better" churches.

"If the triangles could conceive of a god," said Montesquieu, "he would be in the shape of a triangle." Alas, the squares do the same.

Not Going Too Far, But Too Fast

WE ARE CHANGING our environment faster than we can adjust to it. That's as simply as anyone can state our problem—which has less to do with the *substance* of our affairs than with their form and shape.

This is really what upsets everyone so much, and makes us overreact to political and social and economic events. There is a loss of a sense of continuity, a feeling that we are disoriented and a desperate psychological need to cling to some permanent landmark, the way a drunk has to wrap himself around a lamppost.

A few weeks ago, I drove past a country house we used to live in every summer for some years. This spring it was struck by lightning and totally demolished. It gave me a weird feeling to drive past this empty field where only recently we had eaten and slept and played.

In a way, everything we knew has been struck by a kind of lightning in the last few years. The landscape has been radically altered; fields are shopping centers, lanes are highways, lofts are skyscrapers. All the old familiar signposts are gone, or going. There is an uneasy dreamlike aspect to our everyday lives.

A large part of us remains childlike at heart; and we must remember that children above all cherish the familiar, the known, the established. They are dedicated traditionalists: everything must be the same, a story told exactly the same way, a game played in precisely the identical fashion, or they feel lost and cheated.

The acceleration in the rate of change, rather than change itself, is what bothers us to the deepest roots of our psychic constitution. What used to take twenty years now happens in five, or three; and not only to our neighborhoods, our downtowns, our cities, even our villages, but, more importantly, to our moral and social patterns, our modes of relating to one another, our standards of right and wrong, good and bad, guilty and innocent.

Don't even look at the radical left, but at the conservative right—at that bulwark of traditionalism and continuity, the Roman Catholic Church. Who would have imagined a decade ago the cataclysmic changes shaking and altering the ancient and impressive institution? More fissures have appeared in that church in the last ten years than in the preceding 300 years; little wonder that its most devout communicants feel like Chicken Little watching the sky falling down.

Most of the modern change, in my view, is an improvement, in every area. But this doesn't matter. What matters is that we are not able, biologically or psychologically, to deal with so rapid a rate of change—and so we vent our frustration in conflict, in divisiveness, in resistance and resentment that are not amenable to rational argument or logical persuasion.

We are not going too far, as many fear. But we are going too fast. As the body finds it hard to adjust to supersonic speeds, so the mind even more finds it nearly impossible to adjust to the bolts of social lightning striking everywhere around us.

Nothing is so distorted and unreliable as memory—a fact we cannot fully believe until we have revisited our birthplace after a long absence.

*

Ninety percent of what we believe has nothing to do with the process of thought, but comes instead from the four sources of family inheritance, individual temperament, national culture, and economic self-interest; and while we cannot wholly cast off these shackles, we should at least recognize their cramping and distorting influence upon the free process of thought.

We're Not Fit to Colonize Space

A FEW DAYS AFTER our successful orbiting of the moon, a friend expressed the hope that this venture would teach people humility in the face of the universe.

"If this helps us realize how vast outer space is, and how small our globe is," he said, "then it might make us all feel more united as inhabitants of this tiny speck of dust whirling in space."

This would be a commendable lesson to learn, I agree, but I doubt that we would draw so philosophical an inference from the moon project. Rather, I suggested bleakly, it might lead us in the opposite direction.

Instead of regarding space exploration as a common effort binding mankind together, it is far more likely that we will simply extend our competitiveness from inner to outer space, and look upon the solar system as competing nations once regarded explorations on earth—as places to plant flags, to colonize, to use as economic resources and military outposts.

Unless we make some unexpected quantum jump in our thinking and feeling, we will simply extrapolate to other worlds the same greed and vanity, the same lust for possession and domination, the same conflict over boundaries and priorities throughout the solar system.

What is even more dire, we might also export the contamination of our planet, not merely in terms of wars and prejudices and injustices, but quite physically, in terms of bacteria and viruses and all the assorted pollutions of earth, air and water that are rapidly making our own globe nearly uninhabitable.

Nothing in our history, early or recent, indicates that we are not prepared to despoil other planets as carelessly and contemptuously as we have turned ours from green to gray, from fair to foul, from sweet to sour, in the countryside as well as in the cities—so that even sunny, snowy Switzerland has shown a 90 per cent increase in smoke content and turbidity of the air in the last two decades.

We are no more morally or spiritually equipped to colonize other parts of the solar-system—given our past level of behavior on earth—than a hog is fit to march in an Easter parade. Our technical genius so far outstrips our ethical and emotional idiocy that we are no more to be trusted to deal lovingly and creatively with another planet than a rhesus monkey can be allowed to run free in a nuclear power plant.

The astronauts are bold men, and the scientists who sent them up are bright men, but they are not the ones who will decide what is done once we get there. The same old schemers will be running the show.

Sports Only Exercise Our Eyes

BEFORE I PROCEED a line further, let me make it clear that I enjoy physical exercise and sport as much as any man. I like to bat a baseball, dribble a basketball, kick a soccer ball and, most of all, swat a tennis ball. A man who scorned physical activity would hardly build a tennis court on his summerhouse grounds, or use it every day.

Having made this obeisance, let me now confess that I am puzzled and upset—and have been for many years—by the almost obsessive interest in sports taken by the average adult American male.

Athletics is one strand in life, and even the ancient Greek philosophers recognized its importance. But it is by no means the whole web, as it seems to be in our society. If American men are not talking business, they are talking sports, or they are not talking at all.

This strikes me as an enormously adolescent, not to say retarded, attitude on the part of presumed adults. Especially when most of their passion and enthusiasm center around professional teams which bear no indigenous relation to the city they play for, and consist of mercenaries who will wear any town's insignia if the price is right.

Although I like to play, and sometimes like to watch, I cannot see what possible difference it makes which team beats which. The tactics are sometimes interesting, and certainly the prowess of the players deserves applause—but most men seem to use commercial sports as a kind of narcotic, shutting out reality, rather than heightening it.

There is nothing more boring, in my view, than a prolonged discussion by laymen of yesterday's game. These dreary conversations are a form of social alcoholism, enabling them to achieve a dubious rapport without ever once having to come to grips with a subject worthy of a grown man's concern.

It is easy to see the opiate quality of sports in our society when tens of millions of men will spend a splendid Saturday or Sunday fall afternoon sitting stupefied in front of the TV, watching a "big game," when they might be out exercising their own flaccid muscles and stimulating their lethargic corpuscles.

Ironically, our obsession with professional athletics not only makes us mentally limited and conversationally dull, it also keeps us physically inert—thus violating the very reason men began engaging in athletic competitions. It is tempting to call this national malaise of "spectatoritis" childish—except that children have more sense, and would rather run out and play themselves.

All Demonstrators Aren't Kooks

DO YOU KNOW the difference between a "convertible proposition" and "non-convertible proposition"? If you don't, the chances are high that you can't reason accurately or realistically about many issues and conflicts in the modern world.

Suppose I suggest the proposition (which is true): "Neurotic people are usually unorthodox." Do you then turn it around into the proposition (which is false): "Unorthodox people are usually neurotic"? If so, you are commiting a fallacy in logic, and a sin against truth.

Yet, we do this all the time in dozens of obvious and subtle ways. One of the most obvious ways today is our estimation of events like student demonstrations on campuses.

We take the true proposition, "Most kooks and beatniks will participate in these demonstrations," and we convert it into the false proposition, "Most students participating in these demonstrations are kooks and beatniks." If we believe this second statement, then we become totally incapable of understanding the meaning and the thrust of student action.

Another common (and false) conversion is from "Communists support this position" to "Those who support this position are communists." However, the second statement does not at all necessarily follow from the first. It may, or it may not.

Some propositions can be converted, and some cannot; it is important that we recognize the distinction between the two, if we are to discuss and debate important matters rationally. But what most of us do in argument is the equivalent of saying that because "all cats are animals," therefore "all animals are cats."

Going back to the first proposition I cited, it is true that most neurotic people are usually unorthodox, because neurosis tends to make such people alienated from their fellows. Even when they are right, it is for the wrong reasons.

But it is not true that most unorthodox people are necessarily neurotic. Some are ahead of their time; some have more courage or wisdom than the rest of us; some hold their individuality in higher regard than most of us, some have too much creativity or imagination to be content with conventional attitudes.

We must not let the fact that kooks and beatniks and neurotics seize gleefully on campus demonstrations blind us to the even more important fact that thousands of serious and dedicated students also take part in them, for reasons that are worth listening to. If we persist in converting propositions that cannot be converted, we shall continue to be vexed by the patterns of the present, and baffled by the forms of the future.

Lending an Ear to Our Foes

SUPPOSE AN EDITORIAL in the Communist newspaper *Pravda* said: "The scenic resources of the United States have been so ruthlessly exploited by real estate developers, by polluters, by the raw material extractors and other private interests, that relatively few stretches of unspoiled, high-quality, esthetic natural environments are left along the nation's waterways or anywhere else."

We would look upon this as typical Soviet propaganda, wildly exaggerated, and bitterly biased against the "private interests." Our initial reaction would be to rebut this unqualified attack upon us.

In point of fact, the sentence I quoted comes from a recent editorial in the *New York Times*, a highly respected middle-of-the road newspaper and one of the bastions of the U.S. Establishment. As such, the statement was calmly received and given thoughtful attention by readers.

A long time ago, Don Marquis wrote: "An idea isn't responsible for who believes in it." We have yet to learn this lesson. A statement by a Klan leader or a communist, by a civil rights worker or a pacifist, will be judged more by the source than by the content. The intrinsic truth or falsity of the statement is usually obscured by its origin.

This is the height of folly on our part. We can often learn more from our enemies than from our friends; those who disagree with us can, in many cases, help us broaden our own viewpoint and escape from a "closed system" of thinking that tends to entrap most of us.

We know this is true in personal relations. The astringent comment by someone who doesn't like us may reveal an unattractive part of our personality that we are unaware of, and that our friends would never disclose, even if they saw it.

Likewise, in social and political matters, if we talk and listen only to like-minded people, we will hear nothing but what we want to hear, we will merely be confirming our prejudices and comforting our preconceptions. This is why any private club is so insular and so stultifying, whether it is a club of reactionaries or revolutionaries.

When we refuse to listen to our adversaries, or automatically discount their comments as "propaganda," we have relinquished a valuable tool for self-discovery and self-improvement. The best argument for full freedom of speech is a practical one: that clamping down on unpopular sentiments is as self-destructive, in the long run, as listening only to doctors who tell you that you are well, and repressing those who suggest you are ill.

"Obscenity" Is Matter of Intent

THE MOST RECENT SUPREME COURT decision on obscenity—in which the judges divided 5 against 4—only further points up the utter impossiblity of deciding what is "obscene" in any legal sense.

Not only does one generation disagree with another about what is "obscene," but within the same generation different classes and groups of people will disagree about it. There may be some absolute standard, but no one has found it yet.

It might be useful here to compare the idea of "obscenity" with the legal concept of "fraud." In order to prove fraud in a court of law it is first necessary to show "intent to defraud." If it can be shown that a man did not intend to commit fraud, he may be guilty of something else, but he is not guilty of fraud.

In the same way, "obscenity" resides in the intent of the author. And how can one demonstrate such intent, or lack of it? The court has used as a yardstick "whether the material has some redeeming social value." But this is a foolish criterion: I might write a novel consisting of 90 per cent pornography, and put in 10 per cent of "redeeming social value," simply to placate the authorities and satisfy the letter of the law.

"Intent" is a highly subjective matter, and does not easily lend itself to legal probings. I have seen, for instance, foreign movies which the average person would unhesitatingly call "obscene," yet in my view they sprang from an honest attempt to depict reality as the scenarist saw it.

On the other hand, I have seen Hollywood movies which the average person would call "light sex comedies," yet in my view these have been more obscene than the foreign films, for their whole intent seems to be to titillate the subject of sex in a coy and vulgar manner.

Who is right or wrong about this? There is no way to tell: it is a matter of taste, judgment, background, conditioning and cultural atmosphere. It may be that obscenity, like beauty, lies in the mind of the beholder; or there may be an *evolutionary morality,* as Teilard de Chardin put it, whose value depends on "collective feeling, common insight and the culture of the time."

Furthermore, I don't happen to believe that obscenity, of any sort, is as harmful as some people seem to think. The profound immoralities of our time are cruelty, indifference, injustice and the use of others as *means* rather than as *ends* in themselves. If everything deemed indecent or obscene were wiped out overnight, it would not make for a conspicuously better world, or for a more "moral" citizenry.

We Need Security to Do Our Best

ONE OF THE REASONS that organizations don't work as well as they might—and I am thinking here, particularly, of large business organizations—is that most of us have a defective theory of human motivations.

We think, for instance, of "security" and "initiative" as being opposites, in the sense that the more security a person is given, the less initiative he will display. This seems to me a gross misreading of human behavior.

In modern industrial society, the best rewards and the most solid developments are achieved by those organizations that are willing to make innovations, that are unafraid to take risks and to question the conventional wisdom of the past.

When leaders and executives fail to take such risks, it is more usually because they are *insecure,* rather than being *too secure.* They are fearful of their position, scared of being wrong or thought wrong, dubious about their talents or uncertain about their status in the organization. It is this kind of anxiety that makes for conformism, timidity and a lack of initiative.

Giving a man security—so long as his performance justifies it, of course—is giving him a firm place to stand. Without a firm place to stand, he will be afraid to move, lest he topple over. The chap whose philosophy is "don't rock the boat" is the one who feels that the first wave will knock *him* out of the vessel, not the one who is securely tied to a cleat.

As Wilbert E. Moore remarked in his provocative book, *The Conduct of the Corporation*, which won the most distinguished prize in sociology a few years ago: "The freedom to disagree, to suggest improvements, to question time-honored but irrational formulas, requires for most men in most times a relatively stable place to stand."

We can perceive the same tendency in that embryonic organization called a school: The child who is anxious about his academic status, who is too worried about keeping up or passing, will do much worse in his studies than the one who feels that as long as he is doing his best, he will not be thrown to the wolves. A sense of assurance motivates us positively; a sense of fear motivates us negatively, if at all.

Oppressed, insecure and frightened people show little initiative; they are not free enough from inner conflict to stand up boldly and say new and possibly unpopular things. Only the strong can practice freedom, and only the (relatively) secure can feel strong.

Challenge of Psychic Cancer

THE DAY THAT the "guilty" verdict was brought in by the Speck jury, I overheard a group of people at the luncheon table next to mine discussing the trial and conviction.

"Why does the state go to all the trouble, time and expense?" asked one of them. "He's guilty—everybody knew it—so why not give him the electric chair, or put him away for life and forget it?" Everyone else at the table nodded in strong agreement.

I didn't nod in agreement, even mentally. One must recognize that theirs is the attitude of most people, but I happen to think it is a wrong, dangerous and ignorant attitude.

Quite apart from the civil rights involved in the matter—and the blackest villain is entitled to the same trial rights as a cherub, or the law means nothing—there is another equally important consideration: We learn absolutely nothing by sending such a man to the chair, or even by putting him away to rot in prison for a lifetime.

If he is mad, we should study the causes and course of his madness; if he is bad, we should study the origins and evolution of his badness. If he is a mixture of both—as we might suspect—we should study the relationship between moral character and emotional sickness.

Society hates, fears and resents such men, and wants to obliterate them. But such obliteration does not deter or prevent similar occurrences, nor does it help us to detect, in the early stages, the behavior patterns of other men who might do likewise.

It seems painfully obvious to me that if we understood more about such matters, not only might the eight nurses be alive today, but also the young sniper who committed mass murder from his tower in Texas could have been spotted as a potential menace long before that dreadful day. Such actions are almost always prefigured in early behavior—if we are alert to the deeper meaning of such behavior.

Acts of what we call "senseless violence" are increasing enormously in this age. But though such acts may seem senseless to us, they make a kind of insane sense to the persons who perpetrate them, and if we obtained a better grasp of their convoluted mental processes, it might help us prevent incidents of this tragic kind—just as an improved knowledge of symptoms enables us to prevent physical illness from worsening to the incurable stage.

What is a "waste" is not the long and cumbersome trial, but the fact that after the trial little is done to probe the psychic cancers of such men. Simply to execute them or shut them away is the surest guarantee that future tragedies will be neither prevented nor anticipated. If we handled physical disease the same way, who would be alive?

All genuine love comes from strength, and is a kind of surplus energy in living; false love comes from weakness, and tries to suck vitality out of its object.

*

To feel *and display anger without becoming* less, *but becoming* more, *is the surest sign of emotional maturity; for most of us in anger regress to childishness and resort to insult, which diminish the righteousness of our cause rather than support it.*

III.
Of the
Social Animal

What People Fear the Negro Most?

WHITE PEOPLE IN AMERICA are feeling very sorry for themselves these days. That is the meaning of the so-called "white backlash"—it is a form of self-pity.

But, actually, who is the real victim of the Negro's alienation from American society? Not the white man, but the Negro himself. For every white person who feels threatened, a thousand Negroes feel even more so.

For the Negro is victimized, not merely by the white man, but also by his own worst elements. Their gangs threaten him much more than they threaten the whites. He has to live with it all the time—his women-folk afraid to walk the streets at night, his children afraid to come home from school.

In our full-blown compassion for ourselves—and in our fear of invasion, attack and injury—we whites tend to forget that the Negro lives with this, and within this, 24 hours a day, seven days a week. He is the one who is trapped in a jungle society—and his desire to move out is not so much an urge to live with the whites as it is to get away from those Negroes who corrupt and debase his neighborhood.

Negroes rob more Negroes than they do white people; kill more Negroes than they do white people; and even in all the "riots," it has so far generally been the blacks, not the whites, who are left bleeding to die.

In the ghetto, the level of life inevitably sinks to the lowest. The ghetto is run by the toughs, by the venal, by the exploiters, by the dregs—for it has no responsible power structure. "Law and order" has little meaning in such a society; it is only raw power that is respected.

We whites have as yet paid a very small, almost negligible price for Negro servitude. It is the decent, hard-working, responsible Negro who has paid the highest price—being forced to live in an environment where his women walk in fear, where his children grow up stunted and vulnerable to all the vices that accompany poverty and despair.

Whatever the historic causes of this ghetto—and they are complex and contradictory—it is this decent and responsible Negro who must be rescued from the cesspool; his children, at least, must not be allowed to start life with 2½ strikes on them. This is what all the marching and shouting are about—children without a chance.

It is a terrible problem, and there is no easy answer. We are in for a bumpy ride, whites and blacks alike, in the next few years. And we whites who are made uncomfortable by "civil rights" must remember the Negro has lived so long with civil wrongs that he is almost beyond caring to distinguish right from wrong.

When a City's Night Life Perishes

ON MY FIRST TRIP to St. Louis in three years, I took a cab from the airport to the downtown district. It was like arriving in a strange city I had never visited before.

Old buildings had been torn down and new ones put up. Many of the landmarks have disappeared. Expressways and parking lots have changed the whole skyline: even the cab driver was a little puzzled by the detours and dead ends.

This is happening in every large city in America, but of course we can see it more dramatically in a city we haven't visited for a while. It is considered a sign of "growth" and "development," but in my view it is largely a waste of money and energy.

The revitalization of downtown districts is not a matter of office buildings and corporate headquarters, of new city halls or banks or post offices. These are just part of the "daytime" city.

For every true metropolis has two cities downtown—the daytime city and the nighttime city. Unless the latter flourishes as fully as the former, all the new buildings are simply monuments to pride and vanity, and cannot restore the city in any meaningful way.

In the daytime city, everyone pours out of the office buildings and department stores at 5 o'clock, and goes homeward mostly to the suburbs. Downtown then becomes a cavern, dotted only by a few hotels, restaurants and movie houses. It is inhabited largely by out-of-towners, drunks, bums and restless juveniles.

True urban areas, like London, Paris and New York, have a nighttime city that is equal to the daytime city. A whole new population takes over after dark—an active and affluent population that uses and enjoys all the diverse resources of the nighttime city: theaters, cabarets, first-class restaurants and whatever cultural or artistic events the city has provided.

It is the nature and quality of the downtown facilities that transform it from a hick town to a metropolis, and not the height of the buildings or the cost of the rejuvenation. Unless people are made to want to enter the nighttime city by attractions they cannot find elsewhere, all the new buildings and civic centers are doomed to decay.

It takes money to revitalize our drab and dying downtown areas, but money is not enough. In fact, money without ideas is the surest way to speed the disintegration of a downtown, like an oppressively expensive party at which the hosts have supplied everything in embarrassing abundance—except the entertainment of the guests.

Our Apathy to No. 1 Killer

ALL RIGHT, ALL OF YOU good citizens who are so concerned about crime and violence in America. How many of you are willing to support a campaign against by far the greatest menace to life and limb in this nation?

Automobiles take 50,000 lives a year—many of them young children. Last July alone, motor vehicle deaths reached the unprecedented high of 5,130—a 20 per cent increase over the previous monthly high.

Injuries in the first seven months of 1966 disabled 1,000,000 persons, many of whom will never walk again or see again. And the innocent suffer along with the guilty—even more so, for the guilty are scarcely punished under our present system.

The so-called "violence in the streets" that arouses all you good citizens does a tiny percentage of the damage that is done by auto accidents. But there is a very big difference between the two—the violence is committed by *them*, but the auto accidents are by *us*.

Are we willing to discipline ourselves? To submit our cars to more rigorous checkups? To undergo physical and emotional examinations each year? To stiffen the penalties for reckless driving, drunken driving, juvenile driving?

I have seen no evidence that we are. No public committees formed, no meetings held, no petitions passed, no flood of letters to our elected officials, no angry outcries against the senseless "violence" in the streets and on the highways.

For we are afraid of losing our own privileges, and for that cheap and cowardly reason we are willing to permit 1,000 auto deaths a week. We demand tougher laws against criminals and rioters—who make up less than 1 per cent of the population—but not against the 99 per cent of "respectable citizens" who are responsible for the carnage on the highways.

Not many weeks ago, in the county where I spend my summers, three boys roared through a stop sign at 80 miles an hour, hitting a car and killing five members of the family. The boys were fined a total of $27 and given a 30-day sentence (suspended). I heard nobody complain about this travesty of justice: those who might have complained were all dead.

This happens every week, every day, every hour. It is the largest and most relentless slaughter the world has ever known, claiming more lives than we have lost in all the wars we have fought since the Revolution. Statistically, you are far safer walking down the toughest street in the toughest neighborhood in the toughest city in America than riding along a half-mile from your house. That's where the real violence is to be feared. Are you listening, all you good citizens?

Hardy, Tax-Consuming Pioneers

A LITTLE JOKE I READ in a magazine not long ago went: "The man whose great-grandfather built a railroad through the wilderness with nobody's OK now has to get a permit to remodel his front porch."

This is a part of the American myth, and it is surprising how many contemporary Americans still believe it. The fact of the matter is that great-grandfather not only needed permission to build the railroad, but he also was subsidized by the federal government for doing so.

We look upon our Western settlers and pioneers as the prototypes of the free enterprise system, as hardy competitive types who struck out boldly for themselves—but this is a gross misreading of American history.

Actually, the competition was in the East, in the growing towns and the burgeoning industrial activity of the early 19th Century. Many, if not most, of the men who went westward were not able to compete in that vigorous society.

They were offered free land and other inducements by the government. The granting of rights-of-way to railroads, the Homestead Act, the newly-created land grant colleges—all these were designed to provide an economic cushion as an inducement to get more settlers into the West.

This is not to disparage the admirable traits of some of these settlers, who were courageous, resourceful and hardworking. But it is to suggest that they were *fleeing* competition rather than *seeking* it, and usually with government promises of assistance and protection against loss.

The pioneers, assuredly, faced hardships—but these were hardships they chose in preference to other hardships. They opted for space and seclusion and withdrawal from the market place, and accepted whatever government help they could get to withstand the adversities and anarchy of life in raw communities.

Indeed, many of them were looking for "security" of a sort they could not find in the Eastern towns they emigrated from. In the hurly-burly of young industrial capitalism, they had only rustic skills that were not adapted to the urban and technical needs of the growing nation. Their westward migration was motivated as much by nostalgia as by the need for independence.

Certainly there were virtues in the pioneer attitude, some of which have diminished or disappeared today. But it is foolish to perpetuate the mythology that those men were rugged individualists seeking new lands to conquer, when in fact they were the foremost beneficiaries of government aid.

Experts Are the Safest Drivers

SHORTLY AFTER I bought my first sports car, I picked up a flock of motoring magazines to learn a little about the strange new world I was timidly entering.

What impressed me first of all, and most of all, was the repeated emphasis on "safety" in all these racing journals. On the track, or on the road, the driver who neglects safety is considered a moron and a menace.

And I wished that more of the young men who tootle around town so carelessly in their hopped-up cars would read what all the great racing drivers and teachers have to say about safety as a primary consideration in driving.

These young men are being killed at the rate of 8400 a year. Auto accidents slaughter more Americans between the ages of sixteen and twenty-five than any other type of accident or disease. Ignorance, arrogance and carelessness are the three horsemen that accompany the fourth horseman of Death in motoring fatalities.

Contrary to popular opinion, if such young men knew more about cars and about racing, they would drive more prudently. It is the pro who knows how vulnerable he is, how thin the line between courage and folly.

Racing experts are unanimous in declaring that they feel safer taking a specially equipped car across the Bonneville flats at 400 miles an hour than in driving an over-powered, under-steered, nose-diving, tail-wobbling stock car down a highway at seventy miles an hour. "I'm scared to death in highway traffic," admits one racing champion, who knows how much there is to be frightened about.

As an interesting sidelight on racing philosophy, another American expert pointed out that "the aim of racing is to win at the slowest possible speed." Ponder this curious sentence for a while, and you will see that it makes great sense.

The racing driver wants to win—but not by much. A nose is as good as a mile, so long as you pass the flag before the others. The experienced driver holds his car down to the *slowest possible speed* that will enable him to win. Anything more would be foolish and perhaps fatal.

Contrast this mature attitude with the driving habits of the young men you see on the highways every day. Their aim is to go as fast, and as recklessly, as possible; to prove that they can beat you at the getaway and pass you on the straight. When you see an idiot of this kind, you may be sure of at least one fact about him—he is not an expert, and he would be ruled off every racing track in the world.

A lady in town tore the decal daisies off her station wagon and replaced them with an American flag decal; she reports that with the daisies on her car she was stopped at least twice a week by police squads; with the flag she hasn't been stopped once in two months.

A Topsy-Turvy Tax System

WHEN I PUT some expensive improvements on my house, my real property tax goes up. If I let my property run down, my tax would be lower. I can't imagine a more inefficient and illogical way to run a community or a government.

Much of what we currently deplore as "urban blight" is the result of this topsy-turvy state of affairs. It encourages speculators, slum owners and absentee landlords. It discourages owners who want to improve their homes or their farms.

The real property tax is based on the market quality of the property. If I buy raw land and do nothing with it, waiting for the price to increase (as it inevitably must in our expanding population), I pay comparatively little in taxes. But the more I put into it, the more I must pay.

Under such an Alice-in-Wonderland system, it is hardly surprising that the nation's urban complexes are filled with blight, sprawl and greedy speculation; and that any program of urban rehabilitation, construction and development is hamstrung from the beginning.

But what if we took the tax off the improvements and put it on the land? Then nobody would be penalized for improving his property and adding to the value of the community; contrariwise, the incentive to speculate in land would be removed, and both the urban slums and the suburban sprawl would no longer pay rich dividends.

Every year our living, working and playing space gets more cramped and more expensive. The population explosion is driving more and more people from little towns into the big cities; and from the heart of the cities to the peripheries, where suburban slums are now springing up.

The whole theory and practice of our real property taxes cuts across the grain of American history and political economics. We grew strong and prosperous by encouraging people to own and cultivate their property, to make improvements, to add to the wealth of the community.

If we took the tax off the improvements—as we take the tax off other activities we want to encourage, such as charitable contributions—then the land-grabber would no longer get rich by sitting on his property until the need for space is so great that the potential buyers are willing to pay almost any price. And the speculator would no longer profit by squeezing the most housing into the smallest space, as so many of those shoddy suburban development firms have been doing.

Today the more a landlord lets a building deteriorate, the less he pays in real estate taxes, even though he may be making unconsciona- ble profits by converting three apartments into 12. And the owner who wants to rehabilitate such a building pays a high premium for restoring the community value. Wouldn't it be exactly the other way around in a well-ordered society?

Fine Police: One Answer to Crime

MOST PEOPLE innocently think that the way to "do something" about crime is by concentrating on the criminals.

This is looking into the spyglass at the wrong end. The only way to cut crime is by concentrating on the police. Police work must be turned from a trade into a profession—with professional standards, profes- sional prestige and professional pay. Any measures short of this will leave American cities wallowing in lawlessness.

As long as political influence can be brought to bear on the police department, the honest and independent policeman will become in- creasingly cynical about promotions.

As long as patrolmen are paid less than many skilled laborers, the force will not attract the caliber of men who are so desperately needed.

As long as the payoff—by restaurants, hotels and parking lots, among others—continues to operate as flagrantly as it does today, our young people cannot help but feel contempt for the forces of law.

These are facts the public refuses to face. The public wants crimi- nals put in jail—but crime *prevention* is the only way to achieve crime *reduction*.

Anyone who has visited England, for instance, knows what a police force ought to be like. The men are well-trained, courteous and proud of their jobs. They respect themselves, and the public respects them.

Crime in England is low not because punishment is severe—the av- erage jail sentence is shorter there than in America—but because it is swift and certain. No delays, no fix, no payoff. The British public would not try to bribe a policeman. And the police, on the other hand, do not bully and badger the public. They recognize that a civil servant is supposed to be civil, as well as to give service.

We are sentimentalists about crime, although we call ourselves realists. We think that tougher judges or longer sentences or stiffer laws will reduce the crime rate—but this is futile daydreaming.

What reduces crime is the knowledge that the police are above influence and avarice; that they are well trained and well paid; that they are recruited from clean-cut applicants eager for the life, and not sadists or misfits who talk and think and act pretty much like the men they are pursuing.

Some American cities have been highly successful in creating and sustaining such a police force. We will not be a civilized nation until every city has done the same.

High Cost of Compromise

SCHOOLCHILDREN WHO ARE TAKEN on visits to Washington generally tour the Library of Congress. There, in a glass cage, they can see a copy of the Declaration of Independence. But this is not a copy of the original Declaration as written by Thomas Jefferson.

The original sheets, which have been seen only by officials and scholars, are kept in a safe, and they contain a clause which was omitted from all later copies. No reference is ever made to it in history classes.

In this clause, Jefferson denounces King George and the British government for acquiescing in slavery and the slave trade. The clause was knocked out by pressure groups from the South, who agreed to accept other parts of the Declaration only if this part were deleted.

Nobody knows, of course, what history "might have been," but it seems reasonable to assume that the whole social pattern of our country would have been different if the clause against the slave trade had remained in the Declaration, putting the new nation on record as favoring its abolition, along with the other civilized nations of the time.

We would have abolished slavery when it was comparatively easy to do so, and the whole tragic and inconclusive episode of the Civil War would have been averted—an episode for which America is still paying a heavy price today.

This is the terrible paradox of politics—that, by its very nature, it is incapable of solving basic political problems. For the essence of politics is compromise, and Jefferson was forced to compromise his ideals and his good sense in order to obtain the requisite signatures on the Declaration.

But political compromise usually defers, rather than resolves. It closes its eyes to the deeper causes of a problem, in order to treat its symptoms—and meanwhile, since the causes go unchecked, the disease breaks out in more virulent form in the future.

The delegates from South Carolina and Georgia, who pressured Jefferson to delete the slavery clause, were also politicians fighting for what they thought were their regional advantages. But slavery actually dragged down the South in the long run, and the Civil War engendered only bitterness and revenge. Slavery deformed the Negro, denigrated the South and dragged its evil consequences into the 20th Century.

All political issues, if they are fundamental, are at bottom moral issues. They cannot be settled at the political level, and certainly not at the military level. Yet we cannot work out our moral problems outside the political process, outside the give-and-take of practical compromise. That is why genuine progress is so slow. As a man, Jefferson knew slavery was wrong; as a politician, he had to condone it. And we pay the price.

What Is True Patriotism?

MOST PEOPLE FAIL TO UNDERSTAND the difference between "patriotism" and "nationalism."

Patriotism is wanting what is best for your country. Nationalism is thinking your country is best, no matter what it does.

Patriotism means asking your country to conform to the highest laws of man's nature, to the eternal standards of justice and equality. Nationalism means supporting your country even when it violates these eternal standards.

Patriotism means going underground if you have to—as the anti-Nazis in Germany did—and working for the overthrow of your government when it becomes evil and inhuman and incapable of reform.

Nationalism means "going along" with a Hitler or a Stalin or any other tyrant who waves the flag, mouths obscene devotion to the Fatherland and meanwhile tramples the rights of people.

Patriotism is a form of faith. Nationalism is a form of superstition, of fanaticism, of idolatry.

Patriotism would like every country to become like ours, in its best aspects. Nationalism despises other countries as incapable of becoming like ours.

Just as we fail to understand the difference between patriotism and nationalism, so many people fail to understand what "Americanism" really consists of.

"Americanism" was something utterly new in the world when it was conceived by our Founding Fathers. It was not just another form of nationalism—indeed, it was a repudiation of all the then existing nationalisms.

It was conceived as a form of government unrestricted to one geographical place or one kind of people. It was open to all men everywhere—no matter where they were born or came from. In this respect, it was utterly unique. Its patriotism was potentially worldwide.

The word "Americanism" must not be narrowed or flattened or coarsened to apply to one flag, one people, one government. In its highest, original sense, it asks that all men become patriots *to an idea,* not to a particular country or government. And this idea is self-government by all men, who are regarded as equals in the law.

This is why American patriotism—properly understood—is the best patriotism in the world, because it is for all the world, and not just for us. To confuse it with nationalism, to use it for ugly purposes, is to betray the dream of those who made it come true.

What Gun Control Can Do

PEOPLE WHO DON'T LIVE in big cities find it hard to understand the need for gun control. I was in Montana last month giving a talk, and during the question period many in the audience were resentful that I have come out for stricter gun laws.

"No laws will stop criminals from getting hold of guns," they keep repeating—and, of course, they are right. Criminals will always get guns, just as addicts will always get narcotics and prostitutes will always get customers.

What they fail to recognize, however—since they live in areas where guns are used largely for killing animals, not people—is that most violence in the city is not committed by criminals. The professional criminals, in fact, shoot only one another; and even the small-time crook is not statistically a great menace with firearms.

I returned from Montana on a Saturday and picked up that night's paper in Chicago. Five separate shootings had been reported—three of them ending in deaths, including one "innocent bystander" to a quarrel. In none of these five separate shootings was a criminal involved.

One youth peppered a police car as he rode past on a bicycle. Two men fought in a tavern; one left, returned with a gun and killed his antagonist and a stranger at the bar. A 17-year-old girl was shot in the face as she sat on her front porch. An altercation between a tenant and his landlord left the landlord in undisputed possession of his property. He shot the tenant through the head.

This is the pattern of gun killings in the big cities. Most homicides are not professional jobs, in felonious pursuits, but are committed by relatives, friends or neighbors, in the home or nearby. They are sparked by liquor, by lust, by jealousy, or greed, or a burning sense of injustice. And most are committed by people with no previous record of violence.

It is these who will be restrained by stricter gun laws, who will find it much harder to go home, pick up a gun and shoot an adversary. The liquor will pass, the lust will die, reflection will replace passion if the instrument of death is not so readily available.

No one suggests that tougher gun control will reduce organized crime, or will inhibit the crooks. But the majority of fatal shootings in a metropolis are more emotional than criminal in intent, more impulsive than premeditated. And if the gun isn't there, the impulse to shoot cannot be so hastily gratified.

"The Most Typical American"

PERHAPS THE MOST IRONIC aspect of the whole racial conflict in America today is the fact that, to most Europeans, our Negro is the "most typical American."

I was having dinner with a group of Europeans not long ago, when the racial subject came up. All of them nodded in agreement when a Swiss gentleman remarked, "You know, we look upon the Negro as embodying most of what we call 'American characteristics.' "

What he meant by this, I found out, was that the very traits we American whites identify with Negroes are called the most distinctively "American traits" by Europeans.

These are—vitality, friendliness, openness, disregard for tradition, impulsiveness, generosity, a tendency toward physical violence, optimism, impatience with philosophy or theory and lack of social polish.

"Every one of these traits, both good and not so good," said the Swiss, "are the ways in which you white Americans characterize your Negro population. And they are precisely the ways in which we Europeans characterize all Americans, black and white alike—only the Negroes seem more representative of what we call 'the American character.' "

White Americans tend to look upon Negroes as "childish"—but Europeans look upon *all* Americans as childish. We fear the violence of the Negro in the slums—but Europeans fear the whole Western-saloon inheritance of violence in America's white culture. We regard the Negro as crude or even primitive—but Europeans see a kind of primitive crudeness as an integral part of the *whole* American scene.

Now the point is not whether the Europeans are "right" or "wrong" in their estimate of our national character; perhaps there is no objective right or wrong in such matters, but only stereotypes conditioned by different cultural patterns and varying canons of taste.

The point *is* that when we blame the Negro for certain characteristics and modes of behavior, it is possible that we are gazing at an exaggerated representation of ourselves—and nobody likes to see himself in a magnifying mirror, with all his pores enlarged a dozen times.

The modern Negro who calls himself a "black" and turns toward his African heritage rather than identifying with his American background is just deluding himself in seeking for such spurious roots of identity—for, in any sociologist's meaning of the word, he is more "American" in his outlook and reactions than most of his detractors, who bear far deeper marks of their foreign ancestry than he does.

Conventional society has as its guiding, if unspoken, maxim the censorious attitude: "If we can't make the unconventional people act like us, the least we can do is make them miserable."

*

We delude ourselves that we want to implant "honesty" in our children; what we really want is to imbue them with our particular kind of dishonesty, with our culture's dishonesty, our class's dishonesty, our cult's dishonesty.

Judgment Isn't Tied to Intelligence

ONE OF THE most serious mistakes we can make is to confuse the thing we call "intelligence" with another thing called "judgment." The two do not always, or necessarily, go together: many persons of high general intelligence have notoriously poor judgment.

One reason I cling tenaciously to the democratic doctrine is that I respect the overall judgment of the people, even though the average intelligence may be relatively low. Let me explain what I mean.

Every psychologist knows that, generally speaking, the larger the group the lower the intelligence level. When you expand a group of one hundred into a thousand, your intelligence curve flattens for the group as a whole. This can be demonstrated without any dispute.

Now, because of this phenomenon, there are those who maintain that democracy in a large society, such as ours, is unworkable and self-defeating. With 180,000,000 people, the average intelligence must be low indeed—and how can we then expect the electorate to rule themselves rationally and wisely?

But such people reckon without the quality known as "judgment," which is not directly related to intelligence as such—a fact that is painfully known to the wives of many intellectual men.

For instance, it has also been proved by extensive psychological tests that *the larger the group, the better the judgment.* If you ask a dozen persons to estimate the weight of a desk telephone, the answers will vary widely, and the median answer is likely to be quite inaccurate.

But, if you ask twenty-four persons, and then forty-eight, and then double that again, by the time you have asked a thousand persons, the excesses on both sides have canceled each other out—and the median answer will be uncannily accurate.

So, while the collective intelligence of a large group is low, the collective judgment of a large group is quite high—and often much better than the individual judgments of the most intelligent persons within the group.

This is the rationale of democracy as a system of governing, apart from any moral or historical or political reasons. The more people who are enabled to judge a matter—provided, of course, that the society gives these people enough information on which to make a judgment—the more valid is this judgment likely to be.

When democracy does not work, or works badly, it is not because the intelligence of the "mass" is low, but because native judgment is impeded by lack of information, or emotional blocks, or the cumbersome machinery of administering a democratic society. It is not a lack in the people themselves.

Choking Our Cities to Death

THE CITIES OF AMERICA are strangling to death in their own traffic. Yet almost all we do is build more highways to take people out of the cities at night and bring them back in the morning.

Has it been wise to build and sell more cars than we can park? In a free economy, I suppose this is a foolish question—as many cars will be supplied as there are people who want them. But, then, shouldn't the people be asked to pay more for glutting the streets with their cars?

During the epic winter snowstorm in Chicago, we saw what a few inches of snow did to the city. Tens of thousands of cars sprawled all over the roads, like huge wounded animals, with no place to go. When the cars were towed off the main arteries, there were not enough garages, parking lots or side street spaces to accommodate them.

The snowstorm only made more dramatic the plight of urban traffic. Even in dry weather, the downtown districts are suffocated by private cars, trucks, buses, taxis—so much so, indeed, that many merchants have moved to shopping centers in outlying suburbs. But the same thing is already beginning to happen there: Valuable and productive space is being transformed into parking lots, which are a dead loss to the economy and a blight on the landscape.

If we want the comfort, convenience and status of private transportation, I suggest we shall soon have to begin to pay a lot more for it. Motorists will have to pay a "use tax" to come into the city—and this tax will go directly toward alleviating the monstrous traffic problem confronting every American city, and many suburbs as well.

We may have to start thinking about a "double city" in the downtown districts. This would be a system of either elevated or underground roads for vehicular traffic only. The surface level would then be free for walking, for arcades and plazas connecting shops and theaters and restaurants. Beauty and comfort, as well as utility, would be served by such a plan.

The inner cities are corroding and dying, despite massive efforts at rehabilitation by the municipalities and a few large corporations. They are dying because it is too hard to get in and out; and it is too hard largely because the automobile has delivered almost a death blow to mass transportation. And soon the suburban centers will suffer the same fate, for auto traffic increases far out of proportion to the facilities for handling it.

As someone has said, the automobile is the greatest convenience among nuisances, and the greatest nuisance among conveniences. Unless we can find a way to diminish its nuisance-value, its convenience will become a Frankenstein's monster, devouring all it overtakes.

What "Police Brutality" Means

WHEN WE READ ACCUSATIONS of "police brutality," we have to understand what the phrase means. Sometimes it means that heads and bodies are hurt; just as often, it means that feelings are hurt. What upsets Negroes, Puerto Ricans, Mexicans and poor people generally is the fact that they are not treated with the same respect (not to say deference) by the police as are the more affluent members of the community.

There is no question that most police in most cities are acutely sensitive to differences in social and economic standing. A middle-class person is rarely talked to the way an obviously poor person is talked to. The former is treated as a decent citizen until it is proved otherwise; the latter is treated as a suspicious character until it is proved otherwise.

It is this double standard of approach and handling that gives rise to accusations of "police brutality," even when the police have committed no overt act of violence. If their attitude is bellicose and bullying, the "suspect" may even provoke a pushing around in order to justify his dislike and grievance against copdom.

To the poor, the police are hated, despised and feared figures— which means that the police get no co-operation from them. Their reaction irritates the police, who then become even more bellicose and bullying, and the circle of mutual distrust is never broken.

What they fail to understand, of course, is that the police themselves are fearful in such neighborhoods. They know they are looked upon as enemies—in contrast to middle-class neighborhoods, which look upon them as protectors—and their fear of reprisal makes them talk and act tough. There is a "psychological feedback" in the police-and-the-poor relationship that perpetuates hostility.

The police, in point of fact, are much less brutal than they were even a decade or two ago; the florid flatfoot who swung his club first and asked questions afterward is fast disappearing from the force. But as against this, poor people are more aware of their rights than they were even a decade or two ago, and they are beginning to demand the same civility that is shown to their more affluent neighbors.

"Police brutality" is largely a semantic question, and its solution is more a matter of psychological attitudes than laws. To treat a man like dirt, without reason, may hurt him more than hitting him—and may, indeed, encourage him to provoke physical violence. It may be another decade before our police wake up to this truth.

What Is a True "Conservative"?

WHAT is the difference between "conservatism" and "reaction"? I suspect that many persons who call themselves "conservatives" are really reactionaries and don't know it.

I was reminded of this by a letter from a suburban lady who wrote that she wonders "if Abe Lincoln had been able as a youngster to lean on such words as 'disadvantaged' and 'underprivileged,' would he have done as well?" She imagines she is expressing a "conservative" position, but it is really a reactionary one. In the first place, the poverty of Abe Lincoln was nothing like the poverty in the modern urban slum. He was underprivileged economically, but not culturally and socially as well.

In second place, we don't know what anguish Lincoln might have avoided in later life if his early years had not been so bleak and hard, or how much more he might have accomplished in his personal life, which was not successful.

In the third place, the assumption that being "disadvantaged" and "underprivileged" somehow builds character and enables us to triumph over adversity is not borne out by the very people who utter this cliché. For they give their own children the best advantages, send them to the finest schools, and use their connections to the utmost.

Now a genuine conservative is one who wants to conserve the best that we have; that is, he does not want us to squander our resources. But the most precious resouces of any country are the brains and talents of the younger generation. It is absolutely essential that they be utilized to the fullest. True conservatism would demand that every child be given the kind of education and environment that would summon up his full capacities. It would be shocked at the thought that millions of youngsters have practically no chance to demonstrate what they could do under optimum conditions, and that millions of others fritter away their advantages.

The reactionary position—which is often confused with conservatism—is indifferent to this squandering of natural resources. It confuses an economic and social elite—which is one mainly by chance and accident—with an elite of character and intelligence. It wants only to keep what it has, and to get more, rather than to spread the opportunities on the widest possible base.

If underprivilege were such a blessing, there would not be only one Lincoln for a million semiliterates and unemployables; if it were so good for the soul, the suburban lady would sell her house and rear her children in the slums. But of course she won't; disadvantages are "good" only for the great, the dead and the very remote.

But John Q. Just Doesn't Care

WHAT THE BULK OF SOCIETY really wants is for unpleasant people to go away and not bother anybody. "Unpleasant people" are the poor, the convicted, the mentally ill, the old and the troublesome young.

So-called poverty programs keep the poor just where they are, barely hanging on and discreetly out of sight. "Urban redevelopment" means putting the poor where out-of-town visitors can't see them.

Our jails and prisons are devoted to keeping unpleasant characters out of circulation as long as possible, providing minimum opportunities for their rehabilitation and then throwing them back into cells as fast as they get out and demonstrate their inability to break the law successfully again.

Our mental hospitals are grossly understaffed, relying on drugs to keep patients tranquil instead of positive therapy to make them well. We will spend millions for new buildings to put these patients in, but. we won't pay enough for doctors, nurses and orderlies to establish a system in which hope, and not despair, is the chief climate.

Our old people are simply a drag. Many have no place to live, no income to live on and little to live for. We scarcely even pretend to be concerned about this social problem, embarrassing though it is.

The troublesome young are told to cut their hair, brush their teeth, keep going to school (no matter how rotten school may be) and face the delightful prospect of being drafted at eighteen.

If they get into real trouble with the law, they are either put on probation and allowed to keep doing the same things until the boom is dropped, or else they are stuck into a "training school" where they are trained to be professional criminals in a short time.

Despite our massive programs, and our appropriations, and our public and private welfare agencies, the plain fact of the matter is that the average American doesn't give a damn about anyone outside the mainstream of our society—and everybody outside the mainstream knows it. So do the few dedicated people who work with them.

If we really cared, would we tolerate our Congress spending billions and billions for highways (with no relief of traffic congestion), and a mere dribble for decent, human-scale housing? Or a fifth of our national budget to put a man on the moon (mainly for reasons of pride), while our whole school system is falling apart?

We ought to stop congratulating ourselves on our Gross National Product, and start reflecting on our gross attitudes toward the disinherited, the feeble, the troubled and the torn. They won't go away, and we can't build stockades big enough to hold them all.

"Outside Agitator" Hogwash

IT HAS LONG PUZZLED ME why authorities seem to feel that a bad situation can be made to look better by blaming it on "outside agitators." What does it really matter where the agitation comes from?

In most cases, of course, the allegation isn't true. When a demonstration erupts, or a riot explodes, it's usually because the pressure has burst from the inside, and no safety valve has been provided.

Agitators can agitate successfully only when the community supplies no realistic alternatives. Communists have been agitating in the United States for 50 years, and have not succeeded in recruiting as much as one per cent of the population into party ranks.

Indeed, one of the great testimonials to the loyalty and basic trust of the American Negro was the fact that he—who might have been thought to have the least to lose and the most to gain—never succumbed to communist enticements even during the darkest days of the Depression. Here was a pure "proletariat," and it did not respond.

It was not until the Negro realized that America's promises outran its performance that he changed his name to black, and took on an air of militancy. And, even here, the Marxist influence is negligible.

When the blacks, or the students, or any other group, begin to engage in civil disobedience, the first reaction of the authorities is to blame those "outside agitators." The implication being that without such inflammatory aliens, the natives would be happy and passive.

Obviously, that is a lot of hogwash. If strangers can come into a community and incite the residents to social action, all this means is that the fuse was there waiting to be lit. In fact, it is a bigger insult to the authorities that outsiders have a more decisive influence on their people than they do.

If I were a mayor or a governor, I would be ashamed to admit that a few bedraggled orators were able to lead my constituency into militant opposition; it would imply that I had done a rotten job of tending to their needs, responding to their complaints and assuring their rights.

A good and decent administration would inoculate its people against such agitators—not by banning or jailing them but by making sure that grievances are promptly and justly taken care of, that lines of communication are open, that the instruments of law are equally available to all segments, not used by one group against the other. When peaceful alternatives are available, nobody but a nut will listen to the voices of violence.

Pro Sport Is Mercenary Combat

PROFESSIONAL SPORTS don't interest me, because I think that the phrase is a contradiction in terms. An activity ceases to be a sport the moment it becomes professional.

Some months ago, I noted big black headlines on the sports pages, announcing the trading of a star football player from one team to another. The fans were shocked, but the coach said simply, "It's a cruel, hard business. But I have a job to do and I can't let sentiment enter into it."

It's a cruel, hard business. So is every professional sport—baseball and basketball and hockey and golf and tennis. It's mean and mercenary and basically dehumanized—when the whole idea of "sport" should be its humanity.

Recreation was devised so that men could find release from the grim business of making a living; so that they could glory in winning a contest *for its own sake*. The Olympic heroes of ancient Greece were crowned with laurel and given the highest honors of the state because they showed what men could do with no incentive but victory.

Take sentiment out of sports and you take away their reason for existence. Remove sentiment and you have cut the loyalty that clings to a losing team; and little is left but to raise the money that can buy a winning team.

It is good and necessary that men should work for a living. It is a monstrous perversion that men should play for a living. The whole purpose of play is to escape to a realm beyond necessity, to a glorious never-never land, where the skillful and the fleet and the courageous can find a happy ending that is too often denied them in the cold marketplace.

In true sports, the contestants are ranged against each other. In professional sports, they are all ranged against the public. The ultimate object is to attract as many customers as possible. They are merchandisers and promoters and box-office accountants. And the basic loyalty is not to the city, the uniform, the team—even to the game—but to the contract. Their lawyers compete as ferociously as their coaches do.

Let us not pretend that what we have here is "sport." What we have is business, transferred from the counter to the stadium, with a deadly seriousness that has nothing to do with the pleasure men are supposed to take in their bodily prowess. This is not to say the players do not enjoy playing, or the spectators do not enjoy watching; but their enjoyment has lost the innocence it has for children—which means it has lost precisely the healing and redeeming quality that makes it good.

As the coach said, "It's a cruel, hard business." Sport began as a substitute for war, as a cleansing agent for the spirit of aggressiveness; it has turned into combat between mercenaries with a job to do.

To those who have lived by routine all their lives, leisure is far more menacing than work; it is frightening to have to plan one's own time creatively after decades of having time laid out on a rigid pattern; and many men die soon after retirement not because they have lost their work but because they have never found themselves.

*

How can two countries empathize with each other, when in one most of the adults are starving, and in the other most of the adults are reducing?

Struggle Is Fine—in Moderation

ANYONE WHO KNOWS the least bit about propaganda and persuasion is aware that a half-truth is more dangerous than a lie; a lie can always be exposed, but a half-truth can be manipulated so that its obverse side remains concealed to the spectator.

In a recent issue of the little magazine *Quote*, I ran across a perfect example in the statement by B. C. Forbes: *"Strength comes from struggle; weakness from ease."* There is just enough truth in it to make it a deceptive generalization.

Nobody would deny that a *certain amount* of struggle is necessary for the development of strength; but too much can be as bad as too little. Struggle may strengthen us, but if the odds are too uneven, it may also overwhelm or cripple us.

And, likewise, nobody would deny that *too much ease* makes for weakness; without some challenge, we sink into torpidity and softness. But it is worth remembering that only those civilizations where the people had a broad margin of ease contributed a culture and a technology. Countries where everyone struggles all the time remain brutal and backward in the arts, the amenities, the very flowers of what we are pleased to call "civilization."

The most productive societies manage to achieve a *creative tension* between struggle and ease: enough competition to keep us on our toes, but not so much as to force us to our knees.

Men who have had to struggle ferociously from an early age acquire weaknesses as well as strengths; they tend to become harsh, rigid, contemptuous of any values but conflict and victory, and incapable of adjusting to changing times and conditions. Since such men tend to rise to the top, they generally lead their countries into inappropriate combat, like a Napoleon or a Hitler.

Everyone is aware of the perils of too much ease, but it is not as clear at first that struggle itself can be damaging if the handicap is so great that a man must sacrifice a large part of his personality in order to make King of the Hill. This is why so many public "successes" are private failures.

One of the main objects of struggle is to attain relative ease, so that other and higher values may be aimed at; but when struggle is too relentless, it becomes an end in itself, overwhelming and obliterating the cooperative aspects of living together.

A Keats or a Mozart died tragically young from struggling against insuperable odds; a society which would have made it a little easier for them to give us more of their genius ought to be our object.

The Profit System's Excesses

HOW CAN CAPITAL PREACH incessantly that profit is the main driving force of society, and then expect labor to act otherwise? It seems to me that capitalism has been hoist with its own petard, philosophically and practically.

Workmen don't care about the quality of their work. Laborers goof off from their jobs. All they care about is getting more for doing less. The ultimate survivability of the company doesn't interest them.

These are all charges made by capital against labor, and they are in large part true. But why are they true? What has happened to the "old virtues" of reliability, loyalty, craftsmanship, scrupulosity?

What has happened is that the workmen have been thoroughly indoctrinated with the philosophy of profit above all, profit here and now, and damn the consequences. They are just practicing what has been preached to them from the other side of the hall.

Capitalism is an economic system that works well within carefully defined limits. It is not a social system. It is not a philosophy of life. It is not a gospel. It is simply an arrangement of working, owning and producing; and like any other human arrangement, it has its own built-in flaws that must continually be corrected and rectified.

But if you convince people that profit, that the desire to get more and have more, takes precedence over any other set of motivations—and if you elevate this to a principle of life, not just an economic doctrine—then it is hard to blame them for acting on that principle.

If getting the most you can is what counts, labor will try to get the most it can. If buying low and selling dear is the first axiom of capital, then pulling down the highest wages for the smallest expenditure of effort becomes the first axiom of labor.

It is ironic that most American businessmen are much closer to Marx than they know. Marxism is a purely materialistic philosophy, holding that economic considerations dominate human history. If capitalists agree with this view (as most of them seem to), then they have capitulated to a doctrine that will ultimately destroy them.

Our nation was founded on the belief that man is a social and moral creature, and not just the victim of his appetites; on the belief that justice and honor and fidelity and the common welfare are more important than gain. When the profit motive becomes the mainspring of our society, it signals an ideological triumph for Marx, even though it goes by the name of capitalism.

Goal of Age: the Older, the Better

WE OLDER FOLK like to prate a lot about the "duties" and "responsibilities" of young people, but have we ever thought of the obligation that is entailed upon us by growing older?

I don't mean the financial and social and family obligations, which we all accept and understand, but the obligation to become more appealing on the inside as we become less attractive on the outside.

An older person who gets all dried up and brittle and wrinkled and full of complaints is just a total drag, no matter how rich or influential he may be. Most people allow age to do awful things to them.

It seems to me that growing older imposes a duty upon us to get more like a peach on the inside as we get more like a prune on the outside; otherwise, what's the point of it all?

We have to get cuter and funnier and mellower and more tolerant and more perceptive and wiser, simply to compensate for the external ravages of the aging process. Instead, most older people allow themselves to become more rigid, more disapproving, more psychically constipated, more narrowly opinionated and more querulously self-centered as they pass from childhood to senescence without ever having arrived at maturity.

Actually, young people have a natural love and affinity for oldsters who have maintained the spirit of youth within themselves; what they reject and resent are old people who have forgotten what it was to be young, who have discarded their earlier stages of life instead of incorporating them into the total personality at some deep and permanent level.

Our desperate quest for youth must be turned inside out; an older person who tries to look and act and dress like a junior is simply an object of fun or pity. Youth is an emanation from the inside, not a cosmetic application, and it is the inner spirit of the person that youngsters respond to, not the surface appearance.

Old people who feel alienated from the young tend to blame the "changing times," when in reality it is their own inability or unwillingness to deepen their perceptions and broaden their sympathies. Most of us get worse as we get older, when we should get better—we settle into our individual deformations, instead of emerging from the hard shell of self to meet the new world at least halfway.

There is no more delightful person in the world than an octogenarian who is both childlike and wise, spirited and supportive, more willing to learn than he is quick to advise. Socrates began taking dancing lessons at seventy; most of us just take dying lessons.

Lawlessness Seeps Down from the Top

WHAT IS LAWLESSNESS?

Is it a fourteen-year-old Negro boy stealing a radio through a smashed store window during a riot?

Is it college students marching around a public building to protest the Vietnam war, or blocking a doorway and forcing the police to carry them away?

Is it high public officials in a town on Long Island rezoning land, rigging prices and making illicit fortunes out of crooked real estate deals?

Is it policemen in Chicago stealing and hiding a truckload of tires for resale later, or other policemen in the same city shaking down a poor motorist for $500 because he was driving with a revoked license?

Is it three of the largest pharmaceutical firms in the United States being prosecuted for conspiring to inflate the price of a certain medical drug a thousandfold beyond its cost?

All of these are "lawlessness"—in one way or another, to one degree or another. And does one kind excuse any other kinds? No, of course not.

But—and this is a most important but—one kind *leads* to the other kinds, one kind seems to make the other kinds, if not permissible, at least excusable and understandable.

It is immorality and illegality at the *top levels* of society that filter down their dubious ethic and set the tone for attitude and action in the lower strata of society. It has always been this way, and always will be. What the king does—whoever the king may be—gives the commoners their cue for conduct, both privately and publicly.

When elected officials are flagrantly crooked, when police are venal or responsive to political pressures, when large corporations grossly violate laws against conspiracy or price-fixing, then the general public turns sour and cynical and opportunistic and amoral.

When the worst people seem able to hire the best lawyers, when the voice of the medical profession seems to care more about doctors than patients, when power and profit and prestige (none of them bad in itself) seem to be the *ruling criteria* of worth in a society—then why take it all out on the looters, the demonstrators, the protesters, the frustrated, fearful, angry people who get a shafting whichever way they turn?

Lawlessness? It sinks down from the top, it doesn't seep up from the bottom. Like children, people imitate what they look up to.

We Cheat Our Craftsmen Socially

THE WEEKLY DIGEST *Quote* recently reprinted a paragraph by Hubbard Cobb, editor of *The American Home*. Cobb pointed out that not everyone can become a successful nuclear physicist or surgeon or businessman, and went on to say:

"The individual who can work with his hands is just as important to our society as the individual who works with his mind. A pair of skilled hands is more valuable to society than the output of a second-rate mind."

I couldn't agree more, but I would like to have seen how Cobb pursued this line of thought. Because it seems to me that our society may pay lip service to the skilled craftsman, but at the same time denies him any true social status—and this is why he is a vanishing species.

A good barber, for instance, is a necessary and noble creature; yet not one American barber in a hundred knows his business, and the only satisfactory ones I have found were European in origin. American boys don't want to go into barbering, because it lacks a certain social *cachet* we deem more important than pride of craftsmanship.

Good cooks are in desperately short supply in American restaurants, for the same reason. With the highest standard of living in the world, we have the most abominable cuisine, even in the biggest cities.

Nobody here wants to be a chef, just as nobody wants to be a barber. A truly skilled carpenter is increasingly hard to find, and a mason nearly impossible. Roofers can't recruit trainable employees, and any homeowner who has had spout-and-gutter trouble knows how deplorably low the standard of craftsmanship is in this important area.

The cult of the white-collar has been a self-defeating one—for now that our affluent society can afford the best, we lack the people to provide it for us, or to service it after we get it. Because we look down on manual work, our tailors clothe us poorly, our cooks feed us vilely, our barbers crop us barbarously, our shoe-repairers are a dying breed and our appliance-fixers are futile when they are not fraudulent. (I know a man with a $7,000 new car who took it to the garage four times to be "fixed" for the same thing.)

Giving such people more money is not the answer, for a good chef nowadays can command a salary many a junior executive would envy. It is mainly a matter of social values, of recognizing that a man who can elegantly dovetail the drawers of a cabinet may be a higher specimen than a second-rate signer of papers sitting at a mahogany desk. Computers may soon replace many people who work with their minds; but nothing yet can replace that finest physical tool of all, the human hand.

Try These Questions on Friends

ASK THE NEXT PERSON you meet who uses the word "democracy" or "freedom" to tell you what the Bill of Rights is, and to enumerate those rights.

Ask the next person you meet who uses the word "religion" to name the Ten Commandments, in any order.

Ask the next person you meet who uses the phrase "inferiority complex" to tell you who coined it (almost everyone will say "Freud," wrongly), and what the word "complex" meant to the originator.

Ask the next person you meet who uses the phrase "abstract art" how art can be anything but abstract (it can't.)

Ask the next person you meet who uses the phrase "international law" to define the word "law" (if he does correctly, it won't fit together with "international").

Ask the next person you meet who uses the word "race" to name the races of the world and their distinguishing characteristics.

Ask the next person you meet who uses the word "intelligence" how intelligence can be measured, except crudely and by preconceived ideas of what intelligence is.

Ask the next person you meet who uses the word "science" whether science can ever explain the *causes* of anything.

Ask the next person you meet who uses the word "progress" how you can know you are going in the right direction.

Ask the next person you meet who uses the word "individualism" to explain the difference between order and anarchy.

Ask the next person you meet who uses the word "inevitable" to explain the difference between determinism and free will.

Ask the next person you meet who uses the phrase "it's all a matter of taste" whether he thinks it's better to have a taste for strawberries than for shrunken human heads. And why.

Ask the next person you meet who uses the word "logical" to tell you how to detect an undistributed middle term in a logical discussion.

Ask the next person you meet who uses the word "instinct" to define the difference between "instincts" in ants and in men.

Ask any of these questions and by the end of the week you will have no friends left. You won't know much more, either—except, possibly, why Socrates was given poison by the people of Athens for asking so many uncomfortable questions about things the people thought they "knew."

Open Letter to a Certain Boy Driver

THIS IS AN OPEN LETTER to a boy, about eighteen, who forced me off the road while cutting in sharply and passing me on a hill yesterday afternoon:

Dear Son: You may think you are a good driver, and perhaps you are. But I'd like you to keep in mind that most of your "skillful" driving is due to other motorists.

Anybody can whip along the road as fast and as carelessly as you were going. There's no trick to that—the new cars are loaded with power and pickup—too much so, I'm afraid.

Just remember that it was *my* alertness that prevented an accident on the hill, not yours. And the driver who was approaching us also had to brake suddenly and swerve in order to save your life and his.

It is not your courage or dexterity that has kept you alive as long as this, but the prudence and politeness of other motorists. You have been trading on our good will and sense of self-preservation.

I wish it were possible to point out to you that your kind of driving is nothing but bad manners—it is not heroic, or adventurous, or manly.

Suppose you ran down a crowded street, pushing people out of your way, knocking packages out of ladies' hands and kicking children into the gutter. What would be so heroic or manly about that?

Nothing, of course. Then why do you suppose that having two thousand pounds of steel under you makes it any better? There's nothing to be proud of in driving fast—any fool can do that. It's a form of cowardice to threaten other drivers, not courage.

Suppose you beat me at the getaway, or up the hill? What does that prove? Nothing, except that the car you *bought* is faster. You didn't make it; it's a commercial product. Anybody can buy one like it—and anybody can drive with a maniacal disregard for safety.

So don't take any pride in your deadly accomplishment. A *real* man is considerate and polite—and takes chances only when it counts, when his honor and conscience call out for it. On the highway, most of all, it's easy to tell the men from the boys—for the men have to save the boys from the consequences of their foolish and needless bravado.

Three Factors Really Deter Crime

THE PEOPLE WHO would increase punishment for crimes are not stupid; they are just innocent of any historical sense. For the whole history of mankind has shown that severity of punishment does not reduce or deter crime.

Punishment has become less severe over the centuries not because we are more humane or sentimental than past generations, but because hard experience has shown that punishment in itself is futile.

Men used to be subjected to the most horrible tortures and deprivations for even the pettiest of crimes; but the crime rate did not decrease with this treatment. When pickpockets were publicly hanged on Tyburn Hill in England, other pickpockets used to circulate among the crowd during the executions.

There are only three things that really deter crime—the *swiftness* of punishment, the *sureness* of punishment and the *justice* of punishment. It has nothing to do with the length of confinement (which merely brutalizes men), or with the privileges that are given or denied in prison.

If we are not able to work out any rational and effective preventive program for crime, it is our obligation to see that our penological system is sensible and workable.

The crime rate is embarrassingly high in the United States because punishment is slow, it is anything but sure and it has only the vaguest relationship to justice.

The length of sentences depends upon the criminal's wealth and type of legal help more than upon the seriousness of his transgression. Court procedures are slow and cumbersome. It is the poor and stupid criminal who gets the heaviest sentence—so the aim of criminals is to become rich and cunning, and thus avoid the harshest penalties.

It may surprise people who point to England's low crime rate to know that the average prison sentence there is shorter than in the United States. But the English system of justice is swift and sure— money and politics do not intervene between the prisoner at the bar and the judge on the bench.

Meting out heavier sentences is fanatically idiotic (and cripples the reformative powers of prison), as long as the lawbreaker knows that skillful legal talent and the right connections can long postpone or easily ameliorate his punishment. There is not a penologist or a prison warden in the country who is not painfully aware of this contradiction.

When we demand greater punishment for lawbreakers, we are really confessing our inability to cope realistically with the corruption of justice in our amoral society.

Tollway Tremors Have Got Sydney

AS A MOTORIST, I appreciate the speed and safety of those new expressways, tollways, throughways, and freeways that are unwinding all over the American landscape these days.

But, as a middle-aged man whose eye and brain are not as quick on the reflex as his foot is on the pedal, I find myself getting befuddled and panicky on these supermonster roads. I am suffering from a new mid-twentieth century disease called "Tollway Tremors."

The other evening, for instance, I drove out to a distant suburb to make a speech and almost wound up near the Grand Canyon. As I approached the juncture of a new tollway and an older superhighway from my expressway, I saw dozens of grinning green signs beckoning me into as many diverse lanes.

I felt for a moment as if I were being sucked up by some man-eating plant. "Rockford," beckoned one sign; "Aurora," said another. A third invited me to visit Toledo. And yet another winked me seductively up to Milwaukee.

Along with these were another dozen signs, wholesaling travel information incredibly faster than I could absorb it at sixty miles an hour—and I couldn't slow down or I would surely be rammed from the rear.

"Make Two Right Turns To Go Left," said one. "Take Right Lane Into Cloverleaf to East-West Tollway," proclaimed another. "Toll Booth 1 Mile Ahead," warned a third. There were arrows, branching lines, dividing barriers and at least four vertical layers of traffic intertwining like some fantastic vehicular maypole dance.

Not long ago, I made a premature turning on Chicago's Calumet Skyway—or was it Tollway, Throughway or Expressway?—and found myself in Gary when I really meant to be forty miles west of it. Sartre's ominous play *No Exit* has a nightmarish application to modern traffic—once you're on the high road there is no getting off for twenty-two long, bitter, frustrating miles.

No doubt as I become more used to it all I'll be able to fight off the mounting sense of panic as I am swiftly confronted with a dozen choices all at once. But right now Tollway Tremors has me in its grip, and if the speaker of the evening is late for your next club meeting, I just want you to know why. He's cruising down U.S. 264, near Cape Hatteras.

Suburbanite Sealed Off from Reality

"I'M LIVING LIKE a country squire," said the man who had just bought a large house with extensive grounds in an exclusive suburb. "This is the way the gentry used to live."

He is deluding himself. He is living in exactly the opposite way. The old-time gentry saw almost nobody but the "lower classes." This man sees almost nobody but his own class. All his close neighbors are similar to him, in background, station and convictions. He belongs to a country club of his peers, and spends his days shuttling between his office, his club in town and his club in the suburbs. He is effectively sealed off from reality.

The real gentry, in the nineteenth century and before, lived in country houses with no peers around them for many miles. Except for occasional parties or hunts, their daily lives were spent among the common people of their districts.

They mingled with the farmers, the craftsmen, the laborers, the shopkeepers. They understood the problems of these people, their feelings, their frustrations, their special funds of sense and nonsense both.

In a way, our modern society is much more stratified than during the "aristocratic" periods of life. The rich man is almost totally divorced from the actual making of things and the growing of things; and, conversely, the poor man feels no bond of any kind connecting him with his "superiors."

Democracy, in a way, is less democratic than feudalism. Social intercourse between the classes is limited to the service trades; there is little reciprocal understanding of problems, and therefore little sympathy for them. Organized "charity" is a poor substitute for personal charity.

Of course the feudal system had grave drawbacks; and democracy, as Aristotle said, is at any rate the *least bad* of all possible systems. But let us not delude ourselves that we do not live in a sharply defined class structure. It is less formalized than before, but just as real.

It is this artificial separation of classes (which is not so prevalent in an agrarian society) that provides the entering wedge for Marxism. Isolation always perverts; when a man lives only among his own sort, he soon begins to believe that his sort are the best sort. This attitude breeds both the arrogance of the conservative and the bitterness of the radical. The country squire and the suburban executive are worlds apart—as the squire and the hostler were not.

Time Is Relative to All Our Affairs

EVERY NEW ROLE in life requires a new sense of timing, and I feel sorriest for those persons who cannot easily make such adjustments. For "time" is not only relative in the Einsteinian sense, it is relative to all the ordinary affairs of mankind.

I was thinking of this Sunday afternoon, when I was babysitting for a few hours. The children wanted to go out and play in the snow, so I dressed them—sweaters, leggings, overshoes, hooded jackets, scarves and mittens.

It took me nearly a half hour to complete this arduous process—and in ten minutes they were back in the house again, complaining of the cold. The whole process then had to be reversed.

Contrariwise, the day before I took them out sledding in the park for "a half hour" after lunch. I stood on the hill an hour and a half, trembling with cold, while they tumbled in the snow. I practically had to lasso them to their sleds to get them home again.

"Time" with children is very different from time without them. Unless we understand this, and make allowances for it, we will either go crazy or drive the children crazy. They live only in the present; past and future mean nothing to them.

And marriage, generally, requires an exquisite sense of timing. As a single person, time is relative to one's needs and demands; as a married partner, time is a joint venture—the husband may be an hour late getting home, while dinner grows cold; the wife may be an hour late dressing for a party, while her mate grows hot under the collar.

Time does not belong to us alone; we share it with those we love, those we work for, those we play with. It is an elastic concept: we must, as we grow older, be willing to be bored for someone else's sake. And it can be as fatal to be stingy with our time as with our money.

I have often seen mothers pulling their small children along downtown streets, while shopping. But nobody should take a child shopping unless she is prepared to be generous with time. A child has no sense of urgency, and to pull him along hectically is merely to make him stubborn, anxious and resentful. In such cases, the mother is more childish than the child.

Each area of human activity has its own special tempo. This tempo must be respected, if any harmony is desired. You can't play the "Minute Waltz" in thirty seconds and still have it sound like Chopin—but most of us keep trying.

Take away grievances from some people and you remove their reasons for living; most of us are nourished by hope, but a considerable minority get psychic nutrition from their resentments, and would waste away purposelessly without them.

*

Basically, all ideologies aside, there are only two kinds of states: those in which the police are an arm of the government, and those in which the government is an arm of the police.

When Death Could Be the Lesser Evil

LAST NIGHT I MET a young man who has just spent two years of his life lying flat on his back in a hospital bed following an automobile smashup that miraculously turned out to be non-fatal for him.

"You know, I had a lot of time to think," he said, "and I believe that our whole emotional approach to auto accidents is wrong. The National Safety Council, and the other agencies, are emphasizing death too much."

"Why do you think this is wrong?" I asked.

"For three reasons," he said. "First, nobody really believes he is going to die. Death is something that happens to other people. Even when I was a split-second away from the truck I crashed into, I thought to myself, 'Nothing can really happen to me.'

"Secondly," he continued, "many people are fatalistic about death. They step into a car with the attitude, 'If my number is up, then it's up.'

"And thirdly, there are some motorists who are self-destructive and don't know it. They actually have a yearning for suicide, which they disguise from themselves by driving fast and recklessly.

"For these three reasons," he pointed out, "the safety appeals that are based on the desire to live, and the fear of death, are pretty ineffectual. It's time we tried something else, and I think I know what it is."

"And what is it?" I prompted.

"The fear of being disabled," he said. "The fear of being crippled or blinded for life. Safety propaganda should point out to motorists that they might not be 'lucky' enough to die right away.

"The chances are greater that they will be permanently crippled, and become a burden to their families or to the state. They may be condemned to a living death, which most people find more repugnant to think about than the swift oblivion of actual death.

"Dying is a concept we avoid thinking about, because it is so immense and mysterious. It is almost an abstraction. But a broken back, or twisted insides, or amputated limbs—these we can understand and reject with a shudder.

"Nobody wants to be helpless and utterly dependent, withering away in a hospital ward.

"I thought about this a long time after my accident," he stood up and grasped his cane, "when I felt I would never walk again. Why don't the safety posters tell us that death can be a lesser evil?"

Why Should a Killer Show Remorse?

"THE KILLER showed no remorse."

In how many newspaper stories have we seen this sentence, or its equivalent? We are expected to be surprised that the perpetrator of a brutal crime is not immediately overcome with shame and repentance.

But in the modern age, in our society, the shame lies in being caught, in going to jail, in failing. Most criminals regret they were caught, and resolve—not to get caught again.

The emotion of remorse belongs to the conscience; and conscience is not an automatic mechanism within the human mind. It must be built in, carefully and patiently, during the early years.

We live in a success-oriented society. Our criterion is "getting away with it," and we respect the man who gets away with it, if his loot is large enough. We despise petty criminals not so much because they are criminals but because they are petty.

Children grow up not listening to what we say, but watching what we do. Their conscience is shaped by our conduct.

If they see that the law can be twisted out of shape by those with the right connections and the power to do so, then they want connections and power.

Why does the automobile mean so much to boys as young as 14 and 15? Because it means so much to their fathers. Because it has become a deep emotional symbol of status and influence and independence. This is why, by far, most car thefts are committed by boys too young to vote.

Why are the most abominable sex crimes perpetrated by youngsters who in our fathers' time would do no more than wreck a fence on Halloween?

Because sex, along with success, has become a mainspring of our social order; because most of the material goods advertised in American life are keyed to the seductive lips, the searing bosom and the shapely leg.

It is not enough to blame "the parents" for the delinquencies of their children. The parents, too, are victims of our insensate drive for profit and pleasure as final goals in themselves.

In a real sense, all of us are "the parents" of all young children—because we help shape the culture and determine its values.

Young people learn from everyone around them; family influence has declined as technology brings more things into the home and takes the children more easily out of the home. They are exposed to a hundred influences unknown or unobtainable a few generations ago. They are exposed to everything except that old-fashioned notion of "conscience."

So why should the killer show remorse?

Don't Judge a Book by Its Uses

THE OTHER EVENING I heard a man arguing that a certain book should be suppressed because it contained material that could be "dangerous" and "harmful" if it fell into the wrong hands.

His attitude—so common and so wrongheaded—reminded me of what Jacques Maritain, the great Catholic scholar, had to say on the same subject: "If books were judged by the bad uses man can put them to, what book has been more misused than the Bible?"

In the 1,500 years since it was codified and made canonical, the Bible has been used by innumerable sects and rulers to justify (and indeed to exalt) the burning of witches, the torture of heretics, the practice of slavery, the extermination of peoples, the subordination of women, the custom of polygamy and scores of cruelties, barbarities and bigotries of the most odious nature.

Almost anybody can use almost any book for almost any purpose. I have been recently going through a collection of Nietzsche's works. All most people know about him was that he apostrophized the "superman" and that the Nazi movement seemed to take much of its philosophical impulse from Nietzsche's writings.

But a careful reading of his work shows quite the contrary. He was violently anti-German, and considered himself a "good European." Some of his finest passages indict nationalism and war; he opposed anti-Semites as vulgar and brutish. His "superman" was the diametrical opposite of Hitler's "Blond Beast." And he anticipated many of Freud's deepest insights into the irrational character of prejudice and hate.

Our own founding fathers provide a similar example. We can find in the speeches of Washington and Jefferson and Madison and Franklin enough to provide us with ammunition for nearly any cause. I could easily compile a selection of Jefferson that would make him sound like a revolutionary Marxist; and a selection of Franklin that would make him sound like a pacifist and a toady to King George.

To repress a book because it contains "dangerous" or "harmful" material would be to extirpate 90 per cent of the world's great literature—for the greater a work of art is, the more universal, the more embracing, the more it can be misused for every perverted cause.

The only book that cannot be dangerous or harmful is the bland book, the meaningless book, the insipid and characterless book that discourages thought, feeling and reaction. And it is such books that proliferate when controversial works are suppressed; censorship, whether in Russia or America, always leads to the tyranny of the commonplace.

Whose Face Is That in the Mirror?

THE SENSELESS MURDER of the President was a mirror we were forced to hold up to ourselves—and we did not like, or believe, the image that we saw.

"How could it happen here? In this day and age? In our country? I thought such things happened only in history. In Europe. Somewhere else and long ago."

These were the reactions of Americans. They bespoke a tremendous ignorance and delusiveness about ourselves. For, as I have written many times in the past (and have been assailed for so writing), we are a violent people who do not know the range and force of our primitive feelings.

Why should it not happen here? The last three Presidents out of four have had assassination attempts on their lives. Nowhere in Europe is this true; in most such countries, the chiefs of state walk about virtually unguarded.

In this day and age? This is the age of the most ferocious war the world has ever known, the most bloody dictatorships, the gas ovens, the concentration camps, the bombings of Hiroshima and Nagasaki by a "peace-loving" nation.

In our country? Why not, with our staggering homicide rate, our casual and callous auto fatalities, our shocking prevalence of firearms, our frontier relish for combat and conflict, our contempt for courts, our cynicism about the effectiveness of orderly processes.

If anyone still doubts this, consider the cry of applause that went up from the crowd gathered outside the Dallas jail when it learned that the presumed assassin of the President had himself been shot down.

This reaction is, to me, more appalling and more revealing than anything else in the whole nightmare of the weekend. Here was a man not known for sure to be the killer. He had not confessed, not been brought to trial, not defended, not sentenced. And he was killed while in the very hands of the police.

And the crowd outside shouted its approval of this bestial, stupid and irrational act. This is frightening, this is disgusting, this discloses the profound failure of our society to instill in its citizens any real sense of civilization, any idea of the meaning of law and justice. This is what turns our country into little better than a jungle.

If this dreadful murder of a President makes us see ourselves more clearly, makes us re-examine our feelings, makes us determined to purge the violence within each of us and all of us, it will not have been in vain.

Radical Righters Are Fascists

IT'S AN INTERESTING peculiarity of our social order that while the term "communist" is flung around frequently and often carelessly, its opposite number, "fascist," is hardly used at all.

In Europe, this is not the case. People have no hesitancy in speaking of the right-wing radicals as "fascists," for this in what they are. To speak of them as "extreme conservatives" is a foolish contradiction in terms.

And it seems quite plain to me that there are many more fascists and fascist sympathizers in the United States than there are communists and their sympathizers—unless, of course, you care to adopt the fascist line and suggest that everyone who favors staying in the UN and retaining Social Security is a Red fellow-traveler.

We seem to be so exercised about communist influence in this country, which is negligible, both in numbers and in appeal to the American temper. Yet, year by year, one sees a fascist spirit rising among the people, although it is called by many other and softer names, and has even achieved a certain dubious respectability in some circles.

There is no reason why there shouldn't be a fascist movement in this country; nearly every nation has one. But it should be called by its right name, and it should be willing to accept the consequences of its position, as the fascist parties do elsewhere.

It has no business masquerading as "Americanism" or "conservatism" or "patriotism," when its whole philosophy of man is based on a hate-filled exclusiveness that would shock and affront the conservative American patriots who founded this country.

What is distressing about this movement is the tacit or open support given it by men who genuinely think of themselves as "conservatives," and who do not understand the implications of right-wing radicalism any more than the German industrialists understood what would happen to them when Hitler swept into power with their support.

Just as communism always begins with an appeal to "humanity" and "equality" and ends with inhuman despotism, so does fascism always begin with an appeal to "nationalism" and "individualism," and ends with a military collectivism far worse than the disease it purports to cure.

These twin evils are the mirror-image of one another. It would be the supreme irony if, in rejecting the blandishments of communism, we fell hysterically into the arms of fascism disguised (as always) as Defender of the Faith.

Who Oversees the Overseers?

THE COMMONWEALTH enforces morality on its citizens—but who enforces morality on the commonwealth?

We are punished, as individuals, if we lie, steal, use violence or kill—but what effective restraints prevent the commonwealth from doing the same?

What is murder for a citizen in peacetime is bravery and glory in wartime. What is theft for an individual is conquest for a nation. What is lying for a person is diplomacy in foreign relations.

There is a common morality among citizens of a community; but there is no common morality among nations. Nations are above the law; they make their own laws, and break them at will—if it serves the "national purpose," if it is for "self-defense." And every war is, of course, for self-defense.

When our children look at the behavior of nations, throughout history and up to the present day, what can we tell them about their own morality? How can something be "wrong" if an individual does it, and "right" if an institution does it? Especially since institutions are supposed to exist for the benefit of individuals, and not the other way around.

Who has custody of the custodians? This ancient Roman question has not even yet begun to be answered. The commonwealth is the custodian of our conduct, but its own conduct is often at shocking variance with what it prescribes for us.

This is perhaps less true in a democracy than in a totalitarian society—but who would say that the American people decide where we are going, what we are doing and how we are doing it? If we plunge into war, will the American citizenry have any more to say about it than the Russian citizenry? Do we have the information, the time, the resources at our disposal, to make such an irreversible decision?

The world has grown too big and too small at the same time: too big in its complexity, and too small in its dimensions. What affects one affects all—and yet the problems are so intricate, the variables so many, the controls so sensitive, that everyone feels paralyzed and ineffective and overwhelmed, like an ant in an avalanche.

All people everywhere want basically the same things for themselves and for their children. It should be the task of governments to reconcile these common ends with the functions and needs and different systems of each society. Instead, the differences are exaggerated, and the common ends obscured. Can anything short of a global catastrophe bring us to the light? That is the only question worth asking today.

Oh, for the World of the Artist

WATCHING THE GREAT Pablo Casals conduct a chamber orchestra in a Bach suite (in the closed television-circuit program for the National Cultural Center last month), I was forcibly reminded again that the world of performers and artists is in many ways a model of what the outer world ought to be.

Despite the backbiting and envy and childishness of so many performers, there is an immense respect for talent and ability, skill and discipline, imagination and interpretation.

The world of the artist is supremely the world of the *individual*; compared to it, business and trade (which use the word "individualism" merely as a synonym for making more money without restraint) are impersonal and anti-individualistic. The modern corporation, indeed, is a prime example of high-level collectivism.

In the arts, a man or woman is judged *solely and wholly* by what he can do and how well he can do it. There is a true democracy of merit, which means that there is also a true aristocracy—made up of those who have proved themselves as individuals, regardless of their background, their national origin, their private failings.

The veneration given to Casals by his fellow musicians is a moving example of what the entire human family was meant to be. This dumpy, bald, hobbling, ailing old man, without money, without power, without even a country of his own, commands the utmost respect of artists throughout the world—because of his vast ability and his fierce dedication to the highest goals of his craft.

What an artist (if he is really an artist) wants to be is the *best*—not the biggest or the richest or the most famous. His end is a *value*, not a *commodity;* and true civilization can survive only when we place values above commodities. The least practical, and most destructive, thing a society can do is to enshrine the practical above the "idealistic."

What is immensely appealing, in a deep human sense, about the arts is that they remain one of the few areas in which true individualism can flourish; in which the creator and performer is a person directly communicating with other persons; in which his ancestors, language, connections and superficial traits are totally subordinated to his professional skill.

A state which cannot produce and sustain such art is doomed, however tall its buildings or powerful its armaments; and both "democracy" and "individualism" can be measured by the ways in which those who are gifted in other areas shape their lives to give fuller expression to the higher parts of their nature, and not merely to the appetitive part we share with all animals.

It is easier for most men to submit to a great evil than to suffer a slight vexation; and tyrants flourish by providing the masses with minor pleasures while destroying their major freedoms.

*

What the average business organization seems to be looking for today is a young man of thirty with twenty years of sound business experience.

How We Can Master Our Technology

FIRST we invent something. Then we put it into production. Then we buy it and use it. Then, and only then, do we begin to wonder if we haven't been too heedless and hasty.

It's happening now with the snowmobile, as the latest and most dramatic example of this process, but by no means the most important. Only now, after millions have been produced and bought, are we starting to recognize and control the possible damage they can do.

If we are going to become the masters of our technology, however, and not be dominated or overwhelmed by its consequences, it is imperative that we set up a new agency to work alongside the old United States Patent Office, to determine the "social utility" of new devices.

The Patent Office decides only whether a gadget or process will work and whether the applier is entitled to an exclusive right. The new agency should have the power to determine—after the broadest public hearings—whether any invention should be permitted to go into production before its social costs and consequences have been adequately worked out.

This would slow down our rate of technological progress—which is not a bad thing in itself—and would also give us time to prepare for the environmental impact of industrial changes.

While the snowmobile is both a boon and a blessing to winter-bound citizens in many areas, it is already a blight and a menace in these same areas. It came on the market unregulated, without strict registration or licensing, and has been dangerously abused by thousands of idiotic and unqualified operators.

No rules were set up, no trails laid out, no speed limits established. Snowmobiles have chased animals to exhaustion and death, have killed off plantings of seedlings in forests and have upset the whole ecology of wildlife and wilderness in places never before touched by human predators.

This, as I said, is only a minor example of our past indifference to the social consequences of new technology, but one we can see quite vividly. There are others, more obscure and more dangerous in the long run, which must not be allowed to proliferate before it is too late to take anything but the most drastic measures to curtail them.

We have treated our future with the utmost contempt, using our world as a place to plunder, to pollute, to create massive problems for short-term gain. And we have consistently failed to calculate the social costs of these "advances"—for which we are paying, not only through the pocketbook but through the nose, eyes and lungs as well.

Paradox of "Free Enterprise"

THE POPULAR PHRASE, "free enterprise," is an interesting example of what the linguists call "telescoping." It is made up of two separate phrases: "free competition," and "private enterprise."

Private enterprise is what we have in America. In order for private enterprise to work at its best and fairest, we must also have free competition along with it. And that's the rub.

The reason that the phrase "free enterprise" has become such a meaningless political slogan is that many of the people who believe —as I do—in private enterprise do not at the same time really believe—as I do—in free competition.

Not long ago, the State of Illinois recovered nearly a half million dollars from seven rock salt suppliers charged with a price-fixing conspiracy against the state. All these suppliers, no doubt, are ardent believers in private enterprise; but they seem a little short in their fidelity to free competition.

Yet it is impossible to have the one without the other. This would be "socialism at the top"—companies reaping all the benefits of private enterprise without running any of the risk of free competition.

Anyone who follows the proceedings of the antitrust division of the Department of Justice knows the number and variety of large business and industrial firms that have over the years tried to administer prices, fix profits for the whole field and achieve a monopoly or dominance that would really stifle free competition.

It is hard to escape the conclusion that these companies really do not like competition, or the operation of the free market, and seek to replace it with a closed system that assures them profits and gives the consumer no real choice between so-called "competitors."

Now it may be possible that competition is destructive, wasteful, or unnecessarily expensive; and perhaps a few large companies would offer better goods at lower cost than many smaller firms fighting each other. But, if such is the case, then we had better stop using the slogan, "free enterprise," and find something more fitting and accurate to describe the operation of our market.

It seems to me that many leaders of our business community want two contradictory things: freedom to make unlimited profit without interference, and also to protect themselves from the nuisance of free competition. Until they resolve this paradox, they cannot address themselves to the electorate with authority, consistency or conviction.

A Hundred Years of Patience

LOOKING OUT OF MY OFFICE window on St. Patrick's Day, I could see the big parade starting to march through Chicago's Loop—thousands of Irish, with as many "honorary" Irish marching alongside them.

Being Irish is a pride and a pleasure in America today—so much so that many people like to claim spurious Irish ancestry. The Irish are an immensely likeable group, and even their defects are warmly human.

Yet it is worth remembering that it has not always been so. In London, when I was born, the Irish were still considered vaguely subhuman, and generally treated as such. They occupied the most menial jobs, and opportunities for advancement were blocked by prejudice, if not by law.

And even in the United States, until the turn of this century, the Irish were violently discriminated against. "No Irish Need Apply" was a common sign in shop windows in Boston and other Eastern cities for many years. Of all new immigrant groups, the Irish were perhaps the most disdained, feared and shunned by the earlier settlers.

But within a generation or two, in the free atmosphere of a growing and prospering nation, most of this prejudice had dissipated, and today it is only a dim memory that many of the same charges we level against the Negro were once leveled against the Irish.

Yet let us imagine that the Irish had been forced to remain in servitude here; that they had been denied adequate schooling, forbidden to move where they liked, condemned to manual work and even prohibited from voting. Much as I admire them, I doubt that under such pressing conditions they would have reached a fraction of their present eminence in American life.

What they *would* have done, I am sure—knowing what we do of the mercurial Irish temperament—is rebel against those conditions as strenuously as they rebelled against British domination in Ireland. They would not have waited a hundred years, as the Negro patiently has, before they erupted in passion, violence and righteous revolution.

We are alarmed today at the manifestations of Negro unrest, but instead we should be amazed that there is relatively so little of it. The Negro has been astonishingly patient, docile, hopeful and calm in the face of monumental frustration, cruelty and hypocrisy. He has turned the other cheek often enough to embarrass the apostles of official Christendom, and he is now rebelling because cheek-turning has not seemed to work too well.

The Negro has practiced what we have only preached, and now he is beginning to preach what we practice—power. It frightens us to be confronted with our own attitude staring balefully back at us.

Blue-Collar Men in White-Collar Jobs

I WAS CHATTING with a British auto mechanic who is now working in the United States. "Living conditions are wonderful here," he said, "but the standards of work wouldn't be tolerated anywhere in Europe for a moment."

The man is a craftsman of a high order, and he is appalled at the sloppiness and negligence going into many American products. "Most of the men here don't care how poorly they do their jobs," he shrugged.

I am convinced that the main reason for this lies in our insensate drive toward a college-education for everybody, ending in a white-collar job, which alone confers "status" in our society.

American parents, on the whole, do not want their sons to be artisans or craftsmen, but business or professional people. As a result, millions of youngsters are being prepared for careers they have little aptitude for—and little interest in, except for the dubious prestige.

I know a newly-married couple near Pittsburgh who have just moved into their first house. The husband has drifted unsuccessfully from job to job in the business world since they were married.

Yet, almost single-handed he has transformed their ramshackle house into a thing of taste and splendor. He is magnificent with his hands, but he will not use them for occupational purposes because somehow it is thought to be "demeaning" in our society.

But he—and many thousands like him—would be both more prosperous and happier performing tasks of manual and mechanical skill. His family would be horrified at the thought, however, and he would be ashamed and embarrassed. Good family, good school, nothing to do but work in an office and drink too much.

Our culture has elevated the businessman to a status unprecedented anywhere in the past. The price we pay for this is an alarming, and growing, scarcity of willing apprentices in the field of craftsmanship.

There is little incentive here for an artisan to be proud of his work, if he cannot be proud of his position. Shoddy goods and poor servicing are not so much an economic matter as a psychological one. The pay is high, but the prestige is low.

The young man near Pittsburgh would be leading a much happier and more productive life in overalls than in a button-down shirt. He would also pay off his mortgage faster, but we have made clean fingernails a symbol of superiority that keeps many from doing at all what they can do best.

What It Takes to Be a "Square"

PURELY PERSONAL PREJUDICES:

A "square" is a person who takes dessert because it comes "on the dinner," even though he doesn't want it, and will only nibble at it;

Who keeps plastic covers on the furniture, so that it will still "look like new" when the owner is ready to die;

Who believes that the "friendly" voice of the announcer or master of ceremonies really indicates a friendly personality behind it;

Who is filled with compassion for a kitten trapped in a tree, but thinks that the starving people in India wouldn't be in that fix if they had more get-up-and-go;

Who is fond of telling you that he "loves people"—but is careful to associate only with those who do not basically differ from him in background, prejudices and personality traits;

Who wants the most "modern conveniences" in everything from his bathroom to his barbecue pit, and then complains that this modern generation is "growing soft";

Who spends all Sunday morning in washing and polishing his car, so that he can spend all Sunday afternoon driving bumper-to-bumper with other squares in their washed and polished cars;

Who terms anything "highbrow" that he is too lazy to try to understand, and terms anything "sordid" that he is too self-righteous to try to sympathize with;

Who has an "old saying" to fit every situation, which he habitually uses in place of analysis or reflection, which saves the trouble and discomfort of thinking in individual cases;

Who is convinced that the Golden Rule would solve all our problems, but doesn't see why *he* should be the first to put it in practice;

Who feels that "experience" has made him wise, when it has only made him wary;

Who despises "hypocrisy," but comes to terms with it by calling his own brand "getting along with people";

Who finds it hard to believe that, if Jesus came back to earth, He wouldn't really prefer to make His home in some nice, respectable suburb, with trimmed lawns and picture windows;

Who solemnly assures you, as a fragment of eternal wisdom, that a person who attracts dogs must have a "good heart";

Who speaks glibly of something called "the criminal class"—until a member of his family happens to commit a crime.

The Poor Ones Take the Rap

PEOPLE WHO ARE ALARMED at the rising crime rate believe that "getting tougher" will act as a curb on crime. Nothing in criminal history or past legislation bears out this hope. Severity of sentence has no relation to the incidence of crime.

Americans also mistakenly believe that countries such as England, where the crime rate is much lower than ours, give longer sentences than we do. Actually, the sentences are much shorter in England—but the chance of being convicted and sent to prison is much higher.

It is the equality of justice, not the harshness of punishment, that deters criminal activity. Young criminals in America know that the amount of money you have, and the lawyer you can afford to hire, play a much more important role in your defense than the enormity of your crime. Therefore, their aim is not to go straight, but to get rich. A successful criminal rarely gets hurt by the law.

The Atlantian, an excellent magazine put out by the inmates at Atlanta federal prison, recently commented on two new prisoners who arrived in two different federal penitentiaries for the same offense: dealing in narcotics.

One was a pharmacist, a college graduate, who had smuggled in more than $1,000,000 worth of heroin. With a fine defense attorney, he received a sentence of only five years, with eligibility for parole. The second was an addict peddler, who probably never had over $50 in his pocket at any one time. He was given a lawyer by the court, and received a sentence of 60 years—without eligibility for parole and cannot be released until he is 97 years old.

These are typical, not unusual, examples. In the same issue, the magazine mentions a convict in New York who had served 34 years for stealing $5 worth of candy. If he had stolen a thousand times that much, and had the proper connections, he might have served a year, or not at all. There is almost an inverse ratio in such matters.

"Crime" is not an isolated factor in society. When the crime rate is high, it is generally because the whole system of jurisprudence is perverted. When we "get tougher," it is only the poorest, the clumsiest, the dumbest, who are hurt more. The slick professionals continue to beat the raps, laws or no laws.

There is little democracy in law enforcement in America—and this is what breeds contempt for the law in young criminals. And harsher punishment only makes them resolve to get more successful, not to get honest.

Avoiding a Police State

IT IS A HISTORICAL FACT that, throughout the history of the world, the liberties of people have much more often been threatened by the forces of "law and order" than by criminals.

We easily forget this fact when we worry and complain about crime running rampant, and demand that more power be put into the hands of the various law-enforcement agencies.

And it is richly ironic that the very same people who are concerned about the growing influence of government over individual lives are the ones who are clamoring most loudly for increased police powers against lawbreakers.

Yet the quickest way to get a police state is to give the police all the power they ask for. I would be much more worried about a police force that had too much power than about a criminal element that was perhaps treated too gently by the courts.

Individual criminals can always be kept in relative control by a police force that is professionally trained, well paid and free from corrupt political alliances. But a police force cannot be kept in control once its authority has been broadened to a dangerous degree.

Any society has much less to fear from crime—organized or unorganized—than from a ursurpation of power by its own law-enforcement agencies. Protecting even the worst criminals from unfair treatment is a small price to pay for avoiding the greater danger of police transgressions against the civil liberties of all.

This whole question of "handcuffing" the police by high court rulings is a smokescreen to hide the obvious fact that the police would much prefer to have no restraints on their power to badger, to harass, to intimidate, to wiretap, to wring confessions out of suspects without doing the hard work that good police investigation calls for.

The way to reduce crime substantially is not by giving the police more license, but by giving them more of everything else: more pay, more professional pride, more independence from political pressures, more status, more serious technical training.

We cannot make criminals any better, if they want to be criminals. But we can make policemen much better, as they do in England and a few other sensible countries. Law enforcement, on the local urban level, is mostly a cheap racket today. When we are willing to pay enough to turn it into a respected occupation, then crime will no longer be so rampant—among the criminals, or among the police.

Now, Is It Any Wonder We Wonder?

AMERICA IS A COUNTRY where everybody has a car, and nobody has a place to park it.

Where a man is judged by the size of his bankroll, and a woman is judged by the size of her bosom.

Where every parent wants his children to have the "best education," but where a truly educated man is looked upon with suspicion.

Where all the citizens are peace-loving, and prove it by annually piling up the world's greatest total of murders and auto fatalities.

Where everybody screams for greater "economy" in government—except when the shoe begins to pinch his own toes.

Where we spend dozens of millions to support mental patients in state hospitals, but spend hardly a trickle to prevent the stresses that put them there.

Where a man's "good credit" depends on how much he owes—and the more he owes, the more credit he can get.

Where families move from the cities to the suburbs to get away from congestion, and then find that they have brought the congestion with them.

Where husbands work harder and more intensely than their grandfathers did, in order to provide "security" for their children—and then find that the children grow up emotionally insecure because they scarcely know their fathers.

Where an entertainer can earn more money in a year than the aggregate salary of the whole U.S. Congress—and then we wonder why more high-calibered men don't enter the field of politics.

Where we push our children into nursery schools at an absurdly young age, and keep pushing them to grow up fast—and then are shocked when a child of 10 demands privileges that we didn't get at 16.

Where a man who can hit a little ball over a fence is accorded the status of a national hero and then we complain that our age isn't producing heroic figures such as America knew in the past.

Where we publicly praise "free enterprise," but privately permit the big fish to gobble up the little fish in the name of "expansion."

Where, despite all these flaws and frailties and contradictions, we retain the power to criticize ourselves, our institutions and our leaders—for which saving grace, thank God!

For Good or Ill, the Past Never Dies.

ONE OF THE MOST monstrous and dangerous of phrases is that pat and familiar combination of words "dead past." The past is never dead; it is very much alive, for good and ill.

We are not, as a whole, a people with a vivid sense of history. We live in the present and in the future—and are proud of so doing. But without an acute sense of the past, the present is meaningless and the future is fraught with peril.

It is not so much the old cliche that "history repeats itself" as the fact that history *anticipates* itself. Today and tomorrow are prefigured in yesterday's patterns of events.

Hitler is dead; the spirit he generated is not dead, and will never die. Unless we learn what that spirit means, and how it acts under certain circumstances, we will not be able to cope with its return.

Ancient Greece is dead, but its problems remain: especially the one problem that great democracy could not solve—how to achieve both freedom and security at the same time. Learning why Greece failed may help us find some happier solution.

We know that, in an individual life, the past remains active and influential, even when we are most unconscious of it. The same is true of nations and epochs; the waves keep widening for centuries, and slowly change the contour of the shore we stand on.

The past often seems "dead" because it is presented in a deadly fashion. Good teachers of history are almost as rare as good teachers of mathematics: They know far more than the dates, the capitals, the principal commodities, the dull details that can easily be found in any World Almanac.

To make the past come alive requires *imagination* as much as learning. The good history teacher must be more of a poet than a pedant; he must grasp the philosophy of historical events, or he has grasped nothing.

Unless we understand American history, for instance, we cannot effectively defend the Bill of Rights, or even know why it should be defended.

If we lose any freedoms, it may be because we pay too much attention to the temporary needs of the present, and too little attention to the permanent foundations of the past.

People die; objects perish; but ideas persist forever. History shows us how ideas have changed men, and how men have changed ideas. Lacking this knowledge, we can only be blinded by false passions and betrayed by false hopes.

It is axiomatic that the person who is not pleased with others is never pleased with himself, no matter how egocentric he seems to be; the chronic faultfinder is always projecting a profound sense of dissatisfaction with himself.

*

I am always saddened and amused by our unconscious arrogance in speaking of the "Dark Ages" — as if we were living in the age of light, reason and humanitarianism.

The Biggest Snob: No-Snob Snob

IF ONE WERE WRITING a book of snobs, as Thackery once did, it would be necessary to include that modern type—the No-Snob Snob. Today he has become the most prevalent member of the species *homo snobbimus*.

The No-Snob Snob, as his name indicates, feels superior about his inferiority. He is proud of his humility. He revels in the knowledge that he knows little. He feels exceptional to be so ordinary.

If he reads a book that is somewhat beyond him, he does not blame his own limitations for failing to understand it; rather he says beamingly, "I don't go for those authors who won't write English for the common man."

If he hears a piece of music too intricate for his ears, or sees a painting too subtle for his perception, he does not resolve to cultivate his taste in these arts; rather, he puffs himself up and declaims proudly, "Those fellows just don't know how to communicate to the public."

In the political realm, the No-Snob Snob distrusts and derides any candidate with a good command of language, urbane manners and a background that does not encompass the bowling alley and the beer hall.

And if he does elect a Rockefeller to office, it is only after Rockefeller demonstrates that he can eat as many hot dogs, kiss as many babies and pump as many moist palms as the grizzled ward heelers of the River wards.

The No-Snob Snob has lost sight of the Jeffersonian goal of democracy, which was to raise every citizen to the level of excellence; to him, democracy means lowering every citizen to the common denominator of amiable mediocrity.

He condemns the intellectual for his "arrogance," and the aristocrat for his "pride," but actually he is the most arrogant and proud of any.

The intellectual is arrogant about knowledge, which is a good thing; the aristocrat is proud of tradition, which is a good thing; but the No-Snob Snob is arrogant about ignorance and proud of self-centeredness, which are bad things.

As a poor man, the No-Snob Snob is merely pathetic; as a rich man, he is intolerable, for he assumes that his ability to make money has conferred upon him the wisdom of Solomon and the authority of St. Paul.

He feels competent to make majestic pronouncements in all fields of human endeavor, on the false assumption that his pecuniary shrewdness is a mark of God's special favor. Snobbery can go no further than this.

Conversation No Road to Success

I WISH I COULD have believed the advertisement I saw in a magazine last week. It was offering a correspondence course in conversation, holding out the promise of "new heights in the business and social world" to those who mastered the course.

"In your conversation," the ad vibrated, "may lie the opportunity for social and business advancement . . . new contacts . . . promotion . . . in short, SUCCESS."

Would that it were so. But I can't think of anything less important or decisive than conversation in the modern world—and especially in modern America.

The few charming conversationalists I have known were failures in the eyes of the world; and the most successful men have been nearly inarticulate. Most of them could not even verbalize their own businesses.

Conversation is a dying, if not a dead, art. We are too busy getting and spending, listening and watching professional entertainers, to develop our own powers of communication. And when a delightful talker does come along, we sullenly suspect him of being frivolous and insincere.

Our social conversation, in the main, is as deadly as our business talk. The most "fashionable" parties I have attended were accompanied by conversation scarcely above the Cro-Magnon level; but if the liquor is flowing freely, nobody seems to care.

Somebody once said that good conversation should be like a tennis match, with each player gracefully sending the ball back across the net; instead, most conversation is like a golf game, with each player stroking only his own ball, and waiting impatiently for the other to finish.

Success, in the worldly sense, depends upon one thing only (beyond a minimum of cunning), and that is: single-mindedness. You have to care about nothing else, think about nothing else.

This monomania is guaranteed to take you straight to the top, without the need of any correspondence course—but it will do little to expand your talent for self-expression.

It is the manipulation of things, not the mastery of words or ideas, that characterizes our society. We mistake solemn dullness for profundity; and dismiss the verbal graces as mere trifling. Today, the good talker is out selling things for the grunter who makes them.

Harris Scores a Hit on a Foul

THERE IS A DOORMAN on our block who is wild about baseball. He also knows that I am vaguely associated with some newspaper, perhaps in an exalted sporting capacity.

Each morning he greets me with a little baseball observation, and I haven't had the heart to inform him that I know less about baseball than I do about the second law of thermodynamics—about which I know nothing except the phrase.

I have found, however, and I suspect that millions of other American men also have, that it isn't necessary to know a single thing about the game in order to conduct a fairly intelligible conversation about it.

Our regular morning dialogs run something like this:

Doorman: "Well, I see where Frizzle got two out of four at bat yesterday. Guess he's out of that slump now."

Harris: "You just have to ride them out, I guess. You can't force a thing like that.

Doorman: "That's very true. Lookit how Schmangerpamf picked up when he was sold to the Carnals. Best switch hitter in the league now."

Harris: "Of course, a good coach makes a lot of difference, too."

Doorman: "And how. Remember how in '54 Osskewitz was tightening up at the plate until Chicken Licken Jones got him relaxed? He'll murder 'em with that short Los Angeles fence now."

Harris: "Boy, you can't argue with the facts."

Doorman: "You said a mouthful. These Frisco Pygmies are really zooming up there—whaddayuh think of that Chris Cringle making an unassisted double-play yesterday?"

Harris: "Heluva player, that Cringle. He can play on my team any day."

Doorman: "Mine, too. And didyuh notice that new sinker ball Les Fauves is using this year? He oughta win 20 easy this season, if they plug up that hole in center field."

Harris: "They sure gotta plug up that hole, all right; you could drive a fleet of trucks through there right now."

Doorman: "You're not kiddin'. They never shoulda sent Buddy Myopia to the minors—that manager is a moron."

Harris: "Well, that's the way the ball bounces. We ought to pick up steam pretty soon."

Doorman: "I hope so. And if you run across a coupla passes you're not using—don't forget me, Mr. Harris."

Tough: Being Your Own Policeman

WHEN YOU ASK a man to be his own judge, jury and jailer, you are asking too much of him. Nobody can be objective in his own cause.

It is for this reason that professional societies have set up their own bodies to guide their members and to chide them when they have broken the rules of the profession.

But what if these societies turn into mutual protection agencies, who are interested mainly in shielding their members from the consequences of their misdeeds? Then who is in charge of the custodians?

This, I think, is largely what has happened to such powerful and stubborn groups as bar associations and medical societies—and explains, in part, the widespread public resentment against doctors and lawyers.

Everyone knows that it is virtually impossible to get a bar association to take punitive action against a lawyer, or a medical society to reprimand a doctor.

These groups are in business to protect their members more than to protect the public from the folly or fraudulence of legal and medical practitioners. It requires a scandalous crime of the first magnitude before such groups will take action against a fellow professional.

Ironically enough, it is these groups that declaim most stridently against "government powers." But government rushes in only to fill a vacuum. If an organization does not police itself adequately—as, for instance, the Stock Exchange did not in the 1920's—then it paves the way for government intervention.

The way to maintain what we call "free enterprise" is for private organizations to enforce their regulations so stringently and impartially that there is no excuse for the government to step in.

Doctors simply will not testify against other doctors in lawsuits, nor will the average medical society pay much heed to a patient's complaint. And bar associations are notoriously reluctant to disbar or even suspend a member unless he has murdered a judge downtown at high noon, in the presence of the entire Committee on Ethical Practices.

To be a "professional" means to profess, to take a vow, that the welfare of the client or the patient is paramount, and that profit must take second place.

A profession differs from a mere "occupation" in that the latter is done mainly for money; this is why we confer more status upon professional men.

But this status must be earned, maintained and zealously guarded. At present, the guardians have lost much public confidence and respect.

What Is Happiness in a Marriage?

A COLLEGE STUDENT asked me, during a bull-session on campus last week, "How many happy marriages do you think there are in our country?"

Of course, it is an impossible question to answer, even on a rough percentage basis. But the question itself interested me more than the lack of an adequate answer.

Most people don't know that the idea of "happiness" in a personal sense is a relatively new one—no older than the French Revolution. The idea that happiness as such should be the controlling or dominating factor in human life rarely occurred to the ancients or to the medievals.

Along with the vague concept of "progress," happiness is a product of the last two centuries, when man began to feel he had overcome the forces of nature and when the idea of the individual personality became more important than the family, the tribe, the city, or the nation.

People in the past were not supposed to aim at happiness as an ultimate goal; they may have hoped for it as a by-product, but they did not judge the worth of their lives by this standard. Marriages then held together not because the couples were "happier," but because they weren't looking for happiness in marriage.

We can see this even as late as our grandparents' time. Divorces were infrequent not merely because the laws were stricter and morality more severe. The couples themselves were content if they rubbed along together, had enough to live by, reared decent families and died with a sense of conjugal accomplishment.

We today ask a great deal more of marriage—just as we ask a great deal more of life generally. The average married couple is not satisfied short of "happiness," however this happiness may be defined—and its definition usually includes some idea of romantic love that was irrelevant to marriage in past ages.

I can see good in both attitudes. The past was more realistic, and we are more ambitious. Our grandparents didn't expect too much out of marriage, and were satisfied with mere "adjustment." We expect a great deal—perhaps too much—and are unwilling to settle for less.

We have a much different idea of the *individual* than they did, and this accounts for the restlessness and instability of modern marriage. We want marriage to be more than an economic and social contract (which I think it should be) but we have not yet matured enough to realize that "happiness" cannot be *found in* someone else—it must be *built with* someone else. We have not yet grown up to our vast emotional wants.

Still a Bargain: Cost of Being Crooked

EVERY ITEM HAS RISEN steeply in the cost of living—except the cost of being crooked.

Most fines, for both criminal and civil offenses, are still at their laughably low 1940 level. The cost of being honest has more than doubled, but the lawbreaker has not felt the dwindling value of money.

Every day the newspapers report stories of swindlers and thieves who have made off with vast sums—and are fined $500 or $1,000, and perhaps given a year in jail.

I do not believe that long prison sentences do anything but embitter men, but I am convinced that large punitive fines can be effective deterrents to crimes.

A slum owner who persistently defies the law and exploits his wretchedly poor tenants is required to pay some piddling fine while he retains his swollen profits from human misery.

Frauds and fleecers take billions from the public annually, but the law is powerless to do more than assess some trivial fine that was not even adequate a dozen years ago.

A psychopathic drunkard who breaks into a shop and steals a carton of merchandise in order to buy more booze and drown himself in oblivion is sent to prison for a considerable number of years—but the sleek and bloated criminal who uses craft instead of force, and can afford a cunning lawyer, generally is tapped on the wrist with a feathery fine.

We live in a money culture, and money is the only language such men understand; but our justice seems to be in inverse ratio to the magnitude of the offense. The aim of the thief is to be a bigger thief, because size brings relative immunity from punishment.

All our efforts at reform and rehabilitation will prove futile so long as youngsters can plainly see that a man is disgraced not for being a crook, but for being a failure as a crook.

Society's worship of success has extended itself to the enemies of society, and irony can go no further than this.

What we require is a brisk overhauling of our criminal statutes, bringing the fines into more sensible proportion to the value of the dollar today, as well as to the gravity and scope of the offense.

Fines have been doubled for illegal parking, but the upper reaches of lawbreaking have scarcely been touched by the magistrate's hand.

All You Have to Do Is Explain

I WAS IN A STRANGE restaurant yesterday, waiting for my luncheon order, when the waitress came over and said smilingly: "There's a foulup in the kitchen; one of the cooks took ill this morning; can I get you a newspaper to read?"

With these rare and wonderful words, she won me for life. As I am sure she has won hundreds of friends for her employer over the years. For she understands that impatience thrives on ignorance.

Most of us don't mind waiting (most of the time) so long as we know *why* we are waiting. It is the feeling of being neglected that breeds dissatisfaction in patrons, not the mere fact of a delay.

A former airline stewardess of my acquaintance has confirmed this psychological fact: "Whenever we had a delay," she said, "I would explain to the passengers exactly why, and I'd make them feel they are sharing in the workings of the organization. It's surprising how this knowledge converted them from angry patrons to members of the team."

Too often, alas, airline passengers are merely told "there will be a delay," and no other information is forthcoming. This is infuriating and frustrating—and creates a mass of ill will.

Knowledge is a great healer of emotional scars. The dentist who carefully explains to his patient (as mine does) precisely what is being done, and why all these laborious procedures have to be gone through, has made the patient a *participant* in the work, and not merely an *object* that is worked upon. His technique removes fears and anxieties as well as decay.

Everybody has a natural affinity for belonging. We are willing to share in the problems of a service organization that is having trouble—if we can be made to feel that we are an important part of the operation, and that our good will is an asset earnestly desired by the company.

What we resent is being treated as an anonymous mass, too stupid to be told what is going on, and forced to wait until the demigods in the inner office decide to push the proper buttons.

There is a huge reservoir of co-operation in the public that has rarely been tapped. Service organizations may be financially astute, but they are psychologically shallow in not recognizing that the best service consists in giving their customers the facts when things go wrong.

The Degradation of Graduation

A FRIEND OF MINE has a daughter who was "graduated" from kindergarten last month—white gown, mortarboard, diploma and all.

Now I suppose that the theory behind this cute and cunning ceremony is that it makes the children feel important as they step into the primary grades. The primary grades do the same nowadays, and the high schools have long imitated the college graduations.

But the theory actually works in reverse: instead of dignifying the lower "graduations," it merely degrades the graduation from college, which used to be a solemn and unique occasion.

If everybody gets a cap and gown and diploma—from kindergarten right up through the Ph.D—then nobody's cap and gown and diploma has much significance. It all becomes an empty ritual, important mainly for demonstrating the virtuosity of parents with a camera.

This has happened even more blatantly in the field of honorary degrees.

A generation or so ago, an honorary degree was an honor; today it is more likely to be a publicity stunt for the college or for some more commercial enterprise: Bob Hope, after all, was last month made an honorary "Doctor of Laws" for telling jokes in Moscow.

I trust this is not mere stuffiness on my part. It matters little to me personally who gets an honorary degree or a diploma, who wears a mortarboard or a dunce cap. But it does matter to me that standards of excellence have become blurred and blotted by our excess of democratic fervor.

The traditional cap and gown was something students had to work hard for, through 16 years of schooling.

It symbolized both a termination and a commencement; in Europe, where the custom originated, it represented a recognition that the student was ready to accept both the responsibilities and the privileges of the adult world.

Putting these ludicrous costumes on kindergarten children is unconsciously an insult to and a repudiation of the value of higher education.

It is on a par with awarding an honorary degree to a building contractor who has provided the new gym at cost, or making a Doctor of Laws out of a performer who recites the jokes other men have written for him.

Without firm standards of excellence, without special recognition for higher levels of achievement, a democratic society becomes a perversion and a corruption of its original purposes. Perhaps it is time to ask whether much of our love of "equality" is not merely the embrace of mediocrity.

When a politician calls a proposal "unthinkable," you may be sure that a great many people are thinking of it.

IV.
Of Men, Women and Children

The He-Man and the Homosexual

A READER IN MASSACHUSETTS wants to know if, in my opinion, the United States is seeing a rise in the number of homosexuals, and if the same rise is discernible in Europe and the rest of the world.

Nobody has the statistical answer to such a question. For one thing, since our laws and mores are now more permissive than in the past, a larger number of homosexuals feel free to disclose themselves; and this, of course, makes it seem as if the number has increased.

My own feeling is that there is a smaller percentage of homosexuals in Europe than in the United States, principally because the American ethos is aimed at turning out one particular kind of boy.

We are still very much a frontier country in our ideal of the "masculine image." The kind of man we most needed in conquering the wilderness and settling the West is still much the pattern for defining "masculinity" in American society. Europe has had time for other, and differing, masculine "types" to compete with that primitive image.

In the United States, it is still considered suspect for a young man to be interested in aesthetic matters; to like poetry, or enjoy opera, or appreciate the ballet. Indeed, these activities have been institutionalized mostly by females in our society.

In Europe, the concept of masculinity does not exclude such interests—the Italian males enjoy opera as much as the women do, the French consider a poet no less virile than a stockbroker, the Russian male dancers in the Bolshoi ballet are as masculine as any prizefighter.

Americans have always insisted on pushing their boys to one extreme or the other; there is little room for the balanced personality. If a boy at an early age exhibits interest in aesthetic matters, this is often considered "unmanly." And so, because he cannot or will not adjust to the prevailing frontier ethos, he moves toward those who "sympathize" with his bent—which already includes a large homosexual community.

No doubt, the Freudians are right that the early family pattern and the roles played by both parents are tremendously important in shaping the psychosexual life of a boy; on the other hand, the cultural pressures cannot be ignored, either, and a wavering and sensitive boy is more likely to turn away from the mainstream in the United States than in Europe, where he can find plenty of heteros who share his interests.

It is significant that even confirmed homosexuals do not behave so flagrantly in Europe as they do here, for they are accepted casually as an ordinary fact of life. Our frontier mentality not only produces more such men; it also keeps them alienated, anxious and aggressively defensive about their place in our society.

Why Frown on Women M.D.s?

I HAVE WRITTEN about this before, a dozen years ago, but the situation is now worse than it was then, and still nothing much has been done. I refer to the shortage of doctors in the United States, and our provincial prejudice against women in the medical profession.

Our country could use another quarter-million doctors, but many young men are not able to go through the lengthy and expensive period of medical education; on the other hand, hundreds of thousands of college-trained women could take up the profession if they were encouraged to do so.

The majority of doctors are women in Russia, and in the Scandinavian countries and throughout Europe generally there are many times more women doctors than we have in the United States.

Male chauvinism does not run nearly as high in those countries as it does here. Even female lawyers are frowned upon in the United States (both inside and outside the legal profession), are paid less, given more menial assignments and rarely elevated to positions of any real responsibility in public service, as their male counterparts are.

It may be a plausible (though not, to me, persuasive) argument that women lack the toughness of fiber to make first-rate lawyers; but surely no similar argument applies to their potential abilities as doctors.

In the first place, women tend to be natively more sympathetic to physical ailments than men; women are more aware of their bodies, more sensitive to biological processes; more emotionally engaged in the arts of nursing and nutrition and conservation of health.

Secondly, and just as important, women have a naturally deeper understanding of psychosomatic ailments—which are at the bottom of more than 50 per cent of all cases seen by doctors—because their own minds and bodies are so intimately related, so delicately interpenetrated by one another.

And, so far as the technical skills of medicine are concerned, these can be learned by any competent and ordinarily intelligent person of either sex. What chiefly distinguishes a good doctor from a mediocre one is precisely the area in which women excel: the ability to *identify* with the patient, to *communicate* and *interact* on a level beneath the merely verbal and intellectual and clinical.

It is one of the scandals of our society that we fail to extract the vast potential from our women, and still condemn them to second-class citizenship in the profession that needs them most.

Why College Kids Don't Go Home

I WAS SPENDING the weekend in a wealthy city in the Southwest recently, and two of the leading citizens complained that "our young people aren't coming back here after college."

"After they've been away at college a few years, they don't want to come back here and settle down," said one. "Even though they may have the best business opportunities here, through their parents and other connections. I can't understand their reason, when they know this town needs young people so badly."

What could I say to him? I knew the reason, of course, since I visit dozens of colleges and universities throughout the year. The young people don't want to go back because they can't stand the atmosphere of their hometown, when it is smug and provincial.

This is an atmosphere the older citizens cannot feel, the way a fish does not feel water. If you have lived in a specific environment all your life, it is not an "environment"—it is what you call "life." But to the young people it is suffocating, unreal and unutterably dull, both in spirit and in substance. This is why so many gravitate to large, cosmopolitan communities.

Having talked to college students about this subject, across the whole country, I find that these are their chief objections to going back to the town or city they grew up in:

It is deadly conformist, in its thinking, feeling and acting.

It is static in its beliefs, and reactionary in its activities.

It lives by clichés and platitudes that bear no relation or relevance to the twentieth-century world.

It is totally self-delusive, thinks itself to be the repository of all virtues, while wholly oblivious of its defects of vision, imagination, flexibility, tolerance and social responsibility.

It lacks verve, humor, insight and, most of all, a capacity for genuine self-criticism which alone could change it in the future.

The virtues it pays homage to are riches, respectability, power and acquisitiveness; it has little or no use for the energies of the mind and spirit unless they are harnessed to conventional civic goals. This, right or wrong, is what many of the brightest and best college students think of the communities they come from. If they are right, they should not go back; if they are wrong, how did they get these notions?

This is what the town fathers should be asking themselves, instead of scratching their heads and sighing in perplexity.

Help Stamp Out Fourth Grade

How DO YOU get an institution to change without putting a firecracker under its tail? If our colleges and universities had changed when, and in the way, they should have, the riots and disturbances of the late sixties would have been not only avoidable, but unnecessary.

This same discontent is now seeping down to the high schools, and the dead hand of institutionalization will soon be lifted by force if it is not raised by consent. For the quality of education is even worse in most secondary schools than it is in colleges and universities.

We could go right down to the elementary grades for an example of administrative paralysis in the face of modern educational knowledge. For instance, it has been known for more than twenty years that young children cannot be best educated by the present "grade" system of keeping them in the same class for all subjects.

That is, there are no "fourth grade" children. Students of the same age have differing abilities in different fields, and cannot be effectively schooled on a mass assembly-line basis, as they are almost everywhere today. Individual differences must be taken into account.

A child who is in fourth grade in English should not necessarily be doing fourth grade math, but third or fifth. Another might be doing sixth grade art and second grade music. A few might be working at the sixth or seventh grade level in history.

The fiction that abilities are roughly even at comparable ages makes for badly taught pupils and frustrated teachers, but eases the path for administrators, paperworkers and schedule planners. And, of course, the schools are mainly run for the benefit of these people, not for drawing upon the fullest potentialities of teachers or pupils.

All educational experts who have seriously studied the matter agree that the kind of "grade regimentation" we have in the public schools is regressive—this is why so many pupils entering high school have to repeat the last year or two of grade school, and why so many entering college are simply repeating the last year of high school. The "water" in the educational system must be wrung out.

But it will not be wrung out until parents and teachers begin to attack the status quo as expensive, time-consuming and ineffectual. Necessary reforms, however, are rarely implemented by the people who find it simpler to keep the old machine running in the old way; and this is what foments revolutions. An institution that has lost its capacity to be self-correcting invites its own eventual overthrow.

Don't Trust Anyone over Sixty-five

MOST OF US live in mentally airtight compartments; the left hemisphere of our brain doesn't know what the right hemisphere is thinking.

Our luncheon table the other day included the head of a large company, who was complaining about the present generation's lack of respect for age. He compared it with his own time, and deplored our modern youth's contempt for anybody middle-aged or older.

Yet this same man defends a rigid policy at his company which compels employees over sixty-five to retire, no matter how active, bright, healthy or capable they are.

And, while it is not official, his company will not hire anyone over forty-five for a middle management position, because it would put too much of a strain on the firm's pension and welfare structure.

This is the attitude of most companies in our time—which is not only psychologically, socially and economically devastating for many men of sixty-five who still have a decade or more of productive life in them—but also increases the "dependency ratio" of nonproductive people who are being supported either by the government or by the employed portion of the population.

If we callously discard older people regardless of their individual worth, we are obliquely saying to young people that they are right in their disdain for age.

We are confirming their belief that people get "useless" as they get older, and thus undermining the sort of respect for pickled wisdom that has sustained all traditional societies in the past.

Young people today, who reject the past out of hand, who have no patience with "tradition," seeing only its negative and not its positive aspects, take their leaf from our practices, not from our preachments.

If we profess individualism, but cut people off the payroll collectively at the same age, regardless of individual competence; and if we pay lip service to "maturity" but deny responsible employment to people over forty-five, youth will pay more attention to our acts than to our words.

And, as we put older people out to pasture, instead of drawing on their experience and judgment, we are disvaluing age and tacitly concurring in the contemptuous attitude of youth toward its elders.

Such contradictions within our socio-economic system play hob with all our pious platitudes about "reconciling the generations." By our own refusal to give status and dignity to older citizens, we lay the groundwork for the widespread contemporary heresy that youth is all.

Producing Large Family No Big Deal

IF WE ARE GOING to cut down seriously on our population growth—and I think it is an absolute necessity—then we will first have to change our simple-minded attitude toward the parents of large families.

Most people who meet me for the first time ask about my family, and when they find I have five children they emit little murmurs of admiration and respect, as if I had done something notable.

Now I am pleased and proud to have these children, but there was nothing especially meritorious about their conception. Their existence does not testify to my virility, or even to any exceptional fertility, and certainly is no evidence that I am suited for parenthood.

Anybody with the nominal equipment can have children; it is no great achievement. Indeed, in most cases it happens during a fit of absent-mindedness. No child should ever be called a "mistake," but some are certainly miscalculations.

Parents with four children are not twice as good or twice as loving or twice as intelligent as parents with only two children. True, they have more experience, but as Bismarck said of his donkey, "He has been through nine campaigns with me, and knows no more than he did after the first."

Apart from our population problem, I am convinced that an immense number of people who have children should not have them, and do not particularly want them, except as "symbols" of family life. What they want are ideal children, not real ones; and as soon as the real ones show no intention of conforming to the ideal in the parent's mind, they are treated as burdens, shipped away to school or otherwise neglected.

Somebody once said that if many people had not read about romantic love and seen it on the screen, they would never look for it themselves. I believe this, and along with it I believe that if many people were not ashamed to be thought deficient in "family feeling" they would never have children.

Nor have I noticed that the parents of large families exhibit any more proficiency in bringing them up, except in terms of establishing a barracks-room regimen which is necessary for simple survival. Some studies have indicated, in fact, that children coming from large families suffer from a loss of sharply defined personality and lack a sense of individual identity.

At any rate, we have to begin to recognize that it is the *quality* of parenthood that is more essential than the quantity. Rousseau, be it remembered, wrote a masterly book on education—and then sent his five children to a foundling home. He was more honest than most.

Parents today seem to be divided into those who blame themselves too much for what isn't their fault, and those who don't blame themselves enough for what is their fault.

*

The whole trap of parenthood consists in the melancholy truism that by the time the third child comes along, the parents have only just learned how the first one should have been handled.

Children Think, If We Let Them

IT IS ABSURD and condescending to suggest, as so many adults do, that young children are incapable of dealing with "abstract" ideas. Abstract ideas fascinate children almost from the time they are able to think—but most formal education buries this interest deep under the debris of "hard facts."

Not long ago, the smartest nine-year-old girl I know (who is conceited enough without getting her name in print) said to me, "Daddy, there's something peculiar about that whole story of God and the Devil and Hell—it just doesn't hold together."

"Oh," I said, in that tone of false brightness a parent puts on when he thinks a child is out of its intellectual depth. "And why doesn't it hold together?"

"Well," she pondered aloud, "God is supposed to love good people, and the Devil is supposed to favor bad people, right? The good people go to God, but the bad people go to Hell, where the Devil punishes them forever. Isn't that the story?"

"Pretty much," I replied. "What's wrong with it?"

"It doesn't make sense," she continued. "In that case, the Devil couldn't be the enemy of God."

"How do you mean?" I asked.

"I mean if the Devil really was on the side of the bad people, he wouldn't punish them in Hell, would he? He'd treat them nicely and be kind to them for coming over to his side. He'd give them candy and presents and not burn them up."

"You've got a point," I admitted. "So how do you work it out?"

"It seems to me," she reflected, "that if the whole story is true, then the Devil is secretly on the side of God, and is just pretending to be wicked. He works for God as a kind of—secret agent, testing people to find out who's good or bad, but not really fighting against God."

"That's a remarkable theological insight," I said. "Do you think there's any proof?"

"Well," she said, "here's another thing. If God is really all-powerful, no Devil would have a chance against Him. So if a Devil really exists, it must be because he's secretly in cahoots with God."

Here is a child who is busy learning the multiplication table, the capitals of states and the proper use of punctuation marks. All of them necessary, of course—but how long will it be before such metaphysical speculations are stifled out of mind under the pressure of a pedagogical system that imagines young children can't think?

Parents Have Their Limitations

THE COMMON PHRASE, "a good parent," can be a misleading one, because it tries to take in too much ground. There is practically no such thing as a good parent for all of a child's various ages and stages of life.

Some parents are at their best when the child is an infant; others operate most effectively in the toddler and preschool range; still others make their finest contribution to older children, or teen-agers.

Temperamentally, all of us are more or less sympathetic to one age or another, and can identify better or worse with any particular stage of growing up. It is the rare person who possesses the same capabilities along the whole spectrum of growing up, from infancy through adolescence.

A mother might be "a good parent" from the time a baby is born until it is three, while it needs her protection and loving care; but the start of a child's independence might upset and alarm her, and she might then become ineffectual for a few years.

A father might be awkward and uncomfortable with a small child, but could turn into a superb parent when the child is old enough to be taught skills or taken on trips. Some parents feel easier with boys, and others with girls—and then only at certain ages or stages.

It is important, I think, for parents to understand and accept their own limitations in this regard, just as they must accept the child's limitations of temperament and talent. Otherwise, they will feel guilty and blame themselves for inadequacies that are not their fault.

If we know we are not particularly congenial to a certain age or stage of growing up, we will not try to force ourselves or pretend to ourselves (or the child, who has an uncanny faculty for detecting emotional fraudulence). We will simply do the best we can and wait for a period in the child's life when we can genuinely be more helpful. (Hoping, meanwhile, that the other parent can take up the slack at present.)

Much of the guilt of the modern parents comes from the misplaced feeling that he or she ought to be all things at all times to the child, which is manifestly absurd. In past ages, grandparents and uncles and aunts lived with the family, and provided different kinds of impetus or support; in our present ''nuclear'' family, too many roles are demanded of the two parents, which they cannot possibly fulfill.

Just as a child operates better at some stages than at others, so do parents. Recognizing and accepting one's natural abilities and antipathies is surely the first step to sensible and realistic parenthood.

More to Divorce than Meets the Eye

I ENJOY HEARING GOSSIP as much as the next person—although I sometimes pretend not to—but gossip about a broken marriage always exasperates me. Who really knows why any couple separate? All we know is what we see on the surface, and a marriage is like an iceberg, with most of its bulk submerged beneath the public view.

Even when we genuinely regret the breakup of couples we know and like, a little *frisson* of excitement and pleasure runs through us when we hear the bad news. There is a touch of malice in our sympathy, a fleck of superiority in our friendly headshaking.

He seemed rather brutal toward her; perhaps that was it. She failed to keep up with his growth; possibly that started the split. And, of course, there were money troubles . . . anyone could see that.

So the discussion goes, with a kind of half-baked psychiatric jargon: he wanted a mother, she was looking for a father figure, they were both ambivalent—a conversational mixture of ignorance and nonsense and truths ripped out of context and a smug sense that we are made of sterner, and more sensible, stuff than they.

We render verdicts on incomplete evidence, pass judgments on perjured testimony, draw morals that cannot be justified by any of the known facts, and sit back to bask in an atmosphere of self-satisfaction. If only people were more reasonable, if only they could see as clearly as we, if only . . .

And of the true inwardness we know nothing—as little as we know of our own deepest drives and motivations. Of the hidden forces inexorably moving toward the dissolution of a relationship, we are blandly unaware. For a good marriage is a grace as well as a fact in law, and who among us can penetrate the mystery of grace?

Some, the loveliest and the best, have failed to win the hotly coveted chalice. Others—trivial, shallow and selfish—have somehow managed to find a kind of serenity and satisfaction with another soul equally trivial, shallow and selfish.

The rain falls on the just and the unjust alike. A happy life is a free gift from the blue, which nobody really deserves; this was the hard lesson that Job, that most virtuous and pious of men, had to learn, sitting in sackcloth, on his boils.

"He was too this, she was too that." All such words are noise devoid of meaning—and, worse than that, devoid of true charity.

Anti-Smut Weapon: A Happy Home

IN ANY DISCUSSION about "pornographic" literature, the people who would censor it always make a last-ditch defense of their position by bringing up "our children."

"Even granted that adults should be able to choose their own reading material freely," they say, "would you allow your children to be exposed to such trash?"

I am quite honestly puzzled by their attitude. They seem to have such a low and nasty opinion of children, and to have little faith in the training and character of their offspring.

During my youth, all my schoolmates and myself were exposed to the most pornographic kinds of cards and pictures and illustrated jokes. We weren't amused, we weren't shocked and we weren't corrupted; we were simply bored by the graphic dirtiness, after the initial curiosity wore off.

Children who are at all affected by that kind of thing are already the victims of a poor upbringing at home. If sex is portrayed as something dirty, or cruel, or contemptible, or unnatural, or shamefully furtive, then the children will respond to such attitudes by taking a pathological interest in the subject, pornography or not.

Of course, if any community wants to "protect" its children from smut, it has a perfect right to do so—but it should not be surprised if the results are negligible. Children reared in an atmosphere of love and trust and decent values are not "corrupted" by dirty books or pictures—and the others are going to wander into the ways of depravity no matter how vigilantly we may guard against it.

By the time a child is six years old, his basic attitudes have already been shaped. If these attitudes are not healthy and productive ones, he is going to look for other outlets, in sex, in violence, in lying or stealing or playing truant. No police power or censorship power can be a substitute for the moral function of the parent and the family.

The parents who are so angry and worried about pornography falling into the hands of their children are really expressing deep doubts or fears of their own effectiveness as parents. They feel they have failed in some way, and hope that some outside discipline will take up the slack for them.

We cannot ask the schools, courts and police to do our job for us. Character is built only at home. Let us keep the dirty books out of the children's hands, by all means, if we want to—but let us not imagine for a moment that the feverish fantasies of an unhappy or unstable child can be curbed by burning books or prosecuting peddlers of smut.

Good Reason for Parental Pride

ONE OF THE GREAT JOYS of parenthood that I have never heard, or read, much about is the blossoming sense of "fairness" in the child.

There is a great deal of sentimental satisfaction when the young child takes his first step, or utters his first word, or exhibits any of the "cuteness" or "brightness" so endearing in little ones.

But what should be most celebrated by parents—if they know what a human being ought to be—is the beginning of a sense of justice and fair play in the child's mind and character.

That is a lovely thing to see, much more admirable and worthy of comment, encouragement and praise than the showoff antics we customarily give our approval to.

When the child first returns a toy to its proper owner, when he admits the blame for an action, when he wants no more than his fair share, when he absolves another from guilt and when he displays the charity that goes beyond justice—then we have reason to be proud.

But this budding sense of fairness, this tender flower of humanity, is too often ignored or neglected by parents who lavish their praise on smart sayings or self-conscious precocity on the part of the child.

It is curious and depressing that proud parents will place so high an evaluation upon the child's mental or physical prowess but will pay little regard to his development of character. Yet in later life, as we know, if the character is stunted or twisted, not all the mental or physical skills can compensate for this poverty of soul.

It is interesting, too, that while parents pay so high a tribute to the child's "brightness," this brightness comes to be regarded with suspicion and resentment if it is continued into adolescence and young adulthood.

Most parents do not feel easy or comfortable with extremely bright children; and, indeed, our whole society views intellectual superiority with a sullen eye. Why, therefore, do we place so high a premium on the small child's "brightness," if we want to stifle it when he grows older?

I think the reason for this is that parents who excessively encourage smartness in their little child often do so at the expense of the child's general character. They would rather have the child be shrewd than fair, quick of tongue than warm of heart. Thus, many bright children grow up deficient in character traits, for these traits have not been nurtured in the family.

A "cute" child is a delight; but a fair-minded one is a blessing beyond all value, long after the cuteness has disappeared.

They Separate Fantasy and Reality

WHEN AN EDUCATOR or psychologist suggests that children are frightened, and then brutalized, by programs of violence and sadism on television, someone is sure to bring up the old-fashioned fairy tale. "Have you read the Grimm Brothers?" they will ask. "What could be more scarifying than those bloodthirsty fairy tales? And yet children have been reading and enjoying them for many generations."

But it is a serious mistake to compare the two. I learned this while taking Michael to the children's theater on Saturdays. He was not a bit upset by the fierce giant in *Jack the Giant Killer,* or by the evil witch in *Hansel and Gretel.* But when he watched a gangster film on a friend's TV he couldn't sleep all night.

A child maintains a firm dividing line between fantasy and reality. He may pretend to believe in giants and witches and ghosts, but he never confuses them with "real people." The world of reality, he feels, is safe and orderly and kind. When, however, this world of reality is shown in a cruel and barbarous light, he becomes truly frightened. Then, because this fear must be at all costs repressed, he adopts a casual and hard-boiled attitude toward robbing and beating and killing.

The old-fashioned fairy tale kept this distinction in hand at all times. Evil comes from *outside* the human realm; from creatures that are non-human or sub-human or supra-human. Yet in the end, humanity always triumphs. As the psychiatrists might say, it represents a victory of the ego over the dark irrational forces of the id.

In the modern TV tales, this difference between the specifically human and the non-human is blurred. Good men and bad men belong to the same order of being; and even though a shallow moral may be tacked on at the end of the program, the child is (at the best) confused and (at the worst) paralyzed by this sadistic behavior on the part of presumably mature human beings.

I am not suggesting, by any means, that children should be sheltered from the knowledge of good and evil within the human order; but such knowledge should be carefully and lovingly directed by the parents and by teachers, and should not come via the lurid exaggerations of "shocker" programs.

A child loves the thrill of pretending his father is a lion and will eat him up, for he knows his father is not and will not; but when "real" people, not lions or giants or witches, are shown as sadistic villains, then the callousness becomes his only means of fending off fear.

Telling It Like It Is at Christmas?

SINCE IT TAKES US about a month to get rid of the Christmas tree, you can believe that we only now got around to tossing out the mound of Christmas cards. And the ones I most gladly parted with were those long, rambling recitals of "what the Guck family has been doing" all year.

These invariably come from families we hardly know, or have long forgotten, and we have to remind ourselves who these people are and why they feel driven to broadcast all these precise biographical details.

But what I most object to is their uniformly warm and cheery tone. They try to give the impression of being a model family, busy and creative, having gobs of fun, winning honors, enjoying jolly family reunions and going on yachting vacations at the drop of a hatch.

Maybe a few of these chatty Christmas notes vaguely approach the truth, but I doubt it. None of the families we know well would dare send us such literary treacle, because we are acutely aware of the scars and schisms in the family circle, from Papa and Mamma down to the littlest sibling who happens to be in intensive psychiatric care.

How refreshing it would be, for a change, to receive a dour and candid Christmas missive that more closely approximated the facts of family life, something on this order:

"Hi, friends across the continent. We're Jim and Betty Glum, and our three children, Ham, Shem and Impetigo, who used to live your way before Jim got demoted and his company moved him to the paraffin factory in Moose Jaw, which is the end of the business road for him.

"Well, we're still hanging on, folks. Last month marked our twentieth wedding anniversary, and we hardly thought we'd make it. But Jim found a new mistress up here, and Betty keeps herself busy as a Nurse's Aide, so the marriage keeps rubbing along, God knows how.

"Our oldest boy, Ham, was thrown out of three schools before we found one that allows pot-smoking in the dorms. He was briefly engaged to a little tart from town, but fortunately she became pregnant and married the milkman's son posthaste.

"Shem, our second boy, is still sleeping all the time, and keeps promising to look for a job 'tomorrow.' He's become the world's leading expert on afternoon TV soap operas.

"Impetigo, our dearest young daughter, writes that she's happily weaving burlap loincloths in Haight-Ashbury and intends to come home for a visit in two or three years.

"Jim's job looks more precarious than ever, and we haven't been asked anywhere very much since Betty started drinking and crying at parties. Merry Christmas, and the same to all of you!"

The Sad Tale of the Synthetic Shirt

HAVING NEGLECTED to send away the laundry while living *en garçon* for a few days, and finding myself on the verge of a dinner engagement without a clean white shirt in stock, I whisked around the corner and dashed into the nearest haberdasher's.

"I'd like a white shirt," I told the clerk—who looked more like a clark. "Size 15½-33, please."

"Very good, sir," he said. "Here is one of our new Butron shirts."

"What's that?" I asked.

"Well," he explained, "it's a new synthetic, just fresh out of the test tube. Much better than Micron, Pluton, Gadron or Skilon. You wash it out, hang it up and it's dry in a half hour. No pressing."

"Sorry," I said, "but I don't wash shirts—I just wear them."

"How about this Acetate Vitaflex?" He shoved a shirt in my face. "The newest thing in summer synthetics—chock-full of pores. This shirt literally breathes through millions of little chemical air pockets."

"I don't want a shirt that breathes," I said patiently. "Just a plain white shirt so that I can go to dinner tonight. I'll do all the breathing for both of us."

"Of course," he murmured, not listening to a word I said. "Perhaps the gentleman would be interested in our special Porlon shirts. An interesting combination, these. Quite unique."

"How so?" I inquired, ignoring his solecism, and wondering how long it would take before he gave out; if this were a battle of wills, I wasn't going to crack first.

"You see," he purred, "this Porlon shirt doesn't have the clamminess of Micron, it dries faster than Pluton, its reinforced collar is guaranteed to last twice as long as Gabron and it won't crease or wrinkle after washing, like Skilon."

"I'm afraid you haven't quite grasped my shirting needs," I purred right back. "What I'm looking for is a shirt that washes itself, that not only breathes but also makes dinner conversation, that will light up in the dark so that oncoming motorists can see me weaving across the street and that will transform lipstick smudges into atomic energy."

He laughed coldly. "Very amusing," he said, twitching his nose and putting away his impressive stock. I wore an old blue shirt to dinner that evening—one that I affectionately christened Frayon.

Frustration Can Be Good for Child

FREUD IS REPORTED to have said, "I am not a Freudian," just as Marx is supposed to have remarked, "I am not a Marxian."

What both these men meant, of course, was that their theories became exaggerated and perverted at the hands of their ardent followers. The people who champion a cause often do it more harm than the enemies of the cause.

I thought of this today while reading an article about "frustration" in which the author assumes that it is always a bad thing. He warns us that children must not be "frustrated," using the word as if it were some sin or crime. Yet Freud, who was a balanced and sensible (and highly moral) man knew that some frustrations are necessary and some are harmful. It is our job as parents and as adults to learn to distinguish between the two.

"Frustrated," in its original sense, before the psychologists made it popular, simply meant "baffled or defeated." Now, it is a good thing for a child to be occasionally baffled or defeated. It is one of the means by which character is built.

Everybody is frustrated in something or other throughout life. The way we gain maturity is by learning to cope with frustration, to accept it and to transform it into a positive source of energy.

We must not frustrate a child's efforts to develop his emotional and mental capacities, but we are called upon daily to frustrate those demands which will only make him spoiled and querulous and resentful of loving authority.

Parents who are too strict and parents who are too lax are both failing in their duty—which is to give freedom to the child's real needs and to frustrate only his illegitimate needs. It is often hard to tell the difference—but who ever said that parenthood was easy?

Intellectual laziness is often at the root of both these attitudes. Strict parents are like judges who decide that all criminals are unworthy and should be given long sentences; and lax parents are like judges who decide that all criminals should be given another chance. But the judge is supposed to judge individual cases, not to make arbitrary rules.

"Frustration" is a neutral word, like "sex." It can be either good or bad, helpful or harmful. It must not be used by psychologists as a verbal boogieman to scare parents into letting their children become unfrustrated little monsters.

Children Need Freedom to Dawdle

"THE TROUBLE WITH the children here," said a school principal to me, "is that they are regimented into freedom."

This struck me as an unusual phrase, and I asked him exactly what he meant. He is the principal of an upper middle-class school in a suburb of Cincinnati.

"Well," he explained, "we all know how children in slums don't have *enough* to do, because there aren't enough facilities or money. In the opposite way, children here have *too much* to do, because we have a super-abundance of money and facilities.

"What I mean is this: almost every child in our school system is involved in a dozen different activities—scouting, dancing class, painting lessons and whatever the current fashion happens to be at the moment.

"These children are pushed into these activities by their parents, because the parents want them to have 'free expression' of their personalities in all directions.

"But what the parents don't see is that by giving children so much to do, they are actually regimenting their freedom, and forcing the children to compete in many areas where they shouldn't be at all."

"Does this seem to be bad for the children?" I asked.

"It certainly does. Most of our children are over-stimulated all the time. They have too much to do, and hardly a free evening for themselves.

"A child needs time to dream and dawdle and whittle and learn to appreciate a kind of languid solitude. When everything is planned by his parents, or his school, or his community, he has no *real* freedom of expression, any more than a child who is treated repressively."

"Why do the parents do this?" I inquired.

"It seems to me," he answered, "because they confuse *material* giving with *emotional* giving. Many of the parents believe that by sending their children to this club or that class or the other activity, they are showing affection and understanding.

"But often—not in all cases, of course—this is merely a substitute for real understanding of the child.

"They want their children to excel in a number of directions, and a child soon resents it when he learns that his parents are giving him material things so that they can bask in his reflected glory when he leads the group or makes a record.

"Freedom is a funny thing," he shrugged, "when you try to force it on someone, you usually end up by being a benevolent tyrant."

Young people know *less than we do, but they understand more; their perception has not yet been blunted by compromise, fatigue, rationalization, and the mistaking of mere respectability for morality.*

*

Children can accept the wickedness of giants and demons and dragons; what they find hard to accept is the wickedness of humans—which is why the violence in so many TV shows is far more upsetting to them than the goriness of ancient fairy tales.

Rear the Child to be a Good Parent

AS WE WERE PACKING to leave for the country, an acquaintance stopped by and observed the mountain of equipment we were taking along for Michael—which necessitated our borrowing a station wagon, in addition to the family car.

"What a job!" she sympathized, her eye running over the disassembled crib, the teeter-babe, the play-pen, the Johnny-jump-up, the buggy, the stroller, the sterilizing can and the stacks of diapers. "I don't suppose he'll ever appreciate what you do for him."

I was too busy struggling with the stroller ("Collapses with a twist of the wrist," the ad fatuously promised) to answer her, but it occurred to me what a curiously twisted notion she has of the parent-child relationship.

Parents who expect or want their children to "appreciate" what they have done for them usually find that the children feel resentful or rebellious when they grow older.

The devotion and respect of a child cannot be bought by "doing" things to him—but only by an attitude that tells the child he is loved for himself, and is under no obligation to respond in kind.

Theodor Reik, in one of his books, points out that the love of the parents goes to the children—and the love of the children goes to *their* children. A parent should try to rear a child not so much to be a dutiful child as to be a good parent.

It is of the essence of the marital relationship that love be returned; it is the essence of the parent-child relationship that the love be *transferred* to the next generation. Conjugal love is based on reciprocity; parental love is a link in a generational series.

I don't want Michael to "appreciate" what we do for him; we are doing it for our own pleasure, anyway, as much as for his own good. I want him, rather, to like me as an individual when he grows up, not because I "sacrificed" anything for him, but simply because he finds me an interesting companion and a good friend.

Most of all, I want him to be able to give to his children the same attention and affection he is being given.

This is the only "repayment" of a parent's love that we have any right to expect, or to hope for.

"Model" Home? Don't Believe It

THE ONLY THING WRONG with those new "model homes" is that they don't come fully equipped with model children. After a few weeks, those lovely plans for "comfortable living space" might as well have been drawn in vanishing ink.

My own menage has spacious quarters. The little ones have their own rooms, with a connecting bathroom. There is plenty of play space. Also, Mama and Papa have a separate wing: bedroom, study, hall and two bathrooms "for grownups only."

And where do you suppose Michael and Barbara park themselves all day long? Naturally—in Mama's bedroom, in Daddy's study, and in the bathrooms that don't belong to them.

I have yet to shave in the morning without two little ones twining themselves around my legs, tossing a sailboat in my washbasin, tangling themselves in the electric shaver cord.

In our "private" hall, I continually stumble over drums, tractors and doll beds. In my study, when I look for a copy of Fowler's *Modern English Usage,* I have to wade through *Chicken-Licken, The Rattle-Rattle Dump-Truck,* and an assorted mound of coloring books.

You would think that the children's own rooms were perpetually quarantined. Nothing is duller to them than an area that is not inhabited by adults. "Go to your room and play," sounds to them like a death knell; they would much rather punch holes in my hi-fi speaker, or climb up the draperies in the living room.

And these are, on the whole, tractable and obedient children. But, good as they are, they are children—and to a child, unless he is severely repressed, there's no business like the old folks' business.

If the phone in my study rings, Barbara is there to perform her incoherent answering-service. If the doorbell rings, Michael the Butler is out in the hall (usually trouserless) to greet the startled visitor.

If we had put them into airless dungeons, with prison bars and snarling tigers ready to leap out at them, the children couldn't be more disinclined to stay in their rooms. On the rare occasions when they do, we immediately phone the doctor; illness has set in.

This is just a friendly note to young inexperienced parents about to make delicious plans for a "model home." Don't believe it.

Until the kids have reached the adolescent stage of being utterly bored by all adults, there won't be an inch of space in the house you can call your own. I'm writing this while sitting in the children's bathroom.

Woman's Mind Is Like Abstract Art

ONE OF THE MINOR difficulties in the relation between the sexes is that women speak a language without nouns. Their minds work so freely and intuitively that they feel pronouns are enough to tell you what they are talking about.

In one of C.S. Lewis' early novels, he observes: "If two men are doing a bit of work, one will say to the other, 'Put this bowl inside the bigger bowl which you'll find on the top shelf on the green cupboard.' The female for this is 'Put that in the other one there.' And then if you ask them 'In where?' they say, 'In *there*, of course.' "

While undressing at home after a party, a wife will often reflect aloud to her husband, "She really didn't look very well, tonight." "Who didn't?" the husband asks. "Why, Priscilla, of course," the wife replies shortly. "Who else would I mean?"

A woman's mind jumps gaps, like an electric spark, while a man's mind has to travel through a conductor. He needs some vehicle for transmitting the current of thought; she easily dispenses with logical connections, like an abstract expressionist painter.

It ordinarily takes many years for the slow, ponderous mind of man to grasp the content f this idea-painting. He is normally used to literal, photographic impressions of people and the world.

"Did you notice anything about Daphne tonight?" his wife will say. "That was a pretty pink dress," her husband answers dutifully. "It wasn't pink," she says, "and besides, I meant her *attitude*. not her dress."

Ten minutes after entering a room at a dinner party, a woman can tell if any of the couples had a quarrel that day; a man would have to see a husband hitting his wife over the head with a plate before he realized something was amiss. This almost-animal perception is what makes women talk without nouns—they just assume you have followed their unconscious train of thought.

A couple may be sitting in the living room reading the paper after dinner, when she remarks, "It doesn't feel right." "What doesn't?" her husband asks. "The arrangement around the fireplace, naturally," she retorts impatiently. "Why didn't you say so?" he asks. "I did," she answers. And so she did—whose fault was it that he couldn't follow?

We males are clumsy materialists in a world of exquisite female sensibility—a sensibility that goes far beyond facts and logic and even proper nouns; and no marriage can be called a success which ignores this profound emotional disparity.

An Honest Look at Parenthood

I HAPPENED to overhear these women at a luncheon table next to mine discussing a childless couple they knew. One of the women wondered why the couple hadn't had children, and the second woman suggested that perhaps they couldn't.

"And maybe they don't want to," chimed in the third. "Don't assume that every couple wants children—some couples shouldn't have them, and are smart enough to know it."

Her comment (with which I fully agreed) reminded me of a passage in a Robert Louis Stevenson story, in which a doctor is congratulating himself and his wife that their marital state has not been "marred" by the presence of children.

Looking up the passage later, I found that this was what the husband said to his wife:

"I think of it more and more as the years go on, and with more and more gratitude toward the Powers that dispense such afflictions. Your health, my darling, my studious quiet, our little kitchen delicacies, how they would all have been sacrificed! And for what?

"Children," he went on, "are the last word of human imperfection; health flees before their face. They cry, my dear; they put vexatious questions; they demand to be fed, to be washed, to be educated; and then, when the time comes, they break our hearts, as I break this piece of sugar. A pair of professed egoists like you and me should avoid offspring like an infidelity."

How many other "professed egoists" are so candid and self-discerning? How many others of this type delude themselves that they want a child, when all they really want is the abstract idea of a child? How many have children because it seems the thing to do, but would be far happier without such encumbrances?

Many childless couples genuinely yearn for offspring and would be excellent parents; but just as many prefer their childless state, knowing—either consciously or unconsciously—that they lack the patience or the interest required for rearing a child properly.

The world is full of couples who should not have had children, who resent the obligations it imposes upon them, and who turn the resentment upon the children in obvious or subtle forms. How much more clean and honest to admit that two professed egoists have no room in their lives for another personality, and thus to spare themselves, the child and society from the damaging consequences of this twisted relationship.

Why Parents Must "Abdicate"

THE BEST THINGS work for their own reduction and elimination. If we understand this curious process, we can then judge the value and the direction of our efforts.

"Medicine," said Lord Bryce, "is the only profession that labors incessantly to destroy the reason for its own existence." The aim of the art of medicine—when it is not perverted by greed—is to put itself out of business.

The aim of parenthood, likewise, ought to be to set the child on its own feet and make the parents more and more superfluous. The aim of true education is to make the student less and less dependent upon the teacher and the textbook.

In these three essential realms—the physical, the intellectual and the emotional—the proper end of medicine, education and parenthood is the *freedom of the object*. Whatever binds the object more tightly violates this end and damages the object.

This is the only test we can apply to discover whether our dedication and love are real or counterfeit—for the counterfeit always discloses itself by trying to *possess* the object rather than *liberate* it.

Parental love, for instance, should be a ladder, leading the child upward and outward; too often, however, it is a cage or a chain or a corset of unyielding suffocation. Its aim is not the child's liberation, but the parent's gratification.

We can see how this perverted process works most clearly in education. The most badly miseducated person is the one who must continually use references, appeal to authorities *and substitute what has already been said by others for his own thinking*. His education has crippled him for creative thought and made him totally dependent on "the books."

The readiness (however painful in part) to give up their children is the most profound characteristic of genuine parental love. Just as the doctor aims at liberating the patient from his physical ills, and the teacher aims at liberating the pupil from his intellectual confinements, so the parent must aim at freeing the child from its emotional dependencies.

And the end of this paradox is that only when the child is thus free can he have the *proper attachment* to his parents; only when we allow his independence can he then freely offer us love and respect, without conflict and without resentment. It is the hardest lesson to learn that the goal of parenthood is not to reign forever but to abdicate gracefully at the right time.

"Tough Guy" May Just Be Scared

SOME TIME AGO I was discussing the question of juvenile delinquency with a man who worked in the field. "There's one thing I've learned," he said. "When a boy acts tough, it's because he's scared. I've never yet met a 'tough guy' who wasn't frightened beneath his swagger."

This conversation came to mind a few weeks ago in New York, when I was lunching with a friend who had been having job trouble. His boss and he had quarreled, and my friend had taken a belligerent attitude, which made a reconciliation almost impossible.

"Then a curious thing happened," my friend said. "I met a man I knew at dinner one evening, and mentioned my trouble with the firm. He immediately offered to give me another job, at the same salary—and I knew he meant it.

"Well, as soon as I had this security in back of me, I lost all of my belligerence. I was able to go in and talk with my boss on a calm, friendly basis—and when he saw that I had backed down a little, he backed down a little, and now the situation is better than it ever was before.

"It was only after this happened," he continued, "that I realized why I had acted so tough. I was afraid of losing my job, and didn't know where to get another—and this panic made me so angry with fear that I couldn't behave in a normal way. As soon as the fear was removed, so was the fight."

It seems to me that an understanding of this psychological mechanism goes a lot further toward handling tough youngsters than any "programs" or "plans" for community playgrounds and recreation centers and the rest of that well-meaning nonsense.

A hostile child is a frightened child, and it is up to us to discover what has frightened him, and to remove the cause, if possible. A child who feels he must beat up others is afraid he will be beaten up himself.

Putting such a child in a reform school only adds to his fears and doubles his resentments. Aggressive behavior is a symptom of a sickness in the soul; and mere punishment of a delinquent is as ineffectual as punishment of a tubercular.

St. Paul said, a long time before Freud, that "love casts out fear." A delinquent child did not get enough love, or got the wrong kind of love, or got it too late—and it is up to society to redress the balance, rather than to penalize these victims of emotional malnutrition.

Want Not—and Lack Everything

VISITING SOME FRIENDS' HOMES shortly after the holidays was somewhat like touring through an endless juvenile junkyard: dozens of toys, already broken and discarded in disgust, lay strewn in every corner.

And I reflected how astonishing it is that so many otherwise intelligent people keep their beliefs in separate airtight compartments. They believe in the Law of Diminishing Returns; but not, evidently, in terms of their children.

The Law of Diminishing Returns tells that the more we have, beyond a certain point, the less will we be satisfied with what we have. The person who has nearly everything is dissatisfied with nearly everything.

We can see this quite plainly in the case of adults. All of us know successful and prosperous people who are bored and restless, perpetually seeking new diversions and just as perpetually tiring of them. In our common wisdom, we say that such people get things too easily to appreciate them.

But, in this fantastically child-centered culture of ours, we seem blind to the parallel fact that the Law of Diminishing Returns works even more swiftly and more surely with children.

To give a child one toy is to please him; to give him two is to elate him; but to give him ten is to bore, confuse and frustrate him with the multiplicity of easy choices.

Not only that: but this seeming kindness is a cruelty in another sense. For it robs the child of initiative and imagination, those two most priceless ingredients of a full personality.

A child, while he is still relatively unspoiled, loves to make and loves to imagine. He makes a helmet out of a saucepan, and he readily imagines that an egg-beater is a submarine; in these natural ways, he cultivates his powers of invention and creation.

But if he already has a helmet and a submarine—along with a dozen other expensive and fabricated gadgets—he soon comes to believe that everything can be bought and that everything will be given to him. The grown-ups who believe these things are cold, unhappy and ungrateful creatures. What else can we expect such children to become?

Right and Wrong Love for Baby

IT IS IMPOSSIBLE, as every parent knows, to convey to a nonparent the sheer delight of a baby's first smile. It only sounds fatuous or sickeningly sentimental.

Yet, while I have deep sympathy for those who do not know, or will not know, this delight, I have something approaching contempt for the parents who think that "a baby is so cute it's a pity he has to grow up."

Genuine love for a child, it seems to me, must include a desire for his maturity and ultimately his independence. Watching a personality unfold is perhaps the deepest pleasure of parenthood; wishing, or trying, to retard this growth is one of the deepest sins.

Personal relationships are so difficult because there is only one right kind of love, and so many wrong kinds of love. And the wrong kind of love of a parent for a child is the love that dotes on the baby's smallness, his helplessness, his utter dependence.

This love is compounded of vanity, inferiority and a need to grasp and keep power over some individual who is too small, too weak and too uncritical to judge the parent as a person.

And most of the failures in parent-child relationships, from my observation, begin when the child begins to acquire a mind and a will of its own, to make independent decisions and to question the omnipotence or the wisdom of the parent.

Some parents—too many, alas—simply cannot bear the thought that this creature that was recently so dependent and so accepting is now exercising judgment, reflection and criticism.

A child owes respect to a parent, but there is no natural obligation to *like* a parent—unless the parent makes himself likable as a person. If Michael, in later years, treats me with indifference or even with hostility, I shall consider the failure mine, not his.

In one sense, it is blasphemous to say that a child is "ours," when a child is given by God into the custody of parents, and belongs only to God and to himself. A genuine piety would prevent many parents from looking upon a child as a possession, a tool for their vanity or toy for their pleasure.

I enjoy Michael enormously as a baby, but I want him to become older and stronger and more independent. Then, if he likes me, I shall have the real thrill of feeling successful as a parent, judged and accepted as a real person, not merely regarded as a provider, a protector or a household deity.

The Child Needs Incentives, Too

I AM CONSTANTLY surprised at the number of parents who train their children negatively, rather than positively, without ever realizing what they are doing to cripple the child's confidence.

In the park yesterday, I heard a mother keep saying to her young son: "No you're too little for that slide—you're too weak to lift that rock—you're too small to walk that fence."

The point she should have made was that soon the boy would be bigger and stronger and older—and able to do these things. Michael keeps looking forward to "when I'm a big boy," and he understands, at least vaguely, the concept of growth and development.

Speaking of this to a woman at dinner, she reflected, and then said. "Do you know, I believe I was about 12 years old before I realized that I wasn't always going to be a child! I guess I always thought that childhood was something permanent—that the world was divided between big people and little people."

We recognize the importance of incentives for adults, but we often fail to apply the same psychology to children—who need it just as much, if not more.

Emotional studies of delinquents have shown that most of them secretly feel weak and small and defenseless, and strike back at the world in a kind of desperate fury. It is usually the runtiest and skinniest boy in a gang who exhibits the most daring, for he is actually fighting against his own inner sense of helplessness.

Even a child of 2 or 3 can be imbued with the idea that some day he will be able to do what the bigger children are doing; that everybody was once a baby and grew into adulthood; that life is a constant process of growth.

A child needs to be taught to look forward at the future: "Next summer you can go into the water by yourself," not "Little boys like you can't go in the water alone."

The first statement holds forth a bright promise: the second merely creates frustration and resentment.

I am firmly convinced that the child who is given confidence in his increasing powers, who is provided with incentives for development (and thus for self-control), will not grow up into a troubled and trouble-making youngster with a nagging need to test his powers against the authority of the grownup world. Only the people who feel little need to act big.

Why "Good" Father May Have "Bad" Son

IN STUDYING Shakespeare's *Henry IV* for my Great Books class, I glimpsed what seems to me the real reason that the sons of so many sober, respectable men become rounders.

When the King, in the early part of the play, voices disappointment in his frivolous son, he remarks about himself, "My blood hath been too cold and temperate."

Thus, the instincts and feelings which the King had repressed and disciplined broke through violently in his son. The sportive and passionate elements in his nature, which he had ignored in his quest for power, found their revenge in the next generation.

Nietzsche well understood this when he wrote, "What the father has hidden comes out in the son, and often have I found the son to be a father's revealed secret."

Prince Hal, rollicking with rogues and consorting with bawds in the Eastcheap taverns, was expressing his rebellion at his father's one-sided concentration on rank and riches. Consciously or unconsciously, he was redressing the balance of nature.

Only if we accept this theory, I think, can we unlock the eternal riddle of the "good" man with the "bad" son. Most of us are so busy clucking our tongues at the bad son that we scarcely bother to take a long, hard look at the good father.

What we would find, I am convinced, is a man who (in his sober and respectable way) is too harsh, too demanding, too uncompromising, too conscious of his own virtues or too engrossed in success—all of which are denials and repressions of man's natural delight in play for its own sake.

The sons of strong, important and successful men are often weak and willful not (as the world thinks) because they feel incapable of measuring up to the mark their fathers have set, but because they deeply resent the draining off and drying up of their father's instinctual supply of humor, merriment and warmth of feeling.

Next time you encounter a rebellious son, stop and ask yourself, "What is he rebelling *against?*" The chances are better than even that what he is rebelling against is a father whose "blood hath been too cold and temperate."

Parental Goals Can Be Unfair

THE BOY RETURNED HOME from college for the Christmas holidays, and he seemed drawn and depressed. Somebody asked me why, and I said, "Too much pressure."

"Too much pressure of school work?" I shook my head. "No, too much pressure at home. A boy can't carry so big a burden."

The burden I referred to was the expectations of his parents. They are pinning too many hopes on his career; his success is too important to them. And he feels this keenly, and resents it without knowing why.

Even the burden of parental love is sometimes too heavy for a growing child to bear. He feels this warm, moist, concentrated affection pressing down upon him, almost suffocating in its intensity. But most young people eventually learn how to cope with that.

What is much harder to handle is the sense that you have to live up to the mark someone else has set for you. The grades become too important, the competition too frantic, the fear of disappointing those who believe in you turns into an overwhelming nightmare.

And it is desperately unfair to the boy. He cannot live his parents' lives over again for them. He cannot make up for their own lacks, their own unfulfillments. He cannot carry their torch—only his own.

I know boys who do not try—either in high school or in college—simply because their parents' standards are too high for them, and they are afraid of letting down the team.

If they do not try, the parents can always say, "He's very bright, he's very capable; if only he would try, he would do marvelously well." But the boy knows that no matter how hard he tries he will not do as well as his parents' expectations; and so by refusing to try, he is keeping his psychological cake and eating it, too.

All this, sadly enough, is truer of the more educated, higher-income, professional families. It is here that the competition is the greatest, the expectations most elevated. If the boy would be happier as a telephone linesman or a forest ranger, he is in a hopeless bind. His goals have been set for him by his milieu, and he cannot be his own man; so he simply refuses to play the game. He "does not try."

A poor boy has difficult odds to struggle against; but at least he sets the terms of his life-work. A child from a more affluent home is given the terms—doctor, lawyer, business chief—and the Lord help him if he wants to be an auto mechanic or a painter or some other occupation outside the prescribed limits of genteel activity.

As Warden Lawes once said of convicts, no man can be called a failure until he has tried something he really likes, and fails at it.

Another Kind of "Neglected" Child

THE PHRASE "NEGLECTED CHILD" conjures up a picture of slums and broken families, of poverty and drunkenness and cruelty in the familiar pattern of the social worker's case history.

I think another kind of neglect is even more widespread, and just as deleterious in its effects. I am thinking of the ordinarily intelligent middle-class child who is rarely, if ever, treated like a person by its parents, but only as a child.

A few weeks ago I was chatting with an 8-year-old girl of the most appalling ignorance. She didn't know her birthdate, what her father did for a living, how old her teen-age brother was (she guessed "37") or the most commonplace facts that any 5-year-old should be aware of.

This was not a stupid child, but a profoundly neglected one, in the social and psychological senses. It was quite evident from our conversation (and I hasten to add that she was not shy, simply nescient) that her home life is utterly devoid of dialog in any real way. This child was intellectually underprivileged, and may remain crippled by it for a lifetime.

As much as food and drink, love and companionship, a child needs some stimulation at home that can be got nowhere else in the early years. A child requires information, enlightenment, serious discourse at its own age level. More than this, a child desperately needs puns and word games, riddles and jokes, puzzles and poems.

These latter, contrary to popular thought, are not mere luxuries: they are the basic fabric out of which the adult personality is loomed. The parents of this 8-year-old girl will dutifully send her to college, even if they can't afford it, will give her a "good education"—but by then it will be too late. Education, as Justice Holmes said, begins in the womb, before the child is even born.

Like so many millions of others, she has little curiosity, no interest in words or the ideas they convey, no sense of the richness and diversity and wonder of the universe. The parents, perhaps, suppose that somehow she will get all this at school—which is a monstrous fallacy almost wrecking our entire educational system.

Parents, of course, should not push or lead too fast, or expect too much too soon. But for every one set of parents who do this, a thousand do nothing; they are content if the child has surface good manners, is "obedient" and keeps out of the way. They would be angry and horrified to be told that their home contains a well-fed, scrubbed "neglected child."

Split Families Breed Discontent

THE HIGH INCIDENCE of troubled youth in our time—of which juvenile deliquency is only one aspect—is caused by many combining factors, and it would be foolish to isolate one factor for special blame.

Yet it seems to me that, if society is a seamless garment (as I believe), the problem of the young is related to the problem of the old. In our society, in our time, both the young and the old are detached from the core of family life.

This pattern is distinctively new in the 20th Century. We live in the age of the "atomized family"—father, mother and children revolving around the axis of a common income. The old-style "clan family" has all but been abolished, except in parts of Europe or in some rural communities.

I was the last of my family to have been born in a house that contained not only parents, but grandparents and uncles and aunts as well. I was born in a "three-generation" house, but my children were not, nor will their children be. Each family constellation of parents and children is now its own separate galaxy.

As a result, there is isolation at both ends. The old people live alone, or in dreary nursing homes (except for the few who can afford otherwise); while the children grow up lacking that wider contact with the adult world that was formerly provided by clan living.

Whatever disadvantages may have inhered in the old system, I think that its breakdown has a significant relation to the widespread discontent among young people and the increasing sense of forsakenness by old people. Any feeling of continuity through the generations is lacking.

It is this continuity, this sympathy, that we still find (although diminishing) when we visit a country like Italy, where the generations intermingle freely within the same house and neighborhood. But America is predominantly the country of the young middle-aged: the children have their own world, and the old people are pushed into limbo as speedily and as decently as possible.

In the history of mankind, the truncated parent-and-child family is a social novelty and a psychological burden. Discipline is harder, recreation becomes structured and external to family living, indifferent sitters take the place of grandparents or uncles and aunts; in short, the home turns into a launching pad and is no longer seen as a refuge. I have a strong conviction that we will not solve the "problem of the young" until we attack the "problem of the old" at the same time.

Why Do Pupils Lose Their Curiosity?

IF YOU VISIT a first-grade class, as I did recently, you will find that the children are bright-eyed and eager, warm and responsive, direct and spontaneous.

Then, if you visit a sixth-grade class, you will feel a distinct difference in the emotional and intellectual atmosphere. The students are wary; their reactions are calculated; their answers are based on what they think the teacher—and society generally—wants to hear, not on what they themselves think.

One of the real needs for educational research today—and one of the main objectives of a bill now in Congress for that purpose—is to discover how the teaching process actually works best, and how we can prevent it from freezing and formalizing pupils so that their natural curiosity and enthusiasm is not dampened and extinguished.

The whole process of communicating knowledge in the most effective way is still largely a closed book to us. All we can be sure of is that something happens to pupils between their kindergarten experiences and their emergence into high school—and what happens is too frequently a loss of intellectual tone, a cramping of imagination, a resistance to ideas.

I am absolutely convinced that this is not a natural development, but comes from some perversion in the teaching process. All youngsters are normally interested in painting and music; they are fascinated with words and with numbers; they enjoy hearing about strange countries and ancient times. Indeed, the whole curriculum of education is a matter of delight to the inquiring young mind.

The most important thing in the learning process, it seems to me, is an emotional component: the continuing responsiveness of the child. And what is it precisely that turns a child from an eager receptor of knowledge to a dull-eyed reciter of facts he neither cares about nor will bother to remember after the class is over?

This is by no means an academic problem, but an increasingly vital one for modern society. For as knowledge becomes greater, and as the utilization of knowledge becomes more imperative in our national life, we find at the same time that more and more pupils look upon education as merely a tedious preamble to "real life," which means earning a living in the world.

The number of school dropouts is alarmingly high, and rising. More than that, the number of students who are graduated from high school and even from college without a rudimentary education is depressingly high. Modern civilization, if it is to survive at all, calls exactly for those traits of imagination, creativity and curiosity which the schools seem to drain out of their students at an early age.

It is an absolute libel on childhood to say that children resist being taught; children love to be taught, and when they resist it is because something has already gone wrong with the child or with the system of teaching.

*

The most neglected child in the whole educational system is not the backward child, but the gifted one who is bored with a mediocre milieu—and it is a depressing fact that among the upper 20 percent of mental ability, fewer than half ever enter college.

Delinquency Could Be Worse

WE ARE CONCERNED, as we should be, about the delinquency problem. It is growing every year, and its prevalence and intensity threaten the whole fabric of society.

But it is also wise to keep in mind the words of Dr. Lauretta Bender of New York University. Dr. Bender said in a speech some years ago:

"Far more children should be delinquent than actually are. They have an amazing capacity to tolerate bad parents, poor teachers, dreadful homes and communities."

As we look around at our disrupted social order, with its corruption, its fierce competitiveness, its nervous instability, its tremulous existence under the cloud of atomic catastrophe—it can then be seen, more coolly and clearly, that young people do have an astonishing tolerance for growing up under adverse conditions.

For how can we compare the world today with the world in which we experienced our childhood? Within one generation, the world has moved a thousand times faster than in all the previous generations since Adam. Most of the familiar landmarks have disappeared—not only the physical ones, but the psychological, social and moral landmarks as well.

It is hard to believe that when I was a little boy, 40 years ago, there were virtually no automobiles, few telephones, the radio had barely been born, and the child's world was utterly divorced from the adult's world.

My playmates and I moved in a separate sphere; indeed, until the Great Depression of 1929, we were not aware of the adult world. Our diversions were different, the things we heard and saw were designed for children, the activities we engaged in were sharply marked off. There was no such thing as a "teen-ager" in my day.

Now, of course, children are exposed to the adult world from the earliest age. The auto, the telephone, television, impinge upon their senses from the time they can walk and talk. Crime, war, calamities of all sorts are now part of their natural environment. There is no longer a "world of children"; the ages have blurred together into one long continuum.

This fearful acceleration in the physical world has made for an equal acceleration in the emotional world: children become sophisticated before they become wise, cynical before they become knowing, jaded before they become satisifed, ambitious before they become able and sometimes decadent before they become civilized. The real wonder and delight is that so many of them survive and flourish as decent human beings in the setting we have provided them.

Love Is Not Like Merchandise

A READER IN FLORIDA, apparently bruised by some personal experience, writes in to complain, "If I steal a nickel's worth of merchandise, I am a thief and punished; but if I steal the love of another's wife, I am free."

This is a prevalent misconception in many people's minds—that love, like merchandise, can be "stolen." Numerous states, in fact, have enacted laws allowing damages for "alienation of affections."

But love is not a commodity; the real thing cannot be bought, sold, traded or stolen. It is an act of the will, a turning of the emotions, a change in the climate of the personality.

When a husband or wife is "stolen" by another person, that husband or wife was already ripe for the stealing, was already predisposed toward a new partner. The "love-bandit" was only taking what was waiting to be taken, what wanted to be taken.

We tend to treat persons like goods. We even speak of children "belonging" to their parents. But nobody "belongs" to anyone else. Each person belongs to himself, and to God. Children are entrusted to their parents, and if their parents do not treat them properly, the state has a right to remove them from their parents' trusteeship.

Most of us, when young, had the experience of a sweetheart being taken from us by somebody more attractive and more appealing. At the time, we may have resented this intruder—but as we grew older, we recognized that the sweetheart had never been ours to begin with. It was not the intruder that "caused" the break, but the lack of a real relationship.

On the surface, many marriages seem to break up because of a "third party." This is, however, a psychological illusion. The other woman or the other man merely serves as a pretext for dissolving a marriage that had already lost its essential integrity.

Nothing is more futile and more self-defeating than the bitterness of spurned love, the vengeful feeling that someone else has "come between" oneself and a beloved. This is always a distortion of reality, for people are not the captives or victims of others—they are free agents, working out their own destinies for good or for ill.

But the rejected lover or mate cannot afford to believe that his beloved has freely turned away from him—and so he ascribes sinister or magical properties to the interloper. He calls him a hypnotist or a thief or a home-breaker. In the vast majority of cases, however, when a home is broken, the breaking has begun long before any "third party" has appeared on the scene.

Why Our Children Don't Trust Us

STEKEL, THAT BRILLIANT and erratic psychiatrist, said near the end of his life: "When I look back upon the long series of nervous diseases that I have observed, I see that invariably the parents have failed to practice what they preached to their children."

This comment, more than anything else, seems to me to sum up the chief reason for the resentment, the restlessness, the rebellion of so many American youths today.

We are living in a culture which shows all the symptoms of a split personality. And our children do not know which part of us to believe, to trust, to follow.

On the one hand, we preach the Judeo-Christian system of ethics: to treat our fellow men decently, to extend mercy, to behave with honor, to place the welfare of our community above our own self-interest.

On the other hand, we secretly (and sometimes openly) respect the qualities of cunning, shrewdness, self-seeking, duplicity and the aggressive accumulation of material goods.

On Sundays we worship the God of our fathers; on weekdays we make supplication before the idols of the market place. We send our children to Sunday school in the morning; and in the afternoon we bribe a policeman to refrain from giving us a ticket for speeding.

Children take in more with their eyes than with their ears. They recognize that our homilies about honesty do not always jibe with our personal practices, at home, in the office or on the road.

If we tell them to value the quality of "sharing," and then we boast about our "sharp deal," they intuitively know that we are not handling our lives the way we tell them to handle their toys.

What Erik Erikson, in his magnificent book *Childhood and Society*, calls "basic trust" is the most important legacy we can leave a child. But when the child cannot trust us, when he witnesses the gross disparity between our preachments and our practices, then he feels baffled and cheated, and runs wild because he has no guidelines he can cling to.

When parents talk about "discipline," they mean a rigid set of rules to prevent the child from misbehaving.

But the only discipline worthy of the name lies in providing a solid framework of ideals—not for the child to live up to, but for the parents to live within.

You can beat a child until he is black and you are blue, but it cannot make him any better than the examples he sees around him every day.

You Needn't Be Big to Be a Bully

WHEN WE THINK of the word "bully," we commonly conjure up the picture of a red-faced, blustering man with ham-like hands and a voice like a foghorn.

This is the bully of fiction and melodrama; it is not the bully of real life—who is more likely to be pale and soft-spoken, sickly and long-suffering.

Of course, the fictional bully exists, but he is comparatively easy to cope with. For one thing, you know exactly where he stands, and his loudmouthed ranting can be ignored or firmly opposed. A simple show of moral strength is often enough to deflate him.

But not so with the soft-spoken bully, the "sensitive" tyrant. He (or, more usually, she) is devilishly practiced in the black art of making those around him (or her) feel guilty and unworthy.

We have all seen the small, quiet wife with the martyred expression, who seems to be dominated by a vigorous and demanding husband. Yet, in many cases, she is skilled in domestic tyranny, and while seeming to make untold sacrifices for her unappreciative family, actually manages to get her own way in every important matter.

The obvious bully just needs a puff of opposition to blow him over. The subtle and "sensitive" bully cannot be blown over, for it would seem a cruel injustice to oppose someone so frail, so prone to headache, and heartache, so meek and undemanding.

But the demands of weakness can be more powerful than the demands of strength. We are proud to resist a monster; we are ashamed to resist a mouse. And, with true psychological cunning, the mouse plays upon our sense of shame and guilt and ingratitude.

More husbands are driven to drink and infidelity by this kind of subtle bullying than by any open marital conflict; more daughters make hasty and ill-advised marriages because of it; more sons remain tied to the silver cord, resentful but ineffectual, because of it.

The soft-spoken and long-suffering tyrant exacts a high price for the role of seeming to be imposed upon.

If you can make those around you feel guilty and ungrateful, you have forged bonds of servitude that are stronger than any physical chains. You have enslaved the psychic apparatus of freedom.

Using the three-dimensional technique of Freudian analysis, we are only now beginning to understand this devious despotism, beginning to learn that the big man with the big voice is only a cardboard caricature of the true tyrant in family life.

How Our Attitudes Become Frozen

A MAN I HAVE KNOWN, on and off, for years arrived from New York recently, and we had a long lunch together between planes. I ventured to ask him about the state of his previously turbulent domestic life.

"It's a curious thing," he said ruefully. "About six months ago, I decided to reconcile myself to the situation and live out my life with Susan as peacefully as possible. I make every effort to be nice—but I've been nasty to her for so long that I find it impossible to change."

His plight—which is real enough—reminded me of the old story about the vaudeville knife-thrower who had used his wife as a target for years, outlining her body on the board with only a hairbreadth between her skin and the knives.

One day he learned that she was unfaithful to him, and decided to kill her during the evening performance, when it would look like an accidental slip of the knife.

He tried for a week's performances, and couldn't hit her—he had practiced just missing her for so many years that his reflexes wouldn't allow him to come any closer.

Most of us are in the emotional position of the knife-thrower. Our attitudes toward those around us tend to congeal with time, and even when we want to change them, we often find that fixed habit makes us revert to the old and easy attitudes—even when we have, in a way, outgrown them.

"Habits, if not resisted," warned St. Augustine, "soon become necessity." The habits of the mind are even stronger than those of the body. It is easier for a man to quit smoking than to stop bullying his employes; the first merely satisfies a physical craving, while the second soon becomes a consuming spiritual necessity.

There is a great danger in our reactions becoming rigid toward anyone with whom we work or live in close association. It is commonly observable that young people are nicer to strangers than they are to their own parents: this is because they resent the parents' fixed attitudes toward them as they grow older and demand to be treated as emergent adults, not as infants.

We periodically re-evaluate our possessions, our position, our standing in terms of material achievements and goals; it is a pity that most of us are not able, also periodically, to re-evaluate our attitudes that have grown encrusted with habit. After all, the core of neurotic behavior consists in reliving the past without knowing it.

Why Vice Raids Mean Nothing

PERIODICALLY, CHICAGO, like all big cities, features "vice raids" by flying squadrons of police. In these raids, a few saloons are closed down, a handful of prostitutes and panderers fined, a bartender sent to the county jailhouse for a minimal term.

When the heat is off, in a few days, new places open up for the same old business—girls soliciting at bars, phony champagne at $30 a bottle, and cab drivers carting conventioneers to "where the action is."

It is a futile, farcical and hypocritical affair. All seasoned newspaper men know it, the police know it and the denizens of *le milieu* know it; this is what makes them so cynical about "crusades."

There is one simple and efficient way to stop it, or at least to reduce the business to a minimum; but few officials in any city would care to invoke it. And that is to stop applying the double standard to prostitution.

The so-called "respectable" patrons of these joints are never fined or arrested; it is always the disreputable elements who take the rap, such as it is. Since they make their living out of this, they shrug it off stoically and charge it up to "business expenses," as a kind of insurance premium they must pay to stay in business.

They provide the supply. The demand is generated by respectable and responsible members of society: by conventioneers from small towns, by suburban paragons of virtue sneaking into the city for a night of fun, by companies subsidizing the expense accounts of salesmen "entertaining" customers.

It is not riff-raff who patronize these girls and these places. It is the small-town vestryman, the suburban dentist, the loving husband and father who over-subscribes to the Girl Scout Cookie Drive back home. Ninety-nine per cent of the customers are what the *milieu* contemptuously refer to as "square Johns."

What if these square Johns were arrested in raids, fined or jailed for taking part in an illegal transaction? What if their names and addresses were publicized in the newspapers? How long do you imagine the business would continue to thrive under such conditions?

Naturally, this will not be done. We maintain the fiction that the prostitutes are culpable, while the men are innocent victims. But, of course, that is nonsense. The men know exactly what they are looking for, and what they are paying for. Thirty bucks for a bottle of champagne isn't for the bubbles, John.

I am not suggesting that we should engage in this painful exposure of middle-class hypocrisy: merely that until we do, the raids are silly.

Semi-Literates Clog Colleges

WHAT IF THE NATION's high schools simply refused to graduate most of their students next June? What if the whole educational process were backed up a year or so?

Apart from overcrowding, this radical suggestion might be the only solution to the growing problem of illiteracy in the nation's schools. If pupils can't read, write and spell, should they get a diploma and go on to college or to work?

And they can't read, write or spell—even at the highest levels. The University of California, for instance, takes only the top *one-eighth* of the state's high school graduates, and gives them a three-hour English test before admission.

This year, as in past years, about half of these "top one-eighth" incoming college freshmen flunked the English test. Of the 9,000 admitted to the University of California, nearly 5,000 have to be given "bonehead" remedial English courses, at a great loss of time, money and energy.

You can well imagine what the other seven-eighths are like, in terms of having a command of their mother tongue. Yet, they are being turned out of high schools by the millions, to clog up college class-rooms, to hold back the efforts of the minority of serious students.

If pupils, however, absolutely knew that they could not get out of high school until they had a basic grasp of the reading and writing process, then holding them back a year or so might be the fastest and cheapest way to break the log-jam of illiteracy at the college freshman level.

Why can't these students read and write? There are three main reasons: (1) The parents don't care enough; (2) many, if not most, teachers of English are unqualified or under-qualified; and (3) even the qualified ones have too many students and too many classes.

A concerted attack is needed on all these fronts. If the students are held back, the parents will quickly care enough. If they care enough, more school bond issues will pass—and perhaps more of this money will be earmarked for salaries and staff, and less for homecoming games, beauty queens, swimming pools, brass bands and driving instruction.

The National Council of Teachers of English recommends no more than 100 students and four classes per teacher, to obtain the optimum results. But in the state of Illinois, which is fairly typical, only 10 public high schools out of 706 meet this minimum requirement. The pupils can't learn if the teachers can't teach.

Meanwhile, the colleges are flooded with semi-literates, and the whole educational process is bogged down in mediocrity. Maybe it's time to stop the machinery and retool for the next season.

A good teacher will not only make his pupils aware of the half-truths and beguiling fallacies dangled before them by propagandists, but he will go further and guard the pupils against his own, the teacher's, prejudices and preconceptions. (This is perhaps the hardest task in teaching a "live" subject.)

*

Even though education is our largest industry ($39 billion a year), while business spends about ten percent of revenues on research and development, we allocate less than one-tenth of one percent of our educational expenditures to research, and thus still don't know the best ways to teach children.

How We Would Treat a Child

I DON'T BELIEVE those white people who are fond of repeating that "the Negro is just like a child." Not only don't I believe that the Negro is just like a child; I don't believe that those white people believe it either.

Because if the Negro is just like a child, why hasn't he been treated as well as we treat a child? If he is not quite up to the rest of us—a little slower or duller—why haven't we treated him as we treat the slowest or dullest child in the family?

If the parents have any sense or feeling, what do they do with a child who is behind the others? Why, naturally, they treat him better than the others, to try to make up the difference.

They give more sympathy, special tutoring, extra considerations. And, surprisingly often, this "dull" child turns out to be just as smart as—and much nicer than—the others.

But we in America have done exactly the opposite with the Negro. If we sincerely believed that he was slower than the rest of us and that we all belong to the family of man, we would have honored our obligation to give him the most help and understanding, as we would a child.

Instead, we have used his alleged "inferiority," first, to enslave him, then to break up his family, then to deny him a decent education and livelihood and make him fit for nothing but servile work.

Many of the unattractive things that white people say about the Negro are undeniably true. But they are true because *we have made them come true*.

If you treat someone under your control like a dolt, he will react like a dolt; treat him like an animal, and he will respond like an animal; treat him as an object of contempt, and he will become filled with a self-contempt that must sooner or later erupt in rage, hate and violence.

If we are so insecure that we cannot treat Negroes as equals, let us not pretend it is because they are like backward children—for we treat our backward children with love and patience, encouraging them in their schoolwork, making the biggest fuss over their achievements, and trying to provide them with the greatest security for the future.

If we were willing to do for the Negro what we are willing to do for the retarded, we might find that we are not dealing with a backward child at all, but with a flawed and deprived adult who is capable of all we are capable of—and perhaps much more, having suffered so long, having patiently borne the full measure of man's inhumanity to man.

Dual Objective of Education

IN HIS CLASSIC LITTLE BOOK of a generation ago, *The Aims of Education,* Whitehead makes the point—too often forgotten or ignored—that education in its best sense really consists of two things, not one.

It consists of knowing a great many different subjects fairly well, and knowing one subject very well. A person is not truly educated if—like a doctor or lawyer or engineer in modern America—he knows only one thing very well, and other things hardly at all.

By the same token, the generalist is not truly an educated person, if he has only a smattering—or even more than a smattering—of many subjects, and is able to move easily among them. This is the fault, and fallacy, of a "liberal arts" education that concentrates on nothing in particular.

It is easy to see that the narrow specialist is not educated, for he does not grasp the relationship between his field and other fields. It is harder to see that the glib generalist is not educated either, however fluently he may discourse on a number of "cultural" topics.

The value of learning one subject thoroughly is this: not merely that we come to *know* the subject, but that we come to know what *knowing* really consists in. This is of the utmost importance.

Rigorous application to a particular subject—no matter what the subject is—shows the student what knowledge consists of, so that he is aware when he possesses it, and when he does not. For it is the invariable hallmark of the half-educated person (who is much more dangerous than the plain ignoramus) that he thinks he knows what he does not know.

The whole point of learning one thing well is to learn how extremely difficult it is to attain knowledge; how much labor, patience and precision it calls for; and how modest and tentative we must be in assuming that we "know" something before we have given it such labor, patience and precision.

The trouble with a specialized education is that it overlooks whole areas of human activity; the trouble with a "broad" education is that it ranges too widely and diffusely, and enables the student to sound (and feel) knowledgeable without having taken the pains to learn exactly what knowledge is, as opposed to prejudice, opinion, speculation and theory.

Knowledge is like love: it must be directed toward a specific object, it cannot be held in the abstract. Only when we learn to love someone can we detect the counterfeits of love; and only when we know something specific can we compare this knowledge with our ignorance in some other field. In humility lies the beginning of wisdom.

Ten Commandments for Parents

A COLLEGE CONFERENCE on "Parents and Children" has asked me to contribute a few lines to its symposium, since I am unable to attend in person. Knowing full well that almost all advice on child rearing is futile, I am nevertheless tempted to suggest the following Decalog for Parents:

Thou shalt honor no other gods but God, steadfastly refusing to make thy child a minor deity in thy household.

Thou shalt make no promises that are broken, whether these be promises of pleasure or promises of punishment; for unless thy child learns to respect thy word, he will not respect any person.

Thou shalt teach thy child by example, and not by precept; for a parent who teaches a child religion and morality and yet lives by greed, passion and hypocrisy must expect his conduct to be followed and his counsel ignored.

Thou shalt worship the Sabbath communally, with thy family, and not seek solitary pleasures which plunge each member of the family into social and spiritual isolation when they should be most together.

Thou shalt instill no fears into thy child, but rather impress upon him that love casteth out fear; and that he who commits no wrongs because of fear is merely weak, whereas he who pursueth righteousness because of love is truly strong.

Thou shalt help thy child accept the variety of mankind with joy and wonder in God's creative originality; and not breed in him that terrible false pride of superiority, which stunts and twists the personality of man.

Thou shalt be not too much a parent, allowing thy child freely to make his own mistakes, and not protecting him unduly from the painful consequences of his errors.

Thou shalt not expect nor demand love from thy child simply because thou art his parent, but thou shalt try to win his respect as a person by justice, humor and understanding.

Thou shalt not force thy child to develop in thine own image, but assist him in becoming the best kind of person his own nature requires.

Thou shalt look daily into thine own heart and examine thy motives; for when thy motives are unpure, love curdles into possessiveness, and thy child is no longer a creature of God but an instrument of Man's misguided passion.

Inspiring a Lust for Learning

AT ITS HIGHEST LEVEL, the purpose of teaching is not to teach—it is to inspire the desire for learning. Once a student's mind is set on fire, it will find a way to provide its own fuel.

What made me think of this was a luncheon I attended at an Eastern college not long ago, given by the English department of the school. On my left sat a "sound" scholar who knew his field intimately. On my right sat a young whippersnapper who was glib, amusing and superficial. And it was evident that they loathed each other.

Now, of course, the ideal teacher is one who combines both traits: the power and diligence to master a subject thoroughly, and the ability to communicate his knowledge in an interesting and stimulating fashion. Unfortunately, not one teacher in a hundred meets this rigorous standard.

If we are forced to take our choice, I should prefer to have college students (undergraduates, at least) taught by the shallow scholar with zest, rather than by the "sound" scholar with dryness, dullness and pomposity.

Children, for instance, do not "naturally" rebel against mathematics; they rebel against the terrible way it has been taught in the past. Much as a teacher may wince at the thought, he is also an entertainer—for unless he can hold his audience, he cannot really instruct or edify them.

Sound scholarship is necessary in the graduate school, which presumably has weeded out those of limited intellectual attainments. But undergraduates must first be made to feel that a subject is appealing and *relevant* to their concerns; unless this happens, they will not retain what they have learned 24 hours beyond examination day.

Except for the professional schools, teachers should be chosen more for their personal attributes than for their scholarship: for if they cannot make their field seem exciting and challenging to young minds, then they are in the wrong profession, and should devote themselves to research or some other solitary occupation.

The teacher who knows all the answers is not always the one who knows the right questions to ask; the teacher who makes us want to find out the answers for ourselves is the only one who has genuinely contributed to the real end of education—which is a lust for knowing.

That's the Way It Is, Baby

NOTES FOR A NEW COMMENCEMENT SPEECH:

There are three ways to be young, and two of them are dumb.

The first dumb way is to be young-simple-trusting, accepting, believing, going along with the crowd.

The second dumb way is to be young-cynical-doubting, rejecting, suspecting, despising whatever the majority does or thinks or says.

The third way to be young is the only smart way—and, like most smart ways, it is a combination of the other two ways.

And this is to be trusting when you must and doubting when you should.

To accept what has to be accepted and reject what ought to be rejected.

To go along when it doesn't matter much, and to stand alone when it does.

To be young-simple today is to be a sap. To be young-cynical is to be a sucker for cranks and crackpots and spooks of all sort.

This is the way it is, baby—a mixed-up world of black and white and gray. With phonies on both sides of the fence—on the Establishment side and on the Rebel side. With patches of goodness, and blotches of badness, and huge gobs of indifference between them.

How do you know when to trust and when to doubt, when to accept and when to reject?

You know in two ways—by looking into yourself, and by looking out at the world. If you concentrate on yourself, you're a fool about the world. If you concentrate on the world, you're a fool about yourself.

It's that simple. And that hard. It calls for balance, for judgment, for coolness, for honesty. Most of all, it calls for deciding things *on their own merit,* not because you read it or were told it or grew up believing it.

The young-simple way leads to stagnation, to dead people walking around repeating highminded nonsense they don't really understand.

The young-cynical way leads to another kind of stagnation, to living for sensations that offer no possibility for growth.

Life is, if anything, the art of combination. Of discrimination. Of freely picking one's own personal pattern out of a hundred choices. Not letting it be picked *for* you—either by the Establishment, or by the Rebels. Conformity of Hip is no better than Conformity of Square.

This is the way it is, baby. The way it's always going to be.

Double Standard on Children

WE'RE ALL AWARE of the double standard about sex, but few are aware of the even more pervasive double standard about children. I thought of this the other day, while listening to a man talking about the "shiftless" young people in the slums.

This man, I happen to know, has a son who is lazy and not overly bright. Yet he has a responsible and well-paying job with a firm owned by a friend of his father's.

The lad was about to flunk out of school, and was given special tutoring over the summer. He finally got his diploma from a third-rate prep school and managed to enter a fourth-rate college, where he barely squeezed through.

He has had all the advantages a young person could have—in parents, home environment, counseling, financial support, special schools and camps and tutors. Yet, with all this help, his job is still largely a matter of nepotism. Left to himself, he would sink.

Now this is unfortunate, but no disgrace. He is simply not a very energetic or mentally gifted person. But his deficiencies are skillfully camouflaged by his protective environment.

While this is an extreme example, it is by no means an unusual case of what happens among the more affluent, when their sons find it difficult to cope with the competitive world. Everything possible is done to lift them up to the level of the family's expectations.

But we have a double standard about other people's children—especially if they come from the disadvantaged classes. If they lack parental supervision, have a poor home environment, no counseling, inferior schools and not much motivation for success—we still expect them to make it on their own, or we condemn them for "shiftlessness."

If the children of the privileged were thrown into the same cultural cesspool, there is no earthly reason to believe they would do any better; in fact, even with their advantages, many still find it hard to make good marks and meet the world head-on. It is a tough race today, even with all the help available.

What is remarkable about the slums is not that so many fall, but that so many rise. That even a minority is able to surmount the nearly-killing environment is a tribute to human tenacity and courage and talent. The ones who make it have to be twice as good as anyone else; and how many of our children could we say that of?

V.
Of War
and Peace

But Who Speaks Up for All Mankind?

"HUMANITY" IS AN ABSTRACTION. "Mankind" is a word. It is hard to feel passion or loyalty for words and abstractions. Hard, but necessary.

Everyone gives his loyalty to something larger than himself—the father to his family, the communicant to his church, the citizen to his country, even the juvenile delinquent to his gang.

But who is loyal to humanity? Humanity has no flag, no song, no colors, no troops, no salutes, no rituals, no face nor body. It is a word like "justice" or "peace"—cold, perfect and dead.

Yet all the crises of our time can be rolled up into one crisis—that nobody speaks for mankind, even though mankind today is threatened with annihilation as a whole species.

Watching the UN proceedings early this summer, I thought of how fluently and ardently the partisans of each nation spoke up for their sides. But nobody spoke up for everybody, for that faceless, stateless man called "humanity."

Almost every other species of animal is loyal to its own kind, and not merely to its own pack or flock or den. Only man and the shark mortally attrack their own kind, and represent their own worst enemy.

The other species are loyal by instinct; and we must learn to be loyal by intellect. But the time is running out for us to learn that it is not enough to be a good parent, a good communicant, a good citizen. It is time to be a good man.

This means that no loyalty must override the survival of mankind, that in any conflict of interest between this and lesser loyalties, the lesser loyalties must be curtailed or surrendered. If no one speaks for humanity alive, what is there to prevent humanity's death?

Space and time have shrunk with terrifying compression in our age.

Ancient boundaries are meaningless, except for political purposes; old divisions of clan and tribe are sentimental remnants of the pre-atomic age; neither creed nor color nor place of origin is relevant to the realities of modern power to utterly seek and destroy.

Yet we walk around as if nothing had changed, mouthing the same old platitudes, waving the same frayed flags, imagining somehow that we are invulnerable to the tremors that are shaking the whole of the earth. It is hard, almost impossible, to cherish mankind beyond all else. But nothing less, in our century, will suffice. This crisis in loyalty may well be the watershed of the human race, leading to survival or extinction.

Man's Ingenuity Is Misdirected

A FRIEND IN FROM Washington was telling me about our complex and elaborate defense program—our warning system, our lines of communication and our enormously ingenious means of anticipating a sudden attack.

He told me nothing secret, of course, and nothing in detail; just the general outlines of the program, and its vast technical ramifications. As I listened, I became more and more glum.

His story did not make me feel safe, but sorry. The contrast was so appallingly great—between our technical ingenuity and our lack of machinery for keeping and holding the peace.

If one-fiftieth of the brains and money and time and energy the nations put into arms went into devising a world system for peace, we would be well on our way toward a solution of present international difficulties.

Why should so much of our intelligence and cunning and resources go toward creating a war apparatus, and so little toward the common problems that face the human race: food and shelter and disease and population explosions and economic justice?

It is not enough to blame the Russians for this impasse; long before communism was even a word, nations behaved in exactly the same manner.

The difference today—the dismal and depressing difference—is that now we have the scientific and technical ability to provide a decent habitation, and subsistence, for most of the world. Imagine what the tens of billions spent for armaments could mean in terms of productivity in every corner of the globe.

The problem extends far beyond politics; it is the central moral problem of humanity, of survival itself. Are we to perish wholly, because we mobilized our vast resources for annihilation, and not for creation? Is it the final irony of the human race that we deliberately use our wealth and skill and intelligence for mutual destruction?

And this problem cannot be solved at the political level, the diplomatic level, the ideological level; it can be solved only at the moral and spiritual level, only when enough people stand up as individuals to protest against this lunatic betrayal of the human race.

How can we invent such magnificent machines, devise such brilliant technical systems, co-operate in such scientific ventures—and yet fail to use any of our God-given reason to construct a world order that is sane, just, and truly civilized? Our means are miracles of ingenuity, and our ends are barbarous remnants of prehistoric times. We are living in the most crashing paradox of history; and it may be the last one.

Sometimes There Is No Solution

"ALMOST EVERYTHING HAPPENS to you if you live long enough." This is what a wise old man of my acquaintance told me many years ago, when I came to him with some problem that was bothering me at the time.

It is a simple sentence I have never forgotten. And it is remarkable how comforting that thought can be in times of stress or crisis. The only way to avoid trouble is to avoid living.

Americans, particularly (because we have been so favored by geography and history), tend to think of life as a series of problems and solutions. But less fortunate peoples, in other parts of the world, know better. Life is *not* a series of problems and solutions—it is a predicament.

There are some problems that have no solutions. There are some questions that have no answers. There are some situations that must simply be lived through, and cannot be worked out.

It is this kind of acceptance, of stoicism, that seems to be lacking in our ebullient American nature. We cannot bring ourselves to believe that life is a predicament, and not a group of neat equations that we can solve satisfactorily. This is as true in our national outlook as it is in our personal viewpoints.

Part of our resistance, and resentment, and frustration about the present world situation springs from this attitude. We simply cannot believe that the continuing crisis in international affairs cannot be solved or resolved by turning the right key, or taking the right posture, or being more aggressive, or being more conciliatory.

Yet, all the realistic evidence points to the fact that we are going through a long period in which there are no satisfactory solutions. The Russians cannot be wished away, or frightened away, or talked away, or even fought away. They are here, and we are here, and the alternative to living together—in some uneasy symbiosis—is surely dying together.

This is what we find so unpalatable: that we are no longer the sole masters of our own destiny, that we are caught up in a web of history, and we cannot act with the freedom and boldness we have long been accustomed to. Control of atomic fission gave us unprecedented power—but it also made us the slaves of its consequences.

The world is now balanced precariously on the edge of a precipice. Survival calls for delicacy, for the ability to sustain the tension without fight or flight. We have no answers, because new questions have been propounded by our scientific breakthroughs. The ultimate test of our maturity may consist in our willingness to accept the predicament, and to treat it with tact, not with cowardice or bravado.

Bombs Kill People, Not Ideologies

GLANCING THROUGH A MAGAZINE the other day, I stopped at an advertisement for Japan Air Lines, inviting Americans to fly to the Orient with "perfect hospitality in the tradition of Japan."

The ad went on to speak of "the enchantment of Japan," "the classic Japanese manner," "the calm beauty of Japan," the delicacy, the courtesy, the charm of the Japanese culture. All too true, as any visitor can testify.

And then I thought back to less than 20 years, and wondered if those could be the same people we were fighting—those "apes," those "inhuman monsters," those "grinning little devils," those "yellow fiends."

Now they are our allies and friends, as they should be; and so are the Germans, and so are the Italians. And I wondered about another ad, 20 years hence, if the world should survive and rebuild after an atomic catastrophe.

I could see the four-color splash for Samovar Air Lines. The charming Russian stewardess serving tea to the American passengers. The (completely truthful) statements about Russian warmth, Russian hospitality, Russian service in the classic Muscovite tradition.

For there is really no doubt that those of us who are left—if any are—after the next holocaust will do the same as we have always done: will make friends and allies out of our former enemies, will suddenly perceive their virtues and their talents, will admit them as full-fledged members of the human race, will even help rebuild their economy and restore their civilization.

The truly terrible thing about the war spirit, about the fear and hate and hysteria it generates, is that it forces us to think and talk and feel in terms of abstractions—those "communists" this time, those "fascists" last time.

But those we are fighting and killing are people—men, women and children—not political, geographic or economic abstractions. They are, in the main, as decent and fearful and confused as we are. And they regard us as abstractions as much as we do them.

It is only after the conflict that enemies emerge as people much like us, hoping the same things for their children, full of the same anxieties and prayers and puzzlements. It is not abstractions we kill, but people.

Communism is an idea, and it cannot be killed—any more than fascism was killed the last time. An idea can kill itself off, but it cannot be murdered; this is the fatal mistake in all ideological warfare. All that can be murdered are their children, and ours.

When a nation begins talking about its "honor," the chances are better than even that national leaders are preparing for some dishonorable action toward another country.

*

A jolting statistic to all parents, from a UNESCO bulletin, is that the nations of the world spend on the average of $100 a year to teach a child how to read; and a few years later, $7800 a child to teach him how to shoot.

The Last Dozen People on Earth

WHEN THE LAST DOZEN inhabitants of the Earth crawl out of the rubble and find themselves miraculously still alive, they will start the tedious and heartbreaking task of rebuilding a civilization—that is, if the world is still inhabitable, which is unlikely.

They will then, and only then, begin to educate themselves and their children—mutations permitting—in the lessons nobody paid attention to before the Big Bang.

They will point out that nationalism is impossible, that the remnant of mankind must forever unite or perish. They will see clearly (and how painfully!) that war against our own kind is the supreme act of treason toward God and man.

They will comprehend the piercing truth—as ancient and ignored as Isaiah and Jesus and Buddha—that our species is indissolubly one; that not color, nor national origin, nor religious belief, nor political conviction, can divide man from man in any essential way.

These distinctions will, after the Big Bang, seem as trivial and irrelevent as the differences in height or weight or color of eye or pattern of fingerprint.

And they will teach their children—if there are still children who are teachable—that it was not the communists who "started" the last war, nor the fascists who "started" the one before that, nor the Kaiser, nor Napoleon, nor Caesar, nor Hannibal.

It was rather, the absence of law for all men, the wild anarchy of nations, each pursuing its own selfish ends, each blaming the others for greedy motives and evil ways.

There will be no "good guys" or "bad guys" in the history books of the future—if there is a book, if there is a future. For "bad guys" are created by the "good guys" who are too self-concerned with their own prosperity, their own success, their own dominance, to recognize that prosperity, like peace, is indivisible on this shrunken globe.

The last dozen inhabitants will not preach a new philosophy, but a very old one. And they will, finally, be forced to practice what they preach—for the words of Isaiah and Jesus and Buddha will be justified in every demolished city, every stricken land, every polluted sea, every cubic inch of poisoned air.

After the Big Bang it will happen, as was promised to us, that the meek shall inherit the earth. But what an earth, what a price to pay for learning the first lesson handed down to us!

Death Sentence Without a Trial

IN FLORIDA RECENTLY, a pair of unsavory characters were acquitted after a long and nasty murder trial, because the jury found a "reasonable doubt" of their guilt. This was quite just and proper.

At the same time, however, thousands of American boys are being drafted and shipped overseas to their possible death while there still exists a "reasonable doubt" that the war we are waging in Vietnam is either valid or necessary.

This doubt has been expressed by responsible members of the U.S. Congress, by a Supreme Court justice, by an esteemed military leader and by scores of professional, technical and scientific figures who have seriously addressed themselves to the problem.

Putting aside for the moment all the pro and con arguments about our involvement in Vietnam, what strikes me as grotesque is our insistence that no individual be sent to death while a "reasonable doubt" remains—yet our willingness to send thousands of our sons to the bloodiest of battlefields in a cause that many good men think is unreasonable and unjust.

Nations, apparently consider themselves above the rules and laws which they invoke for their citizens. The United States has broken three treaties and is in violation of the U.S. Constitution in its undeclared "war" in Vietnam—and how can we ask citizens to observe laws when nations feel free to break them at will?

We may be right or wrong in doing what we are doing there, but that is not the point of my objection. Even if we are right, we do not convict an individual as long as a reasonable doubt remains; yet the doubts many of us have about Viet Nam are reasonable, and still they do not impede the flow of human sacrifices to the battlefront.

A nation, of course, cannot always wait until *everyone* agrees, especially if it is seriously threatened. But there is no evidence that we are threatened or under attack; indeed, many of the neutral nations, and some of our so-called allies, privately regard *us* as the threateners and attackers in Southeast Asia.

There is much conflicting evidence in this matter, much still to be debated; while we do this in a trial, we do not at the same time send the defendant marching along to the electric chair. But nations are like the Queen in *Alice in Wonderland*, with her shrill, hysterical cry of "sentence first—verdict afterwards." And if the verdict runs out to be "not guilty," how redeem the lives of these young men?

We Live in Two Kinds of "Time"

THE STRANGE, NIGHTMARISH quality of living in the world today comes from the odd juxtaposition of two kinds of time. For we are living both in "real" time and in "psychological" time.

In terms of "real" time, we are living on a globe no bigger than a walnut, and just as easy to crack. Or, to change the metaphor, modern science has packed us all into a tiny rowboat in the middle of a large sea, and a hole drilled under anybody's seat will drown us all.

But in terms of "psychological" time, most of us are still living in centuries past, stirred by ancient grudges, controlled by obsolete prejudices, driven by buried fears.

What brought this shocking contrast most vividly to mind was a recent item in the newspapers about riots between the Flemings and the Walloons in Belgium. When I read the item, I felt rather like Mark Twain's Yankee pulled back abruptly into King Arthur's Court.

This bitter dispute between the Belgians of Dutch ancestry and those of French descent seems as unreal and irrelevant as the fight between the Guelphs and the Ghibellines, or the Yorkists and the Lancastrians.

In "real" time, it is not only far too late to be a Fleming or a Walloon (except on commemorative occasions), but it is too late to be a Belgian. It is almost too late to be merely a European—and Europe is just getting around to that idea in "psychological" time.

In an article not long ago, a scientist remarked that he had been accidently locked up all night in a museum room with exhibits of dead crabs and lobsters. The experience so unnerved him that when the guard opened the door in the morning, the scientist embraced him, saying, "Thank God—you don't know how good it is to see a vertebrate again!"

It is too late to be anything but vertebrates, anything but members of a species called *homo sapiens*— the only species that seems bent upon its own destruction. We now have the tools to do what no other living creatures have ever been able to do before: to arrange our own extinction.

This is the prime fact of "real" time today; in the light of which, the rioting Flemings and Walloons seem as anachronistic as the Battle of the Frogs and Mice. Mankind is haunted by its past—like a neurotic patient, it cannot throw off its bondage to infantile memories, and remains fixed in an attitude of childish antagonism—living compulsively in psychological time, and unaware that real time is fast running out on all of us.

Men Do NOT Like War

IN ANY DISCUSSION of the possible ways to abolish war from the world, one is always likely to hear a strident voice raised in the ringing declamation: "You'll never do away with wars—because men really like them."

There is not, and never has been, the slightest evidence for this statement. Anthropologists tell us that primitive man, in fact, far from being a fighter, was a peaceful farmer, fisherman and hunter—until his economic survival was threatened.

Nor is fighting an "animal instinct." The most ferocious animals do not kill each other, and hunt lesser species only for food. Darwin's "survival of the fittest" did not mean survival by combativeness but by adaptation to the changing conditions of the food supply. (Otherwise, the dinosaurs would have conquered the world, instead of perishing.)

The history of the human race offers more than sufficient proof that men do *not* like war. If they did, millions would not have to be drafted, and then carefully trained in sophisticated savagery. Armies spend many millions in making legal murderers out of average men who would rather switch than fight.

Even in the American Revolution, when the colonists were trying to overthrow a tyrant and establish self-government, Washington's most difficult task was getting and keeping enough troops on hand to meet the Hessian mercenaries hired by the British.

Men had to be bribed and paid increasingly large bounties—and still not enough volunteers were to be had. Washington complained to Congress that many recruits took their bounties and then deserted.

In the War of 1812 and the war with Mexico, three months' pay in advance plus 160 acres of land were offered to each recruit—and the results were disappointing. Desertions were also rife in the Civil War; and in 1863, when Lincoln called for another 100,000 militia, only 16,000 responded, and the Union was forced to draft 35,000 men—of whom at least 25,000 were "substitutes."

Men may sometimes enjoy fighting to obtain release for their animal spirits, but they are not natural killers. In a well-run society, their aggressive drive is safely channeled into sports and other forms of non-lethal activities.

Wars occur because of national pride and economic rivalry, and it is a libel on the human race to suggest that we have a built-in "instinct" for mass homicide. Men may go to war for patriotism, or under compulsion; but no one in his right mind goes to war because he loves the smell of blood.

A World Ruled by Anarchy

FRANCE HAS RECOGNIZED Red China. Israel has signed a pact with West Germany. We are co-operating closely with Japan and Italy, our former enemies. Russia is cuddling up to the United Arab Republic.

The day before yesterday, we shot at one another. Yesterday we shook hands. Today we kiss. Tomorrow—will we shoot at one another again? This is the way children play, from day to day, only their shooting is not for real.

Can anyone still take "international politics" seriously? It is deadly serious, of course, in that the possible consequences are catastrophic for the whole globe. But it is not intellectually or spiritually serious, in any high and meaningful sense of the word.

We are "against communism." But whose communism? The Russians? The Chinese? The Poles? The emerging African nations? The Latin American versions? They seem to be against one another more violently than against us.

The truth is that the world is ruled, as usual, by anarchy; by short-term self-interest; by strategies that cannot deter, deflect or divert without destroying. The only "policy" of the great nations is to keep on top; of the small nations, to ride with the winner.

We are better than the totalitarian countries in our principles, but little different in our practices. We use the UN when it pleases us to (which is not often), and ignore it when we want to (which is often).

We are for "free elections" in foreign countries when we believe our side will win, but against free elections if we believe our side will lose. We willingly support rotten and corrupt reactionary regimes against rotten and corrupt revolutionary regimes.

The citizens of the United States do not know what is going on; which makes us even with the citizens of Russia and Red China. We have as little voice in foreign affairs as they do, because matters are too complex, too variable and too "restricted" for public consumption, discussion and decision.

Tomorrow, Russia might be our friend, and France our enemy. Where will the Turks be at 4 p.m., and the Yugoslavs at midnight? It is an international game of drop-the-handkerchief—only it is not a handkerchief that is threatened to be dropped. It is everyone's future.

We would not let our children play this way with dangerous instruments. We insist on rules to be followed, for the sake of the whole group, and we punish the child that refuses to follow such rules. But we do not punish ourselves for breaking the rules—and thus it becomes logically and morally impossible for any honest parent to explain world affairs today to any reasonably intelligent child.

Will the Past Bury the Future?

NEXT YEAR WE SHALL enter the last third of the 20th Century. More drastic and fundamental changes have taken place in the world during the last 30 years than in the 300 years preceding.

More significantly, the *rate of change* has accelerated to a dizzying degree; science can hardly keep up with itself, and nothing else can keep up with science.

The whole nature and direction of the human problem has changed in one generation. Throughout the entire past, man's prime purpose was to get food and shelter from a hostile or indifferent environment, to obtain a decent measure of goods and security.

Almost all our social, political, and economic institutions were founded on the premise of a world of scarcity. But it is no longer for many of us, and need no longer be for any of us, a world of scarcity; it is now possible to share the abundance technology has made available.

Yet, our modes of thinking and feeling and acting are still attuned to past centuries, not to present needs and capacities. Today's problem is, simply and massively, learning how to live together. It is not a scientific or technical or political problem, but a moral one, in the broadest and deepest sense of that much-abused word.

Man's relationship to the Earth he inhabits has undergone a radical transformation in our time. Wars in the past were fought mainly for *sources of energy*—for slaves or coal or oil or gold that could be turned into labor and thus into wealth. There was not enough to go around, and war was the classic means of getting more.

We are now on the threshold of the release of thermonuclear energy, the most Promethean breakthrough since man discovered how to use fire. It will soon no longer be necessary to compete for scarcity; modern technology will be able to provide abundant energy everywhere on the globe. This is the great promise of nuclear fusion.

But the great promise is matched by an even greater threat. As rational, moral creatures, we are still at least a century behind our scientific times. This "cultural lag" cannot be deplored too often or too strongly. Most of our ideas are obsolescent, most of our social and political arrangements are unfitted for today, much less for tomorrow. This is lamentably true on both sides of the Iron Curtain.

Is it man's tragic fate to be demolished by the most sophisticated weapon on behalf of his most archaic passions? The real race is not between nations, as we mistakenly think it is, but between man's new power to provide a decent life for all, and his ancient reactions of fear, hate and suspicion. Will we allow the past to bury the future?

Let's Let the Moon Alone!

SOME MISGUIDED PATRIOT packed a tiny American flag into the Surveyor, which made a soft landing on the moon last month. I suppose this could be the equivalent of planting the flag on newly discovered territory and claiming it for our own.

In this symbolic gesture, we did not promote the cause of "Americanism"; rather, we simply extended the Earth's anarchy to another planet. If the moon is going to be a "colony" of the Earth, we might as well abandon the whole project now.

Science, as we know, is completely international; the men responsible for our technological progress have been Germans, Norwegians, Italians, Swiss, Russians, Englishmen, Frenchmen, as well as Americans. Without their shared knowledge, few of our 20th Century achievements would have been possible.

If we begin to export nationalism to the moon, we are defeating the very purpose of science and exploration. What will then happen on the moon will be a rapid duplication of what has happened on Earth—claims and counterclaims, invasions and reprisals, conflicts and conquests, all trailing the customary consequences of hate, misery and death.

The moon must represent a radical break with human history, or else it will merely provide an enlarged arena for our enmities. If it is to be used and developed, it must be as a huge laboratory for learning more about the universe we live in, not as another source of space and power and exploitation by rival states.

The power structures have always bent and corrupted knowledge for their own special needs; science has always been subservient to politics, and to its logical extension, war. If this terrestrial tragedy is going to be repeated on a lunar scale, then the billions we are spending for exploration on the moon are more than a waste—they are a menace.

It is not inconceivable that some military power might like to use the moon as a gigantic sentry-box from which to rule the Earth. This would have seemed like the wildest of science-fiction even a dozen years ago; today, it is more than a remote possibility. "Who controls the moon controls the Earth" may be the military slogan of the 21st Century.

The need for some abiding form of international law has never been greater, to transform the struggle for outer space into a co-operative effort to harness all the forces of nature to bring a better life to all peoples. This is the only hope left in the Pandora's box which science has flung open into the startled face of modern man.

Maybe We Need a "Peace Chief"

ONE OF THE CHIEF CONCEITS of so-called "civilization" is that war and conflict were more prevalent in what we call "primitive" societies. But most anthropological research does not bear out this view.

Studies of primitive tribes, whether in Africa or among the American Indians, indicate that only as the tribes advanced further into more "civilized" states did they relax their efforts at peace-keeping and intensify their warlike activities.

Indeed, most of the North American tribes had "peace chiefs" as well as "war chiefs." The peace chiefs engaged in elaborate ceremonials with other tribes to enable potential conflicts to be resolved amicably without loss of face on either side.

And these "primitives" were so psychologically shrewd that sometimes they arranged for the tribes to engage in mock battles, with the exchange of hostages, to drain away the hostility and release pent-up emotions without going through a real war.

The higher the level of civilization, the fewer provisions are made by society for resolving conflicts. Every modern nation has a department of war; none has a department of peace. As society becomes wealthier, stronger and more technical, more of its resources are allocated to military preparations.

A good case could be made that the Johnson administration's decision to stay in Vietnam—despite the deteriorating political situation—is not based on military, political or moral considerations, but simply is an unwillingness to lose face there. Politicians, even more than most people, hate to admit they were wrong; phrases like ''national honor'' are often used as a camouflage for persisting in such tragic mistakes.

Methods of maintaining peace were part of the essential fabric of primitive societies, because it was realized even then that deterrence did not deter; tribes that prepared for war went to war, unless there was some means of turning off the war machinery and turning on the peace machinery. This is a lesson we seem to have lost in our advancing technological society.

For several years, we have been involved in ''disarmament negotiations'' in Geneva, but nobody pretends that these are much more than feeble efforts to strike a moral posture, while at the same time most of our energy and funds go into building the most powerful armament factory the world has ever known. It is a ludicrously unequal contest between the ''war chief'' and the ''peace chief'' in our tribe— especially since no one knows who the peace chief is or what he is really doing.

Perhaps it is time we dropped the illusion of being ''civilized,'' and restored some of these ''primitive'' methods of keeping our young men alive.

Murder one man, you're a villain; murder a dozen, you're a hero; murder a million, you're a World Leader.

*

Because the world spends annually on armaments a sum 25 times greater than the total spent in all foreign assistance countries, the gap between the per capita incomes of rich nations and poor nations is widening rather than narrowing—thus making certain that sometimes those armaments will have to be used by the haves against the have-nots.

"Who's Trying to Stop War?"

"IF I GET DRAFTED when I'm 18," asked my son the other day, "where do you suppose they'll send me to fight?"

I looked at him. He is just 11—barely old enough to join the Scouts. And asking about his military service.

"I don't know," I said. "Maybe there won't be any war by then."

He shook his head in a mixture of scorn and sorrow. "Sure there will, Dad. Who's doing anything to stop it?"

When I was 11, war was something remote and fictional and dramatic. Today it is not only immediate and real but also it seems a permanent state to youngsters. Life consists of going to school, then getting drafted and getting shot at.

"Who's doing anything to stop it?" Nobody, I thought, almost nobody. Fathers give their sons the best they can but once the boys turn 18, we are powerless to protect them from killing and being killed.

It used to be called "defending your country," which is a glorious concept. But it is foolish to pretend today that war "defends" anything. War can only destroy the victors as well as the vanquished, the women and children as well as the combatants.

In some way, the children understand this better than their parents do. They have grown up in the shadow of the bomb and they know that the fingers that press the buttons—kill here, die there—are beyond their parents' control.

We pretend to be knowledgeable and authoritative and ethical figures; but, when the showdown comes, our children are painfully aware that we have little to say about it. We will do what we are told to do, will sacrifice our lovely boys to whatever slogan we are ordered to chant.

We instruct them in morality—but the monumental immorality of war laughs at our petty sermonizing. We give them the finest education—but, before they are barely civilized, they are trained in barbarism. We hold out promise of the "future"—but turn it into a nightmare for them.

Of course, we are fighting for "freedom." So is every country, since prehistoric times. The freedom to fight another war, some other time, some other place, with some other fathers' sons, for some other slogan which will be forgotten or repudiated the day after armistice.

Where do you suppose they'll send him to fight? Seven years is not so long, if we make it. Seven years to fatten him up, smarten him up, make him strong and capable and virtuous and loving. And ready for death at 18. Why not? Who's doing anything to stop it?

Leaders from the Stone Age

IF WE ARE ALIVE then, we won't recognize the world 20 years from now. A dozen different revolutions are taking place—in industry, universities, medical clinics, laboratories, government projects.

These revolutions are changing every field of human activity: transportation, communication, merchandising and marketing, health, weather control, education, the whole structure of work and home life and leisure.

Only one thing is not changing. The most important thing of all— the way in which we conduct our relations with other countries. And this one thing may easily negate all the other things we are doing.

What the professionals call "conflict resolution" is limited largely to a few textbooks and lecture halls. No money is being spent on it, little research is being done, and hardly any progress is being made.

Our machinery for aiding people to live together amicably on this alarmingly shrinking planet is still as creaking and rudimentary as it was 2,500 years ago when the Athenians and the Spartans ruined themselves in a war that meant nothing and settled nothing.

All the lessons, learned by philosophers, social scientists, economists, psychologists and historians in these 2,500 years have not moved us one inch closer to a rational resolution of national conflicts.

This is the most fantastic, and frightening, paradox of the late 20th Century—we seem able to control and improve everything except the one factor that may spell the doom of the human race. In this area, we are still living in the Stone Age—but with the capability of blowing up the whole Earth in one day.

We are employing our best brains and talent—and immense sums of money—to enable people to live better and longer, to enjoy leisure, to take full advantage of our brilliant technological breakthroughs. But whether any of us will survive the next decade still depends upon the ancient (and proved ineffective) devices of power politics.

The world's leaders are the same kind of men they have always been; but we can no longer afford that kind of men, any more than a modern corporation can afford to have a caveman as its top executive.

The world desperately needs professional managers to integrate and implement the new knowledge of the 20th Century, not the same old power-driven, honor-ridden, cliche-mouthing politicians.

The disparity between our New World technology and our Stone Age statesmanship would not be tolerated for a moment in any company, or college, or hospital, or any other institution of our time. Only in the field of government—most crucial of all—are we still trying to operate with the crude instruments of a vanished age.

Only the "Improbable" Is Left

"WHEN YOU HAVE ELIMINATED the impossible," Sherlock Holmes told Dr. Watson, "whatever remains, however improbable, must be the truth." This piece of reasoning applies to much more than just the solving of crimes.

From my study of history, for example, it seems clear that everything we have tried in the past to keep the peace has been impossible of success. Pacts, treaties, balances of power, even conquests—perhaps conquests most of all—have given us only an uneasy truce for a few years.

The idea of some kind of world government is fraught with peril—it is Utopian, idealistic, the time is unripe, the people are not ready and it could pave the way for a world dictatorship. It does not have one chance in a thousand—but nothing else seems to have any chance at all.

The idea of a genuine democracy, likewise, seems highly improbable, for many of the same reasons—there are not enough people who are mature enough to make the important decisions influencing the course of history. Yet, again, no other system is workable, and all others we have tried are worse. As Aristotle said, it is the least bad form of government, in a practical sense.

What is so puzzling and distressing about the human race is that we are more willing to keep trying the impossible than to take a chance on the improbable. We want easy answers to hard questions, even though history, again and again, tells us that easy answers are no answers at all, and only raise harder questions when they fail.

We do not want to pay the price for world unity, which is giving up some of our sovereignty; we do not want to pay the price for democratizing society, which would mean spending more on education for intellectual growth and emotional health than for our physical plant and our military hardware. So, in the end, the price we will pay must be incalculably higher.

We want to choose between the good and the bad, but we do not have this range of choices—usually we have to decide between the relatively bad and the absolutely bad. And since the absolutely bad— like settling national disputes by war—never works, we have to take our chances with the relatively bad.

The development of nuclear weaponry has eliminated all past ways of "solving" our problems as impossible. The resolution of conflict by other means is difficult, delicate, hazardous, demanding a maturity most statesmen and citizens do not possess. But, however improbable, it is the best we have left to us. May we only know it in time.

60 Years of Peace "Progress"

IT WAS EXACTLY 60 years ago this summer that the great "civilized" nations of the world ratified the Hague Convention of 1907, which was widely hailed as a tremendous step forward in "humanizing" warfare.

Under the terms of the Hague Convention, all the great nations agreed that the "laws" of war did not allow unarmed civilians to be killed, and that belligerents did not have unlimited rights to injure the enemy by any means at their disposal.

Since that time, of course, the civilized nations of the world have become more, not less, barbarous. World War I and World War II were bad enough, in terms of civilian atrocities; what has been going on since then is enough to make Attila the Hun seem like Florence Nightingale.

War is now nothing less than wholesale murder. Nuclear weapons make no distinction between fighting men and their women and children. The latest weapons permit us to press a button and annihilate millions of people half way across the world. Wars are no longer "declared"; battle lines mean nothing; and "international laws" are laughed at, both by those who espouse them and those who flout them, when it suits their diverse purposes to do either.

I repeat these truisms at length, because their truth has not yet been absorbed by the millions of people who are now sleep-walking to their own possible—nay, probable—destruction. Most people still think and talk about war as though the old conventions and restraints were still operable. But they have long since been morally repealed.

As Lt. Gen. E. L. M. Burns of the Canadian Army has remarked in his new book, *Megamurder*, the nightmare of the Western world and of the Soviet Union is that at any day instantaneous death may come to millions upon millions of our population, with the simultaneous destruction of our cities, structures, machines, and the stored knowledge upon which civilization depends.

"The military profession," this general points out, "derived whatever respect it enjoyed (in the past) because it was supposed to protect the lives and property of the noncombatant populations. Now, in the conception of nuclear war, the armed forces of each side take the civilians of the other side as their targets, and are unable to safeguard the lives of their own people."

In 1907, he observes, it was declared to be against the laws of war for armed forces to take hostages whose lives would guarantee submission. Now, whole populations are hostages. Does anyone suggest we have made "progress" in the intervening six decades?

Germs May Inherit the Earth

OF ALL LIVING THINGS on Earth, which is the one most resistant to nuclear war? No, not the elephant. Or the whale. Or even the cockroach or the beetle. It's the disease germ.

What does this tell us about the evolutionary process "culminating" in man? When we finally see fit to blow up the Earth—in a temper tantrum over who gets the most toys—the best chance for survival lies with the disease germs.

This is not my jaundiced opinion, nor the whining of some sentimental pacifist. It comes out of a computer programmed by the Rand Corporation, that cold-eyed, logistical, unemotional research company that is financed mainly by the U.S. Air Force.

In its last 22 reports on the biological and environmental consequences of nuclear war, Rand also projected that four families out of five would lose at least one member; that an attack in which 54 per cent of the general population would die would also kill 74 per cent of all children and 87 per cent of all persons over 65.

Along with us would go virtually all animal life, fish, birds, invertebrates and you name it. Only the little bacilli which transmit diseases to living creatures stand a good chance of shrugging off such exposure to nuclear radiation.

When the dove of peace lies dead on the ground, a wilted olive branch dangling from his beak, the germs shall inherit the Earth. At least, according to the latest mathematical formula calculating expectation of loss of life in proportion to exposure to radiation. And those who live by the Rand shall surely die by the Rand.

Then we shall have—for the first time on Earth—true survival of the fittest. For the fittest, in the ultimate nuclear showdown, is neither man nor beast, American, Russian, Chinese or Eskimo—but a tiny creature we cannot see with the naked eye, a thing scarcely to be called a living organism, a silent invader who has been waiting patiently for millions of years to assert its dominance over this little patch of dirt whirling in space.

And if, eventually, the evolutionary process should be started up again, millions of years hence, when the protozoic slime is again fit for living—what a new Bible could then be written! It would make the Book of Genesis sound as prosaic as a railroad timetable. For who then, in the new epoch, would believe the myth that Man himself— expressly forbidden to kill—had killed himself and every other living creature but the disease germ?

How do you like *them* apples, Adam and Eve? For what we are on the threshhold of doing makes your caper seem like a Sunday school picnic.

War a Far Cry from a Game

ONE OF THE MOST sickening aspects of the news coverage in the Vietnam war is the daily scoreboard: "14 Viet Cong Ambushed; Only 2 Yanks Killed." That sort of thing.

It makes the war seem like a football game—so many downs, so many yards gained, so many opposing players knocked out. Only the players are knocked out forever.

Apart from the vulgarity and banality of listing such figures, there is the psychological impact upon the public. After a time, we no longer regard the contending soldiers as human beings: they are numbers, just like the numbers galloping down a football field.

But the Viet Cong are not just numbers, any more than our soldiers are numbers. They are boys, no better and no worse than ours. They are fighting because they are told to fight, and most of them are just as confused about the reason as our boys are.

War dehumanizes people as it progresses, and it dehumanizes the noncombatants even more than the combatants. We are in the stands, cheering as the other side fumbles the ball and our side makes a recovery. But our cheers mingle with cheers from the other side of the field, and after a while it is hard to tell the fans apart.

Every day we read the scoreboard; and every day we become more insensitive to the fact that these are our sons—and their sons—being killed. They are not "Yanks" or "Viet Cong"; they are boys who were meant for better things, who were not born to die in a senseless conflict over policies that could change in the next conference.

Twenty-five years ago, we were fighting the "Japs." They were terrible people then, and now they are our friends. But that war resolved nothing, any more than World War I did. There is more trouble all over the globe today than at any time in our century.

Nor will the end of the Vietnam war resolve anything. The Bad Guys will continue to run wars, and the Good Guys will continue to fight them. The old men will plan, and the young men will die. The power structures will push the buttons, and the people will blow up.

So many of us are worried about "the power of government," but few seem to be worried about the greatest power of all—the power to call and conduct a war. And this is the one power the people of the world can no longer afford to grant their governments, for nobody can be trusted with the new weapons of warfare.

War is not only too serious to be left to the generals; it is too dangerous to be left to the politicians. In the next World Bowl, the score will be 0–0, and the stands will be empty.

The Stuff of Which Fascism Is Made

THE WIDESPREAD CONFUSION about the phrase "law and order" is not confined to the general public; it extends into some high and frightening places.

Recently, Retired Air Force Brigadier General Robert Scott (ironically enough, the author of God Is My Co-Pilot) told an American Legion meeting in California that a military takeover of the United States "by devious or direct means" may become necessary if politicians cannot control lawlessness.

It is hard to know if Scott is a wicked man or merely an ignorant one;

but it is not hard to tell that God is no longer his co-pilot. For the doctrine he preaches is the doctrine of the Devil.

If the military takes over in the name of "law and order," it would be breaking the law as much as if any other unauthorized gang took over. The military has authority only because it is invested with it by the civilian government; and a military putsch would be as much of a revolution—and a gross violation of our Constitution—as a takeover by Black Muslims or White Klansmen or Riders of the Purple Sage.

A military officer, like a police officer, is simply a private citizen who has been temporarily delegated authority by the state. He has no inherent legitimate power, and is subject to all the normal rules and restraints of civilian society.

If the professional politicians cannot keep law and order, we rectify the situation by electing other and better officials—not by mob rule. For the military is just a mob in uniform, once it decides to administer the government on its own terms.

It is a fascinating example of tortured psychology to hear a man deploring "lawlessness" in one breath, and then in the next breath advocating the most dangerous and diabolic lawlessness any nation could ever face—control by a military junta responsible to nothing but itself.

This is the stuff of which fascism is made. Fascism plays on the fears of the middle class—fears of communism, of anarchy, of crime, of any change in the status quo—to impose its own form of dictatorship, which is as dreadful as the disease it purports to cure.

The twisted thinking of the extreme right is as fearsome as the twisted thinking of the extreme left—perhaps even more so in this country, where left-wingers are customarily suspect, but right-wingers assume all the false trappings of respectability and responsibility.

Children play at being soldiers, and the ones who never grow up tend to become generals.

*

To suggest that war will end only when "human aggression" is subdued is to fail to understand both the nature of man and the nature of war; aggression is biological, but war is social, and new social mechanisms can eliminate war, just as the older mechanisms eliminated cannibalism, slavery and the burning of witches.

War Is Cancer of Mankind

WE SAY THAT THE AIM OF LIFE is self-preservation, if not for the individual, at least for the species. Granted that every organism seeks this end, does every organism know what is best for its self-preservation?

Consider cancer cells and non-cancer cells in the human body. The normal cells are aimed at reproducing and functioning in a way that is beneficial to the body. Cancer cells, on the other hand, spread in a way that threatens and ultimately destroys the whole body.

Normal cells work harmoniously, because they "know," in a sense, that their preservation depends upon the health of the body they inhabit. While they are organisms in themselves, they also act as part of a substructure, directed at the good of the whole body.

We might say, metaphorically, that cancer cells do not know enough about self-preservation; they are, biologically, more ignorant than normal cells. The aim of cancer cells is to spread throughout the body, to conquer all the normal cells—and when they reach their aim, the body is dead. *And so are the cancer cells.*

For cancer cells destroy not only all rival cells, in their ruthless biological warfare, but also destroy the larger organization—the body itself—signing their own suicide warrant.

The same is true of war, especially in the modern world. War is the *social cancer* of mankind. It is a pernicious form of ignorance, for it destroys not only its "enemies," but also the whole superstructure of which it is a part—and thus eventually it defeats itself.

Nations live in a state of anarchy, not in a state of law. And, like cancer cells, nations do not know that their ultimate self-interest lies in preserving the health and harmony of the whole body (that is, the community of man), for if that body is mortally wounded, then no nation can survive and flourish.

If the aim of life is self-preservation—for the species as well as for the individual—we must tame or eradicate the cancer cells of war in the social organism. And this can be done only when nations begin to recognize that what may seem to be "in the national interest" cannot be opposed to the common interest of mankind, or both the nation and mankind will die in this "conquest."

The life of every organism depends upon the viability of the system of which it is a member. The cancer cells cannot exist without the body to inhabit, and they must be exterminated if they cannot be re-educated to behave like normal cells. At present, their very success dooms them to failure—just as a victorious war in the atomic age would be an unqualified disaster for the dying winner.

For a New Definition of Lunacy

IN DISCLOSING MORE about her family life and background, Stalin's daughter declared that, in her opinion, her father was not "insane" when he ordered the political purges of the 1930s, although he may have become paranoid a decade later.

I think the world of the future—if there is to be one—will require a new definition of the word *insane*. Heretofore, we have looked upon insanity as a mental aberration; it seems to me that there is something called "moral insanity" as well.

There is no doubt that Stalin was out of his mind in his last years, or that Hitler was a psychopath from the moment he entered the Munich beer cellar in the 1920s. But what of the men around them? What of the cool, plausible, efficient functionaries who did their dreadful bidding?

In some ways, indeed, it is easier to forgive a lunatic like Hitler than a Goering, a Goebbels, a Himmler or an Eichmann. He was possessed by a demon burning in his brain; they had no such excuse for their coldly bestial behavior. Likewise, the men around Stalin who helped murder all the Old Bolsheviks were morally insane.

Our current definition of lunacy is too narrow, too clinical, too conventional, to serve as a socially useful yardstick in judging the actions of public figures. True, we are all reservoirs of private wickedness, and it takes no Shadow to know what evil lurks in the hearts of men.

But public wickedness on a mass scale is not just quantitatively larger; it is qualitatively different. To be unjust, to be cruel, even to kill, for personal reasons, seems part of the defect we were born with; to kill thousands, and even millions, of people impersonally, simply because they are kulaks or capitalists or Poles or Jews, is a form of moral insanity.

In his book, *Functionaries*, F. William Howton defines such men as those who "view their work entirely in terms of a job well done—without stopping to consider whether or not the job ought to be done."

Eichmann was just doing his job, taking orders, carrying out the function assigned him.

To divorce ends from means, to dehumanize oneself so that a child shipped to a gas chamber means no more than a sausage slipped into a casing, may not be insanity in the medical sense of the term—but if there is a moral norm in human conduct, what else can we call such a diabolic departure from the norm?

The State and "Killer Instinct"

WHAT IF, in the past, the human race had conditioned its children against killing as rigorously as it conditioned them against sex? Until this modern age, the sex inhibition was fairly successful in keeping youngsters out of trouble, whatever other damage it happened to do.

A social prohibition against killing would not do any other damage, and might have inhibited people from slaughtering one another through the generations. "Aggressiveness," of course, will never be bred out of humans, but aggressiveness can stop quite short of killing.

The main reason this has not been done—even though homicidal violence can be shown to be a far greater threat to our species than sexual permissiveness—is that the state has always needed its warriors. If men will not kill, but will instead peacefully try to adjust their differences by reason or by other contests of skill and strength, then the leaders have lost their prime power over the masses.

The commandment "Thou shalt not kill" has been interpreted in all Western countries to tailor Christianity to national goals, rather than to fit the country to the religious model. Private citizens are not allowed to kill for private reasons; but as public soldiers, they are encouraged to kill for "civic" reasons that are often just as evil.

It is extraordinary that copulation, which is a life-giving and joyous activity, has been so hedged with restrictions, inhibitions and taboos; while killing, which goes against all divine, human and rational principles, has always been rewarded with honors, rank, medals and supreme power by the state.

The strength of "incest taboos" over the centuries, for instance, indicates how strongly the past can *imprint* repressions upon the young, if it sincerely believes them and carries them out effectively. A similar "killing taboo" against members of our own species could be equally exercised, were it not that the ruling caste of every social order is unwilling to do this for fear of losing its ultimate authority of force.

The state kills "enemies"; it kills "traitors"; it kills "revolutionaries"; it kills "criminals"; it even kills mere "undesirables." And it is rarely the populace itself that decides who such enemies and traitors and revolutionaries and criminals and undesirables are; it is its leaders, who wish to preserve themselves in power by all means.

If we were really serious about it, our children could be so conditioned from birth that taking another person's life would be an unimaginable horror that only the most demented or perverted could commit. Instead, we breed a race of moral idiots who think it is glorious to do for the state what it is forbidden to do singly.

The View from the Saucer

ANTHROPOMORPHIC, as any smart high school senior could tell you, means "conceived in the shape or form of man"; and anthropocentric means "believing that all values and standards center around man."

I think of these two jaw-breaking words whenever I see a cartoon purporting to depict inhabitants from other worlds, like the little men who come out of flying saucers. They are invariably "odd" creatures, with antennae for ears, oblate bodies, and looking somewhat like those mechanical wind-up toys.

It rarely occurs to us, if such creatures exist, and if they should actually capture a specimen of mankind, what *their* reaction might be. Yet it might give us a little healthy humility to try to objectify the human organism from the point of view of a Saucerian.

"What sort of deformed and defective and rather loathsome person can this be?" is a likely response. "The creature has two eyes in front, and none in back, which makes no sense. Its skin is vulnerable to the slightest piercing, and cannot sustain any degree of heat or cold without external protection. And parts of it are covered with a rough and ugly substance called 'hair,' which keeps growing to no purpose.

"The apparatus for hearing," the Saucerian investigator might continue, "consists of two projecting flabs of flesh, connected to a canal that is often filled with something called 'wax.' And the apparatus for smelling is equally strange—a double 'nose' that is usually filled with hideous substances that must be 'blown out.' Likewise, the apparatus for eating is filled with billions of tiny bacilli, which regularly infect the whole system."

He goes on relentlessly: "The interior of this creature is a complex and bafflingly inefficient mass of tubes, tissues and organs, all of them teeming with micro-organisms, and highly susceptible to injury, disease and decay. The eliminatory processes are crude and the reproductive process has an embarrassing propinquity to the former. The less said about all this, the better."

With mingled fascination, wonder and disgust, the Saucerian decides to take back with him a "specimen" of this highest form of life on earth—but first encasing it in a thoroughly sterile covering, so that none of the thousand infections and contagions it is prone to would be likely to contaminate his home planet.

"And the most amazing thing," he tells his colleagues, "is that this polluted and odoriferous creature actually fights with others of the same species, out of a sense of 'superiority.' Incredible, eh?"

"Vaccinating" Nations Against War

WHEN PEOPLE tell me that the idea of any sort of "international government" is impossible and unrealistic—even though they may admit that war cannot be avoided on the national level—I am fond of pointing out that, as early as the last century, certain aspects of international rule were already set up, to promote the common interests of nations.

First there was the Universal Postal Union. This was followed by the Telegraphic Union, the Metric Union, the International Institute of Agriculture, and many others dealing with public hygiene, transportation, literary and artistic property, the slave trade, legal protection of workers, medical and chemical discoveries and commercial statistics.

A half-century ago, Leonard Woolf pointed out (as the British journal, *New Scientist,* recalled recently) that these organizations constituted a true beginning of international government. The international trade union movement, the Inter-Parliamentary Union and the International Polar Year were further steps to make men in different places parts of one community.

And, since the end of World War II, there have sprung up the Food and Agriculture Organization, the World Health Organization, UNESCO, the World Bank and International Monetary Fund and many others in diverse fields of interest.

As the *New Scientist* goes on to enumerate: "The control of nuclear fuels for peaceful purposes, the regulation of broadcasting standards and frequencies, air safety regulations, vaccination regulations for travelers, machinery for the conclusion of tariff agreements . . . all these and many other practical functions of government have been willingly surrendered to international institutions.''

It is quite plain, to any open mind, that the technical requirements of modern society are breaking down the barriers between nations in almost every nonpolitical area of activity, and eroding ''national sovereignty.'' Business and industry have likewise found that narrow national interests have less and less meaning in the modern world.

If international cooperation is necessary and desirable in all the other facets of human life, then obviously it is even more imperative in the vital matter of war and peace. If it is important that we vaccinate people against carrying typhus across borders, how much more essential to ''vaccinate'' nations against the danger of carrying the virus of war across borders? Otherwise, we may find that we have achieved world government in everything except the one area that negates all the others and turns their cooperation into just a prelude to international suicide.

Violence Is as American as Mom's Apple Pie

WE TOOK THIS COUNTRY by violence, in the days when we were still a colony. With muskets and booze, we wrested and defrauded the land away from the Indians.

We shot our way West. We killed off the animals. We killed off the tribes we could not ''pacify.'' Then we began killing each other off, until federal troops had to be called into many towns.

We took Texas by force in the Mexican War that was so unjust that even Lincoln opposed our brutal actions there.

We refused to let the Confederate States secede, though they had both a legal and a moral right to do so—and we plunged the nation into four years of the bloodiest fratricide ever known to man.

We fabricated the Spanish-American War, won it by sheer weight of arms, and started an empire of sorts.

We dropped the atom bombs on Hiroshima and Nagasaki, even though there was no military justification for doing so, and the war against Japan was already won without this hideous act of violence.

We have been involved in more than 100 wars, aggressions and military actions since we shot our way to independence in 1776.

We have hanged, burned, gassed and electrocuted thousands of our citizens who broke the law—and what is capital punishment but a calculated act of violence by the state?

We have broken all the world's records for every category of homicide from manslaughter to murder in the 20th Century.

There are more homicides in New York City in one month than in *all of Great Britain in an entire year.*

There are more guns privately owned in the United States than in the whole rest of the world put together.

We are, and have been for a long time, the most lawbreaking nation in the world, in almost every category of crime—and especially in crimes of violence, in attacks against persons.

Now we are worried about "crime in the streets." As if it were something new. But the only thing new is that the Negro is following the example of the whites.

We have gained, and kept, what we have by raw power. We have been "peace-loving" when it paid, and violent when it did not. This is the example we have provided, while telling ourselves sanctimonious lies about our sweetness and goodness and essential decency.

Now some of our chickens are coming home to roost. And how will we deal with them? By violence, of course. In the good old tradition.

We Astronauts Better Stop Fighting

I WAS LISTENING to a lecture by an astronomer last month, and he mentioned the relative size of our world in the universe. He said that the best modern telescope can now see so far into space that if we took the whole United States as our model, the earth would not even appear on it, when looked at with electron microscopes.

This is a hard image to illustrate with words, so let me try again in another way. If that part of the universe we can already see were the size of the United States, the size of the earth in that area would be about as small as a virus compared with the whole country. Is that clearer?

How provincial of us, the astronomer went on, to imagine that our galaxy with 150 million stars as large as our sun, does not have other planets with life on them—especially since there are 150 million other galaxies in the universe, each containing as many millions of stars.

Other stars no doubt have planets. Other planets, somewhere, must have pretty much the same environmental conditions that bred life on earth; and out of this life must have come what we call "intelligent" life on some of these planets—and possibly millions of years before this planet began to cool off. To believe we are unique is the height of anthropocentric arrogance.

If we could steadily see ourselves in this light—as a tiny speck of dust whirling about in one tiny corner of the universe, with the whole time-span of the earth no longer than a twinkling—we might be able to reach a saner perspective on human and social problems.

Buckminster Fuller's old analogy of the earth as a "spaceship" is another useful concept. We are all riding together in a spaceship that is smaller than the one the astronauts went up in, compared with the size of the cosmos. We are locked into this ship together and forever, and we survive or perish together and forever.

The first and absolute imperative in the spaceship of the astronauts is cooperation, and the subordination of individual will to the welfare of the ship as a whole. Only *after that* is there room for idiosyncratic differences. Disharmony among the astronauts means disaster for all.

Man must begin to take the "astronomical" view of himself and his world if he is to survive. It is far too late for any parochial view; too late for politics, too late for race, too late for class distinctions. Our ship is now so highly explosive, so charged with incendiaries, that we have only two options: We stay up, or we blow up. Not to see this, clearly and steadily and primarily, is to perish in the universe as obscurely and ignobly as we have lived.

Power As a Substitute for Love

"MAKE LOVE, NOT WAR" is the best of the graffiti that today's youngsters have passed along to us. It is a new phrase representing an old truth—the ancient Greeks coupled the god of war with the goddess of love, to symbolize the strange relationship between the two.

Man is said to be essentially composed of an "erotic" and an "aggressive" drive. I believe it, and I also believe that an excess of the one indicates a deficiency of the other. Undue aggressiveness, in my view, is the result of a lack of the ability to love or be loved.

If there were some way we could examine the private lives of public men—with a sort of psychic x-ray—I think we would discover that the loving faculty in them had been dammed up and diverted into channels that ran toward power and position and conquest.

It was easy enough to see without such a device in the case of a Hitler, who had no personal emotive life, and in whom the excitement of hate evidently gave the same thrill that love gives to normal people. I suspect much the same was true of Napoleon, despite his amorous adventurings; he lacked the gift of intimacy, and while he could "possess" women, it was only as possessions, not as persons.

It is no historical accident that leaders are almost always worse than the people they lead, or that their power to summon their subjects' worst instincts for cruelty is far greater than their power to call upon the people's vast capacity for good will and generosity.

We find the same tendency among children, where good or at least average boys will follow the worst of their number—who appeal to their suppressed and forbidden feelings—but will rarely follow the best of their number. Virtue seems individual, while vice is collective.

Since political power goes to those who crave it and combat for it, and since those who crave it (in my opinion) are enjoying it as a substitute for the erotic pleasure they cannot achieve, it is hardly surprising that most leaders have plunged their nations into blood baths with dismaying regularity throughout the centuries.

This is doubtless what Socrates meant when he observed that "power should be entrusted only to those who do not want it." A man whose aggressive and erotic drives are in balance will no more abuse his office than he would abuse his love object; but such a man has to be drafted for public life. Those who volunteer to lead us too often want to lead us into making war, and away from making love.

"Merchants of Death" —New Style

WHEN I WAS GROWING UP, between the First and Second World Wars, we knew all about the "merchants of death"—those shadowy and sinister figures like Krupp and Zaharoff, who made and sold arms to any nation that could afford them.

We naïvely thought, at the time, that if such men and their companies could be prevented from turning a profit on weapons of mass destruction, it might help the world along the bumpy road toward disarmament and eventual peace.

Such men and their companies no longer exercise the power and influence they once had; instead, their place has been taken by the nations of the world themselves. All of us today, through our governments on all sides of all curtains, are the Krupps and Zaharoffs of modern conventional warfare.

This is the inescapable conclusion from reading George Thayer's thoroughly documented book, *The War Business,* which shows how governments themselves have taken over the international trade in armaments, and how billions of dollars a year in arms are sold (or even given away) by so-called "peace-loving" countries—with the United States leading the procession.

In some cases, our rationale for this wholesale merchandising of weapons is that we are trying to "stabilize" a situation and help maintain an equilibrium that will prevent war. But this has never worked, and never will; since both sides are provided with weapons, it merely escalates the hostilities, as it did between Israel and the Arab states a few years ago, and as it threatens to do again now.

All major nations are equally guilty of this traffic; some do it for profit, some for mistaken notions of "balance of power," and some for its pure trouble-making potential. While all these nations speak up for "peace" on the floor of the UN, none of them genuinely supports efforts to create international machinery that would limit their traffic in arms.

The War Business is an ugly book to read, in the sense that a suppurating wound is an ugly thing to look at—but turning our eyes away to lovelier prospects will only speed the moment when death comes to the patient; and, of course, the "patient" in this book is the entire human race.

It is not evil and greedy men, but governments themselves, that sustain and replenish the dangerously high level of weaponry all over the world, and by so doing make a mockery of the "law and order" they preach for domestic consumption only.

When we put a man into a uniform, it matters less than we think which uniform we put him into.

*

Everybody is "against" war, verbally; and the most passionate opponents of war are the generals who fight them and the statesmen who declare them—but the war they are against is abstract, while the one they are waging can always be rationalized as a necessary exception.

Mankind Should Repudiate War

EVERYBODY IS AGAINST WAR. The United States says it is against war. Stalin said he was against war. Even Hitler said he was against war.

What governments usually mean by this statement is that they are against war *as long as they can get their own way by other means.* If the other means fail, they will resort to war.

But to be genuinely and meaningfully against war is to be against the *preconditions that create war and make it inevitable.* These preconditions are: anarchy among nations, the lack of an international court and the absence of an international police force.

Until the nations are willing to give up some of their external authority—just as cities give up some to the states, and the states to the nation—then there is no way to resolve national disputes except by force and violence. It is as simple, and as difficult, as that.

First of all, we must get over the thought that war is a ''natural'' social phenomenon, when it is in truth a disease of mankind. In earlier eras, it was thought that cannibalism was natural; later, it was believed that slavery was natural. Both these practices have been abandoned in the world, and there is no rational reason that war cannot be repudiated by the mass of mankind.

In my view, it will never voluntarily be repudiated by governments as such. Governments have too much of a stake in ruling ever to relinquish any part of their authority—dubious as that authority is in this age of mass retaliation and mutual destruction.

It is the peoples of the world, acting in concert, who must persuade their governments to adopt ''law and order'' in the international sphere, just as those governments urge us to follow law and order in the domestic sphere. How absurd for a government to preach a doctrine of nonviolence to its own citizens, and to practice ruthless violence abroad whenever it so desires. What an immoral contradiction!

In my view, also, the student protest movement is the most heartening sign of a moral revolution in this area. The students are not merely objecting to our involvement in Vietnam; they want to stop war altogether, so that other Vietnams do not crop up yearly.

This can be done only by youth calling across the barriers of nations; by students appealing to students in all other countries, by going over the heads of governments and arousing and mobilizing young people everywhere. I don't think that even the Russians or Chinese could control their own youth in the face of a worldwide movement to stamp out the pandemic disease of war that has for too long afflicted the best, the bravest and the youngest of mankind.

Patton a Most Honest General

I WAS SORRY to miss a preview screening of the film *Patton*, because I wanted to see how this unique general was depicted. Although I did not like Patton, or what he stood for, I respected him as one of the most honest generals of our age.

He was totally free of the cant and self-deception that afflict almost all his military colleagues. He liked fighting, he enjoyed war and he made no sentimental obeisances to peace.

Patton was practically the only military leader I have heard who refrained from the customary gush about "defense" and "security" and "we can't have peace unless we have a strong fighting force."

He enthusiastically accepted the fact that armies are for fighting and for killing, not for keeping the peace. He was restless and unfulfilled out of battle, and felt himself fully alive only in warfare.

This is why men go into the army, and rise in the ranks. They like to command and they can command best in combat. They want victory, honor, decorations, authority and life-and-death decisions to make. This is their form of self-expression.

Barbarous as we may find this, it is at least a far more honest attitude than the public utterances of most military leaders, who pretend that they find peace preferable to war.

Military men, like politicians, are the same the world over, and have more in common with one another (even though they wear different uniforms) than they do with their own countrymen. A "patriotic" American general would be just as patriotic a Russian general if he had happened to be born there.

The combative temperament, like the political temperament, is a supranational trait; it may take on the coloration of its country, but the aim of the general is to win, just as the aim of the politician is to get and stay in office. In both cases, the ideology is subordinate to the conflict. Patton, I dare say, might have been just as happy fighting with the Nazis as against them, and would have found adequate reasons for justifying his role. Generals are not natural democrats.

Indeed, military men often feel themselves "obstructed" under a democratic form of government, and they thrive much better in nations where civilian control has been weakened or usurped. Our founding fathers understood this quite well when they stipulated that a civilian President should be commander-in-chief of the armed forces.

What is tragic is that the combative virtues of such men as Patton must be enlisted in the service of killing rather than of leading us in conquest of our common enemies—disease, famine, flood and, most menacingly, that pervasive prejudice that may eventually conquer us all.

We Don't Need More Treasure

SINCE THE UNITED STATES already owns a vast disproportion of the world's resources and riches, and since the inequity between the rich nations and the poor nations is increasing rather than decreasing, we must obviously find some way to bring the world more into economic balance if we want to avoid widespread rebellion and revolution.

There is one way to do this without sacrificing a single dollar or resource we already possess. It would be a gracious and generous gesture, signifying to the poor and struggling countries of the world that we are not the oppressors and exploiters as depicted in Marxist demonology.

It is agreed by all experts in the various scientific disciplines that the wealth on and under the floor of the oceans is many times greater than our resources on land. The seabeds of the globe—which represent two-thirds of the total area of the world—contain enormous natural riches we are now technologically ready to develop and utilize.

Since the international seas belong to everybody, those nations with the most money and equipment would normally be the first and most successful to take part in this new "gold rush" for underwater minerals and other resources. And the United States would be first of all.

It is my view that we have not only a moral obligation but a practical stake as well in relinquishing all claims to this subaqueous treasure. We should work with the UN's Political Committee of the General Assembly to assure that international regulation will apportion the largest shares to the countries in greatest need.

More than this, rather than giving military and economic aid to nations, which only foments conflict and often keeps corrupt administrations more securely in power, we should offer equipment and technical help (on a loan-and-repayment basis) to the underdeveloped lands for working the seabeds.

The United States already commands some 60 per cent of the world's renewable and nonrenewable resources. Much more will come in when we cultivate our own coastal waters on the continental shelf. Only shortsighted greed would compel us to engage in a new race of underwater colonialism, and compound the anarchy we have created on land.

Our generosity (which is only a form of common sense) would do more to undercut the Marxist attacks on our hegemony of the world's riches than almost any other step we could take. To say "We want no more, and recognize that poverty must be alleviated if peace is to be maintained," would testify most eloquently to our sincere aim of avoiding a nuclear holocaust in a struggle for oceanic treasure.

World Still Living in the Wild West

THE TWENTIETH-CENTURY WORLD, with all its magnificent technology, is very much like a small Western town in the early days of our nation, before sheriffs and judges and courts turned the town into a genuine "community."

Everybody arms himself for what he claims is defense; but the line between "defense" and "aggression" is a thin one, and nobody has the authority to decide which is truly which.

While our scientific and technical achievement staggers the imagination, our civil and political arrangements have not progressed an inch beyond the frontier mentality. There is no common law, no common protection, no peaceable means for adjudicating disputes.

Each nation is its own law, its own sheriff, its own judge. Each has its own arsenal of weapons hidden away, and—out of fear more than out of hostility—each feels it must maintain an "arms superiority" over the others.

The Western towns could not long exist in this fashion, for only the outlaws flourished as long as the law was in private hands. And the country did not grow and prosper until all assented to a common law with enforceable powers.

World law today is in private hands—which means that there is no law, and therefore there is no order. There is only anarchy masquerading as national sovereignty. But there is no sovereignty, either, for nuclear weapons make defense meaningless and victory for any side impossible.

These are the plain facts of the case. They have always been the facts of the case, because all that can ever exist between independent sovereignties is an uneasy truce, never a genuine peace. But the big difference today is that no nation has power to defend itself—it can only retaliate in kind.

War used to be called an "extension of politics," and with some reason. Now, war has become obsolete because, pushed to the ultimate, it can merely end in mutual self-destruction. *Atomic energy has given us so much power that we have lost the power to use it,* as a means of getting our own way by threats or by violence.

The Western town grew too big for anarchy, and the modern world has grown too small for it. We are all locked into the same little cabin, and any shot through the ceiling can depressurize the craft, destroying the destroyer along with his victim. Not to recognize this paramount truth of our time is to betray the act of creation.

No More Time for "We" and "They"

IT IS NEVER WE who want the war. It is always They who want it.

They may be the Persians or the Spartans or the Carthaginians or the Yorkists or the Confederates or the communists. There has always been a They.

But, from their side, We have always been the They. And, to them, We have always wanted the war. So, out of mutual fear and misunderstanding and dislike, We and They have always gone to war.

Obviously, there is only one way to end war before we end the human race. And that is for all of us to become a We. I know this is a foolish, impractical, impossible, idealistic solution. It has always been that.

But nothing else has ever worked. For thousands of years, the world has been guided by the practical, the possible, the realistic. And it has always failed. The next war has always been born within the peace treaty of the old one.

We have tried everything else—pacts and alliances and defense and extermination of the enemy and a League of Nations and a United Nations. We have patched and sewed, prayed and threatened, and ended by making new weapons for the new war against the new enemy.

Only now we have reached the end of that road. War has now become something bigger than We and They. We can no longer march off to war to protect our women and children—war is now coming to us, and the women and children will die along with the men, who have no place to march.

The human race is signing a suicide pact in its sleep. Events are slipping out of our control. No nation is "free," no nation is "sovereign" any more. Every nation owns the seas and the skies. The wind bloweth where it listeth, and radioactivity has no citizenship.

War has suddenly become obsolete as a means of deciding national differences. People everywhere in the world are beginning to know it, but governments do not yet know it. Governments are still a century behind the times, planning to fight with weapons they cannot control.

But there is no creative dialog between the people and their governments: none in Russia, and very little more here. The people feel carried along by forces they can neither guide, restrain nor comprehend. In the great Democracy, we have little more to say about war and peace than in the great Dictatorship. "What can one person do to stop it?"

We can think. We can speak. We can call for new ideas, for a personal, a moral, a humanitarian approach to world problems. If we are going to die, we can at least die as a consequence of our beliefs, not like animals, stunned and hopeless, in a war that nobody really wanted.

The grim prospect of the 20th Century is indicated by the twin facts that while medical science is discovering new ways of keeping people alive, military science is inventing new ways of killing them—the one providing a population explosion, and the other an explosion of the population.

*

Men of power often complain that they are losing their basic liberties when they are only losing their license to infringe on other people's liberties.

We Live in Two Worlds at Once

WE WERE WALKING down to the beach, on the last day of vacation. It was a morning fresh from the hand of God—sun and sky and wind and water, and birds coasting above the cliffs, and children tumbling about the sand.

It was impossible to believe, at that clear and suspended moment in time, that the other world actually existed—the world of bombs and warplanes, of revolts and repressions, of organized bitterness and official cunning and mechanized ferocity.

On a morning such as that, there comes a sudden, piercing knowledge that mankind is living through its own nightmare, that everything we call "real" in the big world is a feverish fantasy, that the only truth of existence resides somewhere here, between shore and sea, sand and sky.

Not that Nature is kind or benevolent; I do not subscribe to that sentimental fiction. But Nature is at least indifferent to our ends; it provides a setting which we can enjoy or mutilate or obliterate entirely. It gives us a choice of action for good or ill.

The other world—the world of headlines—gives us no choice of action. We are mute walk-ons in a global drama we have neither written nor directed. As in a nightmare, we are controlled by forces we cannot comprehend.

Mankind has always known anguish and loss. But with a sense of purpose, with a feeling for the future, with a faith that goodness was recoverable, that wholeness and saneness were the ultimate and attainable ends of the pathetic and noble human struggle to find a meaning and a place in the universe.

We have become dehumanized. We now think only of "survival," like some blind, groping animals clawing their way underground. And not even survival as a people or a nation, but as a tribe, a clan, a family, defending its dwindling supply of water and food and air by machine guns aimed at their own neighbors.

Is the Greek dream, the Hebrew dream, the Christian dream, come to this—that we abdicate our humanity, call ourselves powerless before the forces of history, and retreat to our underground caverns, for the sake of a bestial "survival"?

Man was made to stand on the shore, to celebrate the sun and the sky, to use the wind and master the water, to care passionately for the children tumbling about the sand. He was made to grow in the image of his Father, to embrace his fellows everywhere, to open the doors, to feed the hungry, to return good for evil. Nothing is harder, but anything else is sure damnation.

Wars Just Make Us Worse

IN 1917, the year I was born, we went to war against Germany for the first time. One of the chief reasons we gave for entering the war on the side of the Allies was the terrible "militarism" of the kaiser.

And the worst symptom of this militarism, we said, was the fact that Germany had compulsory conscription. Young boys were drafted against their will into the kaiser's army, even before a war was declared.

Now, 50 years later, we are engaged in an undeclared war in Vietnam. We have a system of compulsory conscription, and have had it ever since Selective Service was set up in World War II, a quarter-century ago. And nearly everybody here takes it for granted.

We may differ and argue about the form of the draft, but almost all Americans agree that compulsory conscription is a necessity in today's world. We beat the kaiser, but the kaiser's militarism has eventually won. We have become what we went to war against our enemy for being.

And this is the great indictment of war as an institution. It reduces everyone to the lowest common denominator of humanity. It makes the victors almost indistinguishable from the vanquished.

One war, and one generation, after we had fought the kaiser, we fought Hitler's Germany. We were appalled when the Nazis bombed Coventry and Rotterdam, undefended cities, killing tens of thousands of civilians—men, women and children.

The Nazis said they were doing it as an act of humanity—for it would bring the war to an end sooner. We rejected this horrible hypocrisy, and condemned the Nazis as bestial barbarians.

Then, not much later, we bombed the undefended cities of Hiroshima and Nagasaki, killing tens of thousands of civilians—men, women and children. We said we were doing it as an act of humanity—for it would bring the war against Japan to an end sooner. And we did not, and do not, call ourselves bestial barbarians.

Now, one war and one generation later, we are burning peasants in

Vietnam, destroying villages and devastating the countryside—
because our enemy is forcing us to behave in this frightful fashion. We
say we have no choice; we must fight fire with fire.

Where do we stand now, compared to that day in 1917 when we first
went to war to "make the world safe for democracy"? If the kaiser had
won, would it have been any worse? Indeed, it was because the kaiser
lost that Nazism was able to take root in Germany. Does war do
anything but perpetuate itself, in more hideous form, a generation
later?

Our Society Has a Split Personality

THERE ARE DAYS, many days, when the world seems a cold and
terrible place. So much cruelty, so much bestiality, so much greed and
indifference and blind anger.

Yet what we call "the world" is something different from the
people who make it up. This is the enormous and stunning paradox of
human society—that the institutions we have created, the mechanisms
we have devised, are so much worse than we are.

For the people themselves, everywhere, are fundamentally decent.
They are honest and well-meaning and wanting the same things for
themselves and their families: a modest sufficiency, a little peace, a
little pleasure.

I have been reading a new book written by a dope addict shortly
before she committed suicide. It is a compelling and frightening book,
for she and the other addicts seem nicer people than those around them.
The police, the courts, the neighbors, the relatives, the whole machinery of our vast social order rolls its wheels mercilessly over these
sick and helpless people.

Her story—authentic to its last gasp—is a bitter indictment of our
behavior in the mass. There is no compassion, no understanding of
the tragic plight of the addict. Our prisons are subhuman, our courts
are Kafka-like nightmares, our police are coarse and venal, our
whole apparatus of society is an expression of our fear, hostility and
ignorance.

If, however, we examined each of these oppressive persons as an
individual, we would find them kind and decent in their personal
relationships—loving their children, supporting their parents, feeding
stray cats, contributing to charities.

There exists a tremendous schizophrenia between our private and our public morality. Our attitude toward addicts is only one dramatic facet of this split. Individually, we would not treat dogs the way we permit migrant workers to be treated in this country. Our frightful housing situation shocks us only when a baby is bitten to death by rats; we think nothing of the others who die more slowly, suffocated by the slums.

And this schizophrenia, of course, is projected outward to the world. Nations behave toward each other as they never would to their own people; diplomacy and war confer a spurious legality upon the most immoral acts. We will not see an end to any of this until we fit together the two parts of our being, and learn to act institutionally in the kind manner we act personally.

The greatest harm done by the Industrial Revolution is that, more than ever before in history, knowledge became enslaved to power, and was directed by power to ends inconsistent with wisdom.

*

In our age, the only practical alternative to war is not something nebulously called "peace," but prosperity for all nations, with a sharp reduction in the differences between haves and have-nots, which is a far greater threat to world stability than all ideologies put together.

*

One wonders how many potentially great leaders have died obscure in a nation of mediocrities that was not ready for them, or that sacrificed them in war before their special talents could come to fruition.

*

It is the sentimentalist, not the realist, who believes that the more terrible the instruments of war become, the more reluctant will mankind be to use them; and the archsentimentalist was Nobel, who actually declared that his invention of dynamite was so fearsome that nations could no longer war against each other.

VI.
Of Words
and Phrases

Of Words and Phrases

WHY IS IT ALWAYS "betrayal" if one of Us goes over to Them, but "conversion" if one of Them comes over to Us?

The woman who impresses her husband-to-be as "vivacious" before the marriage often seems "fluttery" after the marriage; and the woman who was courted for her "serenity" may later be upbraided for her "laziness."

Why do we attach the label "radical" only to those extremists of the left, when the extremists of the right are just as "radical," just as threatening to democracy—and even more numerous?

Our ambassador is "diplomatic," but Theirs is "evasive."

My son is "high-spirited," but yours is a "roughneck."

My daughter is "proud of her appearance," but yours is "terribly vain."

Our team is made up of "gallant bulldog hearts," but your team is composed of "stubborn diehards."

Your homely niece is "plain as a mud fence," but mine has "a lot of character in her face."

Our preacher is a "golden orator," and yours is a "windbag."

Fifty years ago, it was morally condemned as a "sin"; twenty-five years ago, it was philosophically condoned as an "experience"; today, it is gaily dismissed as an "affair."

An "innovator" is a man whose new ideas may benefit you, but a "crackpot" is a man whose schemes might bankrupt you.

I poke my nose into your affairs because I "love people," but you poke your nose into mine because you have "morbid curiosity."

My off-color jokes are "earthy," but yours are "filthy."

The man who steals ten dollars is a "thief," but the man who steals ten million is a "titan."

Your sweetheart's hair is "touched up," but her rival's is "dripping with peroxide."

I have "faith," but you live in a "fool's Paradise."

When I disagree with you, it's a "matter of principle," but when you disagree with me, it's only a "verbal quibble."

The striking colors in our living room are "dramatic"; the striking colors in yours are "flamboyant."

My senator is "peace-loving," but your senator is an "appeaser."

Your children are guilty of "rowdyism," but mine merely exhibit "healthy animal spirits."

My occasional outbursts are caused by "intense emotional stress"; yours are caused by a "miserable temper."

When I am buying, I wonder when this vicious spiral of inflation is going to end; when I am selling, I am just the victim of rising costs of labor and material.

When my candidate reverses his stand after election, it proves he is "open-minded"; when yours does the same thing, it shows him up as "a man of no principle."

You may get "drunk," but I only get "high."

A "theorist" is a man whose theories differ from my theories.

My inability to warm up to strangers is caused by "shyness," but yours is caused by "stand-offishness."

A member of my family went to a sanatarium suffering from "nervous exhaustion," but a member of your family went suffering from a "mental breakdown."

A "conventioneer" is that loud and ludicrous object who behaves in our city exactly the way we behave when attending a convention in his city.

We send our child to pre-pre-nursery school because "it's good for him to have contact with other children"; but you send yours to the same place "to get him out of the way."

I can't reduce effectively because of my "glandular system," but you can't reduce because you make a pig of yourself.

When I do something wrong, I want to be excused on account of my "good intentions," but when you do something wrong, you are beyond excuse, because "only actions count."

A woman's friend who keeps a messy house is "frail," but her enemy who keeps a messy house is "bone lazy."

My forebears, who came here early, were "Pilgrims"; but your forebears, who came here later, were "immigrants."

I call for "justice" when you break the terms of our agreement, but I call for "mercy" when I am forced to break the terms of our agreement.

When I do something disgraceful, I excuse it on the grounds that "I'm only human," but when you do something disgraceful, your conduct is "inhuman."

My teen-age daughter is "popular with the opposite sex," but yours is a notorious "boy chaser."

My boy went wrong because he "wouldn't listen to his parents," but your boy went wrong because he was "neglected."

"You only live once" generally means "Then why not do what I know I shouldn't do?"

"All the other kids are . . . " generally means "Joe's folks and Jim's folks and Bill's folks are weak—why can't you be weak, too?"

"A man has to live" generally means "I'm vaguely ashamed of what I'm doing, but I don't have the moral courage to live like a man."

"If I don't, somebody else will" generally means "If somebody is going to profit from human credulity, folly, greed and ignorance, why shouldn't it be little old me?"

It's a continuing lesson in humility for us to keep remembering that there is only a century or less of difference between an "idle dreamer" and an "inventive genius."

"For your own good" generally means "for the pleasure it affords me in telling you something you won't like to hear."

You stay away from work because of "a little cold in the head," but I stay away from work because of a "severe virus infection."

My objections to a coarse play that you may find funny are based on "common decency," but your objections to a play I find funny are nothing but "prudery."

Their nation has a "network of spies," but our nation takes "security measures."

I run my office strictly because I am a "disciplinarian," but you run your office strictly because you are a "sadist."

Our competitor's company is slow on deliveries because of a "bottleneck," but our company is slow on deliveries because of "a few little snags we're straightening out."

My attorney "knows all the ins and outs," but my opponents attorney is a "slippery character."

A "snob" is anybody on the rung above who feels exactly about us as we do about those on the rung below.

My club is "quiet and dignified," but your club is "stuffy and filled with mummies."

"Our product helps bring the more leisurely, comfortable life to all Americans," declared the manufacturer ten minutes before he dropped dead of a heart attack from too much work and not enough leisure.

When you attack us, it is an "act of war," but when we attack you, it is "a necessary preventive move to maintain our independence and to preserve the peace."

As a junior executive, I am "on the alert for opportunities within the organization," but as a junior executive, you are "on the make."

A "troublemaker" is the generic term for anyone who wants to change the way we have become accustomed to doing things.

"Team spirit" is a phrase to denote that social timidity which inhibits anyone in a group from pointing out that someone else in the group is wrong.

A pre-conference "bull session" is a wistful hoping that no idea plus no idea plus no idea will somehow add up to An Idea.

I take my work home because "my work is my hobby," but you take your work home because you're "overmatched for the job."

I have an appreciative eye for the ladies; you are quite a Lothario; he is an old lecher.

I believe that charity begins at home; you are quite careful with your money; he is a tightwad.

I am a neat dresser; you are a dapper dresser; he is a fop.

I am a man of firm principles; you tend to be stubborn; he is pigheaded.

I am orderly; you are a little fussy; he is an old maid.

I have a few pet peeves; you have some idiosyncracies; he is a crank.

I believe in every man for himself; you are looking for the main chance; he is ruthless.

I read relaxing books; you read escape fiction; he reads trash.

I sowed a few wild oats; you were a gay dog; he was a rake.

I have an occasional fling; you go on a binge; he runs wild.

I vote for the man, not the label; you vote for the personality that appeals to you; he votes for a golden-tongued demagogue.

I believe that children should respect their parents; you believe in making them toe the mark; he is a domestic tyrant.

I believe that marriage is a partnership; you listen to your better half; he is henpecked.

I believe it is the spirit, and not the cost of the gift that is important; you believe in giving a modest token of appreciation; he is a cheapskate.

I am co-operating with our economy's flexible credit system; you are buying on the installment plan; he is over his head in debt.

I have an open disposition; you say what you believe; he is a frightful gossip.

I have to maintain my position; you are keeping up appearances; he is putting up a front.

I enjoy a controversial discussion; you like a good argument; he always wants to pick a fight.

I am involved in making a living for my family; you are engrossed in "the game"; he is neglecting his wife and children.

When my company buys out your company, we are "expanding and diversifying," but when your company buys out my company, you are "raiding" the field.

My dog jumps up on your lap because he is "friendly," but your hound messes up my clothes because he is "untrained."

When my team loses, it goes down to a "gallant defeat," but when your team loses, it is a "rout."

If it was your fault, we had a "collision," but if it was my fault, we just "bumped fenders."

When you interfere in my affairs, you're a "busybody," but when I interfere in your affairs, it's because I feel "it's my duty as a friend."

The people upstairs had a "terrible fight," but we just had a "family spat."

There are no juvenile gang leaders, because according to the parents every boy in the gang was "led astray" by another boy.

Likewise, there are no aggressors in a war, because according to the nations each army was "provoked" into taking action by the open or tacit aggression of another.

My book didn't sell because it was "too far above the heads of the masses," but your book didn't sell because "the public was wise to it."

When I publicly oppose your religious convictions, I am exercising my "precious American right of free expression," but when you publicly oppose mine, you are indulging in "cheap bias and malicious defamation."

A "statesman" is a politician who happens to be saying what I want to hear; a "demagogue" is a politician who is saying what my opponents want to hear.

When I am cruising at forty miles an hour, I am indignant because the traffic cops don't go after the speeders who cut ahead of me; but when I am speeding at seventy, and am stopped by a cop, I am indignant because they aren't out catching criminals instead of harassing respectable motorists.

When I want you to change your ways, I advise you that "a person's never too old to learn," but when you want me to change my ways, I inform you that "you can't teach an old dog new tricks."

I repeat a choice morsel of gossip in "the greatest confidence," but you "blab it all over town."

The difference between "vandalism" and a "harmless prank" depends upon whose child has committed it.

A "longhair" is anyone whose taste is slightly more cultivated than mine; and a "lowbrow" is anyone who calls me a longhair.

I am opposed to your newfangled ideas because I believe in "the value of tradition," but you are opposed to my sensible reforms because you are "blindly clinging to the past."

When I need help from you, I am quick to tell you that "it is more blessed to give than to receive," but when you need help from me, I am equally quick to tell you that "God helps those who help themselves."

A "man of the world" is generally one who has learned how to utilize all the bad things in the world, and refuses to acknowledge the existence of the good things.

Likewise, a "sophisticate" is a man who tries to convince every attractive woman he meets that she ought to relinquish her virtue to him and then spends most of his life looking for a "virtuous" woman he can marry.

When I agree with a political leader who is cautious, I call him a sensible "middle-of-the-roader," but when I disagree with a political leader who is cautious, I call him a "fence-straddler."

The innovation I want to buy is a sign of "progress," but the innovation I don't want to buy is simply "newfangled."

I won't modify my demands because "it's a matter of principle," but you won't modify your demands because you won't accept the fact that "all life is a matter of compromise."

Our party arrives late at the theater because "we like a nice, leisurely, civilized dinner," but your party arrives late at the theater because you have "been drinking Martinis until curtain time."

Daddy isn't very good at math because "he doesn't have a head for figures," but Junior gets poor grades in math because "he's lazy and won't apply himself."

A person who has a nervous breakdown and can afford a private sanatorium is "deeply troubled," but a person who has a nervous breakdown and has to go to a state mental hospital is "off his rocker."

When we find it expedient to do business with a dictator, we call it "adjusting to realistic conditions," but when we are under no such compulsion we can take a lofty spiritual tone about "exercising a moral influence" on world affairs.

A man who takes bold chances in a sport I admire is "adventuresome," but a man who takes bold chances in a sport I am indifferent to is "foolhardy."

My habit of drinking socially makes me a "social" drinker, but your habit of drinking socially makes you an "habitual" drinker.

What a husband calls an "innocent flirtation" is one that his wife detected before he could move it beyond the "innocent" stage.

The "good old days" are those days of which our memory has enhanced the pleasant aspects and conveniently blotted out the unpleasant aspects.

When I agree with the majority, I refer to them as "the public"; when I disagree with the majority, I refer to them as "the mass."

I, who was not caught, merely "cut corners" on my income tax; but you, who happened to be caught, were "cheating."

The fellow who objects to my whispering in a movie house is a "sourpuss," but the fellow whose whispering disturbs me is an "illmannered nuisance."

When I am offering to sell an old-fashioned house, I describe it as "gracious and spacious," but when I am offering to buy an oldfashioned house, I describe it an "an ancient and crumbling barn of a place."

We tell each other that "you can't tell a book by its cover," but in choosing people we too often select by the cover alone and never look into the book until it's too late. (Alimony in mistaken marriages may be said to be an expensive "cover charge.")

A "fanatic" is anyone who actually tries to practice what we only preach—and most of us are secretly like the late Jimmy Walker, the amiably corrupt mayor of New York, who said: "I believe in honesty, but I'm not fanatical about it."

When I want to do something rash, I shrug that "all life is a gamble," but when you want to do something rash, I caution you to "play it safe."

"Realistic" is my solution to a given problem, as opposed to any contrary solution, which is "academic," "idealistic," and "fine in theory but not in practice."

Why is it that Our secret agents are "patriots," while Their secret agents are nothing but "spies"?

When I have one over the limit, I become "the life of the party"; when you have one over the limit, you become a "loudmouth."

I am "strong-minded," but you are "opinionated."

My candidate's plan for the future shows he has "vision," but your candidate's plan for the future makes him a "wild-eyed dreamer."

I am about the only capable and careful driver on the road; all other motorists are either "stick-in-the-muds" or "reckless maniacs."

The British are too "reserved," and the French are too "effusive"; the Italians are too "impulsive," and the Scandinavians are too "cold," the Germans are too "arrogant," and the Japanese are too "diffident"—surely God must be an American.

A "sound" man is a man who sounds like me.

My family, which is poor, lost its tremendous fortune during the Depression; but your family which is rich, made all its money profiteering during the War.

A "realistic" novel is a novel that agrees with the idea of reality I held before I even opened the book.

Why is it that "modern" is an approving adjective for plumbing, but a disapproving adjective for art?

My wife's dress is "simple," but your wife's dress is "dowdy."

Likewise, my summer wardrobe is "casual," but yours is "sloppy."

Everybody knows that We are producing armaments for "defense," but They are producing armaments for "war."

When my party gets loud, we are merely having "innocent fun," but when the party next door gets loud, they are "creating a disturbance."

When my candidate makes slashing charges against the opposition, he is "forthright," but when your candidate does the same, he is "irresponsible."

Likewise, my congressman makes a "probe," but your congressman "goes on a fishing expedition"—and, of course, ends up with a "smear."

A $4 hotel has a "house dick," whereas a $14 hotel has a "security officer."

Jane marries John because of his "boyish charm"—and divorces him because of his "immaturity."

They try to change Our minds by "propaganda," but We try to change Their minds by "information."

When I play a game well, I insist that "it has to be taken seriously or it's no fun," but when I play poorly at some diversion, I remind you that "it's only a game, after all."

Our country believes in a "higher standard of living," but Their country simply believes in "materialism."

A "reliable" subordinate is one I can rely on to do my dirty work.

She married him because he was so "easygoing," but she divorced him because he was so "spineless."

When weather seems to threaten my going to the races, which I like, it's only a "little summer sprinkle," but when weather seems to threaten my going to a picnic, which I dislike, it's an "all-day downpour."

My daughter's face is filled with "merry freckles," but your daughter's skin is "blotchy."

I take you to a restaurant that is "charmingly unpretentious," but you take me to a restaurant that is a "dive."

A "migraine" is a headache with a college education.

A "forward-looking citizen" is any man who happens to be facing in the same direction I am.

When I ask for "constructive criticism," I mean the kind that won't make my mistakes look bad.

A censor is a man who has never got over the initial embarrassment of having been born in bed with a lady.

A realist is a person who is living comfortably off the interest that accrues from the capital invested by idealists of the previous generation.

An orator is a man who never knows what he thinks until he hears himself saying it.

A best-dressed woman is one who wants to be admired for what goes on her rather than for what comes out of her.

A diplomatist is a man who would rather lose your leg in a war than lose his face in a conference.

An engineer is a man with mechanical aptitude—which decreases with each step he takes closer to his home.

A theatrical producer is a man who thinks that Shakespeare might have a hit, if he would only prop up that sagging second act, cut out some of the poetry, and put in a few more visual gags.

A personnel director is a man who flunked so many tests when he applied for jobs that he decided his only hope lay in giving the tests rather than taking them.

Some Tired Items That Should Be Retired

"AND NOW the Club de Crampo takes great pride in presenting . . ."

"Imported, designed and made with JUST YOU in mind . . ."

"A person who really needs no introduction . . ."

"This special offer is good for a limited time only . . . so hurry!"

"Including the latest in brilliant pastel-colored bathroom fixtures."

"Surveys show that our magazine is read by more green-eyed women in cities between 2000 and 5000 population than any other periodical."

"Star-studded . . . spectacular . . . showcase . . . cavalcade . . . panorama . . . stay tuned to Channel . . ."

"And now a few words from the charming chairlady of our program committee . . ."

"For the man (woman, child, dog, parakeet) who has *everything,* we suggest . . ."

"Direct from twelve sensational weeks at the . . ."

"As this columnist predicted last August . . . Remember, folks, you read it here first!"

"You'll think she's singing in the same room with you, when you hear this breath-taking high-fidelity . . . for the first time . . . science . . . unbelievable . . . at this price . . ."

"And that little boy, barefoot and dirty-faced, clutching his ten-cent-store horn in his tiny hand, turned out to be . . ."

"Open your heart and give . . . and, of course, it's deductible from your income tax . . ."

"That distinguished star of stage, screen, radio and TV, whose newest picture, *Hit Me Again, Baby,* may be seen at . . ."

"Due to our expansion program, we are closing our East Side outlet and offering at great sacrifice . . ."

"Bring the kiddies and make it a real outing for the whole family!"

"A combination of medically proven ingredients . . ."

"You can't afford not to . . ."

"And now . . . the Blank of Tomorrow . . . Today!"

"Banishes those Monday (Workday, Washday, Specialday, Anyday) Blues."

"Our research scientists, in test after test, have demonstrated conclusively that no other . . ."

"You'll marvel at its . . ."

"Dad won't believe it when you tell him it only cost . . ."

"Oh-so-good . . . taste-thrill . . . new experience . . . and yummier-than-ever in the sparkling modern Fresh-O-Wrap silver package."

"Boy, Mummie, I never liked beetle juice until you bought Coleoptera Farms special Nutro-Dexamin beetle juice, fortified with powdered slag."

"The ultimate in sensuous perfumes . . . what else could we call it . . . but 'Lust.' "

"For a real He-Man drink, it's Old Cirrhosis, specially blended from a secret formula, and permitted to age for six long weeks in our own fungoid kegs in Sunny Kaintucky, where . . ."

"When Henry died, I didn't know what to do . . . where to turn . . . and the children . . . but then I remembered our all-protection policy from the Make Glad Your Bereavement Insurance Company . . . and our friendly agent . . . through those difficult days . . ."

"And don't forget . . . when you go to your neighborhood Blank shop . . . be sure to look for the Purple Crow . . . the Big Red X . . . the Little Twin Elves . . . the Aztec Voodoo Sign . . . on the package."

"It's Sandblast . . . the revolutionary dentifrice . . . works with hydroelectrical pneumatic action . . . turns dingy teeth to blinding brilliance . . . and why? . . . because it gets off the enamel . . . digs beneath that yellow coating . . . and actually tuckpoints your teeth!"

"We laugh at interest rates . . . just pick up your phone and in a whisk we'll send over our Indian runner with a basketful of gold.''

"In perfect condition . . . owned by an old lady . . . who used it only to go to church on Sundays . . .''

"And now Hollywood dares to . . .''

Rural Dictionary for City Folks

A SHORT DICTIONARY of Ruralisms for the City Tourists:

"Down the road a piece" means either a quarter mile or six miles, depending on how the person who is giving you directions feels at the moment.

"I don't care" means that your offer of a coke or a beer will be accepted, if you ask a couple of times more.

"I'll be around to fix the screens tomorrow" means that you can expect to hear from him in about two weeks—if his crops don't spoil, his chickens don't sicken, his pump doesn't fail, his car doesn't break down or his own screens don't need repairing.

"They're hard to get this time of year" means that some excuse, however lame, has to be found for doubling the price of produce for the summer visitors.

"So-and-so's is a good place to eat" means that the recommender is a first cousin to the man who owns the restaurant.

"The bus is usually a little late" means that the arrival or departure of the bus bears only a coincidental relationship to the times indicated on the schedule.

"He's a gentle horse" means that the riding-stable owner has given you a nag that is too old to run and too tired to care.

"They've got dancing there" means a jukebox filled with polkas, or (on Saturday nights) an accordion, a drum and a musical saw, played by the owner's son-in-law and two of his unemployed cronies.

"Unusual weather for this time of year" means practically nothing, for the area hasn't had "usual" weather this time of year since the polar cap receded.

"You can't miss it" means that you're going to miss it unless you use aerial reconnaissance.

"A quiet homelike atmosphere" means that the hotel has no guests who are ambulatory and under eighty-five.

"One thing for sure—you sleep well at night here" means there is nothing else to do at night here.

"The nicest time of year is just after Labor Day" means it will be a wonderful relief to get rid of the tourists and their oddball habits, and get back to leading a real life again.

In Defense of Worthwhile Slang

A TEACHER OF ENGLISH in a Texas high school has written in, asking me to tilt a lance against the use of slang by teen-agers. "How can we expect them to learn proper English," she complains, "if their daily speech is full of barbarisms?"

Much as I sympathize with her plight, I think that slang fulfills an important function in any language. What she forgets is that just as there are two kinds of English—good and bad—so are there two kinds of slang.

If any language were spoken exactly as it is written, the language would soon dry up and disappear. So-called "correct" speech has a tendency to become increasingly stale and conservative, and it needs constant transfusions of new verbal blood.

What we call "slang" is only a matter of time and degree: many words frowned upon in 1900 are accepted as standard English half a century later. Each word or phrase has to pass the test of time—silly or superfluous slang drops out of the language, and useful and vivid slang becomes naturalized.

Slang is as old as language, and in its own way just as honorable. If you read an ancient Latin comedy by Plautus, you will find one of the characters saying "Do you catch on" (*tenes?*), and another saying, "I put it over on him" (*ei os sublevi*). There is even the modern slang phrase, "I'll touch the old man for a loan" (*tangam senem, etc.*).

And even the double negative—which is still the bane of English teachers' lives—is as old as Latin. One of the freedmen in a story by Petronius remarks, "You ought not to do a good turn to nobody" (*neminem nihil boni facere oportet*). Which would indicate that the level of ordinary speech has been the same throughout the ages.

The ultimate test of any new word or expression is its ability to fill a long-felt need. Slang that supplies no real purpose quickly sounds old-fashioned (twenty-three skiddoo!) and simply drops out of every-day speech; but slang that creates a genuinely fresh image becomes a welcome permanent guest in any language.

No English teacher should be "against" slang, but only against speech that is tired, dull, and drained of vitality. The pompous, and proper, cadences of a banquet orator are a greater offense to the English tongue than any teen-ager's flip innovations.

We Waste Our Gift of Expression

IN THE BEGINNING, we are told, was the Word; but it is no more. The word is no longer honored, respected or believed; not even the Logos of God, which has too often been perverted by men for selfish ends.

One of the most salient characteristics of young people today, not only in the United States but all over the world, is the rejection of the word. The young person will not communicate because he distrusts words; he prefers listening to music to reading books because music is incapable of lying.

We have devalued the currency of communication. The monetary inflation we so worry about is as nothing in the grand scheme of things compared with the verbal inflation we have inflicted on the world. We have taken the most singular gift of man—expression—and forced it to serve our own proud, profit-seeking or petty purposes.

This is what young people resent most of all. Like all innocent youth, they began by trusting the word, by taking it at face value. Slowly and painfully, they learned that society does not say what it means, or mean what it says. Idealism quickly corrodes into cynicism, and the sullen silence of the young in the presence of their elders is a deep repudiation of the whole medium of verbal expression.

The task before us—if any real reconciliation is at all possible—is far more than a political or social or economic one. It is a task that goes to the very roots of human existence: that of restoring the word to its pristine purity and its human authenticity.

Communication—and therefore communion—can survive only when there is a genuine "meeting" between persons, when truth encounters truth, clasps it and returns it. But no genuine meeting is possible when we use words as bludgeons, as blackmail, as screens to hide our bad faith or as brilliant lures to hook the fish we are preying upon.

Even without bad faith—even when our intentions, so far as we know them, are the best—we still manipulate the word to defend our weaknesses, conceal our vulnerability, justify our self-centerdness and erect a "philosophy of life" out of fear, prejudice and ignorance.

We are told that "the letter killeth, but the spirit giveth life," and the letter has all but killed the spirit. Man's most precious gift has been perverted from the beginning, but only in this age of "mass communication" has the letter been able to extend its hegemony over the total range of men's relationships. If there is one resolution worth making, it is the resolve to treat the word as a holy thing, not a dark device for attacking, defending or disguising.

Even English Is Greek to Americans

I HATE TO MEET young people from foreign countries. They make me feel so inferior—and they make me blush for our own young people in America.

Dining with us last evening was a German boy of nineteen, who arrived on these shores a week ago to attend a college in Ohio. His grasp of English was superb, and I asked him how often he had been to America.

"Oh, never before," he said. "This is my first trip here. But, from my reading, I feel as if I know America very well."

"How did you learn to speak English so well?" I asked.

"I had six years of English in school" he said, "starting when I was ten. But English is simple compared to Greek and Latin. I had to study those languages for ten years."

This boy, mind you, while bright, is no exceptional scholar, no intellectual—just an ordinary, educated European youth. He took it for granted that nobody with a decent education would speak only one language.

I was ashamed to tell him not only that most American students cannot converse in any foreign language, but that most of them are not able to express themselves gracefully in English speech or writing.

The language courses in most American schools are a farcical waste of time and money, for many reasons. First of all, youngsters start too late—by the time they reach high school and begin to take a foreign language they are too old, too busy and too indifferent to learn it.

It would be better to cut out languages entirely than to persist in this foolish course of teaching them for only a year or two in high school. Not one student in a thousand can conduct a mature conversation in a foreign tongue after he leaves school.

But the root of the trouble lies deeper than this. English itself is not

understood by the mass of students. And when one does not understand the structure of one's own language, it is virtually impossible to
learn a second, except by living abroad and hearing it every day.

The whole body of language teaching—including English—in
American schools needs a radical revision. And not merely for the
sake of English (important as it is), but because ignorance in speaking
and writing becomes a crippling handicap in all other subjects.

If we cannot communicate coherently, we cannot really achieve a
mastery in any field. America is full of tongue-tied technicians, who
cannot transmit their knowledge, even to their own countrymen.

Study of Latin Is No Waste of Time

A HIGH SCHOOL STUDENT in West Virginia has written to ask me if I
think he should continue with his Latin studies. "Has Latin done you
any good?" he inquires, "and is it useful in your work?"

The answer is "yes" to both these questions. Nobody can speak,
write or understand English properly unless he has some rudimentary
knowledge of Latin. For English is a *hybrid* language—fewer than
half our words are native, and the rest borrowed from foreign tongues,
mostly Latin.

In no other language, for instance, do we find so many native nouns
taking Latin adjectives. The adjective for *mouth* is not *mouthy* but
oral which is straight from the Latin.

Likewise, *nose* give us *nasal*, *eye* gives us *ocular*, *mind* gives us
mental, *son* gives us *filial*, *house* gives us *domestic*, *sun* and *moon*
give us *solar* and *lunar*. There are hundreds of similar cases.

We don't even have native English adjectives for the four seasons:
fall is *autumnal*, winter is *hibernal*, spring is *vernal*, and summer is
estival. The first words a child learns, *mama* and *daddy*, take Latin
adjectives—*maternal* and *paternal*.

English is primarily a "loan language." If you want to know how
much, read any of the books by Otto Jespersen, the great Danish
philologist, and you may be surprised at the enormous debt we owe not
only to Latin and Greek but also to the Scandinavian languages, to
French and even to the Germanic influences upon Old English.

A foreigner learning English would find it insuperably difficult if he
did not have a solid base in Latin.

This explains why educated foreigners are able to pick up our tongue so rapidly, and why some uneducated foreigners can live here thirty years without really grasping the language.

As an important parenthesis, I found my own Latin (shaky as it is) of great use while traveling through Europe. I was able to get along handily in Italian after only six weeks of living in Florence, and my French is at least passable, using the glue of Latin to stick together French and English words.

Studying the classic languages is neither a waste of time nor a form of intellectual snobbishness; it is, rather, the quickest and most permanent way to master one's own tongue and to become a genuine citizen in the community of man, past and present.

Facts Alone Don't Communicate

DOES A MERE DIFFERENCE in a word make a difference in a thing, in an attitude, in a relationship? Of course it does. If we use the wrong word for the right one, then we imagine we are saying something when we are saying something else.

Take the two popular words today, "information" and "communication." They are often used interchangeably, but they signify quite different things. Information is *giving out;* communication is *getting through.*

This is the basic trouble with so-called communication within and between large groups. In most cases, it is simply information that is being given out, not communication that is getting through.

Many large companies, for instance, privately deplore the lack of "communication" they may have with their employees. But what they fondly imagine is communication is really not—it is just information, and only the kind of information the company wants the employees to have.

Communication is at least the beginning of a dialogue; information is a monologue. Communication is alert for a response; information shuts off the switch when the message is ended. Most of all, information *tells what;* communication *explains why.*

Business and industry, among other institutions, expend tens of millions yearly under the mistaken notion that they are communicating with their various publics; when, in nine cases out of ten, they are only processing information in a way that is palatable to their self-image. These publics, being no fools, quite properly refuse to believe official communiqués, house organs, publicity handouts and all the rest.

Strictly speaking, genuine communication can exist only between persons in what Buber has called the I-Thou relationship; anything else is an I-It relationship, where we are not speaking to another person, in the fullness of his uniquely created humanity, but to an "object," a "mass," indeed, a "public."

But, even allowing for this basic difficulty, there is no question but that institutions, organizations, corporate bodies, can move from the information end of the spectrum closer to the communication end. They can do this, however, only by sacrificing some false pride and acting like persons who are fallible, uncertain, sometimes wrong and willing to learn from mistakes.

When we inform, we lead from strength; when we communicate, we lead from weakness—and it is precisely this confession of mortality that engages the ears, heads and hearts of those we want to enlist as allies in a common cause.

Yes, Harris Hasn't Changed a Bit

WHEN I PLEAD, as I often do, for greater precision in our use of words, perhaps it is because I am so prone to confusion. I remember as a little boy reading the signs on some highways and bridges: HEAVY TRAFFIC NOT PERMITTED.

It puzzled me for a long time how the individual motorist was going to decide whether the traffic was too heavy for him to continue on the road or over the bridge. It was a year or more before I realized that the sign meant: HEAVY VEHICLES NOT PERMITTED.

And I may have been more stupid than most, but when I heard in fourth grade that a special class was being formed for "backward readers," I silently wondered how many of my classmates possessed that marvelous gift of being able to read backward.

A friend recently told me of an incident in a veterans' hospital. The physician in charge of the mental ward had a sign on his door: DOCTOR'S OFFICE. PLEASE KNOCK. He was driven to distraction by an obedient patient who carefully knocked every time he passed the door.

Youngsters, and people out of their right minds, are likely to take words more literally than they are meant. Unless we say exactly what we mean, youngsters will read another meaning into it.

Even idiomatic phrases are not without their danger to the growing mind. James Thurber confesses, in one of his delightful books of reminiscences, that whenever his mother would say at dinner, "Dad is tied up at the office," he had a mental picture of the old man struggling to free himself from the bonds that were lashing him to his chair.

Another of my own childhood perplexities was the sign: IN CASE OF FIRE, BREAK GLASS. I couldn't figure out how breaking the glass was going to help put out the fire, and it's a good thing I was never called upon to turn in an alarm.

I am not suggesting that everything should be spelled out in a-b-c fashion, thus reducing us all to the condition of children or savages. But words should be *accurate* and *explicit*; except for poetry, they should say no more and no less than they actually mean.

As Mark Twain remarked, "The difference between the right word and the almost right word is the difference between lightning and the lightning bug."

A lovely example I ran across in California last summer was a sign in a public park: PEOPLE WITHOUT DOGS ON A LEASH NOT PERMITTED. I wonder if the good aldermen realized that this banned everyone not owning a dog from entering the park? As you see, I haven't changed much since the fourth grade.

Is That Man a Patriot or an Agitator?

ANTICS WITH SEMANTICS:

I am taking "medication"; you are on "pills"; he takes "dope."

I vote on "principles"; you vote on "ideology", he votes on "dogmas."

Spying by our side is "military intelligence"; spying by their side is "espionage."

When demonstrators make an unprovoked attack, it is a "riot"; when police make an unprovoked attack, it is a "defense of law and order."

An interesting example of reverse semantic logic is the fact that since so many prostitutes officially list their profession as "model," any woman who lists her profession as model may be suspected of being a part-time prostitute.

And, speaking of this subject, the semantics of sex are so primly twisted around in our culture that the phrase "sleeping with" actually means "not sleeping with."

Our overweight child has a "glandular problem," but yours is "fat as a pig."

If a used car can be advertised as "owner-tested," why can't used shoes be sold as "pedestrian-tested"?

When I look at a nude film of colored people ("natives") it is, of course, "ethnography"; when I look at a nude film of white people, it is "pornography."

Educational euphemisms are the most absurdly amusing in modern semantics—such as "underachiever," "disadvantaged," and so on. In his book, *Translations from the English,* Robert Paul Smith aptly translates the jargon, "The child seems to have developed late in large-muscle control," as "He falls on his head frequently."

One of the earliest warnings on the vicious way we twist words was given by George Orwell (long before Vietnam), when he wrote: "Defenseless villages are bombarded from the air, the inhabitants driven out into the countryside, the cattle machine-gunned, the huts set on fire with incendiary bullets; this is called *pacification.*"

In the same sense, Mayor Daley was correct when he suggested there were no "slums" in Chicago—only "substandard dwellings."

A "patriot" is an "agitator" whose side long ago gained control of the government.

And remember, finally, if you agree with most of the above items, I am a "courageous" and "challenging" columnist; if you disagree, I am "slanderous" and "irresponsible."

When the Wench Was a Man

To MANY PEOPLE, the study of words seems a remote and academic pastime, bearing little relation to the real world. Actually, however, it is in words and their changing use that we find important clues to the social and psychological drifts of the society.

For instance, what do all the following words have in common: *bawd, concubine, coquette, courtesan, hag, harlot, hoyden, shrew, termagant, wench* and *witch?*

Of course, they are all demeaning words for women, and today are used only in reference to women. But the really interesting thing about them—and many more—is that originally they were used to denote *either sex.*

Over the last few centuries, however, these words became pejorative and were used only for women—which indicates how male chauvinism in the real world translated itself into the verbal downgrading of the opposite sex.

Bawds, concubines, coquettes, courtesans and harlots initially referred to both men and women of loose sexual practices. Chaucer, Wycliffe, Beaumont and Fletcher, Shakespeare and countless other writers use these terms interchangeably for either sex. Then they suddenly die out as words applying to men, and become "feminine" only.

Why should a "hag" be only an unattractive old woman, when there is no correlative term for such a man? Why should a "termagant" become only a female who rants and rails, when just as many men are nags? Why should a "shrew" be only a woman, when masculine shrews abound everywhere? And a "witch" was at first of either sex; that is why so much Elizabethan literature referred to a "she-witch" when such was intended.

Only 200 years ago, the word "hoyden" was more often applied to a clownish, ill-bred man than to a girl; now it is exclusively used to designate a certain type of female. We really have no masculine equivalent—even such Victorian terms as "cad" and "bounder" were quickly dropped from the language of epithet.

Our speech accurately reflects the prejudices of the ruling group. Since the rulers and the rich and the educated (who directed language) generally lived in cities, we developed such words as "villain," which meant a rustic; "heathen" and "pagan," which also indicated those who dwelt in the country; "boor," which meant a farmer; and many other such words which downgraded rural inhabitants.

The use of a word wrongly understood can affect great events. Some believe that Darwin's *The Descent of Man* evoked such a storm because "descent" seems to indicate a dropping down from the apes; when he really meant it in the sense in which we speak of "descending from royalty."

I'm fond of the little boy's definition of "chivalry," after studying knighthood in school: "Chivalry," he said, "is going around releasing beautiful maidens from other men's castles, and taking them to your own castle."

*

"Obscenity" is not a disease of the lewd mind, but merely a symptom of society's suppression and distortion of natural sexuality; when we grow up to our sexuality, in all its manifestations, then obscenity will disappear as a social phenomenon, and will lurk only in a few immature and pitiable personalities.

Hear We Go Splitting Some Hares

A HOMOPHONE IS A WORD that is pronounced the same as another, but differs in spelling or meaning, like "pair" and "pear" and "pare." There are many of these in the English language, and in most cases the wrong word is written for the right one.

Even so literate a journal as the *New York Review of Books,* in a large headline offering special holiday subscriptions, wrote "Christmas doesn't phase me," when the word it meant was "faze." It is a common error; most people think "phase" is proper in this usage, and "faze" is only a slang variant, but they are totally different words.

The *New York Times,* which also should know better, not long ago reported in a story that a person was "hailed into court." The homophone that should have been used is "haled," which means "drawn by force." To be "hailed" into court is to be shouted for, which was not meant. Yet "hailed" has almost driven out "haled" in this kind of context.

Recently I read a story in which one character was described as being "hairbrained." This is a common homophonic mistake for "harebrained," which means giddy or nutty behavior, such as is associated with the March hare and other rabbits that seem to go wild in some seasons. The notion of "hair" has nothing whatever to do with the case.

Every language has such problems. Cinderella's famous glass slipper is the result of a homophonic mistake in French. The original title of Perrault's *Cinderella* was *La Petite Pantoufle de Vair,* or "The Little *Fur* Slipper," but the sound of "vair" was confused with "verre," meaning glass, and the mistake is now ineradicable.

But English is especially burdened with this problem. Some 50 years ago, Robert Bridges, the poet and scholar, wrote an essay on English homophones with a list of 835 entries involving nearly 1800 words. These words are troublesome and self-destructive; also, because we are careless in speech and smudge the vowels, words originally different begin to sound alike, and we lose important distinctions.

Almost everyone calls it "Welsh rarebit," when it should be "Welsh rabbit"; all children refer to "cole slaw" as "cold slaw," and I have seen it printed as such on some menus; "buttonhold" long ago lost out to "buttonhole"; "sweetheart" has nothing to do with the heart, but it a corruption of "sweetard," like "dotard" and "coward."

If I recall my *Alice* correctly, it was the Gryphon who remarked that school hours in the sea grew shorter every day. "That's why they're called 'lessons,' you know," he said to Alice, "because they lessen each day." Alice knew there was something wrong with this explanation, but a seven-year-old girl can hardly handle a homophone.

It Can't Be Said in English

A HUNGARIAN FRIEND of mine once walked into a drugstore and asked the clerk for "a pack of feeble cigarettes." He finally managed to convey that he wanted a very mild brand—he had looked up "feeble" in the dictionary and learned that it meant "lacking in strength."

There are few adjectives that are truly synonyms in any language. And when we try to translate words literally from one language to another, we can run a whole gamut of errors from the tragic to the ludicrous. Wars have been set off by a mistranslated phrase.

Someone operating a translating machine at the UN has explained how easily such mistakes occur. The machine, one day, was asked to put a common English phrase into Chinese, and then out of Chinese into French.

The English phrase chosen was "out of sight, out of mind." It ended up as "invisible, insane." Of course, out of sight does mean invisible, and out of mind does mean insane. But not in the adage.

Mario Pei, the linguist, tells of an American businessman in Russia who received a cable from home about his daughter: "Harriet hung for juvenile crimes."

The cable had been translated into Russian, then retranslated into English; the original version read: "Harriet suspended for minor offenses." Certainly, suspended is hung, and a juvenile is a minor.

Pei also points out that when the UN was in formation, it was found that French has no equivalent for *trusteeship*, that Chinese has no way of expressing *steering committee*, and that Spanish does not distinguish between *chairman* and *president*—so a new UN dictionary had to be devised.

Russia, strangely enough has no word for *efficiency*. In French, and other Romance languages, it is not possible to distinguish *house* from *home*. English has no synonym for French *savoir-faire*, or for the German *Gemütlichkeit*. And no one has yet been able to find an exact and succinct Italian equivalent of our *wishful thinking*.

You may remember that old chestnut about the three French language teachers trying to recall the English word for a woman who is sterile. "Unbearable?" ventured the first. "Inconceivable?" volunteered the second. "You're both wrong," said the third. "She is impregnable!" They consulted their dean. "Ah, I have it!" he exclaimed. "Such a woman is insurmountable!"

That Curious Word "Discrimination"

DURING A RECENT SNOWSTORM, I recalled having read somewhere that the Eskimos have about 200 different words describing and defining different kinds of snow. To us, all snow seems pretty much alike; to those who live with it all the time, it is as strikingly different as leaves to a botanist or stones to a geologist.

The less we know something, the more ignorant we are, the more we tend to lump it in indiscriminate categories. The painter's eye can distinguish 20 shades or tones where the layman can see only a few; the musician's ear can hear a pattern of melody that sounds only like cacophony to the rest of us.

What is true in these matters is true in the field of personal relations as well. The less knowledge, the less intelligence, the less training, the less we are able to distinguish persons as individuals, and the more likely to lump them in convenient categories.

Some months ago, I spent a half-day in a large factory, mingling with the men. What struck me most about their talk was their way of referring to co-workers; they seemed hooked on national origin as a means of identifying and labeling one another, especially newcomers.

There were the Greek and the Dutchman and the Scandahoofian and the Dago and the Mick and the Hunkie and many more. These men were defined and delineated by their ancestry or national origin, sometimes in derogation and sometimes in good humor, but always in terms of their background rather than their individual identity.

This is the way visitors behave in a foreign country that is very unlike their own: the residents are all "natives," indistinguishable from one another. But if one comes to live there a few months or longer, suddenly the idea of natives is dissolved into its component individuals, and the difference between one native and another is seen to be as great as that between one American and another.

"Discrimination" is a curious word, because it means two opposite things: discriminating *against*, and discriminating *between*. At a low level of intelligence, we lump people into categories and discriminate *against;* at a higher level, we perceive the individual characteristics of snow, or leaves, or stones, or people, and discriminate *between*.

What did Einstein have in common with George Jessel, or Enrico Fermi with a Mafia captain, or Albert Schweitzer with Adolf Hitler, or James Joyce with Pat O'Brien? Until we recognize that the differences among persons belonging to the same group are far greater than between one group and another, we are socially and intellectually snow-blind.

Questions Key to Polling

RECENTLY, I RECEIVED a letter from George Gallup, head of the American Institute of Public Opinion, advising that he is at work on a book "which will try to describe and explain polling methods." He asked me to write down any questions I might have about any aspect of polling.

Well, whenever I hear the results of some public opinion poll, I am always more interested in how the questions were framed than in how the answers turned out. Any question can be framed—consciously or unconsciously—to elicit the kind of answer it wants or expects.

I could easily devise two political polls of five questions each, one designed to elicit the answer that the country is drifting rightward, and the other to elicit an equally leftward drift. No trouble at all.

At a college, not long ago, a professor of logic submitted a list of ten questions to his classes; a large majority answered affirmatively to eight of them—which happened to be the ten propositions in Marx's *Communist Manifesto*. Then he rephrased the questions, and just as many opposed them. Both times, they were responding to *words* more than to *ideas*.

Two words may *denote* the same thing, but *connote* different things. Most people do not mind categorizing themselves as average, but they bristle at being categorized as mediocre—which means the same thing.

A recent Gallup poll asked Americans, of all ages and classes, if they were "very happy," "moderately happy" or "unhappy." Apart from the fact that happiness is virtually impossible to define (Aristotle's rigorous definition would not be accepted by any nonphilosopher), people lie to themselves about the way they feel more than about anything else. If they lie to themselves, they cannot help lying to pollsters.

A psychiatrist knows that one has to phrase such a question far more subtly to get an accurate answer. You may recall the old story about two priests arguing whether it was proper to smoke and pray at the same time. One said it was, and the other said it wasn't. To settle the matter, they agreed that both should write to the pope for his opinion.

A few weeks later they met and compared notes. Each claimed that the pope had supported his view, and suspected the other of falsifying the reply he got from the Holy Office.

Finally, one asked, "How did you phrase your question?" The other replied: "I asked whether it was proper to smoke while one is praying, and the pope answered, 'Certainly not, praying is serious business and permits of no distractions.' And how did you phrase your question?"

"Well," said the other, "I asked if it was proper to pray while smoking, and the pope said, 'Certainly, prayer is always in order.' "

Antics with Semantics

MY SENATOR is making a "probe"; your senator is on a "fishing expedition"; his senator is starting a "witch-hunt."

I am "cautious"; you are "timid"; he is "cowardly."

I believe something to be a fact because "I saw it in black and white"; but you mustn't believe something to be a fact "just because you happened to see it in print somewhere."

Our country is engaged in "security measures"; your country is engaged in an "arms race"; his country is engaged in "stockpiling weapons."

My church denomination lives by a "creed," but yours subscribes to a "dogma."

The ceremony I approve of had "dignity and grandeur"; the ceremony I disapprove of had "pomp and ostentation."

I believe in "authority"; you believe in "force"; he believes in "violence."

I am a "man of few words"; you are "taciturn"; he is "unresponsive."

My outburst was "indignation"; yours was "anger"; his was "petulance."

My crude friend is "a diamond in the rough"; yours is "a touch on the common side"; his is "a loudmouthed boor."

If she picks up men in bars, she is a "floozie"; if she picks up men at a Hollywood shindig, she is a "swinger"; if she picks up men at a fashionable garden party, she is a "femme fatale."

I am a great champion of "tolerance"—as long as you let me define the precise point at which it becomes intolerable.

My cutting remark is an "epigram"; yours is a "wisecrack"; his is a "cheap jeer."

I am a "realist" when I am doing to you that which, if you were doing it to me, I would call "ruthless."

There are really no "juvenile gang leaders" because, according to the parents, each of the boys "just happened to get in with the wrong crowd."

I am opposed to your newfangled ideas because I believe in "the value of tradition," but you are opposed to my sensible reforms because you are "blindly clinging to the past."

Why is the female of the species called a "songstress," when the male isn't called a "songster"?

"Know" –A Word with a Defect

ALTHOUGH ENGLISH is an admirable language, rich and flexible, it has its own defects. Among the most serious is the double use of the word "know." There are two separate ways of "knowing" something, and our language does not ordinarily distinguish between them. The first way is to know a thing objectively, from the outside; the second way is to know it intimately, from the inside.

As the sociologist Dr. Robert Angell points out in his recent book, *Free Society and Moral Crisis*, different people know a cat in different ways:

"A physicist knows a cat from one viewpoint, a psychologist from another, a physiologist from a third, but the fond child who plays with the cat daily is really acquainted with it."

Both French and German have two words to describe these different ways of knowing: the Germans make a distinction between *wissen* and *kennen;* the French between *savoir* and *connaître.*

The first expression in each pair stands for objective knowledge; the second expression stands for intimate knowledge that includes a shared feeling.

And until we can go from the first kind of knowledge to the second, we really cannot cope effectively with any of the frictions that continually rise in society. As Dr. Angell suggests: "Thus it is that the other man's moral position has little appeal to us unless we see it from all sides as he does, unless we feel a little of the pull it has from him. We are not likely to appreciate his view in this way unless we have come to know him intimately."

As a prominent modern example, many businessmen who have entered government administration quickly find that their viewpoint about "waste" and "extravagance" and "interference" has changed under the impact of daily personal acquaintance with government problems. As participants, they "know" government quite differently from the "knowledge" as outsiders.

This is not to justify government waste, but merely to illuminate the reason men seem to change when they get *inside* a situation. Real knowledge, full knowledge, includes a sharing of feelings—which also explains why a neurotic person may "know" what is wrong with himself, but cannot help himself until he moves from *wissen* to *kennen*, from *savoir* to *connaître*, from the cat as a bundle of reflexes to the cat as a living organism and an object of love.

Antics with Semantics

OUR GOVERNMENT ISSUES "information"; your government issues "publicity"; their government issues "propaganda."

A "voluntary" confession to the police is one which no one can prove was involuntary.

The young nations which oppose our policies are "backward"; the neutral ones are "underdeveloped"; and the ones supporting us are "developing."

What a bad teacher means by a "good" pupil is one who is immobile, docile, passive and unquestioning; what a good teacher means by a "poor" pupil is one who is immobile, docile, passive and unquestioning.

I lost the match because I was "off my form"; you lost because you were "overconfident"; he lost because he was "too cocky."

Someone we don't know who takes drugs is an "addict"; someone we know who takes drugs is a "victim."

What is called "crime" on a small scale is called "conquest" on a large scale; if Napoleon while still a corporal had seized a farm, he would have been executed; when as a general, he seized a whole country, he was crowned.

When our statesmen say what they do not really mean, they are exercising "diplomacy"; when their statesmen say what they do not really mean, they are engaging in "guile."

What we call an "unforgivable" action is one we cannot contemplate committing; if we could contemplate committing it, it would no longer be considered "unforgivable."

"History" is what we point to when we want to draw some parallel between olden times and today; and what we conveniently ignore when the parallel runs counter to our viewpoint.

Courtroom trials will remain contests of rhetoric, not of rights, as long as only the witnesses, and not the lawyers, are compelled to tell "the whole truth and nothing but the truth"; for the art of the advocate consists largely in repressing those aspects of the truth which do not serve his client's interests. (For perjury by suppression is a far more frequent occurrence than perjury by overt statement.)

A "good marriage" is one in which the initial expectations were so low that no illusions could be shattered by the reality.

Our Language Has Become Fuzzier

IN NUMEROUS STORIES and headlines, the Starved Rock killer has been referred to as a "fiend." In other stories of crimes by juveniles, the boys have been called "toughs" or "hoodlums." But the Starved Rock murderer is not a "fiend." He is a psychopath and a moron. The boys are not "toughs." They are weak. If we are to call them anything idiomatic, "weaks" is the proper word.

This nomenclature is more important than you may think. What we call these people helps determine what they think of themselves. Many boys are out to get a reputation as "tough." In jail they read their publicity avidly. Their pathetic egos are willing to put up with any punishment so long as they can feel important.

Newspapers, which should be most aware of the power of words, often seem the most insensitive to them. Instead of seeking the precise word, they reach for the easy, the dramatic, the lurid word.

Violent criminals, we know, have weak, twisted and unintelligent personalities. They lack the strength to cope with the realistic conditions of life, they are unsure of their own manhood, and they are "acting out" a fantasy of childhood. Most so-called "sex fiends" are actually impotent. These psychopaths thrive on publicity which describes them with fear and horror. They desperately need a "rep," and the worse the rep the better they feel about it. Each wants to be called a "desperado," when he is really just a "thief."

Such thwarted personalities should be described accurately and clinically, not with melodramatic shock. They should be objects of pity or contempt, not symbols of courage, daring and diabolic power. A skinny, pimply youth of seventeen who feels infinitely vulnerable without a gun in his hand will swagger and sneer in the lockup if he reads of himself as a "menace" or, better still, as a "monster."

We laugh at the Victorians' odd use of words, and yet we are less realistic in many areas than they were. A "cad," after all, described a certain type of man; what do we have to take its place? An unprincipled womanizer used to be called a "libertine"; today we call him a "playboy" or a "Lothario." The image he has of himself is much easier to live with than it used to be.

Language has become fuzzier as our values have become diffused. The word "celebrity" nowadays covers everybody from Jonas Salk to Caryl Chessman—and insecure boys don't much care which kind of "celebrity" they achieve, so long as the headline gratifies their cancerous egos.

Writer Needs an Ear for Words

WHILE READING THE ENTRIES, as one of the judges in a collegiate writing contest, I was reminded of Mark Twain's annoyed remark that "the difference between the right word and the *almost* right word is the difference between lightning and the lightning bug."

Most persons—and this includes aspiring writers—simply fail to recognize that there are very few true synonyms in the language, no matter what the dictionary may insist.

The dictionary, for instance, gives "devour" as a synonym for "eat." But no woman would care to have it said of her that she "devoured her dinner," which sounds more like an animal than a human. (Indeed, German has "essen" for human eating, and "fressen" for animal eating.)

Again, a woman's eyes may "glow" with affection, but they do not "glitter," although the two words are roughly synonymous. Eyes "glitter" with greed or contempt, but they "glow" with love or compassion.

Distinguishing between two words that seem to mean the same, but have different colors and shapes and suggestions—this is essential to the art of writing, and also of speaking. The dictionary can tell you only what a word points to; it cannot tell you what it feels like.

An interesting example is the word "fat." The unabridged dictionary gives as synonyms: fleshy, plump, corpulent, obese, stocky, portly, tubby, and thick, among others.

Obviously, different people are fat in different ways—a woman may be "fleshy," but a man is "portly." "Obese" carries the connotation of a glandular sickness. "Stocky" involves size as well as shape. We speak of a "plump" or "tubby" baby, but nobody would call him "corpulent."

The same is true of hundreds of words which only superficially resemble one another. "Unspeakable" in the dictionary means the same as "unutterable"—but the former is always used to mean something base or vile, while the latter usually means some rapturous or divine thought or emotion.

The right word is as important to the writer as the right note to the composer or the right line to the painter.

Hemingway's prose is so compelling (despite his defects of mind) precisely because he always knows the right word to capture the essence of a situation or the feel of a person. A writer needs an "ear" as much as a musician does.

And without this ear, he is lost and groping in a forest of words, where all the trees look much alike.

In the parlance of the film and novel advertisements, "Realistic!" has come to mean "with all the brutality of life left in, and all the beauty of life left out."

*

The best and briefest reason for a good education is that the more effort you expend in sharpening the ax, the less effort you have to expend in chopping the wood.

Textbooks Encourage Bad English

A READER IN AKRON sends me a letter she has received from a firm of educational publishers, replying to her complaint about a children's book her daughter is reading in second grade.

The mother objected to the use of "can" for "may" in the conversation used in the text, and wanted to know why an educational book should inflict this error upon small children.

The answer is illuminating:

"Our writers and editors think it advisable to observe, throughout the Basic Readers, the normal patterns of everyday speech. Particularly when a child is mastering the reading process, they feel that the words he finds in print should be familiar and follow patterns of his daily conversation. . .

"It has been the observation of grammarians for a long time that in cultivated English 'can' has been replacing 'may'. . . If our primary grade books use only 'may,' we feel the children would get only an artificial usage of the word and most of the pupils would eventually use 'can' in spite of the textbook.

"Of course, these questions have different aspects at high school level. There, one can teach students how our language has developed, and can discuss with them what standard of usage they wish to adopt."

Here, in a few concise paragraphs, are summed up all the vices of so-called "progressive" education. The word "may" is to be junked, because most children incorrectly use "can." The aim of the book is to make the children feel at home with their lack of grammar, rather than teaching them the important distinction between these two words.

Then, after the children have been speaking ungrammatically for a dozen years, they will be told the difference, and asked to vote on the way they care to speak English!

Of course, words and usages change, but if we use "can" in all cases where "may" is correct, how then do we distinguish between the two? If a child asks "Can I climb that fence?" is he asking for permission or for a vote of confidence in his ability? True communication breaks down when words are used so sloppily.

According to the editor of the book company, if children customarily use "can" for "may" and "ain't" for "isn't" and "would of" for "would have," we should go along with these barbarisms until they have become such settled habits that the child is condemned to perpetual illiteracy. This is a doctrine of "democracy" in its most debased and perverted form.

Little wonder that our children cannot read, write or speak like cultivated human beings, when even "educational" publishers pander to the soft corruption of the language.

"To and Fro" from "Hem and Haw"

A FEW WEEKS AGO I mentioned the phrase "hem and haw" as a marvelously concise description of a certain type of speaking. Afterward, it occurred to me that neither of these fine little words is used anywhere in the language except as part of that phrase.

Then I began thinking about the Lost Little Words in the English language—words that have been retained in some phrase or proverb or idiom, but which otherwise are not put to use.

For instance, in "hue and cry," the word "hue" has disappeared from ordinary speech. It has become what philologists call a "fossil" word.

Likewise, the "file" in "rank and file"; the "whit" in "not a whit"; the "poke" in "a pig in a poke"; the "bay" in "at bay"; and the "loggerheads" in "at loggerheads."

No one knows why these short and useful words have dropped out of everyday speech, except for one retained phrase. Then there are also "spick and span" and "tit for tat," containing words that have become meaningless by themselves, even though the phrases themselves are in daily use.

Then, too, there are many archaic and poetic words that no longer cross our lips, except in special idioms that have somehow retained their vitality—such as *"hither* and *thither," "to and fro," "might* and *main," "rack* and ruin," *"kith* and kin," "one *fell* swoop," "on one's *mettle."*

Who can say why "fell," which is a fine adjective, has fallen out of favor? Or why the word "mettle" is no longer a part of our verbal currency? Or who voted "rack" out of linguistic office?

The rich puddings of Shakespeare's plays are filled with thousands of such raisins; and one reason his poetry seems so "difficult" to the modern eye and ear is that he was the master of idiom, utilizing every scrap of phrase he had heard or picked up through his voluminous reading in medieval literature.

He also, of course, coined many phrases of his own, which have passed into the language so completely that we no longer recognize them as "quotations."

But the real tragedy of Shakespeare's plays is that in another century they may be unreadable without a "translation" into modern English—so swiftly does our language change its forms and fashions.

There is no logic in language, which only proves that language came before logic—and indicates, perhaps, why words so often confuse a situation instead of clarifying it.

In Russia, It's "It's Chinese to Me"

IN THAT CHARMING new book on language which I recently recommended, *Naming-Day in Eden*, the author amplifies a subject that has frequently fascinated me—how each nation attributes distasteful habits and acts to foreigners.

I have commented in the past on the fact that what is called "the French disease" in England is called "the English disease" in France. Likewise, to "take French leave," meaning to duck out without saying farewell, is known as "taking English leave" in France.

The French also used to call a creditor an Englishman *(un Anglais)*. When he excused himself from entering a theater or cafe because he was in debt, a Parisian would say, *"Non, non! Je suis Angle."* ("I'm broke, I'm in debt.")

When we "gyp" somebody, we are referring to gypsies, who originally were thought to come from Egypt. And when someone speaks unintelligibly, we say, "It's Greek to me."

The Russians say, "It's Chinese to me"; the French say, "That's Hebrew to me"; the Germans say, "That's Spanish to me," and the Poles say, "I'm listening to a Turkish sermon."

"Each nation," remarks Noah Jacobs, "associates a host of miscellaneous vulgarities, vices, diseases and disagreeable traits with foreign countries."

The Japanese phrase for foreigners means "stinking of foreign hair." The Czechs call a Hungarian a "pimple." In Hungary and Austria, the cockroach is known as a "Swabian," in Poland as a "Prussian," and in Germany as a "Frenchman."

The French refer to a louse as a "Spaniard," and the Italians have at times denoted a privy as an "Englishman." (Does anyone know, by the way, how it came to be called a "john" in American colloquial speech?)

A sharper at cards is a "Greek" to the English and French. The Germans say "proud as a Spaniard," the Romanians say "stubborn as a Bulgarian," and the Dutch say "boastful as a Frenchman."

In Czech, excessive drinking is "to drink like a Dutchman," but in Holland it is "to drink like a Pole."

In Spain, "to work for the English" is to work for practically nothing, and in Yiddish "to repay in Turkish" is to do a dirty trick.

We have come a long way from naming-day in Eden to name-calling day in the capitals of the world.

Words Can Be Just Too Divine

A SHORT DICTIONARY OF WORD CHANGES

DIVINE—once meant pertaining to God, religious, holy, proceeding from a deity; now means lovely, cute, charming, attractive, such as "What a divine hat!" and "A perfectly divine luncheon!"

FABULOUS—once meant fictitious, as in a fable, exaggerated and untrue, not unreal; now means extraordinary, better than the best and buy it, such as "Fabulous low price!" and "Fabulous home for sale."

ADORE—once meant to worship or honor a supernatural being, to regard with reverent admiration; now means like, enjoy, am pleased with, such as "I adore going to the circus" and "An adorable petticoat."

PASSION—once meant an enduring pain, or the suffering of a martyr, from the Latin *passus*, to suffer; now it means what a high-school girl feels for a high-school boy after their first date; after the second date, it becomes a "grand passion."

CREATIVE—once meant producing a work of thought or imagination, especially a work of art; now it often means trivial rearranging or elaborating, such as "creative interior decorating" and "a new hair creation."

PERSONALITY—once meant the distinctive inner characteristics of a person, the quality of being individual; now means the obvious social flair, such as "A smile with a lot of personality" and "A fine outgoing personality."

ENTERPRISE—once meant an undertaking which involves courage, energy and daring to try the difficult or untried; now it means any business which attempts to make the most profit for the smallest risk.

DEMOCRACY—once meant (to Jefferson and his colleagues) a system of government in which all the people would be encouraged to rise to the highest level of taste and judgment; now it means a system in which all are expected to sink to the lowest level of taste and judgment; and those who refuse to sink are labeled "undemocratic."

ENTHUSIASM—once meant to be divinely inspired or possessed, to have a zeal for goodness; now it means a "passion" for football or coin-collecting or breeding Pomeranians.

PROFESSION—once meant a calling of high seriousness, in which the practitioner took a solemn vow to maintain standards of truth and fairness above self-interest; now it means any occupation that is guided by self-interest rather than duty, such as "a professional hockey player" or a "professional bartender."

First Names Should Come Last

A FRIEND OF MINE insists I am stuffy because I resent the use of first names between persons who know each other only slightly. "It's just a friendly and informal American habit," he protests.

Strangely enough, I don't think it is informal at all; I think it is quite formal—because it is a mere *formality*, without any true meaning.

When I meet a man and begin calling him "Dick" instead of "Mr. Johnson" within a half hour, I am conforming to a false standard of intimacy. The man is a stranger to me, and I have no right to presume on a friendship that does not exist.

Like the words "darling" and "sweetheart" in theatrical circles (which mean absolutely nothing, since they are applied to everyone indiscriminately), first-naming of strangers is a cheapening and debasement of true friendship.

When an actor calls everybody "sweetheart," what is left to call his sweetheart? When I address a stranger by his first name, what is left to call my dearest friends? How then can I signify the gradations of feeling from politeness to deep devotion?

My objection to first names on early acquaintance does not indicate that I am unfriendly; far from it. It indicates that I value friendship so highly that I am unwilling to bestow its symbol upon a stranger. I think friendship must be earned and won, and not conferred loosely.

Language is a tool—our greatest tool—and can be blunted and broken like any other tool. A man would be a fool to use a fencing sword to cut butter, or a butter knife to hack down a tree—yet we abuse the tools of language even more violently and senselessly.

If we call every minor writer a "genius," then we have lost a word to apply when a genuine genius comes along; if every performer in show business is "great," how do we define true greatness? And if every transitory amour is called "love," we must seek for some other word to describe that rare, elevated and abiding passion.

It used to be, when a man called you by your first name, you knew it signified a change in the relationship—that he accepted you at your worth, considered you a friend and could be relied upon to help.

This is precisely what it should mean; but among today's Dicks and Toms and Sams, it is only a formal salutation of false conviviality.

"I'm sorry, Dick, we have to let you go," says Tom, the boss, smiling heartily and pulling out the rug from under his good old pal.

Poor Translations Can Trip Us Up

I WAS TALKING with a Russian who is in this country on an exchange program, and he said that one of the things that bothered him was our frequent references to Khrushchev's phrase: "We shall bury you."

This, he said, was a poor translation of the idiom actually used. What the phrase meant in Russian was, "We shall leave you in the dust" in the race between the United States and Russia for economic supremacy.

The translation of idioms from one language to another has always posed a tricky problem. Some informed persons insist that a wrong translation was responsible for our dropping the first atomic bombs on Hiroshima and Nagasaki—the Japanese verb *"mokusatsu,"* meaning both "no comment" or "to kill with silence."

As Dr. Mario Pei points out in his revised edition of *The Story of Language*, the Japanese reaction to our demands for unconditional surrender was interpreted as rejecting our ultimatum as "unworthy of notice." What the Japanese premier actually said, according to the story, was that his government had decided to withhold comment until it had time to study the demand further.

The Italians have a phrase, *"Traddutore—traditore,"* which means "A translator is a traitor." Words and phrases take on different nuances and connotations in a different language: Balzac's *Droll Stories* are not what we mean by "droll"; the Spanish *"Los Toros*

Bravos'' does not really mean "the brave bulls"; and Dante's *Divine Comedy* is nothing like what we would be inclined to call a "comedy."

Even the same language has its own pitfalls of misunderstanding regional use. I recall a story about an Englishman, an American and a Scotsman telling their experiences in other English-speaking areas.

The Englishman recounted: "I'll never forget my feelings the first time I had breakfast in America, when the waitress leaned over my shoulder and whispered: 'Are you through with your cereal?' It was some time before I discovered she meant, "Have you finished your porridge?' ''

The American rejoined: "Well, shortly after I landed in England, a waiter came up to me at lunch and said, 'How did you find your chop, sir?' I replied, 'Oh, I looked behind the potato and there it was,' before I realized he was asking me how I liked it."

And the Scotsman weighed in with: "I was once in lodgings in a small town in the west of Ireland. When I'd finished supper, an exceedingly pretty girl came into my room and said, 'Will I strip now, sir?' I fled into my bedroom and locked the door but learned afterwards that Irish girls always talk about 'stripping the table' when they clear dishes."

When Good Points Go Sour

ANTICS WITH SEMANTICS:

She married him because he was such a "dominating man"; she divorced him because he was such a "domineering male."

He married her because she was so "fragile and petite"; he divorced her because she was so "weak and helpless."

She married him because he "danced so well"; she divorced him because he "never takes me dancing any more."

He married her because "she reminds me of my mother"; he divorced her because "she's getting more like *her* mother every day."

She married him because "he knows how to provide a good living"; she divorced him because "all he thinks about is business."

He married her because "we were childhood sweethearts"; he divorced her because "we were both just children when we got married."

She married him because he was "gay and romantic"; she divorced him because he was "shiftless and fun-loving."

He married her because she was "steady and sensible"; he divorced her because she was "boring and dull."

She married him because he was "sweet and attentive"; she divorced him because he was "spineless and indecisive."

He married her because she was "such a beauty"; he divorced her because "all she thinks of are her looks."

She married him because he was so "intelligent and witty"; she divorced him because he was so "critical and wise-cracking."

He married her because "we have such a great sexual attraction for each other"; he divorced her because "we have nothing in common any more."

She married him because he was "the life of the party"; she divorced him because "he never wants to come home from a party."

He married her because "she's so neat and efficient"; he divorced her because "she thinks more of the furniture and the food than she does of me."

She married him because "we have such great talks together"; she divorced him because "he never listens when I tell him anything."

He married her because "she has such a gentle nature"; he divorced her because "she doesn't know how to discipline the children."

She married him because "he swept me off my feet"; she divorced him because "he knocked me off my feet."

He married her because "she was so crazy about me"; he divorced her because "she was so insanely jealous."

Language Is Too Rich to Cheapen

WHAT SCHOLARS CALL (after taking a deep breath) the "pejoration" of language is taking place all around us at a frightening rate. Pejoration means "to make worse."

How are we making our language worse? By cheapening and debasing words, so that they no longer mean what they once did, and still should. Like "divine," which once referred to God, and now may mean anything from a new hat to a cocktail.

Last week I saw an ad for an airline, featuring a large picture of the pilot, with a bold caption: "Jet-Power Missionary." Now a missionary means a person sent to propagate a religious mission, and not an employee who flies a commercial plane around the world.

Another pejorative word is "crucial." A sports story yesterday said: "The Milwaukee Braves' infield faces a crucial test this spring." But "crucial" means "having the form of a cross." It refers to a supreme trial or final choice, such as Jesus' agony upon the cross. It has nothing to do with a baseball team, or any such trivial matters.

I object to this debasement, not because I am a purist about language, but because it robs us of essential words, and deadens their spiritual and emotional significance. If every decision is "crucial," how then can we describe the supreme trial of the cross? If every salesman is a "missionary," what then is a man who carries a religious message afield? If a spring hat is "divine," we shall have to find another phrase for "divine mercy."

In our own time, within the last fifty years, many psychological words have become pejorative—a fact which shocked and disturbed Sigmund Freud, who developed most of them. Today we use "repressed" and "frustrated" as "bad" words, but in the science of psychology they are merely neutral words. Everybody is somewhat repressed and frustrated; what is important is how we *handle* these repressions and frustrations.

Freud never suggested that the goal of psychiatric treatment is to "get rid of our repressions" in the sense that we should behave promiscuously or instinctively; as a highly moral man, he knew this would wreck the social order.

What he meant was *becoming conscious* of our buried feelings, bringing them to light, and dealing with them realistically, rather than allowing them to control us by unconscious direction. The misinterpretations of Freud in the modern mind are a direct result of our loose, inaccurate, and vulgar handling of the tools of language.

There's Poetry in Everyday Talk

A FRIEND WAS TELLING US how he tried to explain the clock to his small son. "Here are the hours, here are the minutes and here are the seconds."

The little boy pondered the clock for a moment, and then asked in puzzlement, "But where are the jiffies?"

A sensible and logical question. We have become so used to idiomatic language that we scarcely think how confusing it must be to the literal mind of a child.

Living with a small child makes one constantly aware of the metaphors we use in everyday speech. If you mention "a stab in the back," he wants to know what you were stabbed with; if you refer to a "queer kettle of fish," he wants to see both the kettle and the fish.

People who pride themselves on realistic "down-to-earth" speech simply don't realize how their everyday expressions are shot through with poetry and metaphor, with tags from Shakespeare and Milton and the Bible.

Without these imaginative springboards, we would be reduced to grunts and squeaks.

The most factual people in the English-speaking world every day use such expressions as "in my mind's eye," "more in sorrow than in anger," "the primrose path," "the milk of human kindness," and dozens of others—wholly unaware that such phrases did not exist until Shakespeare invented them for his plays.

And the most pious atheist daily makes use of scores of poetic idioms from the King James Bible—"feet of clay," "all things to all men," "filthy lucre," "a drop in the bucket," "a fly in the ointment," "a voice in the wilderness," "a wolf in sheep's clothing," "the blind leading the blind"—I could fill a whole page of newsprint with similar quotations.

But the strange power of metaphorical language is such that it soon ceases to be "quotation" and becomes an everyday part of speech.

This is why professional writers try to avoid such phrases if possible—for they want to devise their own metaphors that are fresh and stimulating to the reader.

Nobody can speak "literal" English, which has no force and no grace. Moliere's comic character was surprised to learn he had been speaking "prose" all his life—we may be equally surprised to learn we have been speaking poetry.

The Man in the Middle: II

I AM THE MAN in the middle; for where I stand determines where the middle is.

I am compassionate; those less compassionate than I are "cold," and those more compassionate than I are "sentimental"

I am steadfast; those less steadfast than I are "fickle," and those more steadfast than I are "stubborn."

I am friendly; those less friendly than I are "stand-offish," and those more friendly than I are "pushy."

I am decent; those less decent than I are "disreputable," and those more decent than I are "priggish."

I am civil; those less civil than I are "rude," and those more civil than I are "obsequious."

I am dutiful; those less dutiful than I are "irresponsible," and those more dutiful than I are "subservient."

I am an individualist; those less individualistic than I are "conformists," and those more individualistic than I are "kooks."

I am brave; those less brave than I are "lily-livered," and those more brave than I are "hotheads."

I am a moderate; those less moderate than I are "extremists," and those more moderate than I are "fence-sitters."

I am firm; those less firm than I are "soft-hearted," and those more firm than I are "hard-nosed."

I am competitive; those more competitive than I are "wolves," and those less competitive than I are "worms."

I am normally sexed; those less so are "repressed," and those more so are "promiscuous."

I am prudent; those less prudent are "spendthrifts," and those more prudent are "skinflints."

I am patriotic; those less patriotic are "un-American," and those more patriotic are "jingoists."

I am reasonable; those less reasonable are "too emotional," and those more reasonable are "too logical."

I am a fond parent; those less fond than I are "authoritarian," and those more fond than I are "permissive."

I am a careful driver; those less careful than I are "reckless," and those more careful than I are "slowpokes."

I am the man in the middle, for where I stand determines where the middle is.

VII.
Of the Fine
and Vulgar Arts

Ghostwriting Never Reaches Level of Art

I RECENTLY SPIED a wistful ad in the classified columns of a literary magazine: "Wanted—Playwright with successful record who can write a Tennessee Williams style of play for a corporation executive with a good story."

There is scarcely a person over 40 who does not think that his life, or portions of it, would make a "good story"—if only he could express it with literary skill.

But a ghostwriter is never more than a ghost, and a ghost cannot write a flesh-and-blood story. In art, the content and the form are really indivisible: the way you express yourself is an essential part of yourself.

It is true that great writers have borrowed, or downright stolen, stories from many sources; but they then bend these stories to their own purposes. *Hamlet,* as refracted by Shakespeare's personality, is totally different from the ancient gory tale of revenge which provided him with the source material.

In truly good writing, the reader feels that the author gleams through his style; which is what Buffon meant when he said, "The style is the man."

A work of art is not an artifact: it is not plastered and nailed together. It is organic like a tree or a flower; it shoots up from the hidden roots of personality, and is all of a piece.

This is the grand fallacy of those people who are looking for a writer to collaborate with them on their "good story." If the writer faithfully followed what they said, the story would be dull; and if he injected his own personality, his own style, it would no longer be their story, but his own.

Writing, more than anything else, is an individual enterprise. It comes from the impact of a unique individual upon his environment, and when it is collectivized it loses its essential truth and vitality.

When a man says "I know what I mean, but I can't express it," he generally does not know what he means—for there can be no knowledge without words; there can only be *feelings*. And feelings are a long way from art.

I hope no one answers the corporation executive's ad. It is better for him to nourish his wistful dream than to learn that it will evaporate in the artful hands of a professional writer.

Success Can Prove to Be a Trap

BEING AN AVID READER of mystery stories—the civilized British variety, I hasten to add—I was interested to learn from a recent magazine article on Agatha Christie that she is bored to death with Poirot.

Hercule Poirot, for those of you who do not savor the delights of literary homicide, is Miss Christie's famous Belgian detective, who has been solving the trickiest of cases for more than 40 years—and, incidentally, amassing several fortunes for his gifted creator.

By frankly confessing her boredom with Poirot, Miss Christie takes her place in a long line of writers and other artists who have become the miserable victims of their creations.

Most famous, of course, is Conan Doyle, who actually killed Sherlock Holmes—and was forced by indignant readers to bring him back to life. Doyle simply couldn't abide his pipe-smoking hero, and wanted desperately to be known as a writer of serious fiction.

Rachmaninoff wrote his celebrated (and trivial) "Prelude in C Sharp Minor" as a young man mostly for the exercise. It eventually brought him more than all his other works combined, but he grew to abhor the silly piece, refused to play it and would even leave the room if he heard its familiar opening bar.

Likewise, Sir Arthur Sullivan felt trapped by his reputation with the D'Oyly Carte Company. He became increasingly disconsolate with the operettas he composed for Gilbert's lyrics, feeling that these enormously popular musicals were unworthy (and unrepresentative) of his talents. Yet his more ambitious work has passed into oblivion.

Even Gelett Burgess, the American humorist, grew weary of being identified only as the man who wrote the four-line verse on "The

Purple Cow." Some years later, he wrote another verse, cursing the day he had thought of the first one.

The tale of Frankenstein's monster is more than a horror fantasy—it is a symbolic expression of the way in which a creator can be trapped by his own success.

Robert Benchley was scarcely fooling when he ruefully wrote: "It took me 15 years to find out that I wasn't a writer—but by that time I was so successful that I couldn't afford to give it up!"

Only those who know it personally realize that fame is a two-edged sword: it gives the artist the recognition he is looking for, but just as often it prevents him from developing, from changing the formula which he has long outgrown.

Bad TV Is Not All Public's Fault

SPEAKING OF THE LOW LEVEL of television programs, as I was the other day, reminded me of a conversation I recently had with a man who insisted that the "mass mind" will respond only to infantile entertainment.

"How else," he asked, "can you account for the fact that whenever 'quality' programs have been offered in the films, radio or TV, they have attracted much smaller audiences than loud, corny and stupid shows?"

I account for it quite easily. Many, if not most, of these "quality" programs have been devilishly dull—long on sincerity, and short on dramatic interest.

For instance, most "serious" Hollywood films suffer from taking themselves too seriously. They are pompous and pretentious and self-conscious about their virtue—which makes them dull.

I would rather see a slapstick comedy or a really exciting Western film than a Movie with a Message, in capital letters. This is because, in the hands of an inexpert craftsman, the message gets in the way of the art.

Nothing is harder than the kind of writing that is both serious and entertaining at the same time. It is easy to write a piece of fluff; it is just as easy to write a solemn and significant tract.

But it takes a literary artist of high caliber to write on two levels at once—one level tickling our senses, while the other level provokes our mental processes.

Shakespeare, of course, is the paramount example of this delicate craft. A teen-ager can enjoy *Hamlet* for the sword-play, the satire, the swirling machinations of the plot. Yet, on a higher level, *Hamlet* says a great deal about the nature of man and his relation to society.

Shaw was one of the few writers in our time who was able to combine these elements. Graham Greene is another. But they are rare in any age; and they are generally not to be found working for movie studios or television networks.

Public taste may be low, because taste tends to become corrupted by what it feeds on. But not all the fault lies on the public's side. Most people favor entertainment that is frankly idiotic, and wisely reject the overblown platitudes of second-rate writers trying to be High and Serious.

I think there is a basic shrewdness in the common mind that prefers an honest mug of beer to a bottle of flat champagne.

You, Too, Can Be an Art Critic

HAVING JUST SLUNK AWAY from a shattering experience at an art gallery, where I was given the Grand Tour by the artist himself, I'd like to offer a little advice to anyone trapped in a similar situation.

One of the most difficult predicaments in the world is confronting a selection of paintings which you privately loathe, but which you are forced to admire and comment upon with some vague degree of coherence.

I have found, in years of painful experience, that you can say absolutely nothing and make it sound both impressive and appreciative, and I hereby grant all readers the right to appropriate for themselves this vocabulary of glittering nonsense.

Long ago I used to mutter (as you probably do), "Very interesting," and cast a desperate glance around for the punch-bowl. This banal comment fools no one, least of all the artist, and you quickly find you have lost a friend and alienated a roomful of people, all of whom are pretending they like the pictures with a grim kind of enthusiasm.

Here is my recipe for Insincere Art Appreciation:

If the pictures are stark and sterile—"I find a lot of power and a deep sense of suffering in your work, old boy. There's a sort of stoical Roman grandeur—but definitely keyed to the modern Zeitgeist."

If the pictures are sweetly insipid—"What we need is more tenderness of this sort, to give a lyrical tone to the bleakness of contemporary life."

If the pictures are totally lacking in form or intelligibility—"I get a great feeling of freedom and a daring sweep of imagination. And the clever way you use color to achieve spatial arrangements is a real challenge to traditional concepts."

If the pictures are stupidly realistic—"I'm glad to see that some artists have maintained a sanity and an appreciation of realism, and are rediscovering the eternal values of the objective world."

Now for a useful list of Don'ts: Don't refer to any painting as "pretty"; don't mention another artist in comparison; don't ever ask "What does it mean?"; don't say "It would go well with our living-room draperies"; and, above all, don't say "I don't know Art, but I know what I like."

The artist knows you don't know Art, and he doesn't really care what you like. All he asks for is a little insincere appreciation, if you can't give him the real thing.

Creativity Isn't a Matter of Mood

"YOU MUST HAVE FELT depressed when you wrote that column," said a friend the other day. "But I suppose it's hard to keep your immediate feelings out of what you write."

Nothing could be further from the truth. Everything we know about the creative process—from giants like Mozart to pygmies like Harris—indicates that your conscious state of mind has nothing to do with what you write, or paint, or compose.

Mozart wrote most of his gayest melodies while suffering deeply, both physically and mentally. Balzac dashed off his *Droll Stories* while rebuffed in romance, pursued by creditors, laughed at by society and wrapped in the gloom of loneliness.

And, of course, Robert Louis Stevenson was racked with pain when he was turning out his adventure tales and his charming poems for children. Such cases could be multiplied indefinitely in the history of all the arts.

The creative person works with his *unconscious* mind, which operates even when he is sleeping. By the time he sits down at the typewriter, or approaches the easel, his task has already been completed—all that remains is the physical job at hand.

An admirer once asked Anton Bruckner, the composer, "Master, how, when and where did you think of the divine motif of your Ninth Symphony?"

"Well, it was like this," Bruckner smiled, "I walked up the Kahlenberg, and when it got hot I got hungry. I sat down by a little brook and unpacked my cheese. And just as I opened the greasy paper, that darn tune pops into my head!"

Much the same is true in original scientific research. Dozens of scientists have testified that their best ideas came to them while they were sleeping or fishing or strolling in the woods—and not while they were consciously grappling with problems.

Creativity is not a matter of being in the right "mood," as so many amateurs think. The man who waits to get into the right mood will find that the best ideas elude him; just as the man who sits down determined to write a masterpiece often finds that his words are wooden and his sentences stiff.

We have scarcely begun to recognize the enormous power of the unconscious mind, which is the true source of creativity. Newton lying under the apple tree discovered more truth than Newton browsing through books and bending over papers.

Give Culture Back to the People

THE WORD "CULTURE" takes an awful beating in our society—from its friends as much as from its enemies.

To its friends, "culture" is something lofty and spiritual and almost sacred; to its enemies, "culture" is a mess of highfalutin' nonsense that is spouted by people who think they are superior to the ordinary run.

Yet the clearest, as well as the shortest, description of the word was given a century ago by Thomas Carlyle, when he said: "The great law of culture is this: Let each become all that he was created capable of being."

The culture-vultures try to be more than they were created capable of being, and so they often sound pretentious and absurd. The culture-haters are content to remain less than they can be, and so they sound barbarous and bigoted. But, in different ways, are untrue to themselves.

A truly cultured person is one who appreciates Beethoven as well as jazz, who relishes a well-written mystery book as well as a literary masterpiece, who knows that a human being is made up of varying and contradictory tastes and desires, and wants to expand his personality to the widest range.

Most people, I am convinced, were created capable of being much more than they are in everyday life. When they allow themselves to be touched, by a play or a poem or a piece of music, you can see how a part of them, beneath the surface, has a deep hunger for something beyond the banalities of their ordinary existence.

But the culture-vultures and the intellectual snobs, and the self-appointed guardians of the Muses, often frighten off the average person from the free development of this appetite.

There is a need for more tolerance on both sides. The barbarian who rejects the unfamiliar just because it is unfamiliar is no worse than the snob who embraces the difficult and obscure simply because it makes him feel superior to the mass. Each attitude, in turn, perpetuates the vicious circle of contempt.

Every human being of average intelligence was created capable of being more than he is. He can appreciate Shakespeare because Shakespeare wrote for him, not for scholars; he can glory in Beethoven, because Beethoven expresses the deepest passions and perplexities of the spirit.

Americans are tremendously interested in "personal development"—and this is all that Carlyle meant by "culture" The term needs to be rescued from the prissy-lipped promoters of afternoon teas and given back to the people, who are looking for greatness, but do not know it.

No Short Cut to Creative Writing

QUITE OFTEN I RECEIVE letters from college students and others, wanting to know my working habits, my literary techniques, my sources of inspiration and my personal recipe for becoming a professional writer.

To ask this sort of question is to disqualify oneself from the beginning. There is no recipe, no formula, no Seven Sure Steps to Selling Your Work. All that sort of thing is a commercial fraud.

Anyone who has read widely in the lives of writers—and painters and composers and all artists—surely must know that working habits and techniques differ as widely as tastes in food, drink and women.

Mozart composed in a noisy coffee house; Beethoven required the grandeur of solitude. Goethe created while taking long walks; Proust wrote in a cork-lined bedroom. And so on, through the whole Dictionary of Biography.

Temperament, not talent, determines how a man works. His technique is derived from his unconscious structure, not from any conscious formula.

His "inspiration" may come from the stars or the gambling tables, the sugared sonnets of Shakespeare or the didactic lines of St. Thomas Aquinas—and sometimes from all of these together.

Our time, and our society, seems to have a peculiarly strong need to believe in a magic recipe for success in every field of endeavor.

Incredible sums are spent annually for canned advice on How to Make Your First Million, How to Write a Three-Act Play, How to Succeed with the Opposite Sex.

As if these basic drives in human nature—for love, for power and for self-expression—could ever be taught or explained or codified. The man who makes a million cannot tell you how or why he did it, any more than Keats could tell you how he happened to write immortal odes, or Abelard could impart the "technique" he used with Heloise.

Of course, there are some primary rules of craftsmanship in any activity; but these rules can be learned by any simpleton in a few hours, and they exist only to be broken by men of original talent.

Oscar Wilde tossed off the lines of his plays as casually as he sipped his absinthe; Bernard Shaw carefully reasoned out every sentence he wrote to the utmost of his capacity before committing it to print.

Each of these men would have given diametrically opposite "advice" to aspiring writers. And both pieces of advice would have been equally useless, for creation comes out of the dark pit of the soul which no textbook can illuminate.

Among the greatest of academic frauds are courses in "Creative Writing"; one can no more be taught how to write "creatively" than to love creatively; one can be taught only to write carefully, gracefully and economically—which has nothing to do with creative power.

*

Literature is not, and can never be, "realistic"; in life, a bore is a person we want to run away from; but in literature, some of the most delightful characters ever drawn have been monumental bores. If an author "realistically" portrayed a bore, we would throw the book down after a few pages.

We Pay a Heavy Price for Gadgets

VISITING FRIENDS the other evening, I observed their three children slumped in the "family room" watching television with a mixture of boredom, cynicism and inexpressible sophistication.

And, for some reason, I vividly remembered the first radio I ever heard. It was in 1924, and my cousins had daringly bought a new "crystal set" with two pairs of earphones.

We were excited and dazzled by this experience. Mondays were "silent nights," when local stations went off the air, and sometimes we could hear a cracked soprano screeching from a station as far away as St. Paul.

But there is a law of diminishing returns in such devices. The worst thing about a man-made miracle is that it soon comes to be accepted as a commonplace.

In a year or so, the radio set meant little to us, just as the television set has already become a "normal" part of the world to today's children.

This is a relentless part of the price we pay for our mechanical civilization. The gadget that delighted us last year only bores us this year; the automobile that we are so crazy to drive on our 16th birthday has become a parking headache on our 26th birthday.

This psychological fact—the dwindling returns of pleasure from mechanical objects, so that we constantly require new gadgets to titillate our jaded emotions—is one of the soundest reasons for giving our children the kind of "humanistic" education I mentioned in my recent column on schooling.

For it is only in the world of the mind and imagination that we can find the eternally recurring springs of enjoyment.

Nobody who has ever taken the trouble to read Shakespeare can ever tire of his poetry; nobody who has learned how to listen to Beethoven has ever been known to grow weary of his "old" music.

Works of art contain their own sources of rejuvenation; and the greater the work, the more "new things" one can find in it year after year. *Hamlet* is an inexhaustible play; you can never get to the "bottom" of it.

Children who grow up with an understanding and an appreciation of this heritage have infinitely more to sustain and delight and console them through life than those children who are given nothing but material objects.

It is not a matter of Culture, it is a matter of common sense, that the soaring mind of man is the only instrument that does not become obsolete with time and oppressive with use.

Why Actors Always Seem to Be Vain

AT DINNER LAST EVENING, the conversation turned to actors and acting. Someone wanted to know why actors seem to be the vainest of all the people in the arts.

It seems to me, if this charge is true (and I think it is), that it is because actors are the only artists who use *themselves* as their instruments.

Notice the loving care a violinist gives to his precious fiddle; the meticulous attention a painter pays to his canvases and palette and brushes; the careful way in which a writer treats his pads and pencils, his typewriter, his notes and his corrected manuscripts.

But the actor has nothing but himself—a body, a face, a set of movements, expressions, vocal effects. His only equipment is his total personality.

Not only is his "equipment," as it were, locked within himself, but it is in a real sense irreplaceable. The violinist can buy a new fiddle, the painter keeps changing canvases and brushes, the writer can use any typewriter or paper.

The actor, however, is guarding an instrument which, once damaged or degenerated, can never be substituted. His hair, his skin, his hands, his voice, his bearing and spirit represent his total artistic resources.

Of course, there are other and deeper reasons for the actor's vanity—one of them being the emotional causes that drew him to the stage in the first place. But these causes exist in virtually all artists of every type—the need for approval and admiration is strong in every creative personality.

We tend to judge actors more harshly than these other artists, however, who can let their work speak for itself, through the instruments they have chosen.

They can afford to be diffident, or even downright negligent, about themselves—rising to glory through the medium of their work.

But the actor is inextricably involved in his medium, living with it every minute of the day, so that the distinction between his work and his life becomes blurred, and his private personality is diffused with those professional strains which seem so unattractive off the stage. He is not to be envied; on the same account, he should not be condemned for treating himself like a Stradivarius.

Found: The Drama Critic's Dotter

HE LOOKED LIKE a shy little man, and he was standing all alone in one corner of the room, as if he wondered why he had been invited to the theatrical party.

I strolled over to him and began making light conversation in the heavy way that strangers do at a party. "Are you connected with the theater?" I asked.

He hesitated, and then answered softly. "Well, in a way . . . You see, I'm a Dotter."

"A Dotter?" I repeated. "What in the world is that?"

"I put the three little dots in between the quotations of play reviews." he replied shyly. "You know, like ' "Exciting . . . Amusing," says Matilda Frump of the Evening Bugle.' "

"What's the importance of the three little dots?" I inquired, in deep innocence.

"They're very important," he said, with a burst of spirit, "especially if Miss Frump's complete remark was: 'Exciting my contempt, this play is amusing only in its unconscious triteness.' "

"That sort of job must take a lot of skill on your part," I ventured.

"Oh, it does," he nodded in appreciation of my appreciation. "Sometimes I have to think for hours before I can put those three little dots in exactly the right places.

"When the musical, 'Nirvana' came to town," he continued, "I had the devil's own time with quotations. The critics unanimously panned it, you know. The most influential one, in fact, declared that it was scarcely better than 'Abie's Irish Rose.' "

"How did you handle that?" I asked.

"There was only one thing to do—put my three dots at the beginning of the quote, like this:' . . . better than "Abie's Irish Rose." ' It was my triumph of the season."

"Do you do the quotes for books, too?" I wanted to know.

"Not any more," he shook his head. "The literary critics pack so many adjectives so closely in each review that there's really no need for three little dots. But those drama critics are mean—and cagey!"

"You have a fascinatingly morbid profession, which I would not find enjoyable," I murmured, moving away.

As I left, he repeated to himself, with deep satisfaction: "Fascinatingly . . . enjoyable."

Do People Know What They Want?

THAT POPULAR SELLING PHRASE, "You have to give the people what they want," has always struck me as a piece of dangerous nonsense.

If Hollywood makes one successful film about alcoholism, then all the other studios rush into production with their own sagas about the battle with the bottle.

If one book publisher climbs to the top of the best-seller list with the story of the sinking of the *Titanic* then a dozen other publishers announce new books on the sinking of the *Lusitania*, the *Morro Castle* and the *Eastland*.

But "the public" which flocked to the first film on alcoholism and bought the first book on marine disaster, may refuse to accept any of the sequels. This is known in selling circles as "fickleness."

It is my stubborn contention that nobody knows what the people want—including the people. If anybody did, there would be no flop movies, no remaindered books, and no records warping in the warehouse.

The men who tell you they have their finger on the public pulse are generally taking their own temperature.

My theory is that people do *not* know what they want—until it is given to them. We are all bundles of vague and conflicting appetites, and the only thing certain is that there can be no certainty in predicting the popularity of anything.

There was no clamor for Beethoven's strangely powerful music until he wrote it. Indeed, the music publishers of his time were so afraid of his "dissonances" that he inscribed one quartet with the ironically reassuring line: "Not too original—borrowed from many sources."

There was no great public demand for Bernard Shaw's plays at the turn of the century; quite to the contrary, his first productions were rejected and repressed, and it was not for some years that he became the most popular and respected playwright of our time.

Greatness, and even goodness, has a way of forcing itself down the public's throat, and creating an appetite where none was known to exist before. It is not true that the public merely "catches up" with talent; the talent shapes public taste to its own will.

If nobody, including the public, really knows what the public wants, then the frantic race to please the people is futile and self-defeating. All that a man of sense and honor can do is to give what he thinks is worthwhile, and hope he is running with the tide.

"Empathy" Is Writer's Most Important Tool

A COLLEGE SENIOR of my acquaintance, who is majoring in what his school hopefully calls "Creative Writing," asked me at dinner last night what I think is the most important single quality that a writer must have.

I gave the question much thought—selecting and then rejecting such traits as "sincerity," "originality," "honesty," "imagination." Finally, the word I think best describes it is "empathy."

What is empathy? It is, basically, the ability to get inside another person and see the world through his eyes. Sympathy is feeling "for" someone else; empathy is feeling "with" him.

Apart from his glorious use of language, what makes Shakespeare so pre-eminently great? It is his empathy—his ability to get inside all his characters, so that we see them as individuals and not as heroes or villains or dupes.

This is how the genuinely creative person differs from the layman: he sees the world primarily in terms of its individual components, and not in aggregates. For the creative person, there is no such thing as a "foreigner," or a "criminal," or a "homosexual," or a "radical." He does not label people from the outside, does not stamp them with a word and pigeonhole them in some neat compartment of his mind.

He knows that every person is a unique act of creation, made up of many facets. He knows he may have more in common with a particular "foreigner" than with his next-door neighbor, or that the "criminal" put behind bars may be in many ways a better person than the men who put him there and keep him there.

Most of us cannot truly like or understand people who seem to be quite dissimilar from us; they awaken old tribal instincts, and inspire us to fear or hate or anger or contempt.

But the creative person knows every man for his brother, in some way. He recognizes that he himself is potentially a hero and a villain and a dupe; and he says, along with Terence: "I am a human being, and therefore nothing human is alien to me."

This attitude, combined with a flair for expression, is what makes a great writer. And this is also why there are so few of them in history.

No Business Like Show Business

A LAYMAN'S LEXICON OF SHOW BUSINESS:

"Negotiating with" means "we've written to a few big stars about appearing here, and while we haven't had any answers yet (and don't expect to), we feel that this gives us a pretext to use their names for some free publicity."

"Fresh new talent" means some performer who has been struggling and starving for 10 years in basement bistros, and has been "discovered" just on the verge of a breakdown from nervous exhaustion.

"All-star cast" often means "we have so little faith in the script that we felt it necessary to burden the cast with a half-dozen Names to conceal the lack of a story."

"Lavish spectacle" usually means the same thing—except this time, instead of Names, the production has been loaded down with garish scenery and flamboyant costumes to camouflage the essential hollowness of the entertainment.

"Pre-Broadway Premiere" too often means "we'll try it out on the dogs before we dare to take it into the Big City."

"Sure-fire comedy" means the same comedy you've been seeing for the last 30 years, with every touch of originality ruthlessly trimmed out—for in show business, familiarity breeds content.

"Raw human emotions!" means a cast of characters who behave toward each other as inhumanly as it is possible to get away with.

"A gay and naughty French farce" commonly means the sort of infantile nonsense that the French public grew tired of two generations ago.

"It is my pleasure and privilege to present . . ." means exactly nothing.

"Direct from 39 record-breaking weeks" usually means that the press agent is breaking new records for brash mendacity. (In some segments of show business, everybody breaks his predecessor's "record," which is about as statistically reliable as a Soviet production figure.)

"And now, for the first time, Hollywood dares to . . ." means that the film is perspiring foolishly over some trite sexual situation that Chaucer tossed off in a couplet of his "Canterbury Tales" 500 years ago.

"Limited engagement" means precisely that, when stated by a reputable impresario—otherwise, it means an engagement that will be limited by the number of people who decide to buy tickets of admission.

Novel Has Gone a Long Way—Down

THE POST OFFICE Department has impounded some copies of the old D. H. Lawrence novel, *Lady Chatterley's Lover*, which has just been published in the first unexpurgated American edition.

Meanwhile, the public is buying all the copies available. My local bookseller reports a brisk sale, adding wryly: "The joke is on the public—because it's not really a dirty book at all, by today's standards."

Lady Chatterley's Lover contains a number of four-letter words and a few frank references to sex, but otherwise it is as fresh and innocent as the Bobbsey Twins series, compared with many modern novels.

A cousin of mine brought back the Florence edition from Italy about 25 years ago, and I perused it with shocked delight as a teen-ager. When I picked it up again last week, it was ludicrous. The book is almost quaintly dated, and really quite dull.

What I find offensive in modern novels is not their candor about sex (which is, after all, a legitimate area of human experience), but their blindness to other values in life.

I would have the same objection to a writer who used a whole novel to describe what the characters ate and drank every day.

Lawrence was coarse, but earthy and wholesome. *"Lady Chatterley's Lover* is a straightforward tale of a love affair. The modern novel, on the contrary, wallows in perversion, violence, hate and squalor—for their own sake, and not for the sake of any redeeming spiritual qualities.

We must not, of course, demand that a novel be "uplifting"—this is a task for ethics and religion, not literature—but we have a right to ask that the novelist present us with a well-rounded portrait of life.

And the author who stresses nothing but degradation is as lopsided as the "inspirational" writer who sees only Beauty and Goodness in life.

An author needs a scale of values as much as he requires talent. Lawrence had the talent (which most modern sex novelists do not have), but he was so busy rebelling against the Victorian standard of primness that he fell headlong into the opposite error of deifying sex.

But whatever his faults in this direction, he was a serious artist and a passionate seeker for what he hoped was the truth in human relationships—unlike the sensational and semi-literate scribblers of today, who seek merely to shock us with scabrous case studies of psychopaths.

We have come a long way in the last 50 years. Most of it down.

Great Art Pays Off Best in the End

WHEN WE SPEAK of the "commercial" theater and of the "artistic" theater, we generally imply that the former makes a great deal of money, while the latter languishes into bankruptcy.

But this is taking the very short view. The paradox of the so-called "commercial" theater—or the commercial novel or music or what have you—is that ultimately it doesn't even do as well on commercial terms as the artistic work.

The reason is perfectly simple. A commercial play has only one life. It flares into popularity for a few weeks or months, and then it dies without hope of resurrection.

One day everybody is humming the same popular song. It cannot be repeated too often; a million records are sold; but a few weeks later, the public will not tolerate it on any terms. And if it is a purely commercial tune, it cannot be, and never will be, revived.

Now this does not happen to genuine works of art. As Shaw pointed out, "the masterpiece begins by fighting for its life against unpopularity, by which I do not mean mere indifference, but positive hatred and furious renunciation of it as an instrument of torture."

Beethoven's Ninth Symphony, for instance, did not have anything like the success of the Intermezzo in *Cavalleria Rusticana;* some eminent musicians of the time described it as an outrage by a maniac. But in the long run Beethoven makes Mascagni look like an organ grinder, even as a money-maker.

The Shakespearean plays have earned more for their producers over 300 years than all the popular Broadway hits rolled into one.

Homer's *Iliad* sells only a few thousand copies a year, while *Gone with the Wind* sold millions—but no longer, and never again.

Even popular works of some merit run a comparatively brief course. When the Sherlock Holmes stories were first adapted to the stage, the public clamored to see the production. A few years ago, however, when Basil Rathbone attempted a stage revival, it was a major disaster, losing a great deal more money in a few weeks than the original play had made in a year.

The demand for a "best-seller" seems to stop overnight. It is not, by its very nature, a long-term investment. But works which are not constructed with popular success in mind have the power of coming to life again and again, in succeeding generations.

Even by a banker's calculations, the commercial is less successful than the artistic.

The Soft Words Are Hard to Come By

IT IS A CURIOUS commentary on human nature—and on human speech, which reflects our nature—that we have so few words to designate good things, and so many to designate bad.

Flying home the other evening, I heard the pilot announce to the passengers, over the intercom: "There's no weather between here and Chicago."

By "no weather" he meant no bad weather. To aviation people, the mere word "weather" signifies a difficult condition; just as, on the ground, the mere word "traffic" often means a tie-up.

If we think a man is a liar or a drunk or a cheat, we have scores of deprecatory words at our command; the English language (like any language) is rich in scornful epithets.

But if we think he is an admirable person, we can only falter and fumble for words . . . and end up calling him "a good guy."

A nice day is just a nice day; everyone calls it that. But an unnice day is mean, miserable, drab, ghastly, chilling, bitter, inhuman, depressing and lots more. We are never at a loss to describe our negative feelings.

This explains, I think, why criticism often seems so much more harsh than it really means to be. When a critic likes a book or a play or a piece of music, he can only murmur a few conventionally grateful phrases. The vocabulary of approval is extremely limited, even among talented writers.

All criticism is therefore distorted, in some sense. Positive feelings, which come from the heart, are difficult and embarrassing to articulate; negative feelings (in which fear or anger or contempt have been aroused) pour forth with hardly any conscious manipulation.

Not only do we express ourselves more vividly and vehemently in a negative way, but we even obtain a greater enjoyment in hearing such criticism.

None of Wilde's or Shaw's or Dorothy Parker's generous comments have ever won wide currency; it is only their wittily devastating attacks that are repeated with relish. No critic has achieved eminence for kindness of heart.

This may be a pity (it is certainly an injustice) but it seems to be an inevitable part of the human condition. The most we can do is reach a private understanding with ourselves that all negative criticism (including our own) shall be discounted at 50 per cent on the emotional dollar.

Harm in Worship of the Sensational

THE GREATEST IMPEDIMENT to the artist in our society—whether he be a writer, a painter, an actor or a singer—is our blind worship of the sensational.

We appreciate and applaud whatever looks difficult—and only the artist knows that what looks difficult is usually easy, and what looks easy is usually most difficult.

This is as true for the lowly tap dancer as for the concert pianist who is wildly clapped for playing fast and loud (which any technician can do), but is unnoticed for his slow, quiet passages, which are incredibly hard to perform.

I remember some years ago I was home with a bad cold and had to turn in a column by 5 o'clock in the afternoon. The "e" key on my typewriter suddenly jammed, and I was faced with the prospect of writing without using the most frequently used letter in the alphabet.

Writing the column by hand was out of the question, for I couldn't read back my own scribbling. So I gaily sat down at the typewriter and in a half-hour or so contrived a column without using the letter "e" once.

Well, when this appeared in print you would think I had composed the Sermon on the Mount. People were dazzled by my tremendous feat; they couldn't believe I hadn't slaved over it for days, and admiring letters came in from all parts of the country.

Actually, it was a crummy column, which said little and said it badly. I have written thousands of others which were incomparably superior; yet readers who never bothered to drop a note about the others took pens in hand to salute my overpowering genius.

This sort of thing is most discouraging to a serious practitioner of any of the arts. It is also tempting for him to perform tricks, to balance the sausage on his nose, to play the piano with his toes and take the cash and credit without giving the public the substance of his talent.

Our modern emphasis on sensation is a profoundly corrupting influence, which only the strongest and most dedicated can resist.

Nor is it confined merely to "high-brow" arts; the jazz musician has likewise suffered because shallow and spectacular performers have overshadowed the real masters of the art.

Only when we develop a discriminating audience can we hope for a genuinely civilized form of entertainment to replace the glitter and the shriek.

Why Can't Admen Sell Culture, Too?

"WE HAVE TO GIVE the public what it wants," is the credo of the advertising man who defends the low standards of radio and television programs.

When I ask my advertising friends why better programs aren't put on the air, and kept on the air, until the public is educated to like them, they reply: "You can't force the public to like anything."

But you can. This is the whole idea in back of commercials. The radio and TV men know that if you plug a product long enough and hard enough, the public will go for it.

This is how they justify the repetitive commercial. This is how they sell products—bad ones as easily as good ones. This is how they sell the immature beer, the harsh cigaret, the brand of aspirin that is no different from anybody else's brand of aspirin.

Public taste and opinion are not considered when it comes to the commercials. Commercials are *didactic:* they tell you what to like, and *why* to like it. They cram the product down your throat, on the theory that if you see and hear a thing often enough, you will want it.

If this is true (and it is), then it logically follows that the public can be educated (or indoctrinated, or whatever verb you care to use) to respond to better music, better plays and better programs generally.

If radio and television devoted one tenth of the energy in elevating its entertainment standards that is now expended in making the "hard sell" for products, within a year the public would be buying a better brand of culture, and loving it.

The argument that "We have to give the public what it wants" is false and hypocritical, because the whole economic structure of radio and television depends for its life on *making the public want what it didn't know it wanted before.*

But there is an immediate profit in selling a product to the public—and no immediate profit in selling a higher level of entertainment. In the long run, of course, poor programs weaken and debase our society; but "society" is an abstract word, while "sales" is a concrete one.

Let the hucksters justify their cynicism and vulgarity any way they please; but let them not blame it on the public.

The public has no taste for dog biscuits, but will buy any brand that is promoted with force, skill and repetition. Radio and television are simply unwilling to employ the same talents toward the propagation of long-range values, and they are responsible for our moronic pattern of mass entertainment.

Who Can Really Define Poetry?

THE OTHER MORNING I received an unconsciously amusing note from a high school student, which asked:

"Our English class is studying poetry. Would you please be kind enough to send me your definition of a poem?"

Who can define a "poem"? The dictionary tells us it is "a composition in verse, characterized by imagination and poetic diction." but this tells us nothing we did not already know.

Learned scholars and literary critics have written tons of books on the subject—and no satisfactory definition has been found which would suit them all.

The Bible, for instance, is not written in verse, yet much of it is great poetry, in terms of diction and imagination. Birthday greeting cards, on the other hand, *are* written in verse—but no one of any taste would call them poems.

Emerson thought that Poe's poems were just "jingles." The critics attacked Walt Whitman's poetry as being not poetry at all, but merely uncouth sounds. Many of the moderns are still suspect in high academic circles.

The word "poem" is an abstraction, and an abstraction is notoriously hard to define. Who knows a satisfactory definition of "love"? Or of "justice"? Or of "freedom"? Or of "happiness"? If these could be properly and ultimately defined, students would not be quarreling about their meaning for centuries.

We cannot be scientific about unscientific subjects. A chemist can take apart a chemical object and tell you precisely what it is made up of—but objects of the spirit, of the mind, cannot be dissected, for when they are taken apart, their essence disappears, and we are left with only a handful of verbal dust.

A good poem can be *felt,* over a period of time, by those persons whose taste has been cultivated. It cannot be defined, described or explained.

It is impossible to convince a man that a Shakespearean sonnet is greater poetry than a ballad by Robert W. Service, if the man's poetic vision is blurred, or limited or distorted by bad habits.

Some things—the most important things—can be understood only by living them. What can a youngster know of mature love? What can a selfish person know of sacrifice? What can a blind man know of color? And what can a man whose whole approach to life is prosaic and "practical" know of poetry, past the level of the greeting card?

"Tough" Mysteries Are Too Real

THE LOCAL LIBRARIAN, who has been cheerfully supplying my limitless appetite for mystery books during the summer, asked me why I am so un-American in my taste.

"I notice you only pick up English mysteries." she said. "What have you got against the American kind? Don't our mystery story authors write as well as the British?"

Well, no, they don't; but this isn't my main reason for preferring English mystery books. Most American mysteries are "tough," and operate in an atmosphere of lawlessness, where the police and the politicians are often no better than the criminals they are pursuing.

The English mystery is set in an atmosphere of justice and order. Public safety is secure in these books, and we are free to follow the story with perfect assurance that virtue will triumph.

The American mystery often features a private detective who is as bitter against the police and the machinery of law as he is against the murderer.

He is a lone wolf, fighting, drinking and wenching amidst a general breakdown of public morals.

What this kind of book loses is the *contrast* offered in English mysteries between justice on the one hand, and crime on the other. When the police are brutal and the courts are corrupt, the line between good and evil becomes blurred, and the mystery is no longer a morality tale but a depressing study in civic depravity.

Murder as an art form can flourish only when the state is safe and solid, when the ordinary person is not threatened by a breakdown of the law, and when the detective hero is something more than a hard-drinking lecher who is interested only in collecting his fee.

My charge against American mysteries is not that they are too improbable, but that they are too real. Reading them, we do not escape from the mundane world, but plunge more deeply into the muck of it. They induce (in me, at least) feelings of uneasiness, rather than feelings of satisfaction.

It is the *incongruity* of the English mystery that makes its appeal: the vicar foully stabbed to death behind the rosebushes, in a peaceful and law-abiding town. But when the town is ruled by mobsters and their political henchmen, murder ceases to be a shock and a scandal, and becomes merely another sordid statistic of a dead body folded in an auto trunk.

"Infancy" Is No Excuse for Bad TV

ONE DEFENSIVE COMMENT of the television addicts that I fail to understand is the argument that television is still in its "infancy" and that it is unjust to compare it to the other arts.

"Give television some time," they mutter. "Think of the other arts in *their* infancy!"

All right, let's. Think of the drama in its infancy—Aeschylus, Sophocles, Euripides, Aristophanes, still the greatest of playwrights.

Think of sculpture in its infancy—Praxiteles and Phidias, whose work has not yet been excelled.

Think of architecture in its infancy—the magnificent pyramids of Egypt, the temples and public buildings of ancient Greece.

Think of literature and poetry in their infancy—the unrivaled Songs of Solomon, the *Odyssey* and *Iliad* of Homer, the *Aeneid* of Virgil, the odes of Horace—which moderns are still translating into inferior versions.

An art form does not develop with *time*—if it did, our playwrights would be three hundred years better than Shakespeare, and we know that they are three hundred million light-years behind him.

Movies are not conspicuously better than they were thirty years ago; they were not helped by sound, by color, nor by technical improvement. Radio programs are not more adult and civilized than they were in the days of battery sets—at least *then* there were no soap operas on the air.

The difference between these two latter forms (and television) and the other arts that came to fulfillment from their beginnings is a difference in *purpose*, not in time or technique.

The great art of the past wanted to express something about life— about the nature of man and the universe. It asked real questions, and tried to answer them in terms of truth and goodness and beauty.

The latter-day arts want merely to please as large an audience as possible—either to lull them into a false complacency, or to make them responsive to a sales pitch. With these ends, you can wait an eternity for movies and radio and television, and they will not grow up. Artistic maturity, like emotional maturity, means *giving*, and they are interested only in *getting*.

Why Glorify Eccentrics on the Stage?

WATCHING a performance of the Truman Capote play, *The Grass Harp*, I thought how each era has its own particular kind of unfairness.

In most literature (and drama) of the past, the respectable and conventional people were considered as norms of behavior. Theirs were the standards by which all personalities were judged; and the eccentrics, the marginal characters, were reviled or ridiculed.

This, of course, was a desperately unfair attitude. Goodness and badness cannot be measured in terms of social "acceptability"; we know that Socrates was worth more to the world than all the Athenians who condemned him.

Today, however, the circle has swung full around—and it is just as desperately unfair. In The *Grass Harp,* and many plays and stories of its type, it is the eccentric who is glorified and the conventional citizen who is scorned or derided.

Writers like Capote are preoccupied with pixie characters who defy society, who do not fit into neat patterns, whose imagination and insight make them alien to their families and neighbors.

It is perfectly fine to interpret, and to sympathize with, such square pegs who sometimes become the most valuable members of society. But it is never right to elevate them at the expense of the ordinary person who has his own perplexities of which he is scarcely aware.

In *The Grass Harp*, for instance, the townspeople are represented as gossipy, malicious, clannish, obtuse and hostile toward anyone who tries to break out of the provincial pattern of life. All these charges may be true, on the surface—but it is the duty of a writer to dig beneath the surface.

One of the purposes of art is a higher understanding of human nature—both its capacities and its limitations. Ordinary people, caught in the trap of their routine lives, are not villains any more than eccentrics or rebels are villains. Essentially, both kinds of people are struggling to be good, through a maze of conflicts and a haze of shadows.

Much modern literature has merely reversed the pattern of black and white, which is both artistically and morally a sin. The stern, self-righteous sister in *The Grass Harp* should be an object of pity and comprehension, not a figure to sneer at. She does not understand her motivations—but if the writer did, he would approach her with love and never with contempt.

Why Actors Prefer the Stage

"WE MURDERED THEM in Cleveland," I overheard an actor saying at the restaurant table next to mine. "We knocked them dead for two weeks."

Phrases don't just happen; they are carefully selected by the unconscious mind to describe the actual hidden feelings in a situation. And performers always speak of "murdering" an audience when they go over well.

For acting is basically a contest between two antagonists—the performer and the audience. The audience comes wanting to be subdued, but ready to turn and sneer if it is not; the performer walks out on the stage like the gladiators of old, to slay or be slain.

When actors are interviewed and they babble away about "the wonderful audiences in your wonderful city," either they are being consciously insincere or else are fooling themselves.

Men and women take up stage careers for many reasons; but the most important, I feel, is neither vanity nor exhibitionism, but a need to acquire the authority on the stage which they feel they lack in real life. The theater transforms dull and drab creatures into magnificent specimens of courage, charm and beauty.

This is why veteran acting coaches stress the importance of "authority" in a performer—that almost mystical ability to walk out of the wings and instantly command the audience's attention and respect.

Without this authority, all the talent in the world is wasted; with it, a little talent can be made to go a long way. In a sense the actor is a kind of lion tamer, forcing the audience to jump through the hoops he has devised for them.

The best performances send a current tingling from the stage down to the seats; this current is suspended hostility, like a truce between two sides in a battle. If the play falters or sags, the lions begin to bare their fangs and snarl.

Rodgers and Hammerstein, in a moment of candor, once referred to the audience as "The Big Black Monster." They meant no contempt, but were simply expressing a psychological fact of stage life. The breathing monster in the dark pit of a theater is a potential enemy to everyone on the stage—and nobody knows it more than the weak or frightened actor.

This is a large part of the allure of the living theater: an element of conflict that is lacking in films, where everything has been predetermined. Actors prefer the stage to the screen, despite the lower pay, because they want to tame the beast and prove nightly that they are heroes.

It's the Pause That Counts in Art

ARTUR SCHNABEL was once asked for the "secret" of his superb piano playing. "How do you handle the notes as well as you do?" inquired a student.

"The notes I handle no better than many pianists," Schnabel replied. "But the pauses between the notes—ah, that is where the art resides!"

He was not being funny or mischievous. One of the most astonishing things about the arts is what they leave unsaid, or unwritten, or unplayed, or unpainted.

What distinguishes a great actor from a merely good one? Bearing, poise, diction, depth of feeling? Perhaps more important than any of these, it is knowing how to make a pregnant pause in a speech that moves an audience more than anything that is spoken. Mark Twain understood this well when he commented on a certain performance of

Shakespeare: "The pause—that impressive silence, that eloquent silence, the geometrically progressive silence, which often achieves a desired effect where no combination of words, however felicitous, could accomplish it."

On the lower level of entertainment, this is what is meant when a comedian is praised for his "timing"—that rarest and finest attribute of verbal humorists. The skilled comedian knows, by intuition as well as by craft, when to pause for a heightened effect; and his brief silences are more important than the jokes themselves. "It isn't so much what he says as the way he says it," is the highest compliment we can pay a comedian.

And this also is where the amateur can be distinguished from the professional. The amateur is always *explicit;* he finishes every sentence, draws every line, and plays every note with the same value. He leaves nothing to the imagination of the audience.

Silence is a positive and compelling force, and not a mere negative. Notice at a dinner, when a silence falls at the table, how the silence becomes an almost palpable thing—and how, the longer the silence endures, the harder it becomes to speak. And couples who retreat into mutual silence when they quarrel find it more difficult to make up than couples who shout and argue with one another.

All art is suggestion and implication. Anybody, with practice, can play the notes in a Schubert sonata—but to play the pauses between the notes—"Ah, that is where the art resides."

Artist's "Realism" Not Like Ours

ONE OF THE HALF DOZEN most difficult words in the world to define or to understand is "realism"; and yet people use it unthinkingly all the time, to make judgments about many things, including the arts.

What does a man really mean when he says he likes "realistic" painting? He means, in most cases, that he likes a picture to represent objects the way the eye sees them. But the eye does not see "reality."

When we look at a chair, we do not see the "real" chair, but an object that is more or less an optical illusion. The "real" chair is a mass of particles moving at incredible speeds with ceaseless energy.

When we look at a person, we see the face, the limbs, the clothes. Are these the "real" person? Nobody would deny that it is the character, the spirit, the emotional structure beneath the bone that make the real person.

The telescope sees big things more "realistically" than the eye; the microscope sees little things more "realistically" than the eye. If we do not expect the scientist to look at the world with our naïve realism, why should we expect the artist to do so?

Both the scientist and the artist are engaged in a quest for the things that the eye *cannot* see by itself. What we call reality is merely the surface of things, the appearance of objects. There is no truth to be found in this appearance, and both the scientist and the artist are looking for the kind of truth not visible to the naked eye.

Actually, we do not even believe in our own realism: we do not believe that the earth is flat, as it seems to be; we do not believe that the man who looks kind *is* kind, as he seems to be. We ourselves apply more critical, more sophisticated and (to use a dirty word) more intellectual yardsticks to everyday things around us.

The artist goes us one further. He accepts *nothing* as it seems to be, for it is his task to throw a searchlight on the caverns and labyrinths of life. Now, his searchlight may be weak, or dirty, or focused in the wrong way, and the art he gives us will then be defective or chaotic.

But whether he is a good or a bad artist, we cannot ask him to look at life the way we do, for then he would see nothing more than we do. If his "realism" and ours do not seem to square, it is cheap and arrogant of us automatically to assume that our vision is the truer or the better, for history proves that the mass of mankind spend their todays in trying to catch up to the artists of yesterday.

Actors Are Often Two-Faced Critics

BEING ONE OF THAT UNHAPPY BREED known as a drama critic—the man blamed for everything that is wrong in the theater—I was wickedly pleased to read a self-revealing article last month in *Actors Equity Bulletin,* the journal of the actors' union.

Actors had been complaining that theater managers were not giving them nearly as many free tickets to Broadway plays as they used to; and a representative of the union interviewed theater managers to learn the dark reason.

It turns out, the official reported sadly, that actors constitute the most critical audience, behaving in a way that drama critics would never dare or care to. Many performers who attend a show free of charge, he said, "and sit next to a person who has spent $6.60 for a seat . . . comment disparagingly upon what is going on on the stage.

That can ruin theatergoing for the people who overhear it . . .

"Then," the report continued, "there were actors in the lobby between acts, who would run down both the plays and the actors on the stage, even though they were guests of the management."

To add sartorial insult to the verbal injury, the fact that many performers attended the theater (free) in sweatshirts, tennis shoes and dungarees didn't make the theater managers especially eager to invite them again in the future.

Drama critics have long been aware of this two-faced attitude on the part of professional actors. Publicly they upbraid the critics for saying harsh and unpleasant things about a play; but privately—and even not so privately—performers themselves are brutally candid about the deficiencies of a production or a cast. I have heard actors and actresses on radio and TV interviews blasting the critics for "killing a play" they are appearing in, and then an hour later in some night spot the very same performers are confiding to all around them that the play is vile, the director is an idiot and the management is beneath contempt.

Even press agents, who are paid (and handsomely) for trumpeting the merits of their production, have admitted to me, on the day the play closed, that the critics were absolutely right, and that everyone connected with the play knew it all along. The critic is usually blamed for saying in print what the professionals in the theater say to each other and to their friends.

You Get Soiled in Hunt for Dirt

SHAKESPEARE'S LINE ABOUT THE LADY protesting too much has been confirmed by modern psychology. We have grown increasingly suspicious of those who aggressively parade their loyalty, their piety or their honesty.

The same holds true, I believe, for the censorious mind. It is one thing to dislike literary dirt; it is quite another to seek actively for it, and often to find it where it does not exist.

I have known individuals who thought they were dedicated to stamping out obscenity—when, actually, they were fascinated by it. Their greatest thrill consisted in finding a "dirty" picture, or a "pornographic" book. They would relentlessly pursue this quest, in the name of decency—but they were really engaging in a lewd activity while at the same time able to pride themselves on their moral superiority.

Thus, they are able to have their emotional cake and eat it: to maintain a good conscience about their "purity," and to indulge in the prurient curiosity they have repressed in themselves.

A famous actress once satirized this attitude when she told an interviewer: "I was disgusted with the dirtiness in *Tobacco Road*—and each time I went back to see the play, I was even more disgusted."

People with normal and decent instincts do not become crusaders against dirt, for they know that obscenity flourishes only when the society itself is sick. The dirt is a symptom, not a cause. It is a symptom of bad emotional housekeeping, of poor parental training and of grownups failing to practice the virtues they smugly preach to their children.

Honesty in human relations is the only way to diminish this kind of dirt: an honesty that candidly admits man is a delicate balance of animal and spirit, and does not close the blinds to whatever is bestial in us.

Schools, and books, and newspapers, cannot develop the proper reactions of young people in this matter. Only the family, in its intimate setting, is capable of putting sexuality in its proper perspective, neither overplaying its importance nor ignoring its vitality.

Until then, the hunt for dirt is as futile as sweeping out the Augean stables—except for the sweepers, who love the task.

Most Autobiographies Are Atrocious

WHAT SEEMS THE EASIEST SORT of book for any person to write? Naturally—his autobiography. And what, actually, is the hardest book for anyone to write? His autobiography.

Hardly anyone you meet does not think, secretly or openly, that his life would make a fascinating book "if only I had the gift of words." Among the ordinary, this remains merely a wistful belief; among the celebrated it amounts to an obsession. Only the very strongest of famous personages can resist writing his autobiography.

I have just finished reading another depressing one, which set off this chain of thought. It is a quite bad book, although the author has been a professional writer and editor for all his adult life. And it is (like most autobiographies) shallow, embarrassing, self-deceiving and utterly pointless.

Even the greatest writers have faltered and failed in this peculiarly difficult task. Mark Twain's worst serious book was his *Autobiography,* which grossly displayed all his faults and none of his genius.

His biographers, although inferior to him as writers, did a much better job on his life than he did.

In our own time, that splendid writer G. K. Chesterton attempted his autobiography, with disappointing results; his biography, by Maisie Ward, is an incomparably superior job. Chesterton's angle of vision, which was marvelously acute when applied to the outside world, was terribly obtuse when turned within.

Not more than a half-dozen worthwhile autobiographies have been penned in the fifteen hundred years since St. Augustine gave us his *Confessions*. After Cellini and Rousseau, after John Stuart Mill and Benjamin Franklin, what do we have? Mostly gossip, vanity, mawkish recollections, dreary anecdotes, self-justification, libel, half-truths and untruths.

It used to be, at any rate, that only genuinely famous persons undertook this task: eminent authors, generals, statesmen, scientists, divines, whose personal contributions provided at least a footnote to history.

Today all that is changed: we find the bookshop tables heaped high with autobiographies (mostly ghosted) by movie actors, comedians, dress designers, innkeepers and—the latest atrocity to arrive on my desk—Perle Mesta.

No other field of writing is so beguiling, so treacherous and so doomed as that of autobiography. Literary skill is not enough; psychological insight is not enough; honest intentions are not nearly enough. Where is the surgeon who can perform a successful heart operation upon himself?

A great autobiography is a miracle; even a good one is beyond the grasp of most geniuses. Let us be grateful Shakespeare never tried—there is no reason to believe he would have succeeded.

The trouble with many profound books is that the reader has to have more learning than the author in order to know if the book is right or wrong; and if you have more learning, why bother to read the book?

*

Historical novels bore me; biographical novels offend me; history and character are cheapened and flattened by being fictionalized, for nothing is more exciting—if well handled—than a real person and a real event.

An Artist's Personality Is Paramount

"I HAVE MET A NUMBER of writers and other artists," observes a college student, "and they are generally not as pleasant or as pleased with themselves as other people. Can you explain the reason for this?"

The explanation, it seems to me, lies in the nature of the work itself, and in the type of person who is attracted to it. A human being is happiest when he can *objectify* himself in his work; in popular terms, when he can "lose himself" in what he is doing.

It is in the nature of art—and especially literary art—that the person making it is engaging in a highly *subjective* task. He draws the material out of himself, as it were, and is perpetually involved in excavating material from the depth of his own personality. This is neither a pleasant nor a happy project; it is merely an essential one for the human race—for great art expresses the deepest and most lasting values of mankind.

But the artist himself cannot find an objective contentment in his work; he is not *giving* himself to something outside himself. By the very nature of his craft, he is unable to lose himself in the task itself; his own personality is always paramount.

In a crude way, one might say that the writer is always scratching himself to find where he itches—and the more he scratches, the more he itches. Art is produced in this introspective way, but it does not make a man pleasant to be with or serene within himself. The so-called "artistic temperament" (when it is not pose) comes from this aggravated sense of self.

Genuine contentment is found in performing tasks that take us out of ourselves, for a purpose greater than ourselves. Only when the personality is subordinated to a higher goal do we attain the serenity we are looking for—this is why the beatitude of the saint, whose life is directed toward the highest possible goal, is unattainable by the rest of us.

It is the burden of the artist that he cannot escape this sense of self and achieve the simple and profound happiness of the surgeon in performing a delicate operation, the researcher at the microscope, the sea captain navigating his craft through turbulent waters. All of them, like the Zen archer, become the bow, the arrow and the target.

The artist has other satisfactions that compensate for this—after all, he provides the future with lasting objects of enjoyment. But he himself is no happier than a patient with a constant itch.

Artists Crave Praise, Not Criticism

ONLY ONCE IN MY LIFE have I heard a critic attacked by someone he had "overpraised." I was at a party with a famous violinist, and he derided a music critic for having given him a "rave" review the day before.

"I played terribly," he confessed. "It was the worst recital I've given in years. That critic should be fired for not knowing his business. Who wants such praise?"

Most authors, artists, and performers do. They rip into critics mercilessly when the critics depreciate their work; but they never object when their productions of peformances are overvalued; as they often are. They insist that what they want is "objective criticism"; apart from the fact that there's no such animal, they don't want it anyway. They want praise, as much and as often as possible, even when they don't deserve it.

In some thirty years of drama reviewing, I have received many notes from actors and actresses thanking me for kind words about their performances. Not once has any of them berated me for a glowing review about a poor performance.

Sometimes, when plays and concerts are good, they receive bad notices, and the performers are outraged. But other times these plays and concerts are bad and receive good notices. Honesty should compel the performers to complain just as vigorously, if they are serious about wanting "objective criticism"—but somehow they never do.

Perhaps an artist or performer cannot be objective about his own work; perhaps he thinks that everything he does is good. But the really top-rank artists I have known are painfully aware when they do less than their best. I have heard musicians curse themselves after a sloppy performance—but they never curse the bestower of unmerited praise.

This is one reason I pay little attention to the complaints about the "severity" of critics. When they are unfairly severe, the artists jump on them; when they are unfairly favorable (because justice does not mean being kind, it means being just), nobody takes issue with them. As a result, most critics attain a reputation for severity.

Only when artists object just as vehemently to undeserved praise as they do to undeserved disparagement will they be able to make out an honest case against the critics. Until then, what they really want is not criticism, good or bad, but simply a massaging of their egos.